BOOK 2 in House OF the Living Sky

The Star in Chains

J.D. GIGGY

Publishing Coordinator – Sharon Kizziah-Holmes

Paperback-Press
an imprint of A & S Publishing
Paperback Press, LLC

ISBN -13: 978-1-956806-86-1

TABLE OF CONTENTS

CHAPTER 1: THE PATH LESS TRAVELLED

Thetrulengo speaks,

*W*hat now entices my mind is not my own being, but the nature of being; the influence that one life exerts on another. As the dawn comes pouring out from Iregruun – the Far Edge, derivation of Az'Rech the Numenlight – I again fondly recall the first understanding that I was. Counting this season of the mortals' Windsong and every season that mortality has yet survived since the last Unravelling, I have been conscious of seventy-three thousand eight hundred twenty-three in all. This account excludes all prior cycles of the Unravelling, only summarizes all which has occurred since. Specifically, it encompasses life since the Nhi'Thaun were maggots writhing in the new flesh of Maengir, compounded in the modern scale of forty-three days for each season. It has taken this many seasons of life, as well as my failure to destroy Zeniquorer, for me to see that to which I have been ignorant for so long.

I have no soul, no light, but neither do I have flesh or bone. I think, feel, sense and experience, yet I have no presence. I can move mountains as easily as plucking a flower, yet the only body I have must be wrought from dirt and air, only to crumble away

1

when I've finished with it. I can control, yet I cannot become. This is my revelation: I exist, yet I cannot possibly exist. I am unexplainable, and therefore the only thing hereto extant which does not fit my own understanding of being.

What does this mean, to 'become'? Everything across the endless expanse changes, grows, withers, weathers, crumbles, learns, adapts, dies, rots. One becomes these. I want to understand how I can, and perhaps have, become something new. I existed when I realized my existence. I became wise (the mating of caution and accountability with experience and insight) through seeing more than what my eyes...what I beheld through various simulacra. What have I become by protecting or ignoring or avoiding or loathing or loving? What have I become with each thought that visits and departs my consciousness? Like wind across stone, they reshape me, yet into what? I cannot know, for I am still becoming.

I contemplate this upon seeing the changes in young Raphenie, in the Vulgoli and in the mantic Artimecian. The living war always, yet some are unfairly chosen by the dead and powerful to become more. By the will of the failed and fallen, they become.

Raphenie believes her power came from her curse, lost to her when her father was finally destroyed. She will realize soon enough he was not all that was trapped in her mind. The death essence of the gods is ever flowing toward the youngest of the line. Though her father hurt her through this bond, it will yet reunite her with her family.

I have never...ached thusly. To save but a single life was the root of my heart's painful journey into longing. At its end, I succumbed to the uncontrollable passions of Maengir. I betrayed the impartiality and detachment I have always believed to be the locus in which my purpose lay. What then can I do to find the answer to my great questions? I do not know why I exist, only that I do. All my life I have searched for the meaning in it. So far, the only meaning I have found – the stimulant of my disloyalty to objectivity – is the same that pries thought and action akin to the unconscionable treason from the afterlings of Escharka's deep Ireapos: the survival of mortality and preservation of this Maengir. This was a terrible mistake. I feel no love for all, only for a few, and not all of them living. Does this mean a life has no importance unless I feel drawn to it? Or, conversely, my devotion is groundless, and I have no ability to determine which life is worth saving. Moreover, am I wrong to only feel compassion for the individual but not the whole? Is there even a difference?

I am confused, unable to keep a clear head. I must away from their dealings for now and find the center of myself, taking the journey mahvaeba, as they say. I think it is a justifiable belief that, if one is aware of one's own existence, then it is wisest to seek clarity first within before seeking it without.

I will engage myself to wander the forests to the Hai and experience the caravan of Hauan Etain. I would like to see how strong the hand of this city is when it reaches beyond its borders. I have seen such strength persist in pursuit of war but never as a gesture of protection, especially not to those parted from their parent nation by its decision and demand. This will gain me time to dwell upon myself, ensuring that I do not disregard great deeds simply because they take place beyond this, the heart of the Mantichaena realm. It is not just their demesne that abides in constant peril, but all things. There is neither time nor compelling cause to attend the continuation of more than a few continents, though I will try with what little time I have. The days left to this world are numbered, no doubt.

~Chronicle of Wonders, Great Riddle of Identity

Now was the end of Longhand, and yet its star's ascent back to deep sky had only just begun. Similarly, the Windsong remained by its side. Their conjoined presence, along with the breaking of the Gate and the sudden advent of the Bone passing, had worsened the unseasonable heat as the bearing took a sudden turn. The effects of the tumult among dead elders had not passed. However, crops did not wither as before, and the rivers still ran heavy.

Zeniquorer was no more, and his empowered youngest was finally free to feel the birthright of Miohaelia within. So, the arrival of white and silent skies over the lands of the Mantichaena brought good yields from the befuddled ground.

The reinvigorated Miohaelia's place in the firmament was one of satisfaction now. She and her lover were appeased by retribution against her cruel enemy, and they shone with pride that their children, Raphenie and Naguza, had survived their ordeal and each had found their destined place in the company of the other.

Oorghunak had finally prevailed in his eternal battle with Zeniquorer and Maengir would suffer Miohaelia's manifest grief no more. The love between the two dominated deep sky as they slowly, imperceptibly retreated together.

Meanwhile, the distant, violet corpse of Zeniquorer languished in loathing of the world it could never return to. It was a new season, not Longhand nor Windsong nor Bone, but a season forever changed by the struggle among them for which those on the battlefield were paying the price.

The seasons were becoming the property of the living; a new generation of gods.

Far from Hanging Gate, many rivers wound through Sekhaadi Ni'ivitnem, their sheer numbers being the root of its namesake. Although wild and often feared by younger Mantichaena the distant tracks of woodland remained an important source of the city's livelihood, hunting its depths a test of a Gazan child's mettle. Compared to the safe conurbation of Hanging Gate it seemed nearly without end, bountiful in flora, fauna, minerals and waters of matchless delectability. However, those who made a life here quickly learned that even paradise tends to be home first to creatures far hungrier and more vicious.

The cliffs below the Gate were only barely visible through the thick green canopy, home to a pageant of tasty and beautiful things that were, nonetheless, deadly predators. The thi'zech of the Tau, those deadly thorns that had once made Keimas' first journey so difficult, were not without relatives in the Hai, many hundreds of which were permanently rooted throughout the trunks of harmless thi. The underwood made an ideal haunt for every carnivore known, as well as some not yet discovered. For safety's sake, the Mantichaena only ventured here with a mature protector or two, though the safety a Mearnum felt under the protection of a Bakul was not felt by the Bakul.

This was the second day in the trek of Nepiur's caravan, dispatched by the former Primarch Sky, traversing the rugged road through the borderlands. This was the land of hunters, where the laws of Hanging Gate barely existed. The city depended largely on the food found here, though there communication between the two was limited to the exchange of fresh recruits and hunted game.

There was no council, hall or hierarchy out here. Every troupe hunted on their own, made their own rules and decided who stayed and who went home to be replaced. It was often only the dead or severely injured who returned to the Gate, as the hunters originated principally in Gazan, and were a proud breed as a whole, who would not suffer the indignation of becoming an apothecary or digger. The children brought up in the arena were often bound to join the militia. However, refusal was not uncommon. The borderlands were where most restless Kulo, Boroo and Kubernu found themselves, either too altered by their brood to fit into civilized society, perhaps innately averse to it, or simply born with a yearning for untamed adventure. They were welcome and celebrated for their services, certainly not as undesirable as Gal'tskhain, but neither did they truly belong at the Gate.

Some members of the caravan were uncomfortable in these savage tracks, where life and death were entirely in one's own hands. Others felt as though they had just come to life, for there was a beauty in Ni'ivitnem's sights and smells they could not have imagined. With each hill mounted and glade crossed, new wonders were revealed.

Kut'ifitre were known to all, but never in such numbers as here. In every shadow the fluttering insects whirled, spinning their gossamer nets and dragging them through the breeze to snare smaller prey, occasional conflicts breaking out when one captured another by mistake.

Upon the Thaun or Dhai facing surfaces of thi and stone, indiscernibly tiny creatures gathered to, and would soon become stuck fast in, a sweet mucus laid down by their natural predator, the simonma. This was a humble cephalopod which settled where its unique coloration best camouflaged it, waiting patiently for its trap to be filled with wriggling morsels, then making the rounds to collect.

Deeper in the jungle and nearer its intersecting rivers and streams, a hushed moan, like the wind across a cavern mouth, could be heard from time to time. While first thought to be the rumblings of brak herds, the absence of shaking ground assured it was not. Rather, it was the lilting song of thi'pobpanaed, a marvel belonging to both the flora and the fauna. On roots which slowly groped across the riverbeds, it navigated the waterways, holding aloft a swaying trunk. Atop this its bloom, not of petals, but long, probing vines, clung to the boughs of any thi they touched, stripped the rich fungus from them, then slowly plunged down its throat-like trunk, presumably to undergo a form of digestion.

Nepiur had a particular fascination with the enigmatic thi'pobpanaed, imagining at every encounter what its insides must be like, then cringing at the thought of finding out firsthand. She suspected the remarkable living thi were a puzzle even to Ms'egol's botanists. While lovely and tantalizing, it seemed the thi'pobpanaed might enjoy anything they found in the canopies, even an unsuspecting body.

There was one among the caravan who felt neither amazement nor discomfort in the face of Nivitnem's exotic dance. The company's Boroo pathfinder, Ms'egol Udai Haxelinopsis, sat in an afflictive depression, effectively neglecting duty while transposing his memories and introspection to verse. Still passing through lands at least minimally occupied by some few Mantichaena and with somewhat familiar surroundings for his leaders to navigate by, he had nestled among the shoulder spines of his great friend, Gazan Udai Dace. There he waxed poetic in a worn pamphlet of leather-laced pages.

While progress would be more efficient with his attentive guidance, Hax was as slothful as he was knowledgeable. Moreover, his reclusive lifestyle and recurring drunken stupors had not overly endeared him to his companions. Though he and Dace were close, and the favored Bakul's word held weight with many, it had been apparent to Hax from the beginning of their undertaking that his presence was not warmly welcomed. The company seemed satisfied that he conceal himself until needed.

The caravan crossed over the last fringes of the borderlands on less travelled terrain, bound for the village of Aes'bethil. From here they knew only the general direction, and so Hax began to periodically rise just enough to ensure they were on the right path, barking in affirmation when Maurus or Nepiur demanded an update on their course. Otherwise, he was absorbed in the pages between his fingers, thereupon which he scribbled his inmost thoughts:

Seeking yet untouching death
A single body's single breath
A captive arm with many hands
All light begotten by our brands
One together, yet always apart
Of love to neither mind nor heart
Brothers, sisters, willing slaves
Knowing pain, but never graves
With memories of death within
Eternal life becomes our si...

"Hax? Hax! There is sign! Hereto bring your eyes!" came the spirited but unwelcome voice of Nepiur, Hax's mistress until such time as this tedious assignment was completed.

His eyes did not go at first, but pressed tightly shut in instinctual outrage at the interruption. He replaced the scroll and dye in his satchel, threw the strap over his shoulder, then vacated his resting place upon Dace with a lazy leap. Whipping his tail around a low branch he swung through the air to join Nepiur where she crouched on a mossy ledge overlooking a river.

She had called him with some urgency and directed him forward in the same way.

"I see no trail on the other side. *Minla,* I suspect Bethaali's priest crossed here, though there is no sign of which direction."

Hax snorted and coughed gracelessly, cleared his throat, and leaned forward on his knuckles. A short salvo of smaller sniffs drew his attention upstream while he mumbled unhappily.

"Would have been easier if we had brought the man with us."

"No good, that," Nepiur said. "They wanted him healed and rested for a report. I am certain there will be more the Council wants out of him…if it be only criticisms by my father's loathing for Bethaali's followers."

Hax was not minding her words.

"That way," he muttered, gesturing impatiently upriver.

"*Quouein?* How do you know?" she asked skeptically.

"The water is moving too fast here. If this is where he came ashore then he would have been swept down from further ahead, maybe…seventy paces or so, judging by the current."

"You are certain?" Nepiur asked.

Hax nodded absently, keenly searching the path he had spied before pointing more precisely.

"I am. There, see you? There is a marring of the algae on that mound up the way. He slid in; most likely lost his footing while looking for a ford."

Nepiur traced his finger and believed she saw the boulders indicated, but they were barely visible through the foliage, the indicated markings barely discernible from where they stood. She chose to believe him, and so patted his shoulder and smirked. Then, she teased him lightheartedly while shooting up into the canopy and crossing interwoven branches toward the far bank.

"Let us say I do," she called back. "*Udai*, no need to show off for your brawny lover."

"M-my…*minaien enta,* outrageous accusation!" Hax spluttered, swinging over to hang upside down from his perch and shrug at Dace, expectant his friend would intervene.

The big Bakul only chortled and stormed up to the river to wade in, winking obviously to Hax and shouting his own jests.

"Heed her, friend. Lie too long upon a man's back and you are certain to become of love to him eventually."

Hax was unamused by the flippant heckling but was quickly distracted as Nepiur signaled to Maurus on his behalf.

Maurus reluctantly drew the Boroo's precious wineskin from his haversack and tossed it to eager hands.

"Only…keep a sharp mind, *la?*" Nepiur reminded Hax. "I swear on my brush I'll strangle you myself and bury you upside down if your fermented brain gets us lost."

Hax guzzled, swallowed, wiped his lips, and belched a mighty belch in reply, causing Dace to stumble with laughter and Maurus to rub his eyes in frustration. Hax then took off through the leaning stalks of the thi, cheering happily.

"Woo-OO! Not to worry, my generous Matriarch! My brain may turn mush, but my nose only gets keener when I've got the fruited tears of Aurba's joy in me!"

Nepiur did not provoke him further, grateful enough that he had managed to address her with some semblance of recognition of her authority.

Meanwhile, Rashala and Ronsha, the Iron Rain witchcrafters who would serve as the caravan's weapons, stole Hax's place upon Dace's back without warning. Ronsha helped her husband aboard before leaning over their carrier's forehead and smiling down into his indignantly upturned face.

"*Eina*, Dace, would you mind?" she implored. "My paws are all but scraped bare!"

Dace growled and rustled his spines, raised onto his hind legs to ford the river. He would rather not carry them, preferring to keep Hax's company.

"*Minla!*" he groused. "After two mornings? Away, freebooters!"

"It's so cold!" Ronsha cajoled, hugging Dace's neck. "And you have no fur! I turn into a tumbleweed if I get wet. It's unthinkable!"

Dace called over his shoulder, bucking a bit to get Rashala's attention.

"*Aienla*, unthinkable. Must be why you married that one, *la*?"

Rashala scoffed, while his wife giggled. In a confident protest he kissed her on the cheek. She blushed, giving him a look that belied Dace's insult.

Forgoing the conversation, Dace begrudgingly bore them across, grumbling all the way.

"Damned Iron beasts, making themselves at home on a man." He then hailed Nepiur, who scrambled among the branches overhead. "Mother, why did we bring these bothersome things anyway?"

Nepiur adroitly landed on the far bank, crouching in wait for the rest of them.

"*Udaiaan*, you want to fight a thuell yourself?"

"Bah! BAH! I fear no monster," he boasted, "Only this ceaseless fawning and chatter. *Svitka*, I feel their mancy burning my skin!"

He had to yell over that chatter. All the while, his riders fell over one another like pups with playful prods and constant joking, most of which was at Dace's expense.

Nepiur sought Hax, whose time seemed divided evenly between sniffing his way down their route and pouring wine down his throat as fast as he could. Part of her felt she was failing as a leader, seeing how these animals behaved. Even the Iron Rain were a shock to her. They were nothing like she expected. Their bodies were cut and bruised all over – from what gruesome contraption she dared not guess – yet they were incorrigibly rambunctious. Was this what all the student witchcrafters were like? They seemed almost innocent, playful in the face of danger, very unlike their teacher. The rest of the company were no different, she supposed, as if none but herself took their task seriously. She began to wonder if it was not their minds that were out of place. With a sudden shift in manner, she turned her half-lidded gaze towards Dace and joined the fun.

"*Eina*, I thought you took pride in protecting the helpless? If the water frightens them so much, then perhaps they should cower upon you permanently?"

The lovers' heads shot upright, forgetting their play.

"*Minaien* mother, I object!" Ronsha cried.

"*Aiatan*, we jest!" Rashala added.

Ronsha thrust her back against one of Dace's spikes theatrically, sweeping the back of her hand over her face and moaning.

"Oh, what shame to have a mother speak of us so! This grievous weight crushes the very breath from my lungs!"

"Gods take us!" Rashala agreed, feigning a slow death and draping himself over Dace's head. "*Vaeba* perish us! Woe forever be upon we, the loveless and forsaken!"

Nepiur rolled her eyes and smiled while Dace groused. As he reached the far bank, the Bakul pitched to his side and heaved his cargo into the moist grit of the bank. Then, not dignifying their remonstrations with a response, he trundled onward with a haggard sigh.

Now all the company but Maurus were assembled along the line of foliage, waiting patiently for the Lugu as he fought through the icy water with only his head and cutters visible. Trembling from the cold, his face was curled in a censorious scowl, eyes squinting against the bright sky overhead.

"I hate…you all…so much," he gasped, breathing between waves across his face.

Nepiur flushed with embarrassment at having left him behind so thoughtlessly. Striving to play her role honorably, she reached out to help him climb up the slippery bank with an apology.

"*Eina malpael udai*, I should have had Dace…"

"Should have had me what?" Dace interjected in good humor. "Shall I not carry the whole troupe, then?"

"*La? Ueinla*! Let's have that!" Came the laughter of the Iron Rain as they shook mud from their fur and clambered back on top of him.

Ignoring the escapades, Maurus clawed up the bank and took Nepiur's hand while leering up at Hax.

"All but that one," he commented. "He had better get us there soon. I tire of these vines and fronds attacking my face. And how long will Laesis sit overhead!? The above ground is torturous: the light, the heat, the people!"

Hax had climbed up onto the high branches of a gnarled thi, now hunched with pointed finger and twitching ears, indicating something visible through the canopies.

"I will not disappoint, *utaneis! Einla*, there is a thinning of the forest far and away, the unmistakable colors of carved stone there!"

"Standing stones? Good words!" Nepiur said thankfully.

"*Aiat*, there can be no knowing," he responded. "I could be terribly drunk, *la*?"

Dace snatched Maurus up onto his back, trampling a trail through the overgrown forest floor with zeal.

"Nothing repeated blows to the head won't fix!" He laughed. "I'll administer the treatment upon our arrival! BAHAHA! Come brothers, sisters, and mother most high. *Hawth*! With Loi's blessing there may be blood for spilling and friends for saving!"

CHAPTER 2: BETHAALI, GAL'TSKHAIN

Hax and Nepiur were, by their humble broods' gift of dexterity, first to traverse the rolling dell beyond the river and reach the meadows where Aes'bethil's domiciles glinted in the veridian light. An overzealous Dace burst from the brush shortly thereafter. Though they had indeed arrived at the place they sought, all their hopes were dashed by the unspeakable ruin before them.

The city had been truly beautiful once. Small, pristine, with two opposing rows of smooth white stone houses built into one another with meticulous artisanship. Across the tops of each, and winding down their faces, were troughs and trellises from which sprang an assortment of phototrophic flowers and vibrant cha'tskthi, both the fruiting and the decorative.

No Mantichaena of the Gate had ever visited Aes'bethil, and there was little left intact to admire. Its serene beauty was a veiled memory, nearly erased by the scars of a bloody battle. Homes had entire walls torn away, others were covered in ugly cracks. The ground all around was churned up, with a particularly horrendous black gouge running the length of the city, from the forest in the Thaun to the tallest buildings near the heart of the enclave. The damage was so extensive that it was difficult to conceive of anything smaller than a Bakul having wrought it. Such was not the work of liquid thuell.

Hax teetered once from inebriation before pressing on, the scene sobering him as he trudged past the city limits with aghast glances cast all around him. The rest followed in silence. Ronsha and Rashala were particularly wary, their instincts awakened as they slunk nervously on all fours, tails stiff and straight.

Nepiur went to stand at the edge of the deep wound in the ground and shuddered.

"Anama's bright blood protect us. What could have done this?"

A lone survivor, a man dressed and soiled much like the messenger had been, emerged from one of the more intact houses. Expressionless, he raised a hand to them, let it fall, then retreated.

The Iron Rain moved to Nepiur's side.

"Mother, if the thuell has infested something so large...I question our usefulness." Rashala said.

Nepiur's face was stern. She sharply gestured for all company on either side of her to advance on the house.

"I do not," she stated flatly. "Here we fight for our own, not strangers. We are the last defense of Aes'bethil, and we will do as needs must."

The interior of the building, a once resplendent villa larger and more ornate than the rest, was no less pulverized. The citizens huddled inside were so dejected that they appeared as dead as those they mourned. Their gloom was understandable. The runner who had come for aid had not overstated the gravity of their situation.

Nepiur braced as she approached a gathering of clasped hands and bowed heads, robed acolytes praying over a terribly injured woman. Just inside, she bowed gratefully to the man who had beckoned them, and quietly commanded accommodations be found for her troupe.

He obediently tried to lead the small group away to the next house, though Maurus resisted.

"Mother, wait, let us present ourselves!" he demanded.

Nepiur silenced him with sad eyes and, keeping her voice quiet, rebuked his attitude in the delicate situation.

"Be silent and go. This is not for you. See to it ours are rested."

Maurus' did not understand, his confusion betrayed by his frown, though there was no gain in arguing further. He nodded to their summoner and gestured for the party to follow. As soon as they were out of sight, Nepiur allowed herself to drop her stately composure and hurried over to fall at the prostrate woman's side, pushing several of the acolytes out of her way.

It was an unwelcome sight, a heartbreaking one, to see a sister in such condition. Even Bethaali the godlike had not escaped the carnage. She wheezed painfully, trembling from the pain of a fetid gash in her ribs. It seeped dark blood through the tight fibers and reeked of a familiar evil. Bandages and herbs were no good to stop it. They never were.

Nepiur's measured voice broke as she took and squeezed Bethaali's clammy fingers, stroked her tangled brown hair and desperately willed her sister to open her eyes.

"Bethaali?" she spoke quietly but firmly. "*Ein eis'mnaek* – can you hear me?" she persisted.

Bethaali's pallid lids fluttered open, soft green eyes and the lips beneath them smiling adoringly up to Nepiur.

"My…little precious…I don't believe it," she whispered.

Nepiur laughed through the tears that silently streamed down her cheeks and pressed her forehead to Bethaali's, kissed her nose.

"*Malpael.* I told you I would find you again."

"Not a day too soon," Bethaali replied with a touch of regret.

"No. No don't say that. Yours here are wise and skilled. They will have you strong again soon."

"Nep," Bethaali groaned, flinching and holding onto her sister's hand as tightly as she could. she tugged at it to keep herself focused as a toxic delirium tried to silence her. "It is just as father feared. It did not die in the Tau." She glanced over at the priest beside Nepiur, and he quickly rose to lead his fellows further away, giving privacy to their conference. "I was not able…to save my people. I am not strong like you."

"*Minla!*" Nepiur cried. "You are! You are your mother's daughter."

"Nepiur, listen to…please. I did this. I brought it here," Bethaali declared.

"*Aia…aien* what do you mean?"

"I went too far. Father was right to send me away. I did something very foolish."

Nepiur's lip trembled as she wiped her eyes, trying to comfort her ailing kin.

"Whatever happened, I know you never meant it so."

"It doesn't matter," Bethaali said dourly. "I have killed my own faithful." Her cheeks tightened as she clenched her eyes in shame. "Nep I...I know I promised you, no more travelling. I j-just...needed to know."

Nepiur was bewildered at her sister's weighty grief, absent now of any joy at their reunion. Clearly, in Bethaali's eyes, this was of consummate importance.

"*Quotis*, what reason have you not to travel as you wish?" Nepiur asked, forsaking her own misgivings. "You've gone afar since you were younger than I."

"This was different, worse," Bethaali mumbled. The look in her eyes was haunted, as if she was only partly present. Some frightening memory tugged at her. Nepiur saw it and, with more a sister's love than a Matriarch's, pleaded for her to explain.

"Betha, what happened?"

"I was so...interested in the stories that Hax used to tell," Bethaali began, slowly meeting her sister's eye. "Do you remember Hax?"

"The name stirs memory," Nepiur muttered.

"He used to make up such ridiculous accounts, wars that decimated the earthplane, how he fought alongside beings of pure light; So detailed, so drunk..." She trailed off with a halfhearted smile and Nepiur patted her cheek nervously and a bit roughly to keep her awake. Revived, Bethaali swallowed painfully and wheezed "Sister, his stories were truth. *Eina enta*, he was, at least about the...the things he fought. I have seen them."

"Betha, what did you do?"

Tears welled up in Bethaali's eyes, miserably bloodshot.

"I wanted see...see the end, the end of everything. I think I have."

Nepiur could not accept that, fumbled for a response but none came to her. Bethaali lay mutely ashamed, stared into space before suddenly returning to the conversation with tense, groping fingers and an urgent tone.

"Nep, *minein*, I was such a desperate fool. I wanted to see where everything led, the reason we are here...the meaning of it all." A shadow drifted through her eyes, a phantom that plagued her mind. "It's right here, all around us but…in the distant future; a dark world, Vaeba flowing over the earthplane. I couldn't move, couldn't breathe. It hurt just to be there. There were these…things, all around me; disgusting, shapeless nightmares that screeched and scraped through slime. And there was someone there, someone watching from above, on a mountain of bones. He was evil Nep. I know it. He was the most wicked thing I have ever seen. His hair, his body and…so many eyes, sick and unblinking…"

As Bethaali faded again, Nepiur shook her lightly and held her head, took up a cup from the assorted supplies with which the zealots had cared for her and put it to her lips.

"Do not go from me!" she cried, "*Prostas*, you must rest."

Bethaali sputtered on the water and her head lolled back and forth, half-conscious.

"I ran…tried to get away…breached…something came with me."

Her eyes clashed with Nepiur's, pleading for forgiveness. Nepiur's throat closed and she kneaded her sister's shoulders in frustration.

"Betha, hold onto me! You're going to be ok!"

"*Minaien.* Listen to me, my light and hope. You have to kill it. Don't…don't let that world come today. Don't let it come at all."

Bethaali then slipped off into painless dreams.

Nepiur allowed herself a small smile. How pleasant her sister's expression was when finally asleep, despite her suffering. Her blood still flowed, and her breath struggled on. It was good that she rested, giving Nepiur the opportunity to carefully inspect the sickly wound. It was unexplainable how the wound refused to close. Her mind reeled with thoughts of what curse or infection could be preventing it. Then, before her eyes, the oozing ceased. The gentle tics of Bethaali's hands and eyes grew further apart, stopped altogether and a final breath escaped her sinking chest. Nepiur sensed the change, grateful for the increasing serenity in her before realizing what was happening to the woman she held. As the warmth began to fade from her and into the ground Nepiur continued to sit with her, wept, tugged at Bethaali's clothes and whimpered imploringly for her to wake.

As hope was leaving Nepiur, a flicker of light traced the edges of Bethaali's body, suffusing her clothes. Entranced, Nepiur watched as her eyes opened. Blood that had fallen to ground rose up and slid back into the bindings that covered her wound, color returned and her whole body vibrated. For just a moment Nepiur dared hope her sister would survive, until Bethaali's creaking voice warbled innocently.

"N...Nep...I don't believe it," the dying woman wheezed, in the same sleepy tone.

"*Quo?* What don't you..." Nepiur began.

"You came...and not a day too soon."

"No...please," Nepiur moaned, her heart aching at the eerie familiarity of the words. She let go, standing and backing away as the scene replayed, every motion, every word she had heard in their first moment back together.

"Nep...Nep it's just as father feared," Bethaali said.

"No!" Nepiur cringed, screeching, "Damn you, NO!"

Nepiur could not take her eyes away as the harrowing monologue continued. The faithful gave no sign of consolation or grief as they gradually trickled back in, only hid their faces and prayed together as Nepiur fled from the room in tears. A goodbye could be endured once, but to relive it forever? How could Bethaali have done such a thing to her body? Had she even been alive when they spoke or was every word just a message left behind? she was in so much pain, travelling the now, binding herself in the same horrible moment just to see the one person she loved on the day of her death.

Thetrulengo speaks,

Misfortune again befalls me, insofar as I seek solace in the midst of a crisis of self and instead find another piece of unwritten history, another distraction from my seeking of truth that simply demands attention.

This woman...this miraculous creature is the closest thing I have ever seen to a being whose limits may exceed my own, a Mantichaena possessed of a power so far beyond normal life.

She is one of the blessed evils, exiles of the Gate. How many there are across Maengir I cannot say, but there are surely no less than six of these most godlike upon Manti. It is well they do not know where they come from, lest they feel they are owed a throne above their kind. One whom I do know could very well take it, but...he is of no consequence at present.

Although the offspring of various stars have appeared on many continents, even outside their forebears' dominion, I have concluded that the invigorating power of Anama in this place has made the Mantichaena especially desired as chosen heirs of the Nhi'Thaun. They develop so quickly here, their Galaila skin absorbing so much of the light. If the struggle between the young of Oorghunak, Miohaelia, and Zeniquorer is any indication, it would seem the elders have a particular interest in this island, as if drawn by its power.

This was the very place where Az'Rech and Escharka touched, the battleground where the offspring of light and flesh purged and remade Maengir. The old grudges and hatred resonating throughout this land are powerful. Is it only for these that they remain? No...there is more to do. The war is not over. The luminous and bloody gather here in wait of its continuation, and it seems the Nhi'Thaun wish to have their own champions in the fight. Desire never dies.

These champions surely are the Gal'tskhain, the chosen heroes of each elder. About forty seasons ago there was one called Klirash, the second of the Hanging Gate to be exiled after Naguza. She was, as far as I have seen, the final inheritor of the essence of Ferraro, daughter of Ethulsula. Imbued with the spirit of flame and earth, Klirash is the antithesis of Lemalie and equally dangerous. The divergence of their respective destinies was more than social position or public respect. Lemalie was older when they arrived, while Klirash was only a few seasons old. She was unable to control the change as her body became like molten rock, scorching the ground around her and igniting whatever she touched. Having seen Naguza's banishment, she knew that if she did not leave of her own accord she would become equally loathed. Largely in secret and informing only her closest family, she left her world behind to travel the deep ground in search of a more fitting home. Secreted as she was from the Mantichaena, I watched as she wound a solitary path north into Nikhaadi Gao. I presume she believed that icy waste would chill her blood and calm her fiery spirit. In a way it was just so. The Gao is vast enough to isolate her, though the mountain she nestled beneath could not contain her. As she melted the frozen stone around her it sought to be free, eventually boiling from a peak that rose higher and higher, like the womb that birthed her awakened power to the world. The fire did not escape the notice of the Kutu, and so they unwittingly discovered the resting place of Klirash, calling it Broken Mountain, a tower of fire in the lands of snow.

One member of Klirash's family was a gifted classical enchanter and had tried for many seasons to contact her little cousin by projecting her voice through the Veil. Eventually she found her. To the great joy of those who loved the exile there were a few chances to speak with her, though it only lasted for the briefest time. One day she went silent. Her house tried and tried to regain her, but to no avail, never again to hear the fate of their lost daughter. I believe, as they do, she simply accepted her time with them was over and embraced her new life, becoming the very soul of the volcano.

Bethaali is of much greater importance right now. She is a beacon of strength, not as difficult to be in the company of as other godlikes, though still a pariah to her father by nature of her inability to be controlled. She always said 'This was the last time', to him and anyone else concerned by what she was doing. I laugh at the thought of a mortal relinquishing such a gift or leaving it unused. Time, like a roaring sea, is navigable only with a vessel. Bethaali herself is that vessel.

Bethaali is a shadow of myself, the equal and opposite reflection of my ability. I am outside of physical constraints and able to be whatever and wherever I wish to be. Bethaali, while she must walk and climb like Galaila, has the blessing of choosing the moment in time which she experiences. From what I have heard her say to her faithful it sounds as though she cannot change her location, only the day and season.

Bethil means 'To see'. Bethaali means 'To see far'. It is a bit of a misnomer for her, yet it is a name she chose for herself after first discovering what she could do. In this time, I could be aware of her location if I wished it, yet the first time she flew outward from the moment I was astounded to discover I could not find her anywhere in existence! Bethaali has proven to me that time is a real concept, the world being comprised of infinite moments that have a definite sequential relationship. It took some careful disguise for me to seem to her like any of her other disciples, though once I was accepted, I learned all these things from her own lips.

I must concede that her unavoidable exile was not merely out of speculation. There were some complications that came with her 'Travelling'. Her early experiments caused some alarm and minor damage but, at one attempt, she had managed to nearly destroy Hanging Gate with the reckless use of her gift.

To me it is a sad story, now that I have become accustomed to the importance mortality places on the relationship between life and death. Bethaali leaves a sort of scar when she breaches. A door she must go through. For an instant after doing so, it is possible for other things to follow her through. No one of her own time ever dared try, either because they did not understand or because they saw her as a deity, not to be imitated. Even so, the result of this weakness was devastating when she returned to the present from a period in the past, having apparently breached to escape from a stampede of feral brak during the pre-Galaila age of Manti. Her ingress was right in the heart of the city and one of the beasts came through with her, smashed into Gazan and caused the collapse of the outer wall that now leaves so much of the hall's inner floors and arena exposed. Even after that encounter, she could not help herself. She was always so curious that she breached without restraint or thought, so her own father commanded her exile to someplace where she could not endanger Hauan Etain.

She was undeterred by the punishment, so obsessed with what she was capable of that the only remorse she felt was in never seeing her young sister again. Not many fought against her banishment after Gazan's breaking but there were some citizens who would not let her go alone. Such appears to be a common loyalty, or simply delusional faith. As Salohel had gathered the lost to him, so did Bethaali gather the philosopher and academic, those fascinated by attaining knowledge of other times. This was in the time of Anama, when the majority faiths were irrevocably divided between her and Loi, so Bethaali was called a bruise on the city and a false idol, while those who followed her called her the true goddess of their age.

I'm no more correct or enlightened than they. Whatever this woman's source, I have never seen anything like it in any of the elder gods. She is a lone ego, an entirely unique being...unless I have missed something. Perhaps she did not merely inherit the powers of a Nhi'Thaun, but has rather advanced on them. If she is the daughter of a god, then I can only surmise that she is more powerful than whichever created her.

In the interest of at least attempting an explanation, I conclude that she may have some connection to Ethulsula. He could not travel as she does, not that I am aware of, but the rising gods of the first era claimed that he so deeply sensed the essences of all living things that he could determine the choices they would make and the inevitable results. Indeed, they whispered that he could see all possible futures. If that were true, if he were powerful enough, I think it is possible that this girl Bethaali is not actually travelling time but simply negating her presence in this time while she views another; not actually allowing other creatures to travel with her but instinctively manifesting them with the power of her own soul. If I am correct, then she is not necessarily seeing the future or the past, only her best guess at what they will become and occasionally recreating what she sees. An unappealing notion, supposing she ever visited a time when the gods were not the dominant life in Maengir...which it seems she has done.

Concerning Ethulsula, the common rumor regarding his disappearance was that he had foreseen that his own death would come if he became involved in the elder gods' war and, for that reason, secluded himself in a place so well hidden that even his peers could not find him. I myself was so distracted by the conflict between the more prominent and influential divines that I failed to seek him out, ignorant as they of his doings until the fall. As the Nhi'Thaun began to appear in the sky, he finally revealed himself alongside them. Taken quite by surprise, I searched and searched through the few places I had felt his presence and found nothing. Nothing at all. I may never know how the patient god met his end or what he saw in the outer time planes that made him hide from the world. I imagine he was simply the most mortal of them all, chained to the same fear that makes one seek shelter from reality. The fear of death is strong. What a wasted life.

I empathize with that force which made him who he was though: curiosity. He seemed to me entirely consumed by knowing all that could be known and frightened only by that which he did not. This leads to two interesting choices: either Ethulsula was murdered because he foresaw something he was not supposed to, or he saw a future so dreadful that he took his own life to escape it. Perhaps this was the very thing Bethaali has seen.

~Chronicle of Wonders, Legacies of Ancestry

CHAPTER 3: AEGIS AGAINST ALL

T he crushing pressure of solid rock suppressed all movement, deafening Keimas to all but his own life as he began to wake from a murky slumber of the spirit. Though the pain and confusion of his transformation had lasted for only the instant of his transmittal through the earthplane, he felt as if he had awoken for the first time in his life. He opened his eyes but could not see, struggled but could not move. The very substance of the world seemed to be bearing down on him, penetrating and filling him. Had he fallen out of it? Beneath it? It felt as though he was buried so deep in the ground that he had become part of it. Though his body and soul felt strangely powerful they were simultaneously inhibited. Some ethereal thing burning uncontrollably inside him also kept him chained in place.

"H…Help," he croaked.

It was a real sound, real vibrations accompanied by the real feeling of grit slipping between his lips, yet it seemed to fall through him rather than into him. The only unreal object was himself. He felt everything he touched, but as he pressed against the stone it was as if his flesh remained in place while his light reached out, began to move through the stone before being jerked back into place by the grasping presence. Harder and harder he fought against it, straining to escape the shackles of the dark earth, gasping for breath between muffled screams. He felt suffocated, but realized he was not breathing. Perhaps not yet dead, with every effort he increasingly felt he was no longer alive.

Time passed, a fleeting moment or a lifetime, it made no difference. His mind repeated the choices that had buried him. Then, in the tranquility of surrender, he made peace with his fate. There were of course periodic questions, in recalling every word he had heard about Loi's purpose with him. Did that mean the god would return for him? Contemplating this, he prayed that the prophet who had swallowed him was good of his word. After all, Golgamet had sacrificed himself for this. This place was made for a soul not his own, and he was merely occupying it. Would it really be endless? The prospect of eternity conscious but unmoving was an undeath he did not know if he could withstand. It was not what he had bargained for, but as time blurred it seemed inescapable.

Trying to comprehend the intent of the god whom he had always ignored, it was impressed upon him that gods were just as fickle and prone to deception as he had often jested.

No, he tried to assure himself, *have faith, and remember for whom you made this choice.*

He calmed his mind with the memory of Lemalie, seeing again each line and shadow of her face, every flick of her expectant eyes. Strong feelings so freshly suppressed welled up. She was truly the only thing in his life worth such a sacrifice. He could not envision her without hearing her, and trembled as he listened deeper. She said something he could not understand, though in seeking her with his mind he felt her close by, touched her and sensed that they were not alone. Her eyes wandered and he tried to follow them, her hands taking his and drawing them to her belly. There he felt the beautiful and unfamiliar, his fingers clenching in hers as she finally looked on him, her entire story shared in a smile.

"No," he groaned through a mouthful of shifting rock. "What have…NO!"

As his blood heated in dismay, he felt a rising of tremors in the bedrock around him. His soul shook with them, and they mounted until they rattled him to his core. The coldness of the rock intensified, perhaps from below, or whichever direction was to the front of him. Feeling its power running through him he felt oneness with it, the paralytic chill of regret. He moaned and prayed for forgiveness of all his worldly flaws, believing that the end of his days had already passed, abandoning him on the threshold of oblivion and all the torments that surely came with it for such a disgrace of a man. His tortured thoughts warred within as the shaking built, both threatening to tear him apart.

Out of the stone horizon there came forking, searching streaks of red light which churned like smoke. A single bolt split into hundreds and tore apart the tomb around him. It wound away in every direction, filled everything he could see. It was not bright, had rather a sinister glow like a flash across the surface of oil. It opened around him like a mouth, feeling its way around a sparkling aura which only revealed itself while resisting the intrusion. Once wound around it, the crimson bolts constricted as if to bite and swallow. Amid distant cries the armor of light began to break, each resounding crack giving Keimas a surge of strength. Finally, it shattered and turned to a roaring tempest through which he could barely hear the voice ringing through it, vengeful and grating:

"*Aposd'maud'tskaposgahl* – Darkness eat and darkness crawl!"

Keimas screamed as he felt familiar, icy fingers clutch him, and the world became a tunnel of colors. Unable to distinguish one sight from another, he experienced visions of countless lands and skies, felt every sound from all corners of Maengir. All around him were mountaintops, the darkest depths of the sea and the rippling coronas of stars that whipped by him so close he could reach out and touch them, yet as far as they had been when he stood at the cliffs of Hauan Etain. He was singular but limitless, ephemeral but eternal, making his peace and prepared for his final resting place. However, death was not for him yet as he broke free of the Veil of his entombment and was drawn up through the outworld by a demon's vermillion web.

Flailing and shrieking, he abruptly plopped onto his back in a puff of sand. Barely able to see as the sudden white brilliance of Windsong replaced the gory red that plucked him from the abyss. Shielding his eyes, he felt the ground shift fluidly beneath him. Familiar with its sensation he reached down to grip the cool ground, dumbstruck as his hand passed through it.

It must be a dream, he told himself as he felt sand on and inside his skin. His left hand was firmly planted, yet his right was almost indiscernible, submerged until he pulled it back to his face. It was faded, images of flesh gradually appearing through a shining and shapeless fog. He saw where they came from; something he could not describe. The sand was flowing into him, tiny leaves, droplets of water, slithering creatures that burrowed below. The air all around him coursed through his lungs and into his hands. His body was rebuilding itself, replacing its missing piece by eating from nature. Like teeth into flesh, his fingers swallowed Maengir. Boggling as it was, his reassembly completed in a few short breaths, and to his scrutiny there appeared nothing to see but the body he knew.

By the softness of the ground and the sweet scent of fruiting thi he knew the familiar calm of the Gate's riverbanks. Such a welcome deliverance could not be possible, yet here he was. Was it possible this was some benevolent afterlife granted by Loi? The thought was a comfort for the future, but the current pain of being assured him it was not for today. His thoughts focused and his eyes searched the area, found the doors of Voddace and Ms'egol and the hungry chlio leaping from the river. He heard the distant roar of the falls as they poured into it. Laesis and the air of Windsong burned so wonderfully, blanketing him with ecstasy at feeling their worldly caress again. He felt and heard the drumming of many feet racing toward him and, from the path to Nesh heard that precious singular song he so loved; his wife and his whole world as she cried out.

"Kei...KEIMAS!"

Instinctively he launched himself to stand and nearly toppled again as he shakily turned toward her voice. She was there indeed, casting aside a basket of newly harvested nuts and sprinting to him across the field, tears streaming above a face-splitting smile and her sapphire hair billowing with every bound. Like a creature hunting, a single wingbeat heaved Keimas up and pitched him down to sweep over the dried gardens and thi'tskreol to land before her. With indescribable joy he took her in his arms and twirled into the air, swinging her round and round while she squealed happily.

Hundreds of incredulous stares ogled the reunion, and the passion unique to love so irrational that only a few days' division was confusing and tumultuous for those mated in it. Aroch soon appeared, saw the light in his son's face and the happiness in his daughter's voice and felt a calmness he had not in some time. Citizens of all halls, with hands clapped over mouth and breast, came thronging to Keimas. Amazed as they were at his return, they were spellbound by his appearance. Though startled by its change, they abided in Lemalie's affection as proof of his authenticity. This was no demon, as Rogan would have had them believe, yet neither was it the same Keimas.

Oblivious to their stares and ignorant of his own visage, Keimas landed and stood in place as his wife released him and leaned back, her eyes searching deep into his own. Absent her kiss he was already craving it again, but the way she gaped at him was alarming.

She breathed softly, taking hold of his wing and guiding it around her, fondling it, and at last he saw his feathers, no longer the pastel colors he had been born to by Soto's flesh. Instead they were as blue as the shallow sky and his beloved's eyes, similarly sparkling like jewels and nearly translucent as the light struck them. The streaming plumes that trailed from them had become so long and flowing that even with his wings fully uplifted they brushed the ground. His eyes were no different, cobalt like her seas, as though his return made him entirely hers. She took his face in her hands again, unable to speak, kissed him again and refused to let go. Nowhere in her touch did he feel concern for his new appearance. She saw only his heart and, for the first time, he really believed that it was worthy of her.

No sooner had their lips touched again than a crack of thunder split the air and the shadow of billowing clouds veiled Laesis. The heat of the Tau's wind was ripped away as it turned fast and cold. Then the heads and outstretched hands of the people felt an enlivening sprinkle started to fall. Longhand had promised water until the advent of Windsong destroyed it but, as the ominous star of Zeniquorer had retreated into the Aurbam Maengiri after his demise, the parched skies and mistaken stars had left the earthplane wanting. At long last the weather broke with a kiss of godlikes. Heat gave way to drizzle, drizzle turned to rain and rain turned to torrential downpour with enough force to drive it against the needful ground.

The two lovers interlocked unyieldingly. Silently lifting up by the whirlwind beneath Keimas' wings, he and Lemalie held one another, turning about in the brutal storm and never parting. Holding their ground and shielding their eyes, the crowd cheered at the power displayed. Lemalie had already shown them what she could do, but these two emergent furies clashing produced a wellspring of blessings. Some whispered reverently, others stomped in growing puddles and laughed up into the storm. A cheer began to rise through the noisome rain, chanting the godlikes' names to the sky: *"Khanem fex'ueaia Keimas'tskLemalie jioumeghen!"* – "To the rainmakers Keimas and Lemalie, prayer and praise!"

Lemalie's conquest had brought a new time, when the godlikes were no longer feared and reviled. Without Sky to turn fear upon them, those once called gal'tskhain were the inheritors of the tribe and seen only as a blessing from Loi and Anama. The reverent welcome of her and Keimas' display seemed a sign that Hauan Etain had become as it was always meant to be; the land new gods would rule.

Thetrulengo speaks,

At first glance I believed a sudden storm to be coincidental and trivial. With a second, I realize it is much more.

When given the opportunity to change our surroundings to our advantage it is almost inevitable that we do so. By 'We' I of course mean the majority of lives as well as myself, by mistake, if not with purpose. Is that wrong?

When an environment changes an animal seeks shelter until it understands the change. When one sees a flicker of affection in another's eye they are drawn to act on it. When a god gains an advantage over lesser beings they shall exploit it. In all these ways and more we attempt to give order to a chaotic world by remaking some element of it in the way which we believe is best. By proving to ourselves that we can bend events to suit our liking we begin to chip away at our sense of vulnerability, realizing the dream of a life that is as we wish it to be. I would infer that this is the very definition of morality; one's understanding of the relationship between the way the world is and the way it could be, most applicably by the change one creates in their own heart and what can come of it. After all, what is the world if not the plant grown from the seed of an individual's conviction? However, this is not a moral world, nor could it ever be, for by remaking an element of the world after one's own morality it will inexorably conflict with the morality of another. This is not a grand time of transcendence, it is merely the repetition of the mistakes made by the Nhi'Thaun.

Sometimes these actions are unconscious, such as in the case of the two newest gods in the long list of those known to the Mantichaena. Until now, Keimas and Lemalie were man and woman, one of whom they called possessed and corrupted and the other they simply called beautiful but secretive. Such paltry intellects have had a change of heart, whether because they needed to see for themselves that their Kutu had not turned into something hideous or if word of Artimecian's confessions dissolved their enmity toward him. As it began to rain this day, many knelt before the lovers and praised them as divine benefactors, believing that they had summoned the deluge as a divine boon. Is it true? Who is to say. I am not part of the veil nor of Maengir. That which I can understand is derived from what I observe and therefore limited in its completeness.

However, there is another sense shared by all beings that has no given name. It is the sense of disturbance, of chills from a change in how the world moves as the threads that hold everything together vibrate from a subtle wind. It is the tingling in the back of your mind that warns of something wonderful or terrible. I feel this sensation now, as I always have when creatures of power begin to ascend for the first time, though this time it is different. I feel waves of light approaching Maengir, at their heart a presence I have long been unable to feel. The machine of Az'Rech has changed, the Vulgoli removed and a new host emplaced. The edges dark and far have felt its thread quiver and both have begun to awaken for the first time since the beginning. Loi's actions have shown the oldest denizens of eternity that Maengir has become unruly.

~Chronicle of Wonders, the Worship of Fear

CHAPTER 4: NEVER APART

Nepiur's delegation had immediately turned the quarters they were given into a worse mess than it had been in the monster's wake. More homey now, the wreckage now closely resembled the deeper rooms of Gazan where recruits slept in piles, half-finished meals and soiled clothing scattered around them. Daylight spread from the front entrance as well as a side pass.

Yet more light fell through a gaping hole in the ceiling, the rough edges of which dripped an insidious sludge. Beneath it was a pile of fallen rubble, untouched for fear it would infect. Having settled a small area for their meager belongings the next order of business was to remove this insidious taint and the Iron Rain lost no time in cleansing the abode. Over each putrid crack and gathering pool they waved their fingers, ejecting arcs of energy that boiled and curdled the muck until only ash remained. Such was always the future of the thuell. They merely hurried it along. As the flash of the witchcrafters' power finally stopped the group relaxed, taking advantage of the lull before they began the greater task set before them.

Nepiur had been gone quite a while. Without her to orchestrate their actions neither solemnity nor caution seemed suitable to the weary travelers, leastwise to those castes of K'hizu whose broods would be found at play during even the most trying times. Rashala and Ronsha feistily wrestled in an illuminated patch of dirt while Hax drank to excess and goaded them on, asking around for stakes on the winner. Maurus, being of a different temperament, sat in the corner and sharpened his claws with only an occasional glance at their antics. Dace should have been at the center of the chaos but instead sat by Maurus and swatted at Hax whenever he wandered too close, or similarly swatted at the air to disperse the acrid odor left behind by the Boroo's inebriated breath.

Ever-alert, Maurus detected Nepiur's approach by the shadow she cast and was stood to order by the time she crossed the threshold. She leaned on the door's destroyed frame, taking in the scene before her with no apparent feelings to share. Her mind was teeming with plans for retribution but, facing her dedicated band, she felt no inclination to speak of it. Their warriors' convictions were worthy of her confidence, though they may not be entirely prepared for what they were about to face. She could barely think of how to describe it. Dace followed Maurus' example and rose, the three fools freezing mid-melee at a snap of Maurus' fingers. Those entangled joined the attentive and they collectively approached their leader, reduced to patient silence by the hollow look in her eyes. She had been trained for this, trained in Nesh since birth to take control and lead with firmness and good judgment no matter what adversity she had to endure, yet her eyelids and cheeks were still red and tear stained and every word she spoke was flat, absent her usual fervor.

"She's…travelling her last," she said, finally.

Hax winced and stifled an undignified belch, delayed in understanding the news while the rest of them thought on what they could say in support. They weren't even sure it was their place to try, given the circumstances and her higher station, so stood at a loss for words. She felt as they did; unsure, out of place. Then, the last glimpse of her sister's face turned her fear of the unknown back upon it and an unfamiliar hatred filled her. She was Nesh, and all other halls were her with her. The full power of the Gate was at her back. Drawing from it she tightened her jaw, almost growled as she spoke.

"*Eina mnaan* my friends, you were chosen for this journey because we of the council believed you suitable to do battle with the thuell, the vilest enemy our kind has known. It seems we are on the hunt for something far more despicable." She bit her tongue and stepped between her fellows, putting hands to Maurus' and Ronsha's shoulders and dispatching orders in a voice ripe with disgust. "The creature is unknown, from another world. It has already taken too many and it could again bring Aes'bethil to the ground unless it is stopped. I want it dead. Do you hear me? DEAD! There will be no further report of its nature to the council or any speculation of its origin. I'll not scrutinize it nor make supposition of its intentions. We hunt it, and we send it to Vaeba." They saluted acknowledgement, claws interwoven at belly height and heads bowed until she spoke again. "Have a rest and fill your guts. We move as morning becomes high day." She then beckoned Hax to her side, said "Except you. I will have a word."

Hax indolently did as told, now in a sour mood as the bottle he carried had run dry. Longingly he glanced back at the satchel where more could be found but, with duty incipient, he had no choice but to go without.

"*La aiat?*" he said, rather rigidly, as he met with her at the door.

Nepiur's unease was obvious as she addressed her tracker. "Hax, let's sit us down outside. Now…go and fetch yourself a drink. It is the only thing coming to you that will be of comfort, and I would prefer that you are comfortable." She left him to his personal pleasure and shuffled out.

Overjoyed by her accommodation and with fresh supply of the cherished liquor in hand, Hax gave chase out the entry and up a shallow gradient carved from the side of the building. It crossed half the front side, then in rounding its corner rose between it and the adjacent home, leading to a rooftop which was only partially intact for a hole bored in its south end. There were some undamaged wooden benches to lounge on but after seeing the ominous storm clouds that inexplicably billowed from the direction of Hanging Gate they were both inclined to stand, wrapping themselves in their arms.

"*Minein*, that is a bit strange," Hax groused at the coming sheets of rain, quaffing his wine. "Surprised to see a single drop come out of that dreadful heat."

Nepiur's seemed not even to hear.

"Hax, I know that…" vexed, she tried to gather her thoughts.

"*Malpael*, I know I once mocked you for the stories you used to tell when we were younger, perhaps too much so."

"*La*. But a childish pup grows to a hunter's Jiaia in this tribe as it does among the *K'hizu*."

She smiled. He didn't like it. She was smiling in the face of an utterly disrespectful remark, which meant she was feeling something worse than offense. He saw only pity cast at him.

"True enough, as you might have. I looked on you only as what you appeared to be. To my great embarrassment, I had hoped you would just leave and stop bothering everyone with your nonsense."

"With propriety to your place, lady, *wektauk autvul*, am I speaking to the archon or the heart?" Wine or not, Hax felt a fight was brewing.

Nepiur's lip stiffened and she tried not to cry, not as concerned with either of their feelings as she was with the truth.

"Hax, you were not ever planning to, were you?" she hesitated, unsure of how to proceed. "You would not leave, *la*? We thought you were one of us, cast away on this island long before we found it, called you a fool when you tried to convince us otherwise. You took to drink and we called you a bum. We ignored you and yet you stayed with us all this time, tried to make your way in a house even when no one welcomed you. Why?"

"*Aien*, lady says this now because she no longer thinks me a liar?" Hax asked.

Nepiur tried to move closer to him without alarming him.

"Convince her," she said.

"Can a beast not choose to be among others of his kind?" Hax mumbled uncomfortably.

"We are not your kind, are we?" she asked indelicately.

His expression soured and he broke eye contact with her, hesitant enough to regain it that Nepiur already had her answer.

"The story makes more sense than what I see," she thought aloud. "All of it, every ridiculous tale around a fire. You are the only Mantichaena to be found before us, so I cannot discount how long you have been here waiting. You...really fought against something of the old world?"

"I would have stood aside, had I known what would happen here. *Minein*, I did...I just wanted to help you people!" Hax stood groggily and paced around the terrace, suppressed self-disdain born of several lifetimes of bitter failure rising and blooming into anger before Nepiur's eyes. "All I wanted was for you to stop killing one another! I tried and tried but no one would listen!"

Nepiur recoiled as Hax released the pent-up hurt, lost control and swung a fist at the parapets of the house, cracked skin and bone on the unyielding marble. The sound made Nepiur wince in sympathetic pain, but Hax barely acknowledged the injury, never favoring it while downing more wine.

"I finally found a god willing to embrace peace," he spewed, "A warrior willing to stay his hand. One is not enough while it still has enemies, and so even that peace amounted to nothing. I succeeded only in getting him killed."

"Hax…how long have you been alive?" Nepiur inquired sternly, feeling herself believe in him.

"Long enough," he huffed wearily. "Long enough to see oligarchies and apostolic monarchies a hundred times greater than yours come crashing down because no one can…let go."

A suffocating quiet followed, and Nepiur hoped that the rumble of thunder in the distance would keep them unheard by the company below.

"Hax…*eina malpaelm*," she said sadly. "I am sorry that you have gone unheard so long."

"Dace heard me. He always has."

"He is the better man, better than the rest of us, to a friend who needs it."

Hax felt the warmth of gratitude and faced her again. That she would now trust him meant the world and moved him to answer her next penetrating question.

"I'm sure it's very hard for you to think about," she quietly continued, "But I need to ask you about your past."

"My answers are yours, *aiat*," he allowed. Then, lifting the drink and smiling slightly, "Payment for the libations and your kindness."

"Is there really a god of gods?" Nepiur inquired. "Not Loi but something more?"

"I have faith there is."

"You don't know?" she asked, disconcerted.

"I have never met it. None of us had. We knew only one lord, the son of god, who assured us of his father's word and existence, demanded we praise him above all else and die in his name. If we diverted from that righteous path we were punished with the removal of the divine grace he had given us."

Nepiur was lost, failing to make sense of his discombobulated memories.

Hax grunted, "You don't believe me anymore, do you?"

She paused a moment, then said, "If you are merely a mad drunk then my sister is too."

"Bethaali spoke of...god?" This was surprising to Hax.

"*Minein.* She told of a future in which an insidious creature has taken hold of all the world and light is no more. What she described seemed to me very like the cataclysm you used to describe, the one you told us you and your kind put an end to. Is this something you would understand?" Her searching gaze connected with his once again.

Hax nodded very slowly, troubled and greatly focused on some inner memory.

"*La.* It is exactly what we were created to prevent. Nepiur, is that the place from whence our quarry came?"

"I imagine it is. Can we kill it?"

And there was the question. Hax sat stone-faced on the edge of the roof, patted the spot beside him and looked far and away into the winds from the Tau, losing himself in the gloomy rain oppressing Ni'ivitnem in the distance as Nepiur sat. Several times he parted lips as if to speak, always resealing them with a new look of disconcertment. Nepiur waited patiently by his side as he worked through the thoughts.

"Tell me, did she conjure a monster, or a man?"

"A...a monster," Nepiur affirmed.

"Then it will die," he said with a sigh of relief.

"And if perchance it were a man?" she asked, remembering Bethaali's description of the harbinger that stood atop the mountain.

Hax's teeth clicked uncomfortably. He trembled in the cold wind but did not warm himself, dreading for the first time in many seasons what might become of this world.

"Then...nothing can save us," he muttered.

Nepiur's throat dried at the certainty with which he spoke. Whether he said it more from faith than fact she could not tell. She had no idea what dangerous new territory this battle would bring them into and could not reassure herself that Bethaali's vision was not indeed the bitter end that awaited. All she could do was hope the thing they sought was no more a man than any other poisoned by thuell, that Hax was correct in believing they could stop it.

"You are right," she said abruptly, looking to the Tau and diverging from the topic. "That gloom and wet is very out of place this season."

"A good omen?" Hax proposed.

"*Einla*, an omen, though not one which we that are untouched by the celestial can interpret."

Hax recognized her ironic joke with some pleasure but his forlorn expression remained. She had never much cared for him but in light of his tales' new credibility she tried to imagine what plagued him if not concerns well above her own. Imagining that he had indeed lived since the old world and walked among gods and demons, she felt her burdens were sadly meager upon seeing how he resented the state of the new one.

"Tell me more about yourself," she again shifted subjects.

"Why?" He countered with wide eyes and disbelieving smirk. "I'm no less a drunkard now than I was before."

She smiled amiably, pressing "Well, it is just so strange to me that a mortal might become a higher being and yet remain who he always was."

"Never have I been mortal as you are," he sighed with indolence. "Once I walked as a beast in the shadow of flesh, then was raised from it to fight upon the shores of light. That light is removed and I am left with memories of the beast and the anointed, yet no memory of freedom."

Nepiur stared sadly. She had assumed he was no longer Deina'itka, as he once titled himself, though the way he accentuated the word 'removed' held a particular resentment.

"*Myela!*" he spat lightheartedly. "The mantle of Deina is unpleasantly kept. Far better to be a fool upon Maengir than a slave in the earth or sky. In the company of my wife I threw it down hoping to annul the price I paid for it. That is the one choice I made for myself."

"You took a wife?" she asked, astonished.

"Amazing that this is what intrigues you," Hax laughed.

Nepiur blushed, clinging to herself again to stave off the cold and regretting having left her cloak below.

"It is now the only thing that doesn't seem to suit you," she said, with no small irony. "What was she like?"

"She was stubborn," he stated emphatically.

"A good woman, then," Nepiur said with a pert smile.

"A stubborn one," he repeated. "But *la,* goodness taken form. She was always stronger than me, more decisive, far more gifted. It never served me well to disagree with her. We were charged with watching over this small corner of Maengir, she and I, with our nine hundred ninety-six brothers and sisters scattered across hundreds of other lands. We were as content as soldiers without a battle could be. Yet the more time she spent here the more she became obsessed with the island's history – the bloodshed we had seen on it and the secrets it still kept from us – until she...turned away from the god."

"Where is she now?" Nepiur enquired.

"I have not the smallest inkling. I resented her for making me choose between her and our calling but still I gave in to her. I followed her until the moment she began to scratch at doors we were warned never to open. She stopped trusting me it seemed, never telling me what it was she wanted, what she was after. It consumed her, stole every shred of her love for me. In the end, I had to let her go the way she wished, for it was clear that it did not lead back to me. She became understandably angry and continued her mortal journey without me, leaving me to protect this place while she searched on."

"That is a terrible loss," Nepiur said.

"She holds no blame. I must forgive her for being who she was born to be. I was content to live and die at her side. She could never be happy without a battle to win."

"Do you know nothing of her doings since parting?"

"I know only that she set out east from where we made camp in the mountains Dhai. It was a few seasons before the time you and your people first arrived. She wanted to...recruit."

"For the Deina'itka?"

"For herself," Hax retorted gruffly. "To join her search. I spied on her a bit to ensure she was not doing anything too rash in her quest, yet all she did was wander from place to place spending many seasons at a time to dig deep with the only two fool enough to follow her; two young fellows called Bandta and Kjan."

"I'm not familiar with them," Nepiur said, searching her memory. "And you've no idea what they were looking for?"

"I discovered it in due time," Hax admitted. "By where she searched, how long, how deep. She was looking for our champion, one who had fallen in the clash. She wanted to find a way to bring her back; the only mother we had known."

Nepiur sensed that Hax was wearied by her interrogation and decided to let him rest.

"Increasingly curious," she huffed, rising again. "Come below for now. Perhaps you can tell me more another time."

He smiled up at her and took her extended hand. "I would enjoy that. To have the ear of one such as you is a gift I will cherish."

Nepiur shared a glinting smile with him before asking one last question.

"Hax, your wife…do you still love her?"

He wasted no time in a warm reply, his eyes roaming through the whispering rain ahead as he stood.

"Deina'itka Aia Takinoxote was and always will be the crescendo of my heart's melody."

Nepiur hummed pleasurably at the way Hax remembered the woman. Her mind wandered briefly as she thought of how Capheif might paint herself in prose. A single, beautiful verse began to form in her mind, immediately vanquished as she looked beneath the storm clouds. The rain came fast, echoing from the bobbing fronds of the thi. As it met the edge of the jungle, she glimpsed a shadow that steamed as the water touched it.

"Haaax…" she hissed furiously.

"I see it," he said with deliberate calm, crouching slightly.

Nepiur gripped his wrist, her eyes piercing the rain.

"I…am I mad, or is it…looking right at us?"

There, where the trunks tangled together, a dark mass gently heaved with spindly extrusions twitching in the shaded mist.

Hax's muscles tightened. He tilted back and forth like a man suspicious of his own reflection. Then, without warning, he surged forward and leapt out through the arriving rain to the ground.

As soon as Hax moved, the grotesque jerked away, cleaving a clump of roots in half as it scrambled into the thi.

Nepiur gasped and bounded down the stairs on all fours, shouting at the top of her lungs,

"*Hawth Thaun*! *Hauan Etainilt,* shake your tails! It is still here!"

CHAPTER 5: PAVED WITH GOOD INTENTION

Even the largest Mantichaena knew not to underestimate the borderland. There were some, however, who challenged it with reckless abandon, believing themselves its masters. Far from the Gate, amid unsettled hills where no Mantichaena was welcome, one was testing the forgiveness of both nature and the divine.

From the rim of a great and lightless pit, a burly Bakul voice echoed down therein.

"Tak? Tak! See you anything?"

The man was not as large as others of his kind, though still a fine anchor for the vine that slid tautly through his hands.

From the deep came the muted reply of his partner, a Boroo woman on a search for fortune and glory.

"Not yet...wait...*EIN LAAN*!"

The walls were slick, despite the recent lack of rain. Moisture seeped out of the ground and vaporized in moments, filling the deeper tunnel with a stale-smelling fog.

As the Boroo's descent jerked to a stop, her small, clawed feet scrabbled to keep her steady. She shouted her irritation to her belayer, though in truth she was not angry with him. She was not patient by nature, less so now, as many seasons' wounds and starvation seemed near their end. She was getting restless, reckless, desperate. A lifetime of dead-ends and cold trails had made her so.

Pulling hard to increase her slack, Tak stepped out, flattening her tufted ears against her head and barely squeezing into a damp fissure that allowed only slight movement. From a side-slung bag she withdrew a candle and knelt with it in hand. Then, pushing her ornately beaded locks of brown hair away from her painted face, licked her lips nervously and gently blew across its wick. Spontaneously, and with great flare, it ignited, momentarily dazzling her as it reflected off the surface of a stone blocking her path, purposefully emplaced yet obviously foreign. With laughter and relief, she kicked off the wall and spun round and round,

"Tak, what is it?" came the voice above her.

"*Bolg'chakeiis*...Bandta, go and fetch Kjan!"

"Is it here? Are you certain!?" he replied excitedly.

"*Mineina*...not just yet," she called, distractedly searching around the hole. The earth is disturbed. We are not the first to cut to the quick of it."

"Do I tie you off?" Bandta asked with concern.

"*Einla*! Don't you strand me here!"

The vine rustled as it was hurriedly hitched to some other object, and the sound of Bandta's retreat reverberated down to Tak, leaving her alone. She ignored a tingling fear as silence seemed to envelop her. Tak placed her hands on the slick stone in unrestrained glee and shoved with all her might. It shifted marginally, enough that she could illuminate the path beyond. It was unsightly, hastily dug and without any sign of offshoots. It was almost certainly no mine, nor was there any practical reason to seal it if it were not a deliberate hiding place.

She silently prayed for an end to the sour luck she seemed to be cursed with and that this would not be another in a long string of disappointments. Did she pray to a god? No. She prayed to herself. Again, she heaved on the stone until a rustle at her back signaled the arrival of help.

"Bandta, tear this big bastard away would y..." She turned away from the irksome obstacle then fell back against it at the sickening sight of a full-grown deghni clawing up from the depths. Its barbed skin steamed in the faint daylight but the hunger in its eyes showed it would not turn easily from a lovely snack. It attacked as soon as it was noticed, dripping pincers that lined its vertical maw snapping against each other as its long body and rattling carapace thrashed against the slim gap, breaking it apart piece by piece amid chilling screeches.

Tak flattened herself in the crook of the wall around the stone, curling her arms in front of her in defense as her mind shook off fear in search of a plan. She gauged the time she had until it broke through. With no other options, she encircled the air in front of her with her palms and closed her eyes. "*Dei'isnir deisay...*" Her incantation was interrupted by the hideous creature's death rattle, a fountain of blood and spittle burbling from its gullet as Bandta's giant fingers crushed its neck. Tak huddled away from the effusions, wincing at the wet crunch of its carapace before the prickly corpse slid back into the ground; soon after, a satisfying sound of chitin against stone.

Tak unwound, and the flickering light in her fingertips dissolved into the air.

Bandta's chunky face popped into view, upside-down and with a pleasant smile.

"*La*, mistress, some days since we had meat."

"Eat later," she said mirthlessly. "Get to digging a path."

She then slipped out to trade places with him, anchoring herself against the wall just as their last companion came sliding down the vine.

Kjan, a mangy and unkempt Kulo, was even less intimidating a figure than the others. Missing several teeth, a foot and half an ear, his companionship was a result of his having very little direction in life, and Tak having a need for any assistance she could find.

Seeing no kills in his possession, Tak was uninterested in hearing how poorly his search for food had surely gone.

Their Bakul set to driving his tusks against the alcove to continue the work the deghni had started until it was thoroughly smashed, wide enough even for his great frame to pass. The hefty, smooth stone within was no more a challenge, easily ripped away and flung to the abyss with one hand. He faced Tak, aglow with boyish cheer and putting a hand to his ear to savor the splat it would make as it struck the vanquished arachnid. He was disappointed when there came instead the bang of rock alone but shrugged and dismissed it.

"Hmm, long drop. It must have tumbled away."

"Or its brood dragged it away for a feast before they come looking for its killer," Kjan reasoned in a raspy voice. "We should not tarry."

Tak pushed past Bandta and into the passage without delay, retrieving her candle and leading the way with its minimal light.

"*La.* One big one means a hundred little ones. Keep a lively pace and be wary."

Bandta followed with Kjan in tow, both jabbering in anticipation of what was to come.

Tak ignored them, immersed in her own thoughts. If not for the deliberate blockade she would have dismissed this as a natural cavern. Though it may not be the hiding place she sought, it was certainly something worth investigating.

Her hunch was rewarded as the company was confronted by a spine-tingling spectacle: a widening of the burrow as it sharply declined, slathered on all surfaces with a sticky black crust and the reeking odor of dead things. She seemed not to notice the stench, was only aroused by the implications of such decor.

Kjan winced slightly from the stench but maintained. He was accustomed to the pungency of his own body. This was little worse.

Bandta, a man of small constitution and once accustomed to comfort, gagged and buried his face in his arm. Despairing that they must travel such a rotten path, he pulled at Tak's shoulder intently.

"*Min*, mistress, I'll not think my own judgement the better to yours, but might we find another way? Perhaps further down the pit?"

As he spoke, they were alerted to the approach of the deghni's many offspring by the distant rattle of pointed feet at the cave mouth.

"No," she smiled grimly, "Unless you want to deal with them."

"I would consider it!" he moaned.

Kjan shoved past Bandta and boldly staggered down the putrid path.

"Come, oaf!" he shouted, the wooden cap on his calf clacking against the sticky cobble. "Infinite glory awaits in the belly of the beast!"

Bandta remained reluctant as they delved deeper, into even

thicker stench. It was of less concern now than being swarmed and eaten. Wringing his rocky hands, he softly hummed to soothe himself.

"Tak, this is neither mold nor mud," Kjan said, poking around him with his clawed toes. "I don't think...what do I feel underfoot?"

"You think not?" Tak inquired.

With an incredulous smirk, Kjan gestured to himself.

Tak sighed at his jest, though convinced the vagrant would know the sensation of such materials. She stooped quickly, swiped a fingerful of the sludge and examined it with nose and eye. Her eyes twinkled, and she smiled with disgust.

"It is a residue left by the thuell, very old, charred as if dayburnt.

"I-is there more down there?" Bandta fretted.

"No, not anymore. This thuell was slain, its remains left here by design. No doubt the tactic of the native ilk to frighten away the feeble."

"They knew you were coming," Kjan chuckled to Bandta.

"They want no trespassers," Bandta muttered, ignoring the jab. "Perhaps another Deina'itka? Or..."

Tak wavered upon feeling some sharp points underfoot and kicked at the obstruction, scattering fragments of crusted bone ahead of them.

"Or the redkin," she concluded for Bandta. "Those of the unravelling must have manipulated the thuell to carve this place out for them, then spread their corpses upon it."

Kjan grew exhilarated and bounded ahead, ignoring the crackle of the black shreds beneath his feet.

"Do you really think she is down here, mistress? *La*, the Vulgoli were tricky to guard it thusly."

"*Udai*, I will not raise my hopes, but I suspect we are getting closer."

Bandta cast a worried glance over his shoulder. The persistent clatter of deghni was growing louder.

"Tak," he warned, "They know we are here. Can you not stop them?"

Kjan perceived the smolder in their leader's eyes and attempted to deflect the thoughtless demand on her behalf.

"It's not worth the risk. You know that."

"Getting picked apart alive seems like it might be worth that risk," Bandta argued.

Conscious now that the danger was upon them, Tak was beginning to consider it.

"Never panic, my friend," she admonished, picking up the pace despite the minimal light of the candle. "I cannot say how much light I could release without drawing the sovereign's gaze to me. I would not dare unless there was no other WAAAY!"

She flapped her arms as her toes slipped over the edge of a sheer drop.

Bandta snatched her arm and pulled her back, staggering a retreat from the precipice.

She likewise gripped him, and together they stared back at the cacophonous shadows gathering at their ingress.

"*Jaiaeis*, now we panic, *la*?" Bandta whimpered.

The three lingered, peering deep into the void with increasing dread as they searched with the tiny light for any route down.

Each then briefly thought on the most preferable death. The deghni's poison was terrible to risk: paralysis, but with nerves fully alert, leaving one awake to endure a long and painful death by teeth and claws. An end far worse than a rocky plunge.

Tak refused to yield, sliding down to lower herself over the edge. Groaning, she reached her toes out in search of any hold or floor. Both evaded her.

"*Taul'khain,* no good!" she cried in dismay, waving the candle beneath her, but seeing nothing.

Kjan similarly felt around the walls, more out of desperation than expectation. He looked back just as the slinking infestation of tiny deghni came into view, and his confidence shattered.

"*Eina khainueg*! Jump for it!" he shouted, recklessly leaping to the far wall of the pit. Latching his claws into it precariously, he felt them slipping on the grime.

Bandta threw himself down prone, reached out to Kjan imploringly.

"Fool! Get back! We can still…"

A pang of terror raced through Kjan's as his grip broke, one foot raking the wall while he strained desperately to catch Bandta's fingers but fell hopelessly short. Stunned at the cruel suddenness of his journey's end, he mutely stared up at his friends until he vanished into the deep. In the absence of his own cries, theirs rained after him, cracking with heartache and drowning out the distant thud of his demise.

Tak dragged her torso over the precipice and slapped furiously at the muck, trembling and screaming. She felt Bandta's powerful arms scoop her up and hold her tight against his chest. For a moment, she looked up at him dejectedly, and he upon her with uncharacteristic serenity.

"Tak...I believe in you," he said with a slight smile. "You showed us a world so much greater than what our eyes could see, a purpose so much bigger than we as simple men could have found on our own. I know you will find her. You will."

Tak latched onto him with all her might, eyes turgid, instinctively resisting as he stepped through her and over the edge. They turned midair, and she barely glimpsed the last flicker of her candle as it slipped her grasp and tumbled away from their deadly plunge.

The fall seemed eternal, then suddenly brief as Bandta thrust his limbs against the wall. Roaring in pain, they were enveloped in swirl of rock, both living and otherwise, as the walls closed in around them. Streaming blood and flesh, Bandta's grip remained unshakeable as he poured his heart into saving a life more important than his own, even unto his own death.

Tak could only hold on for dear life, trying to shut out the cries of her friend while he traded his life for hers.

At last, they met ragged ground in a shower of shattered baktite spines, deep under the skin of the world where neither deghni nor daylight would find them.

CHAPTER 6: BEST REMEMBERED

By the unanimous decree of the Council of Archons, the Iron Sanctum was disbanded until such time as a new archon was found to command it. This decision swiftly followed the examination of its workings and the absolute revulsion on the part of the council that Artimecian could have instituted such reprehensible practices. Of his training methods, the witchcrafters only spoke in defense and with great gratitude. Nonetheless, they grudgingly obeyed when the final order came. At Aroch's command, the devices of torture were dismantled and destroyed. The blood was scrubbed away, the doors were sealed, and lots were drawn by the students for the distribution of Artimecian's meager possessions. In the end, his memory was kept in a few trinkets, while all his clothing was burned, and his furnishings removed to other parts of Ms'egol.

The unseasonable storm continued to rage, adding its oppression to the somber occasion of Artimecian's entombment. He had received no ceremony, no procession, been given no day of mourning as those who died in the struggle against Zeniquorer had. His death was merely accepted, no more noteworthy than the end of a day. The remaining gothic students had not been present as his corpse was drawn from the cells to be bound in silk and placed behind stone in Voddace. His bearers were apathetic to their task, resentful of it even, and so the simple headstone they erected bore only his name without any fond epitaph. Patriarch Saketsu presided over the interment with a somber heart.

Far more burdened by the death, perhaps the only Mantichaena who felt any strong remorse, was his old friend Aroch. Compelled to attend by his own sense of responsibility, he did not harbor the bitterness of most others. Memories of a close bond in youth were as fresh in his mind as they had been in Artimecian's, though perhaps better remembered by the new Primarch than they had been by the master witchcrafter. Aroch believed he understood what had driven his old friend to such extremes. Though he despised it, would not condone it, he felt he understood it, and held onto the hope that it was not true corruption of the heart but merely a confused and misguided hope for the future of the city that had perverted his colleague and made an enemy of him. Melancholic that his once good friend had been so deeply buried in the flesh of such a harsh and obsequious man long before he was buried in stone, Aroch grieved alone amidst the storm and the few attendees.

As the council felt it was their obligation to be present for the interment of one of their order, each wrestled with their own thoughts. Mani was offended by the courtesy offered the man in death and grumbled of it without regard to social niceties. Aroch heard, dismayed by Mani's mutterings but made no reply until the ceremony was complete and the body sealed.

Turning to Mani, he said dourly, "*Eina prostas*, do not wish ill of a dead man. Forgiven or not, debts repaid or increased, this is where he belongs and the only place he should ever be found."

"So near to your own family's tomb?" Mani countered. "With the promised blood of your son on his hands?"

Aroch stared reprovingly but would not defend his judgment. His voice might not be the most adept to politicking, but it was now the strongest the council had. The bitterness of the moment notwithstanding, he knew he had their respect, more so now that everyone knew the impugning of his family's honor was not a conspiracy of many, only the deception of one.

As leader of the family at which the previous Primarch's hatred had been focused it was his right to punish the perpetrators and accessories as he saw fit. Once he had had such dreams of how his vengeance would be wrought but those now seemed small minded.

He was a man of principle. The satisfaction of personal justice meant nothing when the advantage was his, for he felt his soul would scar if he showed so little restraint now that he was in a position of power. There was none who could be trusted to bring wrongdoers to justice more than Sebashni Sky. Still, he would be doing her a disservice not to advise her as wisely against its influence as she had him.

The sparse attendance quickly dissipated until only Aroch remained, lingering at the foot of the great tomb with a blank stare. He was loath to think about the crimes Artimecian had committed, rather recalled the gifts he had shared as a young man: the open doors of his family's home on Ellel, the warmth of their fire and table any time Aroch or Naguza had come to him. Artimecian had been a grandiose man then, still had been at the end, in some ways. It was a critical reminder to Aroch that any could become venal, corrupt, soon after bound, if absent the will to question the beliefs that give order to their thoughts.

It was difficult to imagine the future of the council, considering the deception so recently exposed. Mistrust amongst the people was extensive, who now had to question so much of what they had been led to believe. The idea of electing new archons was laughable until the newly appointed Sky, Aroch's own wife Sebashni, had time to prove her own sense of honor and character. Furthermore, they had yet to deal with those within their ranks who had been so easily misled by Rogan. The new Primacy would need a council that would hold it accountable, not smile and nod obsequiously in order to curry favor.

Aroch aroused himself from his musings, as he remembered his responsibilities: responsibilities that afforded him little time to grieve. His meticulous brand of oversight was required by the crews of Tault, who had already begun repairing the damage to the Gate. Overhead the storm Keimas and Lemalie had supposedly brought on still raged, even out at the edges of Thonsfa. It eased the thirst of the city, allowing them to collect more water for storage and providing hope for one last harvest this season. But it also brought the river levels to a flood stage that was exceedingly rare, such that the mouth at the east end of the canyon where it drained into the winding caverns below was overwhelmed. The excess roiled and carved in the sands, a new stream pushed through the destruction in the great wall and into the dead Tau.

Despite the tumult, the work of resealing the Gate was greatly offset by the pleasant kiss of the cool rain and the flow among the feet of workers as they bore heavy burdens. Lugu and Bakul worked in tandem to bring heavy slices of the blessed rock back where they belonged to close as much of the breach as possible. The scope of the damage was a harrowing testament to Artimecian's strength and the destructive capacity of a gothic master, which served to heighten the residual dread of venturing so near the old land.

Though the laborers' purpose was virtuously inspired and would protect the city from the reemergence of the torrid winds of the Thonsfa, the mood turned grim when they discovered the blackened remains of Raru and his disciples.

Aroch stood aghast as they were wrapped to be returned to the city, feeling the first twinge of real hatred for Artimecian that so many others had felt. Friend or not, he may have deserved less consideration than Aroch had given him. If he had not taken his own life, perhaps Aroch would have ordered it taken from him.

The morbid evidence of the encounter between mantic castes and subsequent revelation of Sky's dealings hung heavy on the workforces as the Gate neared completion. Other Enchanters of Raru's school of classicism stood ready to ignite the repaired portion of the barrier once again. Then, as the final piece was about to be placed, they looked to Aroch for confirmation.

Seeing their expectant faces and thinking deeply, he eventually stayed them with a hand and approached to look out through the downpour to where the gray dunes disappeared into the horizon.

Metaeu, who had been managing construction as acting foreman, now placed his hand on Aroch's back reassuringly.

"Father," he said, "Keimas returns, and his assassins do not. That is reason for resolve, not sympathy."

Aroch huffed uncertainly, then waved off those carrying the last stone.

"*Mingnogheisi* – that is not what I think. Leave it away. So many have been damned these two days that Vaeba will overflow. I would have Artimecian's creatures punished for an attempt, not a success."

"To leave this open will expose us," Metaeu reasoned.

"To what?" Aroch asked without concern. "A puff of heat? *Mineina enta*, look and see the desolation there. There is no great danger but a few sticks and sand. We have blocked most of the crosswind that will arise when it dries again. Now cut that piece in half and fit it. If the Iron Wind returns, they will not be made to die. After a time in that wretched place, and the loss of their father, their penalty must be weighed carefully."

It was done accordingly, but still Metaeu followed in Aroch's retreating steps.

"They were sent to kill your son," he reminded him.

"And they failed. Until Keimas himself speaks against them I'll consider no sentence. It is my family's right to deliberate on what should be done with them."

"Do you think he slew them?" Metaeu asked, a bit hopeful.

Aroch had, to his shame, privately embraced the same hope, yet he could not afford such acrimony if he ever wanted to see his land healed.

"It is possible, though after this ordeal I am exhausted with trying to divine the unknown. As far as this city and this council are concerned, they are still our sons, blinded by devotion and fear of disappointing a teacher. Two lives already condemned will purchase compassion for two more."

"*La*…as you command, father."

In the loveliest of Nesh's rooms, Keimas and Lemalie slept, Lemalie's hands clasping those of her husband. Entwined and uncovered, they were as one, a delicate artistry of contentment. Love had been renewed, rest enjoyed. Presently they awoke to the sight of one another. Embracing silently in the feather-laden bed, each savored the other's every motion and heartbeat.

Keimas inhaled her scent and felt her warmth, the essence of everything he loved in life. They soothed him, raised him above the instincts his blood had previously forced upon him. A sleepy stroke of her fingers brought his eyes to where they touched. It was intoxicating, freeing and captivating; the focal point of his existence in a single marvelous touch. It was a focal point he vowed never again to part from.

He no longer dreaded sleep for fear of that which had pulled him from her. Such things felt surely lost in the past and immaterial now that he was home. With a satisfied eye, his gaze wandered about the room, came to land on the window and saw at last the rain was thinning. The passions of his bride's spirit were finally appeased, her love fulfilled and its manifestation in nature carried on the wind to other places. All Manti would see the sign of their reunion as the storm travelled across its breadth.

He felt different, strange, somehow not himself. At one time he would have spent these moments dreaming of the hunt and combat, yet no such desires now distracted him. He felt no anger, no restlessness, no longing for Ellel nor even for fame. He did not feel any more accomplished, simply contented. His Kutu blood did not burn so hot. His heart, so burdened by the desire for a father he never knew and bitterness against his mother's indifference, was finally calm. It was as though the loss of his body had allowed his soul to heal.

Then, in the very moment he realized he had achieved the quiet happiness he had longed for, his mind began to struggle to understand it.

His task was done, his services rendered. The color of his wings was proof enough that he had fulfilled the demands of his god. Ostensibly liberated from any further obligation, he still could not fully rationalize the unexpected release he had been given. There rose in him an unscratched, subconscious itch: strange words, archaic and barely intelligible, which he could swear resounded through the stone surrounding him in the moment the world turned inside-out and belched him forth. No matter how he tried to reason the blessing of his freedom, his mind was mired in the certainty that he had been purposefully uncaged. Not by a god, nor the prophet who entombed him, worse. A further niggling question started to grow: if Loi desired this body, then how did it now walk on feet and touch with hands? Perhaps, he wondered, the sand and air was all he was, a crass imitation of the man he no longer was.

The students of Nesh, being sheltered diplomats and peacekeepers, were still a bit jumpy as they continued making repairs to the atrium. Zeniquorer's presence still lingered in their home so recently demolished, whispered fear of his possession of the great Kubernu Capheif still prolific. Archons and students could not forget the revulsive sight, ever-wary now of anything out of the ordinary and often recoiling at their own shadows.

Tzychala, the red creature of many eyes, knew nothing of the terrible events that had transpired there, and of Zeniquorer's involvement. Though he had walked dark paths so alien to Maengir, his lifelong vacation from its new age had made him ignorant of much. He had only seen the war of the Nhi'Thaun through the memories of its victims as their light was torn away by his flesh, leaving him with no understanding of why it was waged. He understood greed and power but not their special place in the hearts of mortals and gods. Maengir and those of its creatures not yet ascended were to him as they had always been in the Age of Unravelling; scrabbling, shrieking animals penned for harvest. He had not forgotten his sacrifice, having contracted himself to forsake his natural existence and no longer consume blood, yet he still could not see lesser mortality as anything respectable. He still, as sure as ever, could not resist his want to be like them and possess a soul of his own.

With an aura of jealous indifference he entered Nesh's ruined doors as though he belonged, ebony claws raking the stone as he came in from the windy groves beyond. His matted crimson mane clung around his face and shoulders, heavy with crusted blood from an eternity of dining on the distant ancestors of this place. Without reason or desire to smile, nor to acknowledge the existence of those whose eyes found him, he strode as arrogantly as a predator among vermin.

The tired and nervy inhabitants one by one ceased work entirely as they caught sight of him. They were not afraid but wary as the unfamiliar little man so vilely soiled, entered noiselessly. Claws were commonplace, though his were notably darker and sharper.

The scars on his body would appeal to a warrior. What drew attention was his hair. As confounding as it was intriguing, such a shade of red had never before been encountered among any furred creature. It simply did not exist in their world. He wore no conventional clothing, though to hide the myriad eyes on his arms and chest he wrapped coarse cloth around them as he did his face, apparently dressed in all places except those customary to civilized peoples. He had no concern for appearances, nor any shame of his genitals hanging in plain view. His disguise was successful, for though his skin was the color of burnt ground and his hair as red as the Mercy sky his mortal form was strikingly similar to that of a Kuolt, apart from its extreme gauntness and the five-pointed tail flicking like an anxious serpent. It was this visage that gave the Mantichaena pause.

Tzychala moved through the hall to the great stage, mounted it, folded his hands behind his back and patiently waited. No one dared speak to him. Even the few archons of Tault overseeing the repairs to the nearby avenue did not venture to inquire about his presence. Though terrifying to look on, he was disarmingly passive, thus drawing more curiosity than concern. Indeed, he was not the most awful thing to appear of late, seeming quite like a hunter born to the borderland without ever knowing the comfort or decorum of the Gate. Like any other dangerous creature, he was avoided out of nothing more than prudence, the reasonable desire not to provoke his ire.

Patriarch Metaeu, in a brave moment, attempted to learn the man's identity to no avail. Tzychala deflected his question, stating plainly in his sloppy voice:

"I am not here for you."

The crews returned to their work and Tzychala continued to wait long into the morning.

As Laesis crested the West ridge of the cliffs at the peak of day and infiltrated Nesh's door, glorious blue wings unfurled from the passage to the aviaries as Keimas finally emerged. The latter half of the day he would have to begin his duties anew and hope that his counterparts did not resent picking up his slack.

The workers instinctively moved to welcome him home, eager to give their various assurances that they favored him and had known he would return safely. Not knowing the full extent of the hatred that had been rallied against him he misunderstood the true value of much of the praise, nor did he recognize the duplicity of some. He feigned interest in them as he glanced quickly about the hall, his heart heavy that his obligation to go out on patrol would take him from here while there was still so much work to be done. He had no time right now to heal his own home. The people needed meat far more than another set of hands. He smiled and nodded to the white noise of those approaching him from below as he lamented the state of Nesh, taken aback as his flitting eyes found the creature on the dais, glowered sourly when he recognized its shape from his visions. They stared at one another, a sort of begrudged camaraderie shared between them as they met face to face for the first time. Neither shared any indication of their feelings or expectations, only fixed on one another in a bloodless confrontation. Tzychala's masked eyes turned to him and his cheeks slowly rose with an oozing smile that furrowed his blindfold. With a clumsy combination of eagerness and hesitation, like a child learning in the moment how to greet another, he lifted both hands slowly and wiggled them in a strange wave. Speaking in as pleasant a voice as he could, albeit slurred, he found his first words for Keimas.

"Kutliku-man. Come down. I want to speak."

Others stepped back and watched, captive to their hunter-killer and his unexpected guest as Keimas stepped off the landing and his blue wings glided him gently to the altar, an intense frown growing on his face. A crowd began to form and Tzychala took notice of it. He spun toward them suddenly, more anxious than he at first appeared, hair and tail lashing as he hissed and drove them back with unprovoked hostility. Keimas' unusual ease in the monster's company kept them from panicking, watching him for reassurance. Reluctantly, he held out a hand to urge them back. When Tzychala had subsided Keimas quickly gained the attention of one young Lugu boy and, with a click of his claws, commanded him.

"You, *udaina*, seek me a word of Father Aroch's whereabouts. Bring the man himself if he is not indisposed. I would meet with him when I have finished here."

The boy nodded and was gone. Keimas' attention returned to Tzychala, his displeasure manifest in billowing wings and shimmering teeth.

"It is you, *la*?" he asked, measured but no less threatening. "I know that voice; the voice that tormented me and goaded me into the Tau."

"And the voice that retrieved you," Tzychala replied.

"For further games I suspect, upon seeing how repulsive you truly are. Your voice alone does not do you justice."

Tzychala's eyebrows twitched in surprise but he was otherwise undaunted.

"*Uienla*, Kutu. I hadn't credited you with many a brain. Yet again I'm proven a poor judge of your kind," he said, thoughtfully.

"I should KILL you!" Keimas bellowed, one fist thrust upward in a flash from his side to Tzychala's jaw. It connected, though Tzychala's head only glanced aside momentarily, his resilience far outmatching a lesser god after having received many worse blows from an elder one. He sighed, kept his patience, grimaced as he tried to understand why Keimas was so belligerent despite his own congeniality.

Confused, the demon surmised "I had thought that once your new flesh was given you might be less...Kutu. Have some grace. I did not have to pull you from...ah, *minein,* I suppose it was necessary. Though I could have chosen not to."

His fragmented exposition made little sense. Now that Keimas had vented the bitter memories of the voice and examined the thing that bore it he began to see the creature with more equanimity.

He was surprisingly small, almost stunted, appearing sickly and malnourished. His gray-brown skin clung to his bones and, although some thin muscles wove through him, they seemed fatigued. His tail was yet menacing, certainly the most dangerous part of him. Nearly twice as long as his body, it lilted in small circles.

Now intrigued, and satisfied by the inference that this thing had not come to fight, Keimas was compelled to ask:

"*Ein, vaechaeih*...who are you?"

"Tzychala," was the pleased, grinning reply.

"Why does it grin and glow?" Keimas wondered out loud, shivering at the sight of the dripping, slender teeth.

"*Udai,* because it can," Tzychala explained easily.

Keimas sensed the extreme pride his visitor felt, saw the oddest sort of joy in the muscles around its face. Little by little Keimas explored the outlandish body and, after much deliberation, resolved that the fears of his tribe were rightly placed on this thing they had never seen before. He knew it surely was a remnant of some old god, now used as a threat of religion more than of normal life. It was the closest thing he could imagine to what the pious warned their children about; Demons, the slaves of deities so ancient that there remained none who knew their names.

"Are you...a demon?" he asked at length.

Tzychala growled, huffed, then laughed uproariously, throwing up his arms in disbelief.

"Always am I asked! It is uncanny! Once, if only once, I would be thrilled to be greeted with, '*Ueinla*, and well met! How fare you? *Aurba vulilt*, what unusual hair you have!' Say me, Kutu, is that too much?" Tzychala halted his tirade on seeing Keimas' stupefied expression and fell back to fondly rehearsed cynicism. "*La*. I am demon. Will this satisfy you? I have come to steal you into Vaeba. *Mineina enta*, you've done nothing wrong, mind you, our kind merely despise all things so colored as your sea."

There was still no reaction from Keimas. It appeared his mind had stopped working all together. The silence was deafening. So, with a heavy sigh, Tzychala tried to get the troublesome conversation back to purpose.

"Keimas. This is your name, *uein*? Is my *maen'ghan* poor? For my own benefit, at least gesture if you can understand me."

Keimas twitched back to life and crossed his arms, indignant at Tzychala's manner.

"I can. *Malpael*, we here are simply not accustomed to such repulsive and mannerless things."

"*Uein quo*!? Haha. HAH." Tzychala laughed facetiously. "Well spoken, for a man whose home has already been tread upon by many a crooked god. Just so, I see you've had no complaints at my sister's visits."

"*Ers vineu'quo?* – if this is true, how? Of whom do you speak? None such as yourself have ever presented here..."

"Never you mind, infantile man," Tzychala said impatiently. "I see the godlike kind aren't what they once were, less so now when their only ties to this plane are the inbred creatures of..."

"Stop!" Keimas commanded, tiring of the confusing divergences and rubbing his forehead. "There must be a point to you. *La,* I only want to know by which orifice of Minpaxa or Hosse you've squeezed me out here, through which you've apparently followed. I still have the voice of a talking stone in the bed of my mind and yours is poor company for it."

"You remember?" Tzychala exclaimed quizzically, then began poking one finger into a resistant Keimas, as if searching for any lingering sign of injury.

"I do," Keimas said, trying to avoid the claws. "Images, for the most. I feel some things are missing, though I follow the roots as they spread to other things. I remember the desert, and a...there were people. I was going to..."

Tzychala scratched at his own cheek and hummed curiously as Keimas rambled, secretly admiring the lengths Loi had gone to in order to move secretly into Keimas' husk.

Still lacking the memory of his purpose, Keimas continued to speak of it.

"It is...*eina* you must have been aware of it. By your instruction – unless I miss my mark – I allowed myself to be put into darkness so that Loi might somehow bless me? I remember being made a man of faith before my god and, and this is who I feel myself to be now. My faith belongs with my wife, and I will stand by it. My only worthwhile memory is that this was to be my reward. I did as told, and now here will remain."

"*Udai,* do you not still dream of a war?" Tzychala pressed, with a stealthily extended palm, which Keimas pushed away.

"War I do not desire, nor anything beyond these walls but what my love moves me to."

"There is a hope in me that love will move you against yourself today."

Tzychala's refutation of Keimas' intent was unnerving and Keimas was forced to ponder it without responding. Tzychala moaned and leaned into him, unhappy and feeling exposed at having to explain just how much danger he had put not only the man, but also his people in.

"Keimas....While time is a scarce commodity, there is much I must confess. I begin by offering an apology for my part in this. Then...I must implore you to help me. I have no more tricks to tempt you, *utan,* no more dreams to sway you. But I must beg you follow my voice yet further, to save what little is left to love. I will only give you the truth, and the tale of the monster we have together unchained."

CHAPTER 7: A STRANGER ALLIANT

S houlder to shoulder on the stalk of a fallen thi'haazehil – that species which bore great veridian nuts, perishing and reseeding at the end of each bearing – Nepiur's hunting party gathered to survey a rainswept prairie ahead. They had run a fair distance from the limits of Aes'bethil, though the severity of the rain made scant their time to find their elusive enemy's path. It had led them directly to this open land but no visible thuell sign could be seen in the grasses.

Hax bounded between two high limbs, tail flipping up and down as he scanned the periphery, until he caught in the breeze an odor which singed his nostrils.

"*Ein hawth!* It is off Tau!"

"*Quoein*!? Where is sign?" Maurus bellowed back.

"It's stench only! I assure you it is upwind!" Hax then thought for a moment before moving. "It would not have returned to open ground, *La*? If there is no sign, then we still follow the shade! Laesis would harm it!"

He diligently searched eastward to find a trail to prove his words.

Meanwhile, Nepiur grumbled to herself as she surveyed the meadow.

"Would it?"

"*Aien?*" Maurus asked, sensing doubt in her as well.

Nepiur clicked her claws at the Iron Rain, sending them off in the opposite direction.

"Look at this, all around you," she said to no one in particular.

"I see nothing," Maurus admitted with a shrug.

"That is what worries me. There's no sign for the last hundred paces, no more scarring or even trampled foliage. Is that even possible, after what it did to the city? This place should be plowed like a field and dripping with leavings."

"*La*," Maurus sighed in frustration. "It seems the thing may control the effects of its poison."

"The 'Thing' indeed," Nepiur continued. "Even Bethaali did not seem confident as to what it was. I'm not sure this is what we came prepared for."

"It will burn just the same," Maurus replied. "Our call is unchanged."

Nepiur concurred, pricked her ears up and waited for a telltale sound from either direction. She heard nothing, feeling pressure as her companions stared at her anxiously. Nothing would come of it. They had lost the trail, doomed to trust in Hax.

"Ronsha, Rashala, fall back in! The pathfinder leads!"

The Iron Rain rejoined them quickly and the troupe moved as one, tearing through the jungle high and low with no regard for flora smashed or fauna displaced. Unaccustomed to being above ground and still struggling to see clearly, Maurus repeatedly smacked face-first into trunks and tripped over roots, each with a roar of frustration. Dace was bringing up the rear, so no thi toppled by his carnage would injure the smaller. Seeing Maurus' need, he plucked the grumbling Lugu and bore him without slowing.

"*Hawth, uta,* Stop bonking yourself!" he cheered. We need all in good condition!"

Maurus groaned and nursed his face, grateful for the help but feeling increasingly useless.

"*Prostas*, big brother. I cannot imagine why one so clumsy in the light was wanted."

Dace was too exhilarated by the thought of a battle to entertain pity. Dwelling on hardships was not his nature.

"Clumsy your eyes, yet never your mighty claws! Our lady has no need for a digger. Sharp blades and a strong heart only; these have put you right where you belong! Worry not, my friend. All will believe your little mishaps were the scars of a worthy fight! Hahaaa!"

Maurus held on tightly as their chase gained speed and took them down the slope of a deep, winding ravine. Dace became a juggernaut of rocky fists that smashed through logs and scattered vines effortlessly, howling with glee. Hax and the Iron Rain barely escaped his path of destruction as he passed them by, now barely able to keep up with the careening buffoon. Bakul were rarely seen at such a pace, though when they had the freedom to run as fast as they pleased there was almost nothing that could catch them. Only Hax and Nepiur held a lead on him as they

Hax's tireless snout caught an ill-wind of northern origin and, latching himself to a high bough, sniffed deeply before alerting Nepiur to its worrisome change of course.

"Hooold! *Aiat*, it has turned Thaun!" he yelled.

Nepiur swung up from the underbrush into the canopy and joined him, winded but no less agile.

"How far?" she shouted without slowing her ascent.

"Near…very near, for now," he surmised with a scowl.

"It moves so fast," Nepiur panted. "What in Loi's mercy is it?"

"*Mingnogh*. Not any thuell I know of."

After only a few breaths they resumed their race through the tangle of thi-tops, Nepiur having a sudden epiphany as they flew, panting heavily between conjectures.

"Hax, I think on the scarce trail and how the creature lingered at the city. It must have been injured somehow. The black residue…It's not poisoning the land as thuell would, it's bleeding!"

He did not acknowledge her at first, stopping on a frond to swing down by the tail and bellow directions to those on the ground.

"*Urgtu an'khain!* The thi bend before it in the Tau again! Make right from the stones ahead" then, to Nepiur, he responded "Bleeding like any animal, *la*. And thuell know no retreat."

"*Einla*," she replied knowingly, "Not man, yet not thuell. Hax, what is it?"

"I don't know!" Hax finally admitted.

Nepiur leapt past and snatched him by the hide, stopping them both on a bushy limb.

"*Quouein*!? I thought you knew these creatures!"

"I do, and a thuell this must surely be, but…Thuell infest a host, destroying it even in the absence of the light. It is the nature of the host that eludes me. Whatever poor creature has been taken, it is not dying as it should."

Maurus was heard below, alerting them to movement ahead, and the pair turned on his words to where the thi bowed and swayed on a new course.

"See the clouds! See the rain!" the Lugu called. "*Udaiam,* to the *Tau'tsthaun*! Turn to and *hawth'hway sehel khanem*! It makes for the cover of rain!"

Nepiur's face drooped and her eyes traced the winding path their prey was cutting. Jerking Hax along with her she shouted back to Maurus.

"Get a fire under your paws! Its path is true to Hanging Gate!"

Dace roared and stampeded onward, following Hax's darting silhouette through the canopy. Exhaustion was set aside knowing that yet another city, their city, was in danger. In his charge he barely noticed Nepiur drop down onto him, or Rashala leaping up to join her and Maurus.

"*Aiat,* we face new troubles ahead, I'm afraid," the witchcrafter lamented.

"*Quos ghanwekts?* – what are you saying?" Nepiur demanded.

Maurus saw the pitiful look in Rashala's eyes and slapped his hands across his forehead, shouting over the cacophony of snapping thi.

"*Eina minla*, mother, they are gothics of lightning! If they try to craft in this wet…"

Nepiur stiffened a moment, gritted her teeth at their rotten luck and cursed.

"No…No, no, no! *Eisvulkhaint*!"

The two witchcrafters stared at each other achingly. The bolts of such a storm were their only practiced skill. Surrounded by water they could not risk discharge and their untrained attempts at flame would be snuffed out. The storm only intensified as they neared its center, with no sign of its edge. If they delayed the chase until the skies were clear the creature could well have found their home. Nepiur was not alone in wondering how many lives could be lost, were worth losing, if they delayed for the sake of their own.

Without the Iron Rain there seemed no hope of survival.

Rashala launched off into the thi and joined Ronsha, who shouted irately at no one, her ego unwilling to accept failure for naught but bad weather.

"Surrender is the only true defeat!" she called to Nepiur. "If Loi wills it, then let his strikes reap us as they do our foe! If we are to die for victory, so be it!"

They were on the heels of their prey, so near the rainfall that its early mist could be felt in the westerly wind. The decisive moment arrived with another of Hax's periodic updates.

"Thuell *echmec hway!*"

The signal was mixed triumph and dread. They were out of time if they were to catch it before being doused and could not afford to lose it again. As a wall of torrential rain approached, Dace hunkered down and summoned all his strength, sounding off mightily.

"*Babeidagm*, to my shoulder come! Hold fast or die!"

Each companion obeyed, abandoning their routes to assemble on his back and take hold of his spines. Only Hax remained above, committed to scout with his unmatched speed and calling out when necessary to alter their direction. It was a sound precaution, though the trajectory deviated little from the mouth of the Gate.

All braced themselves as they crashed into the rain. Chilled deeply and instantaneously, they could barely see beyond the next thi ahead. While mounted upon Dace, there was no need. Slashing and trampling, he fought onward without thought to the breaking of his spines and the battery of his flesh.

"Dace, take care!" Maurus shouted, with repeated slaps to the man's back.

"I'll not allow it near our lands!" he bellowed, gasping.

"Brother, your armor!" Hax cautioned from above.

"I'll make more! HAAAH!"

Unbeknownst to the others, it was not mere hatred of the monster that drove Dace but the knowledge of what the cooling of the dry earthplane would mean. He was sped along by fear of what else may be hunting in the jungle. He had never been so deep in the borderlands but knew very well that, after hiding from the heat for many long days, the flesh-eating kuolt, schiis and many more predators would emerge with ravenous hunger. His size and power as Bakul would not deter them from an attack if it meant they could have a feast. They would come in impossible numbers, and with the witchcrafters so limited the others would not last long if he were to fall.

Even in the rain the scent trail grew stronger as they advanced, and it was clear that the fleet horror they chased no longer went stealthily. The scarce bits of black slime in its wake were washing away as quickly as they were noticed but picking them out of the underbrush was gratuitous now, while Hax could maintain the canopy and track their source from above. He was exhausted, drenched and continually weighed down by the storm, fighting to keep up while watching for motion among the thi ahead.

Nepiur knew, as Dace did, of other dangers, had mourned friends lost to storms such as this. Her heart pounded at sudden howls and the sight of mottled fur a stone's throw north; a pack of kuolt, at least ten, which paralleled their trajectory. Dace threw his head to either side and barked threateningly as they raced to encircle the group. The did not hesitate, closing the gap and snapping their jaws in bursts of foaming saliva.

Barreling on to keep from being flanked and cut off, Dace began to tire, despite his great strength. His raspy breath heaved from the burden of vulnerable friends, and his legs began to wobble with each crushing step. Finally, he stumbled, splintered a fallen thi with his knee while his passengers swung around the spikes they clung to.

All held tight but Nepiur, who was ripped away and flung squealing through the branches and vines. Grasping for vines, she could catch no hold, and fell as two of the crazed manhunters pounced after her.

Dace's eyes flared, body bristling as he lunged forward, snatching her with one hand from the jaws and rancid breath of a painful death. With one hand wielding Nepiur overhead, the other thrust down to hold his weight and buried one of her attackers halfway into the soggy peat. The other yelped and fell silent as it tumbled underneath his churning legs. Dace curled Nepiur into his neck and carried on, using his head like a hammer to smash and toss logs and boulders while the first excruciating bites of the kuolt found their way through breaks in his shell. Then, through the sheets of rain he saw Hax swinging ahead on a long vine, shouting frantically.

"Dive, brother! Don't look, DIVE!"

Hax released the vine and plunged straight down, seeming to vanish into the solid ground.

Dace took a desperate gamble in following, throwing himself forward on his belly. Sliding shoulder-first through a narrow gap between ground and a leaning thi he created a wake of mud on either side that hindered the attacking K'hizu momentarily. Pieces broke off him and the grit sank into his wounds until, at the point where Hax had fallen, he broke through a curtain of vines and felt the mire beneath him give way to open air. Like a gondola sailing over the edge of the sea he tumbled into a great void and down a mound of boulders, carried along by a raging river he created. He slammed against every rock on the way down, sent all his passengers flying from his back, then losing his grasp and flinging Nepiur headlong after them.

One by one, each took a punishing fall of twenty feet before landing gracelessly in a churning pool.

The depression was huge, almost the size of Ms'egol's academy. Apart from the landslide, all other walls were naught but loose dirt which continually crumbled from the rain above and roil below. The flow from all sides swirled inward toward a hole at the center, breaking up clumps of clay and turning the saturated ground into a shallow maelstrom. Roots and mycelium were increasingly exposed along the walls, some smaller thi breaking free and falling to be carried away.

Nepiur gathered herself urgently and tromped through the knee-high water to where Dace lay wheezing and writhing.

Maurus and Hax similarly rallied and took up positions between the pursuing kuolt and their downed Bakul. Luckily, the beasts tarried at the precipice and showed no desire to take the deadly plunge. Maurus held there, while Hax and the Iron Rain fought their way back to encircle Dace.

He was badly wounded, more from himself than the attack, having pushed himself so far beyond his limits he could barely keep his heavy head free of the water. The company could only help roll him onto his side and keep him steady.

The kuolt above were increasingly agitated, started to whine and cower, backed away slowly before finally turning heel and taking cover.

As the caravan recovered, Hax took a sharp breath, gaping toward the center of the pool.

Nepiur's hair stood on end at his sudden movement and she followed suit, as did the rest in succession.

Encircling the pit was, sizzling and dissolving in the dim light, a distinct trail of the black blood. Through the veil of rain, they traced it to the eastmost precipice. There, clawing frantically at the base of the cliff in a vain effort to escape the same confinement, was their quarry.

Nearly tall enough to reach the precipice, it appeared almost like a Deghni, though with fewer legs and chitinous plates in place of toxic spines. Like some nightmarish crustacean, it hacked at the wall with heavy pincers, rammed it with headless shoulders and scrabbled upward on pointed legs until clusters of mud collapsed overhead and rolled down its segmented back. It had the black discoloration and rotted texture of a thuell, yet it was not deteriorating, nor having any reaction to the moderate light. The thuell had indeed infested something alien to Manti. Its skin smoldered and shed in small places, though it seemed to grow back just as quickly, continually reproducing its flesh and shell as the disease destroyed them.

With a guttural screech of dismay, the horror realized there was no escaping and turned in search of another egress. Then, upon seeing it was not alone, it went still and silent. Slowly, it raised its folded arms and susurrated through a bubbling goop effusing from a long, vertical mouth which ran nearly the length of its body. The oozing fissure opened and unsheathed row upon row of smaller claws. The creature's only movement or sound was their menacing rattle.

Nepiur's whole body shuddered in revulsion, and she turned to take stock of her company. Dace was incapacitated, the Iron Wind could not cast, and their whole force was frozen and spent before the fight had even begun. Her sharp mind remained stubbornly devoid of a plan. Their defenses were cracked, their weapon blunted, and escape was as impossible as it was unconscionable.

Sudden warmth in Nepiur's shoulder came at Maurus' touch as he pushed a curtain of wet hair out of his face, eyeing her with a quiet determination. The Iron Rain wearily came to her other side and, taking one another's hand, nodded their readiness. Looking back at Dace, Nepiur's heart cried as Hax tried desperately to revive him, moaning like a child over his battered friend.

The hideous creature acted on their vulnerability, lumbered toward them steadily, its maw restless and noisome. It reared back on its hind legs as two more appendages unfolded from inside the horrid mouth, like emaciated arms with skin stretched over three sharp fingers.

Nepiur clenched her jaw and narrowed her eyes against the furious weather. In that moment, all she could think of was the terror on Bethaali's face, and beneath it the sparkle of hope that they could succeed where she had failed in putting this monster down.

Hax appeared silently, brushed past her, his eyes red as he put a hand behind her head. Emoting myriad thoughts with his bloodshot eyes, he growled the same promise he had made her in private.

"*Eins aiat,* if it be a monster…it will die."

Nepiur held his wrist, stared straight ahead and took a slow breath. This was where they would make their stand, possibly their last. She was not afraid, was ready to die like any of Gazan or Ms'egol or Tault. Long had she suffered frequent stigmatic rumor about Nesh: the house that only bred councilors and politicians, poor hunters and unskilled fighters all, save for the Kutu. She had dreamed of being in the wild, proving not just herself but her hall. She had not risen for vainglory, but for the chance to give Mearnum their place among the tribe's legends.

She took a step forward, and her heart filled with fire when Maurus and the Iron Rain moved concurrently. Her short claws scraped together, and she slid carefully across the silty bed.

"Distract from the front," she directed quietly, "Flank and press from behind. Drive it toward the hole." She glanced resentfully up to the sky, then apologetically to Rashala and Ronsha. "Destroyed, no matter the cost."

They understood, repeated together:

"No matter the cost."

They split into small groups around the vortex to close about the enemy. Eyes vigilant, they advanced only to be pushed back by the creature's abrupt warning cry and its long appendages stabbing menacingly into the ground between them.

Nepiur smirked, continued to lead Rashala and Hax on from the left. She surmised from the defensive thrashing that this thing was more K'hizu than thuell, more afraid than crazed. It knew what they were doing, but not how to deal with it. It only pivoted in place and tried to keep them back with a show of force. Attacking would be treacherous, attempting to provoke it to strike first equally so, without first knowing its capability. Most importantly, they could not risk even the smallest injury. Any way the thuell could enter their blood without exposure to air or light meant death, prolonged and unavoidable.

Nepiur's scrying eyes drifted over the blood swirling past them, the rapid healing of the creature's wounds. Something about the water was helping protect it. Perhaps running water prevented the thuell from taking root or even confused its ability to sense a warm body. Was that how it found a host? The idea could become an advantage, but time for planning was up. The battle was on.

Maurus took a long step forward, swiped at the water with his cutters to attract attention, retreated as four sharp points planted where he had been standing. An ear-splitting screech revealed the creature's ire as it overreached against him, swinging wildly. With Ronsha closing in for an opening, Maurus needed only appear as the most present threat.

Ronsha had an idea of her own on where the creature's weakness could be, after noticing the strange absence of any visible eyes. She palmed the slightest spark of her essence, not of lightning but of light; a blinding attack. Leaping out to Maurus' side she flicked the mote of energy into the air, creating a flash as it reacted to the moisture. It was a risky ploy, resulting in an unavoidable jolt spreading through the water and taking everyone's breath away, yet it paid off.

The thuell recoiled and clamped its mouth tight, covering the opening hysterically with its arms as it staggered away into the crumbling wall behind it. Ronsha's hair was on end as she shook out her hand painfully, then shouted her discovery as she stumbled sideways.

"In the mouth! *Betheheisi,* it sees from the mouth!"

"Again! Hit it again!" Hax demanded, perhaps unwisely, as his muscles were still shaking from her discharge.

The thuell tilted off balance. Then, with its mouth fluttering in panic, reverted to aimlessly slashing in search of a kill. Spinning all around, it kicked and stomped and stabbed, leaving no easy approach.

Hax gave Maurus a smirk.

"Not by strength," he said, "But by cunning."

Maurus nodded and braced himself, waited for Hax to make a move.

The disoriented thuell was torn between them. Its seeping mouth had barely opened again, so desperate was the beast to rely on all its senses, which was enough.

Hax leapt through the water, screaming and slapping it to draw attention towards Rashala, who used the cover to close the distance and replicate Ronsha's disabling flash. As Hax passed, he dove, evading the raised pincers so narrowly he felt them brush his chest. With his outstretched palm nearly inside the wriggling mouth, he let fly another burst of light.

While those in the water were nearly paralyzed by the shock, Maurus was already midair as the thuell doubled over in pain and backed into him. His clawed hands and feet bit into its thick carapace as those on his shoulders clamped around its long arms and wrenched them mercilessly backward. Wailing, the thuell bucked back and forth to throw him as he steered it closer to the pit. Loosening his grip more as the flesh he touched began to tear and gush, he was barely clinging on as the black filth streamed past his feet. His spine tingled when he saw the blood writhing midair; tiny, smoking tendrils reaching out from it in search of his flesh. He almost threw himself off in fear of it, but the advantage imagined by Nepiur was shown to him as the rain struck the outgrowths. It was as though it gave up, falling away from its roots and apparently going inert after striking the water below.

Nepiur and Ronsha gave chase, striking in rapid succession at less soiled parts of the thuell's core as it wobbled toward the center of the pool.

As it neared, it became aware of the danger, anchoring three legs to stop its advance and retaliating with the other.

Ronsha dropped to her knees while at speed, slid briefly through the water to get close and barely passed under a swipe at her throat. As the arm coiled and swung back around, its blunt side caught Nepiur square in the jaw and sent her back the way she had come, nearly unconscious. Hax caught her as she was flung into his chest, fell with her before dragging her body out of the fray.

Maurus fought to maintain his hold but, with another shrill cry and a twist of its torso, the thuell spun him to the shallows near the rocky hole with dazing force. Furiously it skewered the sand all around him as he rolled back and forth, barely escaping each impact. His lungs seized as he gagged on the water, too entrapped for anyone to aid him.

Dace suddenly stirred, gasping and shaking his head. The piercing cold of the pool was petrifying but also helped rouse him, sparking his survival instinct as it sped his blood. Though weighed down by cramped and overworked muscles, he was a hard man of Gazan, treating injury as nothing more than discomfort. He grunted and punched the water multiple times, willed himself to ascend, his resolve turning to volcanic rage when he saw the monster with its terrible pincers descending on Maurus. With an urgent roar he thrust against the ground and created an arcing wave all around him as he spun toward the fight. Clamoring on all fours at first, he took the pitfall in a flying leap, landing precariously on its fringe. The rocks cracked under his extreme weight, his heels teetering over the darkness as he intercepted the thuell's attacks. With upthrust hands he seized the snapping claws and twisted them upward at the joint.

The thuell wailed and leaned into him, its long mouth gnashing closer and closer to his face while it scratched in vain at his still-armored belly and tilled the ground beneath them.

Safe for an instant, Maurus lunged up into the drooling torso, grabbed hold of the two lower hands threatening Dace and swung one of his giant cutters down to cleave them free.

Blood flowed, the four legs creaked and bent together, and the frenetic sounds of agony assured Dace he had complete control of the dark thuell.

Dace ignored its size and girth in lifting it up over his head, then knelt hard and shattered its shell over his spiked shoulders, impaling it and crushing its bones while screaming insults up at it.

Squealing, the thuell wormed its legs around Dace's spikes and held its mangled body away from him, the two of them wrestling over the storm of sand and water. Maurus was able to get his fingers between the plates of Dace's cracked chest and heave on him, begging him not to fall and keeping him stable as Nepiur and Hax lined up behind him to help. Though the creature's pincers were maimed, its legs would not release Dace's back.

Dace's left foot slipped to dangle over the abyss, a fatal fall that would drag everyone else with him.

The essence within Rashala and Ronsha glowed, evaporating the water they touched, together racing to either side of the brawl and mounting Dace's arms swiftly. They both gathered their strength and, each palming a whirling flame to the best of their ability, thrust their hands between the man and the monster and released a fiery explosion that forced them apart in a shower of Bakul armor and thuell flesh.

Dace was pushed down and away from the deathly plunge and the thuell up into the air, shrieking and flapping its oozing limbs. It barely managed to clamp down on an outcrop by one cracked pincer, where it swung perilously.

Again, the Iron Rain attacked, gathering their essence and thrusting their charged palms together. A deafening boom echoed as they exerted a force not of lightning but of heat, a shockwave that knocked their allies away, fought back the heavy rain and even threw it back up into the sky, where the storm already overhead was crackling in response to the witchcrafters' call.

Rashala turned and knelt forward, letting Ronsha run up his back and launch off his shoulder.

As Ronsha went soaring over the hole with all the quenching water forced away from it, a white fissure split her chest. Pulled to her, a bolt crashed down from overhead and disappeared into the Veil in its descent, firing out from her and into the ground. It branched and cut through the rocks all around the mouth of the pit, spitting rubble in all directions, but the shaft of the bolt travelled down the crumbling funnel and filled it with fulminating power. It was a risk they had to take, yet righteousness did not spare them the punishment of the strike against water no matter how they deflected the rain. Rocks around the pit shattered and diffused the charges, but still they found water, and from the single attack came enough energy to stop everyone's hearts. The reward for their suffering was the silver flash of lightning tearing through the thuell, a black billow of stench and a horrendous screech as its two burning halves tumbled into darkness among sheets of stone.

The floodwaters momentarily repelled immediately returned in a surf, threatening to throw everyone down after the thuell.

Clawing against it, Rashala was barely able to skirt the downspout in time and hold onto his wife at its edge, bracing his heels against rock as the waves parted across his back.

The rest grasped hold of Dace as they floated past him, recovering slowly while their muscles jerked and dragged in the current.

Hax, who had endured the forefront of the waves, was trying to stand on his own but falling over himself until his legs finally gave out.

Nepiur sat half-submerged in the brown water, one arm hooked over one of Dace's spines, willing away her soreness. The victorious matriarch silently praised Loi. They had won. It was nothing short of a miracle but, by his grace, they had won.

None yet moved when the water settled again, instead laying idle while marveling at their survival. The clouds started to break in the distance, and the rain softened a bit, Laesis beginning to penetrate in scattered patches. A little longer and the high wind would push the storm past them and set free the warmth of a daylit sky.

Gingerly carrying Ronsha against him, Rashala stumbled to Dace's side and lauded the Bakul champion.

Dace could do little else but steady himself on his hands and knees. He might have fallen on his face had Maurus not been there to support him. This was hardly the worst beating he had received, remembering many more in the arena, but none of those had been from a witchcrafter. This was a different kind of pain, yet still a good one that stung of victory and would leave scars to remember it by. Embracing it, he cast a weary smile at Maurus and spoke between coughing breaths.

"Brother...only a moment's rest I had, and still you almost found yourself flayed."

Maurus sighed, bracing himself under Dace's arm and endeavoring to lift him with Hax's immediate aid.

"*La,* though it seems the stars did not find me worthy quite yet. Besides, I would not suffer the embarrassment of perishing before your whimsical little hairball there."

"Hear you that?" Dace laughed to Hax. "*Udai,* it is best you go soon so this one will lose no face."

"After surviving this, I fear we are all of us immortal, you overfed bastard," Hax retorted, his small frame useless in trying to hoist his friend. "The 'Son of a Mountain' indeed. You have the heft of one."

Loosening their grip, they let Dace rest himself in the water a safe distance from the hole. As he sat, Maurus and Hax hurriedly threw water up against his back, desperate to get any remaining traces of the black grime off him. It made no difference. The extreme heat from the Iron Rain's intervention had already scorched his armor to sterility, leaving only ashen flakes that rinsed off easily.

Nepiur wiped her face and shielded her eyes, surveying the surrounding walls. She started to cry tears of joy, then to laugh through them. When the initial rapture of victory had run its course, she stood shivering from the water and smiled at her warriors while speculating on their fate.

"*Laan*, it seems the kuolt lost interest when they laid eyes to the monster. *Einaquom*, if they are lurking further away...*minein*. Lest we be spared the thuell only to freeze to death, I suggest we find a way upward."

Maurus eyed Dace worriedly, though in seeing how quickly the indefatigable brute gathered himself, spoke to his great strength while standing again himself.

"On with it, then. With such a Bakul to rise upon we've no need of a stair."

Dace tried to laugh, coughed painfully, then fell back to his knees. He was well enough, waved off Hax's nervous hovering as he spat blood into the murky water, then smiled through red teeth.

"And here I thought I had carried the load enough for one day. It is my lot in life to toil until I perish. *Einla,* Matriarch, may I remain behind and perish?"

"Not yet, *utan*." Nepiur laughed, heartened by Dace's spirit. "Who will bear the Iron Rain, such as to spare their dainty paws? Also, we do require a stair."

"*La aiat!*" Dace hoarsely agreed, though still he shook and shed broken pieces around him. "Gazan is here for you. Only take care where you step. With my shell so broken, the rest is liable to go any moment."

Thetrulengo speaks,

Fortune is the strangest of phenomena. It strains the mind to imagine a world where lives can be saved and destroyed by events so far removed from them. I marveled so recently at the intricacy of actions which led to the progeny of Miohaelia and Oorghunak finding one another at the truest moment of destiny. Now I find myself baffled by the miracle that has spared these unlikely heroes against all odds.

It was the lovers, Keimas and Lemalie who saved so many of young Nepiur's company. Every touch of the thuell should have killed these people. From a single breath or drop of blood, every one of them should have been victim to madness and burnt to nothing before day's end. However, the gifts of the Nhi'Thaun live and grow with no lost grandeur, shielding their people. The love of two godlikes had indeed conjured a storm from their own light, filled it with the power of their ancestors and let it loose upon a land in need. It was their blessing upon the rain that served to contain and subdue the thuell; their love that covered faraway kin and protected them from its evil.

This remains an unusual day, for not all miracles have brought good. How Bethaali manifested a thuell-taken Balathide is beyond me...if she is even responsible. The Balathide have been beneath this land for many generations, as have the thuell. It is difficult to imagine them surviving until this mysterious end which the prophet claims to have foreseen.

The Balathide have been scattered since Miohaelia's death, a shared mind interwoven with that of their mother and running rampant in the wake of her passing, much like the Hischates of Quetzuaul. While once they were native to the sea floor, the violation of her land by Zeniquorer forced those that survived to flee far and wide. Their connection to one another remained but without a goddess to control them they became an entity of their *own. Unlike the Hischates, clusters of these have formed their own collective mind.*

I have no doubt that Kulibreal, eldest of Miohaelia and sister to Raphenie, must have attempted to regain command in her mother's absence. Clearly she failed, for her suffering in bereavement was as daunting as theirs. The pain of her young memories might be equal to that incurred by banishing her sister, as even the Nhi'Thaun and their purest heirs have their limits. She made the choice to let go of Raphenie so that she could rule her mother's Balathide but it was too late. In what little I have seen of her, I know she was able to draw many of them back home, yet it is a fraction of a fraction of their true numbers. Like locusts they swarm the sea now, directionless, hungry, frightened of the darker things preying within the abyss.

These beautifully crafted beings therefore ventured higher and higher in the realm aquatic and eventually into the caves and waterways beneath many continents, including Manti. They adapted, some even becoming capable of walking and breathing the air, though they found themselves in dangerous territory. Much like the thuell that were buried in Manti's rocks, they could not withstand the heat or light of day, so a hidden war began for the Rokhaadi below; Balathide against thuell. If Bethaali did indeed bring one of these ruinous things back from a distant era, then it would seem the creations of Miohaelia could be the only answer to the errant remnants of the corpse goddess. Never before has a species been able to contain and resist the thuell for so long.

I have often marveled at the resilience of the Balathide species. Despite their limited and very specific nutritional needs, they are able to change their bodies almost at will to suit their environment, all thanks to the healing power of the virginal goddess who shaped them. They could not kill the thuell but neither could the thuell kill them. Their flesh regenerates so quickly that they could suppress the contagion and, every time they became infected, would burst out of the ground and into the light, sacrificing themselves to destroy it. They had bodies to spare so as more gathered to Manti and no sense of self-importance. Verily, the Mantichaena and even Anama herself owe their lives to the Balathide. Without this secret war the thuell would have no doubt found their way to the beating hearts of the land's creatures in unimaginable numbers. Of course, not all thuell are as vulnerable as these. They are all unique, all changing and adapting as quickly as the Balathide. Some have even found ways to survive in full daylight, hiding inside living creatures far more discretely than this wretched thing slain by a company of Mantichaena did. However, a thuell is still thuell; one of many pieces of the Manyflesh that exist purely to consume. Sooner or later they all destroy their hosts.

This secret war will likely go forever unknown to the Mantichaena, for the lands scarred by it are deeply feared by their kind from afar. Seen by the kutliku in their many explorations, they called the southern desolation Nikhaadi Ansax. Unlike the Tau, there was no need for laws against venturing there. It is taboo to them, cursed ground so repulsive that it has the very face of death; gaseous cracks in a black and scorched stone where no thi can grow. After all the death and decay that has filled Ansax and the winding caverns below, the air is choked by the reek of a hundred generations of Balathide corpses putrefying in perpetuity. Many never made it to the surface, while those who did have left a boneyard that would sicken even a god.

Bethaali has spoken of a future all living things must fear and an architect of its coming which can be none other than the most terrible of Vulgoli. Could these Balathide persist even unto that time? Such powerful thuell have become nearly extinct since Escharka faded back into the dark edge and her disastrous presence was removed from her pieces...but what if she rose again? Even the Vulgoli fear the dark edge, calling the time of their mother's return the 'Age of Unraveling'; the ultimate undoing of Maengir as it was consumed by its maker.

Strangely, the day Bethaali predicts is not possible in that future. If Escharka were to revisit from the Dark Edge she would reclaim her lost fragments and there could be no thuell in any future for Bethaali to bring back. More notably, there would be no Maengir left. No – If Bethaali has brought such a foul beast from a distant day then it is not the unravelling she has seen. Something else must be building in the estuary toward which the winding rivers flow. Is there a seed I have overlooked which will grow the future?

~Chronicle of Wonders, The Age Unseen

CHAPTER 8: THE GRACE OF A GUARDIAN

Thetrulengo speaks,

*V*aeba is not merely a concept of the inmost plane. It is a very real place. Due to the stigma that comes from its meaning it is also spoken of as the summation of the many punitive hells in which the mortal have a fearful faith. Its true nature is not so profane, and any truth behind the myth of eternal torment as punishment for wrongdoing is not something I have yet encountered in my exploration. The realm to which they refer is nothing more than the next phase of the inworld; the first layer of the lower and inner veil. When life dies, this is where it goes. It is here that flesh parts from the soul and falls slowly back toward the bottom of everything, back to its mother. The only thing that remains is the 'Aftersoul', their unclean essence, which is neither of flesh nor of light but the parts of their light which have gone dark as it resided in the flesh. It is this anti-life essence from which Escharka molded her firstborns, the Vulgoli.

There is more. Always there are more complications. The Nhi'Thaun could not be drawn into the House of the Living Sky because their essence was too excessive to be controlled without the direct influence of the Deina or their lord, yet they too have *seen Vaeba. All souls do. Each dying soul travels mahavaeba to reach the underlands. There they are pitted against the Ward of Unbirth, the only passageway into the House of the Living Sky. If their essence is too corrupt, touched by Escharka's infection or scarred by the obsessions she herself is wracked with – guilt, shame, bitterness; those things which putrefy the soul – then they will fall among the truly dead and their light will turn to darkness as it lies for eternity upon the reflections of the damned as the few shining fragments of their soul are pulled from them and into the Ward of Unbirth.*

There was a time when Vaeba was a place of peace, order and tranquility, when such grotesqueries were not a tragedy brought on by misuse of power but merely a separation of two parts so they could return to their homes. This all changed on the day the ramshackle truce held by the surviving elder gods fell apart. The last of their wars would reshape the fate of Maengir, all because of that which has vexed the makers of divine law for a thousand lifetimes: forbidden love.

The Veil was as Keimas had seen it when he was pulled in, liberated from the deep earthplane by Tzychala the Eyebeast. Many who part the Veil have witnessed a visual elucidation of all the workings of Maengir; a singular perspective into all that exists across its vast overworld. From where one entered, they could see to other continents, communicate and even travel. They enter the void between matter and energy where the laws of essence and flesh mean nothing. It was exploited most effectively by those who knew its true nature, the Deina lumenspawn and their Vulgoli counterpart, yet mortal magicians have been learning to harness its limitless power. Since they first stumbled onto knowledge of the Veil they have found ways of drinking Az'Rech's lingering essence at an advanced rate due to an ability to farm it from more than just the food they eat and the light upon their skin. The simple truth is that the magicians and godlikes of the new epoch are exactly what the gods of their own time once were. They were the few beings who were more in touch with the Veil, more aware of it and hungrier to taste its bounty. The only thing they did not understand was the balance they fought against, the law that all light lost on their death must return to Az'Rech and the only light the living could gather came from him. The greatest among them grew by stealing it from other creatures, plants, stones, and...more fragile worlds.

At the time I only mocked them, took no real interest in their fights. To revisit it now with fresh eyes and a taste for truth and meaning, knowing as well that I have a better sense of the mortals' fickle emotions, I realize what terrible events were meant to come of a day not so long ago.

Loi was born, ate of his mother, hid in Ephielipax's home, and for some time was unknown to even his own people. When he rose and appeared his people praised him, though he ignored their fealty, seeking a crown for himself that would rule not one nation but all. Overconfident in his stolen power he went to war with his cousins, Kulibreal and Ferraro. However, lacking the foresight or patience to bring together his mother's fallen Hischates, and without the loyalty of Ephielipax's kutliku, he was forced to face them alone. Failing, he recoiled once more into obscurity. He bided his time, dwelt on the memories he had taken from his elders. When the time was right, his final act of defiance brought the day of Ellel's fall.

Love in any form was no concern of Loi's, nor something he had planned for his dominion, so he would not abide the love between one of his children and one of Ferraro's. It was treasonous, at the very least.

~Chronicle of Wonders: Owner of the Wind

Loi's second emergence came in an older, more delicate time; the pivotal period when a few gods had lost control of their designs for Maengir, and their torches passed to their unfortunate children.

The six Nhi'Thaun, being condemned to eternally reach back for the life from which they were taken, were unable to accept any future absent their rule. Still, their greater tragedy was in seeing how their offspring squandered the power each left behind.

Loi had no interest in ruling a single nation and, when the deadly kutliku made in his father's image abandoned Ellel, he had no army with which to conquer any other. Though he tried to destroy Ferraro and Kulibreal at birth he was defeated and forced back to hide in his temple on Ellel, injured and impotent. He waited, watched, went and sought mortal women to satisfy the only need he could have met. Like a monster in the night he kept his base consumption a secret, commanding that virgins be brought to his temple and keeping for himself a harem in his solitude. His priests believed they earned favor, turning their minds from the thought of what fates awaited the victims brought before their hungry lord. Though many of them went willingly and eagerly, these poor girls could not have dreamt that their benevolent Loi had no modicum of kindness in him.

Loi had lost his father's weapons. Unsatisfied with the Galaila, he intended to breed an army of his own. Shortly thereafter, he discovered the difficulties in mating god and mortal, not knowing the secrets to do so. It was a divine seed received as a gift which made a godlike of mortal birth, while physical love could do no more than kill the mortal mate, as it so often did. One by one, Loi murdered his captives to no avail, turning his father's holy temple into a tomb where the pure and innocent were sacrificed to his savage delusions.

One day, against all odds, he finally succeeded. He began to think on the nature of love for the first time, had his first feelings of what it would be like to care for another creature. One tear was shed, and this was enough to blind his next victim to the truth of who he was.

Avocamnta Aia Sohsomi was brought to him, shut inside by his heralds before ever noticing the bog of blood and corpses that filled the blessed halls. Her stomach churned with doubt, her heart raced with fear, yet the god she saw languishing on his gory bed seemed so heartbroken. Curious, and feeling genuine pity, she asked him the simplest question: *'Eis'mgolis, quost'setsiliwekt? – My god, why do you cry?'*

To this he had no reply, looked upon her with gratitude and favor, not understanding the feelings but feeling them nonetheless. It was in that moment that the tiniest flicker of love in her heart fell prey to the one in his, and by nature he gave his light to her. So was his first and only daughter conceived and, in the woman's ensuing captivity, cruelly begotten. The beast could only change when all he desired was out of reach, as all was lost when a good and devoted heart brought it straight to him.

In a house built upon sad bones, Anama was born.

Ellel trembled with Loi's victorious laughter, endless screams of elation that he had found the key to birthing his immortal legion. So overwhelmed was he with fantasies of his coming war that, when at last he became sane and readied to have new innocents sent to him by the hundreds, he saw his child was missing.

Though he had slain his mother while only a day old, he could not imagine that his firstborn would ever flee from him. She must surely have been taken, stolen from him by one of those skulking and underhanded wretches whose eyes never left him: Ferraro and Kulibreal. No more would he be held captive in his own land by their allied power. They had gone too far, traitors to their own claims of peace. For this injury, they would pay with their lives and the lives of all their kind, and the rest of Maengir would follow.

It was the memories stolen from his father that moved him so unrelentingly. Like the pieces of a shattered vessel, he could not order them, knowing only their color and cleavage, yet from that he could still see their original shape. Maengir was not the only world, and it had drawn the eye of something terrible from beyond the horizon.

Ephielipax believed the answer to this coming menace was unity, dying for his hopes while trying to make peace with Quetzuaul.

Loi would answer in his own way. For survival, all light must belong to him. If a thousand nations had to die for him to gather it, then it must be so.

Ferraro's eye had never been further from the doings of her enemy. Her home needed its goddess just as any children needed a parent. Though she listened through the Veil and felt in the bones of the world for any sign of Loi's return to power, she remained the devoted protector and provider of her people. Their lives were simple and happy, as this was the greatest gift she hoped to give them.

Many seasons came and went as the Nhi'Thaun settled into their unfortunate destiny and the times of their stars' prominence became more consistent. Some lands flourished in the absence of their deities while others fell into ruin. Wars raged not by the will of gods, but by that of the mortal, empires rose on one continent, or fell on another, as those left behind gradually turned away from the past.

Then, while the second era of Maengir was still young, Ferraro at last felt a change in the echoes of the Veil. Shaken from her long rest by a distant cry of pain, she knew that one of her oldest and most powerful children was in danger. For the first time in the lives and memories of her people's present generation, the great goddess of mountains vanished, never to return.

Ferraro, supreme inheritor of the deep ground and its undying flames, saw all of Maengir become many and one as she flew across its breadth through the silent currents of the Veil. Only with the empowered eyes of a goddess was she able to discern its individual parts. In the Tau were the lands of Ellel and Gravenje, one which belonged to Loi and the other to Quetzuaul and her Hischates. To the Thaun was Hiwult, the black sands inhabited only by the ruins of a species long dead. To the Dhai, her own homeland of Apos, where her creations were almost indistinguishable from the K'hizu Sekhaadim. Far below the waves was Entedelyan, deep birthplace and sole belonging of Kulibreal. Deeper still was Rokhaadi Haeriobethe, where the earthplane ended and became a void with a lightless sky below.

Far and away across the sea, in any direction and further than any god had yet ventured, there were always more lands. Infinity was untouchable even for one that travelled the Veil, and infinity was truly the distance to Maengir's edge. Not in a hundred lifetimes could Ferraro or any of her peers hope to set foot on every shore.

This perspective of significance gave her wisdom, a love for the small and near, which made her the mother and protector she was. To grasp at the vastness of Maengir was a fool's errand. Truly, the greatest purpose in her existence was in tending what she had created.

The alliance with Kulibreal against Loi was not entirely benevolent. To prevent the decimation of foreign lands was only a consequence of Ferraro's loathing for Loi. She knew him as little as anyone else; hated him only for his parentage. Among the Nhi'Thaun, there were none more reviled than they two who had conquered half of the known world: Ephielipax and Quetzuaul.

Stepping out from a phantasmal avulsion in the fabric of being, Apostaulsm Golaia Ferraro emerged into the vast abysmal foundation of Vaeba, the veil of corpses and secret passages. Here, where fallen aftersouls mounded in a sea of immaterial darkness, she felt the suffering presence of her wandering eldest.

The goddess' appearance was not like others of her kind, deceiving in her size and mortal femininity. She did not hoard her power in order to multiply it and grow her being, rather used it in the rituals of her tribe and in blessings on their jungles. Despite knowing the threat of Loi remained she had lost a great deal of her strength in these pursuits, as well as in reshaping herself to better suit the Apochaena that revered her. Specifically, she had made herself look just like them; what she believed to be the ultimate achievement of beauty, though she was more than twice the height of her mortals.

Her ebony hair flowed like water the length of her body, whispered poetry in praise of the night it reflected. Her russet skin had the warmth and strength of thi bark, overlapping itself in ridges where her bones could separate into segments that slid across one another. Though difficult to master, this anatomy gave her the ability to reinforce any joint or bone at will, as well as provide greater contraction of muscles so as to leap great distances, all while moving with the fluidity of a serpent.

Apochaena skin was not made to absorb energy from Laesis. They relied purely on the food of the land and so were endowed with omnivorous teeth, some sharp for tearing flesh from bone and others smoothed for grinding leaves. However, they did not have claws or other such tools of more barbaric species. They hunted with traps and cunning, as did their goddess.

Her eyes were hunter's eyes, compound and versatile. Toasty golden irises glowed around twin pupils stacked atop one another, squeezing together as they observed what was near, then spreading apart to observe what was far.

Clothed in white and green, a single piece of cloth in hundreds of wraps around her, she had been dressed for ceremony. Her efforts were to entice the love and affection of her most beautiful celebrants. Such romantic appearances were out of place now as she searched for the voice of her child. Like an insect she crouched furtively, her joints and bones collapsing and tensing to move at the slightest provocation.

She looked up once at the underside of Maengir. As far as the eye could see the dark horizons issued forth wandering flecks of light. Small, luminescent bodies they were, the souls of the dead finding their way to an unmarked grave. As they descended, they were drawn to a structure which stood mightily before Ferraro, burning like a white torch to guide the wayward sparks.

The Endmost Tor, as it was known to Ferraro, was the solitary key of grim and unimpressive rock in the dark ocean. It was barren but for the monument containing the light: six pillars of stacked stones which leaned inward to a point as the blinding glow within swirled and flashed around them.

As the last remains found their way to the glow they were transformed and broken beyond repair. Each flickered and was swallowed by the white, separating from any touch of darkness that clung to it. What remained became as a droplet of oil, accumulating in the cracked stone until it flowed over the edge of the mountain. The legend of all gods' great fear lay dying on those gloomy shores, all the lost fragments of souls that could not escape now flooding the belly of the Veil. In the calm, mirror-like surface the streams became the images of those who had possessed them, born again of their unclean essence and desperately straining until the end of time to move their inert bodies. The infinitesimal essence that remained with them was not enough for them to live, too much for them to die. The most polluted of them had the worst curse of all: a half-alive motility that gave them hope of freedom.

Ferraro dreaded to look on what she had already seen once before: the voiceless, noiseless faces of the drowned as they clamored for the embrace of the light, pleading for escape from existence.

She could not allow the distraction of pity, for on the other side of the shining stones was the enemy she had failed once to destroy.

Loi had certainly been busy, eating all the light he could from the living. He had grown, was nearly twice her height, yet could have stood taller judging by how he hunched his back and hung his bulbous head from the weight of giant tusks. His feet were flat and toeless, like hooves of flesh, holding legs so thick and blubbery they could crush boulders with a casual step. The rest of him was no prettier. A shallow chest and an overly muscled back forced him to bend, relying on his giant arms to hold his misshapen weight aloft. His grotesquery was offset slightly by the shimmering crystals that grew from within his skin and tusks, though such decorations were largely hidden by how he clothed himself in skins torn from the hides of his many enemies: Hischates, Apochaena, Balathide, and others Ferraro did not recognize.

One of Loi's broad feet was planted immovably on the arm of a woman with Ferraro's features, her beloved and long-absent celebrant.

She was ragged, beaten, nearly dead, yet a fire of hope filled her eyes when they saw the goddess had come.

By the celebrant's side and clutching her free hand was a much smaller woman of a very strange kind. She appeared Galaila, yet her skin faded in and out of vision as parts of her changed into images of green woods and yellow fields. Among them, fleeting manifestations of claws, fur and horns came and went, as if her body could not decide its shape and wished to be all flora and fauna.

Ferraro had no ill will toward the grieving stranger, was even touched by how she held her daughter's fingers, the sadness visible in her flesh as the pictures within her were filled with rain. A part of Ferraro was indignant that her eldest would be snared by one of an inferior species, but she saw a true desire of the heart in them both, which swayed her to momentary clemency. There were more pressing matters at hand than her daughter's poor judgement.

Pretending herself dispassionate, Ferraro flatly mocked her nemesis.

"*Golina Ellelilt,* you have done little but eat, *la,* while you wallow in your defeat?"

Loi's head turned to her, snorting steam at her disdain for his obvious power but saying nothing.

"You need not suffer the shame of defeat again," she offered.

"Perish your pride and back down, or I will take it from you."

"Pride!?" He thundered back. **"Ferraro is not goddess now. Ferraro is small and soft. You love! Be quiet, lover!"**

His voice boomed profoundly. Ferraro had never been moved by it, or at least had never shown it.

"Eina haten, loose my child," she commanded.

"Your slave? Your pet? I am punishing. Took my Anama," he growled.

"Punish your own. They are accustomed to it."

Her voice wavered as her eyes found those of her daughter's young companion, saw a need far stronger than self-preservation in them. She was of love. The light of Loi radiating from her disgusted Ferraro, yet she did not want to see her child's chosen mate destroyed.

Loi was strong in body but feeble in mind. If Ferraro spoke well she could lead him however she saw fit. Knowing this, she maintained her easy tone and spoke softly.

"Eim, my Golgamet is not deserving of your wrath. She takes what she wants, just as we do. Does that not seem admirable to you? Is that not the example we have set? Our youth have had their fun, now we will have ours. Release mine for my own pleasure and wreak yours on this Anama."

"Nooo!" Loi roared again, stamping down and effortlessly crushing Golgamet's arm into meal.

Anama screamed and flailed as she pulled her maimed lover away and held her tight. Golgamet's eyes were turgid from the shock, kicking her spindly legs, gasping and moaning in unspeakable pain.

Loi's smoking eyes belied how unreasonable his mind was.

"Your woman took Anama! Broke your peace! Stole Anama! Dies!"

Ferraro's temper flared and she could barely contain herself from unleashing everything she had on him, yet she had to take control the situation. Kulibreal was nowhere to be found. She was alone this time and dead certain that she could not fight Loi in his present state and win.

"There are not enough gods left for you to fight!" She reasoned, appealing to his passion with its equal. "What will you conquer when our heads hang around your neck? What pleasure will you find when there is no more killing left for you?"

Loi grinned an evil grin, lips dribbling as he turned away from the children, weighing forward on his knuckles.

"Kill...no. Killing is done, for now. Loi wants your head, fire woman...but not yet. Loi has seen future. New world! New plans. Father had secrets, big secrets about first god, biggest god! This is a secret place...bad place," He looked at the glowing portal, still unknowing of what lay beyond, then back to Ferraro. **"Fur-roh...Ferraro can help. Help Loi breeeak."**

"Eis grao, this bleak hell is the furthest place from any god! What secrets are you jabbering about? What do you know about this...thing?" She indicated the light as well.

Loi scraped at the ground and snarled.

"Golgamet take Anama. Loi take her unless Ferraro help break."

"Father, please stop!" Anama pleaded tearfully.

Loi responded with a bellow and a heavy swing that flattened her against the ground.

Breathing billows of steam, he gave Ferraro his full attention. He paused, inner conflict changing his complexion before he surprised her, confessing, **"Fire-woman, Loi wrong. Loi wrong many times, but peace...peace impossible. Light will poison. Light will kiiill. Loi can stop. Ferraro too! Free ourselves! Break power of big god!"**

"Your 'Big god' is here in Vaeba, is he?" Ferraro seethed, doubtfully. "Then let him show himself, you mindless heap!"

"No. Seeecret god," Loi reached out warily toward the stone-bound star. **"There is power. Biggest god tries to hide, but Loi find. Light-curse kill gods! Kill gods to kill mortals. Keep us slaves! Where dead go, god sleeps. LOI will kill god. End death!"** He lurched back toward Anama and Golgamet and spat at them hatefully. **"Best live one life as *Jiouan* than many as child-mortal, as nothing."**

"Our children are everything!" Ferraro belted.

"Ferraro want because Ferraro weak," Loi grumbled with a dismissive sweep of his engorged hand. **"Want peace because cannot understand war. Ferraro like children. Forgotten the Maengir way! Forgot their place."**

"Minehau, what is their place? Beneath your heel, begging for

what little mercy you have? I have heard their lamentations under your mother's despotism; under your father's neglect, and now hear their lunatic obsession with tall structures and metal clothes while you idly fret over imagined *Nhi'Thauanalt*. They run rampant, worshipping themselves more than they ever did you. Why do you not first conquer your own petty creatures? Because you know no language but fear, and how can they fear you without ever seeing you? You are no more a god than this stone!"

Loi reared to stomp on and obliterate Golgamet entirely, but was struck at the knee by a stream of magma that swept it away and turned him over to crash onto his face, shattering one of his tusks under his own girth.

Ferraro stalked around him, her hair flying up and turning to a roaring fire as more molten rock spilled from her mouth and skin to course along her limbs.

"ENOUGH! Anama..." she commanded, not trusting the woman but forced to rely on her. "...Save my daughter. Protect her, no matter what."

Anama did as she was bid and scrambled along the rough ground to sweep up Golgamet's unconscious body and drag it from Loi's reach.

Loi stared, incredulous, and ignored the hardening stone that burned into his jeweled skin as he glowered hatefully at his child.

"Disloyal!" he roared, pounding his chest and shattering the slag as he hauled himself up, grumbling in confusion. **"If Loi could understand...perhaps Ferraro listen."**

"Go and kill your biggest god!" Ferraro dared with blazing eyes. "Kill all the skies if you so choose, but into those realms belonging to Ferraro and Kulibreal you will NEVER set foot! Do as you wish with Ellel, but that is where you will remain." The lava around her glowed and undulated, pouring forth from her and narrowing to sharp tips.

Loi had stopped listening, now silently watched the luminous columns, his inky eyes reflecting the lustrous beauty.

It was common lore amongst the gods that this final threshold was not to be crossed by any living body, here at the Veil where souls came to rest; in passing through the avenue of the light their bodies would surely fall among the drowned below.

Through the fractured image of his father's memories, Loi saw through the deception, discerned the truth behind the game the insidious light was playing. The 'Deina' were greedy, using fear to keep Maengir in check. This was their place of power, their weapon to be wielded against mortality to keep it vulnerable. If a god took control of it, then even the mighty Deina would be unable to match him. Maengir would finally be safe, protected from the wrath of the unseen god of gods. It would be he, Loi, for none other could hear the voice of danger.

He was so entranced that he did not notice Ferraro's silent glide to stand between him and the light. Snorting and shaking his head, he lowered his gaze to her as she lowered her weapons.

"You spoke of this when last we met...that your father was given a message of the world of light. It seems you have heard half of a story you cannot reason with. I have heard a story of my own, from a father far wiser than yours: 'This wall you must not break. Whether beyond it there awaits power, eternity, or knowledge, it is not our place. What lies therein has been emplaced for a reason, and if you remove it you will set in motion the only death from which there is no return.' I hear your words, Loi of the Siege. I ask you to hear mine."

"Deception...lies. You always lie," Loi reprimanded her.

"I have done this. For that, *prostaan*. But these are the last words of my father. You will heed them, or I will send you to a hell far beneath this one."

Ferraro's flaw was that of many peacekeepers: she believed that bloodless resolutions were always possible. She did not truly wish to kill Loi, neither did she know the full extent of the consequences should he be allowed to continue with his intentions. She had never even heard it called the 'Ward of Unbirth' yet knew its importance by her father's testament. It was more than just a symbol of what afterlife was promised to the fallen, though no curiosity about its designs would move her to risk stealing that afterlife from her people, or any of the dead.

Loi saw her hesitation and, brute that he was, believed it was a fear of him. Opportunity was his to finally rid himself of her interference. In a burst of speed, he charged against her, his knuckles and heels breaking off sheets of rock as he galloped toward the six pillars.

Ferraro fell quickly to her knees and thrust her winding streams of magma into the ground, issuing a tremendous heat which melted the rock between them to catch him in place.

Like stones on mud, Loi's bulky legs sank to the knee at the first touch, eliciting an ear-shattering roar of pain from him as the quagmire enveloped his flesh and set it ablaze. Eyes wide with determination, he slapped and clawed at the rock to drag himself forward, unable to utter any threat or insult through his own cries. Nonetheless, he continued to come.

From her position Ferraro stood suddenly and raised her hands, pulling on the lava like chains and lifting the fiery fury off the ground, raising geysers that wrapped over Loi's shoulders and neck, enveloping him in the inferno.

Hopelessly trapped, Loi ceased struggling.

For a moment Ferraro thought she had won though the attack never waivered. She had underestimated Loi's power before, when she was a young and inexperienced goddess. But Loi, born of the two greatest among Nhi'Thaun, was not to be contained by mere stone. Even as she watched, he gathered his resolve, inhaled deeply, and breathed out an icy wind of such depth and duration that the superheated rock was solidified in an instant. The deep freeze wound through all the streams of lava and straight to Ferraro, nearly catching her in her own element. Panicked by the sudden turn, she was forced to release control, leaping backward and leaving her lava streams solidified in midair, and barely retaining enough of her own heat to counter the ice that built up on her skin.

Loi remained buried neck-deep in solid rock, tiny glimmers of fire shooting out of the crackling rock around him, yet he had never looked so confident. He sneered at Ferraro, struggling to fend off the creeping ice, his bulging forehead nearly hiding his eyes.

"Ferraro was strong. Now is time of Loi! Loi of blue sky!"

In a ferocious whirlwind of ice and stone, Loi broke free of the trap as though it were a pile of leaves, the flesh of his back exploding out into tremendous crystalline wings of such immensity that their tips were almost lost in the distant darkness. All the colors of creation flashed in their every reflective surface, taking the light of the Ward of Unbirth and beaming it across the far reaches of Vaeba and even into the piles of bodies below.

Ferraro was nearly blown from the mountain by the winds, barely held onto the edge of one of the Ward's great pillars. As it began to die, she dangled from high up. She was alone, hopeless to pit her strength against Loi's. She needed a plan.

Loi no longer acknowledged either of the children as they huddled in terror near the precipice. His goal was within reach, nearly in his outstretched hands as he beat his wings to lift from the pit and bounded toward it, shaking the mountain to its foundation with each step.

Her options exhausted, Ferraro had one final ploy to keep Loi at bay. With no regard for the possible consequences, she flung herself from the pillar toward him in a death-defying challenge. Words were not the only gift given to her by her father, though they were by far the most powerful; words of such power that she had been sworn to never speak them unless far more than her own life was at stake. An oath stolen from one of the many creatures he spied on from the shadows of the Veil; an incantation made by and for only the demons of an old and savage world:

"*Aposd'maud'tskaposgahl* – Darkness eat and darkness crawl!", she wailed into the dark.

To her surprise, the dark answered back. Feeling as though the whole of creation was molded in her fingertips, she felt it pulling her in all directions, yet at her command to choose and direct. In her mind she pictured the world above, as far from this place as she could dream, and so that was where the tether tightened and dragged them both.

Sight of the Ward vanished behind a curtain of shadows, and Loi's mind went equally dark as Ferraro's incantation bound their bodies in some otherworldly vessel and set journeyed across the boundaries of the Veil.

Aroused, but seeing double from the disorienting journey, the sky god awoke with his tusks buried in the dirt, face-up on the underside of a landform far above mortality's plane.

They were above Laesis' crest and very near where the higher earthplane broke beautifully free of the aetherplane, each small stone arcing waves of starlight around. Here in deep sky, lifeless rocks drifted across the vast and empty realm, pulled from the greater earthplane by forces so strong that they were caught up in the slipstreams of warped energies that wove upward. These were the roads that especially powerful souls like the Nhi'Thaun had travelled, leaving in their wake a concentration of essence which infused the floating lands with the same pull as the flat world. As Vaeba was dark and deep, so was Aurba dazzling, where all was silent and filled with stars.

"**How...How!? Ferraro...dooms everything,**" Loi fumed as he rose, looking up yet down to see the face of Maengir from his inverted position. "**Golden ones, shiny ones...kill everything.**"

"You share too much common ground, then," Ferraro retorted, standing as he was on a nearby mass. She was ready to take the fight to its bitter end, a long crop of lava in each hand and droplets of the same trickling from her eyes and mouth. Still her hair whipped with flame, illuminating waves of smoke that surrounded her and made her a more inspired image of her former glory.

"**Loi will save. Loi will RULE! Mortals should worship. Loi is all that saves them from biggest god.**"

"Who then will save them from you!?"

Ferraro could not see it for the billowing smoke about her, but Loi wept bits of crystal that spiraled toward the vast auburn mountains of Ellel three-hundred leagues below.

"**Ferraro not help. Not see. Waste of light.**"

Ferraro reared back with twin strikes aimed at Loi's head, though a moment too late. With his colossal wings outthrust he charged her on the air, his gemstone shell growing and sharpening as he bellowed: "**So...Ferraro DIES!**"

For one such as Loi, battle meant heavy blows that devastated anything in his path. For Ferraro it was a dance, her uniquely agile body slipping past every attack and retaliating after every clumsy swing. Like a mite she sprang from one drifting chunk to the next, allowing Loi to obliterate those in her wake while she showered him in liquid stone torn from her surroundings.

Over and over, they repeated this uneven trade, Loi's mounting rage making him ever slower and sloppier.

Just as in Vaeba, Ferraro began to melt one of her mounts at the core, its compromised strength hidden from Loi as she baited him to attack, then left him barreling through a viscous blob that splashed over him, scorching him and weighing him down.

Finally seeing the futility of his tactics, though acting no more strategically, Loi kept his distance and summoned the wind at his back to hold him aloft as he snatched an island from the air and easily tore it in half. With the crystals of his body growing into the two halves of the mass and gripping them, a freely drifting Loi buckled and hurled them toward Ferraro. He was not ingenious, though neither was he entirely daft. The first he threw she escaped with ease but the second was flung at her obvious destination, catching her off guard and punishing her shortsightedness as she tumbled away among the stars.

Free-floating and exposed, she ignited another mass from afar and made its molten skin reach out for her to grab onto. She almost had it, nearly pulled herself to safety, until she saw it freeze in Loi's mighty wind and felt herself struck by his hand. Caught in his grip and trying to sear it with her inner essence, she was swung about and hurled at dizzying speed against ground, feeling the excruciating crack of both it and her bones. Recovering her breath, she screamed as she righted herself, vision clearing just in time to see Loi charging into her. Through blood and dust, she had only a fleeting moment to think of Golgamet before his jeweled fist smashed her and the island that bore her into extinction. A ripple of force tore through the surrounding rocks, shattering them along with the goddess. Like a wildfire her soul spread through the hail of earth, imbuing each meteor with her death rattle as it crashed down upon his own lands.

Loi looked on, with satisfaction. Ellel would die as she had, but it would be born anew in his victory. Once he had control of the hidden lights of the elusive Deina, his father's creatures would worship him at last. Then, they too would be sacrificed for the final battle.

CHAPTER 9: NO SURVIVORS

With his great and final victory, Loi returned, unchallenged, to Vaeba and the gateway of his destiny. It had taken him a great deal of harvesting essence through to accumulate the knowledge and ability needed to move through the Veil. Now that he had learned the skill and found the heart of Vaeba as he had seen it in his father's memories it was a simpler task. It took time nonetheless, far slower and more painful than it had been for Ferraro and her strange trick of darkness. It was a pity that he had killed her so quickly. Eating her would have gained him the same power, as the death of a god or goddess always did. Without it, it took him days to find his way back through the winding passages of each lower plane.

Through strange demi-worlds, Loi sank through the last breath of Maengir and entered Vaeba once again, slamming down upon the Endmost Tor within arm's reach of the Ward of Unbirth. However, it was no longer open. Someone had sealed it entirely. Loi knew immediately who dared such defiance, though it was ultimately inconsequential. He was, however, surprised to see the dismembered celebrant still clinging to life.

Golgamet had outdone Ferraro with such a barrier, though she was clearly near death from using the last of her strength. Both she and Anama were mere shadows of their vibrant selves now, clinging to each other in the encroaching shadows of Vaeba. They had been praying, pleading, bargaining with all divines for Ferraro's victory, now crushed and shrinking in terror at Loi's return.

At a glance, it was no wonder they had languished here in his absence. Golgamet in her condition would surely be destroyed by the journey back to Maengir, and it seemed Anama would not part with her. The prophet had spent the last of herself on the futile wall, and it seemed they were prepared to die for one last desperate bid at hindering him. Pitiful, but tenacious.

For a long time, Loi pondered the sight before him. With Ferraro dead, he now saw Anama was no captive, just a traitor. She had defied him at birth, hurt him, betrayed the destiny they could have shared. There was no showing her the truth now. She was of love, corrupted by that which undermined all great destinies.

"Pretty goddess...dead," he gloated.

Anama screamed angrily into Golgamet's breast, clutching her clothes.

Once, they believed they could survive in secret, hiding their love from their makers in the crevices of creation. To live divided from the suffering wrought by the Elder Gods could have been a dream achieved, though they were cursed to know the malice of Anama's father would one day wake them from it.

Loi moved sternly against them and pulled them apart, though they held so tightly to one another that their fingers tore skin.

"Anama know punishment for betrayal," he growled.

Clasping each of them tight, he held Golgamet in front of his face, his giant jaw hanging as his eyes rolled back. A fog poured from his mouth and nostrils, glistening with droplets of his light and wafting toward Golgamet's near-unconscious body.

Anama's pained keen never ceased as the light soaked into her mate's skin, her limp head twitching in resistance.

Loi's soul was too strong, his essence too overwhelming. A moment later, Golgamet fell limp in his fingers.

Winded from her own cries and stifled by heartbreak, Anama stared in silence.

Loi had finally broken her, grinning and savoring the moment as the fog still trickled from the edges of his mouth.

"Anama love? Then Anama love father. Woman is us now.

Golgamet part of Loi, part of family."

Anama had no words for the hate she felt, shaking uncontrollably as the only creature ever to have truly cared for her was dropped like discarded scraps of a finished meal.

Golgamet struck the ground with a sick crunch, yet rose almost instantly. Limping and bloodied, she stared at nothing with vacant eyes that sparkled with Loi's colorful lights. Turning to face Anama with lips and expression that moved to match Loi's, she and he spoke as one:

"Loi survive. Loi live forever. Anama not worthy of taking. Anama never inherit Loi's power! Watch! Despair!"

With that he cocked back and hurled her away into the higher veils.

Without another sound, Anama evaporated into them, cast into unnavigable planes and unlikely to ever crawl her way back to Maengir or sanity.

There was no need for Loi to issue orders to his new servant. Golgamet was Golgamet no more, only a mouthpiece for the eater of gods. She was motionless a moment as his soul finished settling into her, then her body moved shakily toward the Ward of Unbirth. Sinking into the ground, she drew its protective shell down with her, melding them back into their home and exposing the great, secret prize of Maengir.

At last, and through his own overwhelming victory, Loi was defeated.

Two lifetimes of a dreamless sleep accompanied only by the screams of dying souls ended in a sudden, deafening rush of force and light for the demon whose flesh gave rest to the living. The ache of endless days seeing through the eyes of the destroyed – the paths their lives had taken and the choices they had made – at last was lifted from him and replaced by a still sky and the soft chill of a whispering wind. The pull of chains on his wrists was finally gone, only to be replaced by the force of a solid surface beneath his knees. His blinding coffin became a stair of pure light descending to an open sky below with the hazy blue horizon of the earthplane beyond. Little by little he gathered more sights as he painfully opened his many eyes for the first time since the last Age of Unravelling.

Tzychala struggled to all fours, vexed and disoriented by his release, without any knowledge of how it had happened. His body unchanged, his mind still flush with visions of his own past, he cringed and fought to distinguish his own memories from those of the souls siphoned through him. Those belonging to other entities were like shadows he chased with numb hands, slipping further away the more he reached for them and ever elusive. This world he had saved, had longed to become part of, had changed without him.

He had vowed to serve in exchange for the unequaled blessing of a soul. He had had no idea what he would become if he succeeded, though he had known it would be something wonderful. To his great disgust, he felt no different. Only the world was different; so brightly lit, so stiflingly clean and lacking the savory, erotic odors of blood, decay and panic. This was unimaginable, unthinkable. The memories of the dying had shown him nothing of this hatefully serene reality.

"No...No, it-ch cannot be," he whispered unheard, trying to stand on atrophied legs. They gave way like dry twigs, sending him stumbling and rolling down the glowing steps until he lay prostrate at their edge. From that gossamer precipice he hung and stared in horror at this new and shining world, the light of which was as poison to him.

"NOOO!" He lamented. "What ha...Mother? No, imposssh...the sky? What hasssh happened!?"

His slurring tongue was so long unpracticed that he sounded more like the first form he had taken when Maengir belonged to his kind. His body was equally eldritch; wild hair that drug along the ground, seeping blood from every pore of his skin, many eyes flaring and darting around him in search of meat. He scratched his way back up the stair with cumbersome, overgrown claws, his motion jerking and disjointed, all the while babbling:

"Hm ssshpeak? Shissshter, there you? Deina abounding, you here come?"

No answer came from those he called, though the marvelous

walls thrummed with sounds of rage from within. It had a message and a purpose but he could hear nothing of a voice.

"Who isssh within!? Tell ssshpeak. I am not finissshed! I n-need m…I jusssht need more time."

He knelt, a wreck with eyes pulsating in confusion, until he perceived a moving golden engraving on the wall before him that became symbols of the one language. It was different, no doubt malformed by uncountable days of translation, though still the language of the old world and the very first tongue.

Time.

"Y…yesssh," Tzychala shamefully begged. "I need more. Can they hear? I musssht to be complete."

Enter.

Freedom.

"I cannot, far thing," Tzychala whined. "My body flesssh did be within. It can never again. It is law. Law of the makersssh."

The house shook fiercely and the horrible sound from inside was clearly heard. Tzychala recoiled and wondered reverently at what could have created it. Such power, as though from a true Deina. He recalled a memory that had slipped through him in the infinite instant before he was awakened to the world once more, saw in it the death of a dark goddess at the hands of a roaring beast and thought to himself, *can I yet dream, or have I seen my own escape?*

"Loi. He isssh the name," he ventured at last.

The temple shook again, though not violently. Tzychala laid against the humming wall and communed with it, trying to feel the god inside.

"The terrible godssshon of the Quetzuaul? Ssshon of the dessssciever?"

Loi is Loi.

Tzychala's lips curled darkly, and he pushed aside his unkempt hair to better see the luminous characters inscribed, yearning for more.

"I have ssssheen this, the mountain woman'sssh fire in thisssh world…but not you. Now…I know the ssshuffering you there go endure. We…we can be help ch-together."

There was a moment's tense silence, but Tzychala's words found their mark.

Free Loi.
It must be.

"I can…I will. I will make it…though there isssh ssshomething I want for return…ssshomthing you can make give me…"

Every facet of this long-untold story was recounted by Tzychala himself sixty seasons after the fact.

To every incredible detail Keimas listened quietly while staring into the comforting blaze of Nesh. The fire danced in his wondering eyes but his gaze was far away as he absorbed the demon's recital of the vast and compelling history, culminating in the calamity the Mantichaena kept locked out of their hearts for the misery it had brought them.

"He did it. After all the efforts of the other elders he still got inside," Keimas murmured.

"*La,* trapped eternally by his own ambition," Tzychala immediately replied.

"And Ferraro, she was…protecting us?"

"*La,*" Tzychala repeated.

"She died for nothing."

"*La.*"

"Our land, our home…merely another murder of ambition."

"*La.*"

Keimas was not the only person intrigued enough to stay and hear the demon's history, but he alone was emboldened to demand answers. Over the last handful of days, he had become accustomed to hearing stories so ridiculous, each time from a source closer and closer to the god who sought to use him. In a swift motion with outburst wings he snatched the demon by his locks and dragged him across the floor to pin him against the wall. With each step he loudly recounted everything he had been through: the voice in the temple that had been Tzychala's, Golgamet being nothing but a mouthpiece for Loi to lure Keimas and lock him away, and finally the realization that Tzychala himself had masterminded each event.

"WHY?" he demanded at last, eyes shivering with homicidal

rage. "How could you do this? You hideous little imp!?"

The imp did not struggle or defend himself, merely allowed Keimas to enjoy his retribution.

"I wanted to be like you," was his pathetic reply.

"Like me?" Keimas snarled.

"All of you," Tzychala confessed with a jealous tone. "Mortality. all possessing the freedom of a soul, the freedom to belong in this world, growing in the light instead of rotting in the shadows. Loi...he promised you to me. If I helped to make your body his, your soul was to become mine."

Keimas had few words for his disgust.

"*Khain'ghanilt*! gutless *baemna*, you made me dance in a web of lies, buried me to be rationed like a carcass, so you could play at being a man?"

Tzychala said nothing, closed his eyes and somewhat enjoyed the punitive waves of his own guilt. It was raw emotion, something he craved in any form.

Expecting more defense after his outburst, it took Keimas some time to notice the submission on his captive's face; resignation expressing not only acceptance of punishment but further shame at what confessions remained. It was foreboding, filled Keimas with a nervous dread as he began to grasp the purpose of the demon's surrender.

"It isn't finished yet, this game you started, is it? In Golgamet he said he would use me to strike down Anama. To what end? Surely, this is not about an illicit affair of love."

Tzychala's body drooped, and his voice was resentful.

"This world is...poorly made. To protect the House from being penetrated by any but a Deina – the true masters of the Veil, such as they are – their elder created a single entrance, a secret entrance only accessible through your Vaeba so that souls separated from their flesh might pass through it and be made pure. Memory is the poison that ruins the soul and so their memories were taken into another, cursed with an eternity seen through the eyes of the dead. The House itself is made by and for the light alone. If a flesh should enter there it would become as I was, the catalyst of its function."

"And it worked," Keimas continued for him, "Until the gods became too powerful. Loi knew what it was because his father knew, or because this rogue Deina told him. He knew the entry manifested in Vaeba and went searching for it."

"As you say. This is the Ward of Unbirth. Deina, being as short-minded and arrogant as they are, did not think material creatures capable of cultivating their light, stealing it from their lessers and rising to the heights they did. Thus, there was no plan for if a god such as Loi came upon knowledge of their secret. Though they were clever enough to hide it in deeper planes, the Veil was nothing of a defense against one who knew its nature.

Keimas' eyes flashed as the important words formed a picture of Loi's scheme in his mind.

"He is going back. He is, *la*? With my body to carry him he goes to kill Anama, his daughter; stop his power from flowing into her and steal it back. He means to imprint his own soul onto a new body, then use the Ward to reach his prison and…free himself?"

"Tricking the light with a duplicate," Tzychala affirmed.

The two stared at one another in silence, then a subtle movement caught their attention as Lemalie appeared quietly from the passage overhead. Keimas admired her appearance as fondly as when he had first returned; finely dressed but snuggled in a blanket about her shoulders, still with the mussed hair and bleary expression of one having only just woken. She did not appear disturbed or excited but something of both while she stared at Tzychala frigidly.

Releasing the demon, Keimas quickly ascended with a single wingbeat, settled by her side and put one arm and wing around her, kissed her head and held her.

"My love…" he began.

"You are leaving again, *uein*?" she asked.

"No, I swear to you I have made no such plan," he hastily reassured her.

"I heard plenty," she said agreeably as she leaned against him, sighed and kissed his chest. "Enough to know you cannot stay."

Keimas could not bear the thought, not after how poorly he had handled it prior.

"I will. I must," he fought back. "With all that matters most before me now, I'll not leave your side again."

"Do not be Kutu," she insisted, somewhat jokingly, rousing herself and easing out of his embrace. "When first you left this was a sick fantasy, one you could not explain, I know. Yet, if all you have encountered leads you to believe the words of this...thing," she glanced at Tzychala briefly with a look of distaste, "Then your instincts were rightly followed and must be followed again."

Keimas' face contorted, wishing his bride was not so perceptive and would allow them to stay where they were both comfortably loved.

"*Einla*! She gives her blessing!" Tzychala interrupted brazenly, creeping closer. "Not to interrupt the romantic moment, my attractive friends, but every breath drawn here is another wingbeat for the god who would see you parted by more than distance, *la*?"

In response, Keimas drew Lemalie back to him but spoke harshly to Tzychala.

"There was time for you to tell your own story. There is time for me to relish the only hero in mine."

Tzychala dismissed the spectacle with waving hands, retreating a safe distance to dismount the stage and lean against the Tau wall.

Shyly turning into Keimas, Lemalie rubbed her marginally more protrusive belly and smiled warmly. He put his hand beside hers, reveling for a moment in the thought of their future family.

He asked amorously "*Aien*, this one is why you want me to go."

The full depth of her love shone in her eyes as she confirmed.

"If a bloody end is the fate of all things, then I would face it gladly with you...but I would lose you briefly once more if it means a life for our little beauty."

"Have you chosen a name?" Keimas whispered into her ear as he kissed it.

"No. I will not. We will name her together." Then she clutched his sarong and sternly added "When you come home."

Her words were stubbornly optimistic, though her eyes bestowed an array of warnings not to disappoint her. He ran his fingers over her stomach and sensed the quiet life within her, connected with it and felt its rapidly growing essence.

"In less than a season it will be time to welcome her. I can only hope this good season remains until she joins the world."

"Come back," she abruptly begged, momentarily giving way to her fears. "Be a hero and do as needs must, only come back."

"I obey your every command," he whispered, solemn once more.

She gave him a final kiss for the journey before pushing him along, wanting only for him to feel her full confidence.

He made it more difficult as his gaze lingered on her, his fingers as well, for just a moment longer. Then, he turned and dropped down from the balcony and floated to the waiting Tzychala, aiming his whole body at the ugly thing.

"Do not flee in my absence, *zet'itka vaeamnilt,"* he warned as he landed, taking Tzychala by the throat and pulling him face-to-face. "I'm not finished with you."

Tzychala's demeanor changed immediately, holding up both hands and babbling, "K-Keimas …I n-never…"

Keimas' hold tightened and his other hand clamped over Tzychala's mouth.

"Ssstop. Shut your disgusting hole and listen. Your fortunes of continued life rest on the fine edge on my wife's allowance. Do not think I have forgotten that this is your doing. I no longer care why or how, only that you understand your situation. You are going to stay here, at her mercy and her command. We will finish this discussion when I come back and, I swear on my mother's head, if she is not in better health than she is today, you will die. If I come back and you are not here, I will find you and you will die. If I come back and she has any words but the highest praise for you, you will die. If, on a whim, she decides that you should die, you will kneel before her and die. Do. You. Understand?"

Tzychala cautiously pulled Keimas' palm from his mouth and shifted indignantly, cleared his throat and croaked:

"Ehem…*la.* I am your creature and my life the property of she." He weakly straightened himself and gestured with an objecting finger. "But *utan,* perhaps you will entertain just a tiny deviation from the heroically solitary assault you are surely planning?"

"Your time to speak is short," Keimas cautioned.

"I'll not delay, though I may have neglected to explain the full potency of Loi's essence within your body. It is still connected to him, not a seedling of his soul but a strong bough growing from it. Mortally confined or not, he must not be underestimated. Despite my birth by the most ancient of things I myself was little more than a distraction to him in my current state."

"I will be more," Keimas boasted. "He confessed in the stone that gods were more vulnerable to others of their own line."

"True enough, yet your power is still asleep, spread across the entire family and only beginning to draw into you. You could fight him, perhaps even pose a challenge but…it is a bleak hope."

"And what deviation do you propose to brighten it?"

Tzychala's eyebrows popped and he pursed his lips excitedly.

"I imagine you will enjoy this, *utan*. You are the young heir, the true heir of the Raptor, yet you will recall that Kutu, even kutliku, carry the same seed and are all the peoples of Ephielipax?"

"Proceed," Keimas said shortly.

"That is all," the demon's tongue clicked with a sideways glance. "*Eina*…there are plenty of you here."

Keimas smiled deviously and jammed a finger into Tzychala's chest, beginning to share his zeal.

"You may be right…but hold, will they not be weaker in my presence?"

"They will indeed. And you will be…*laan*?"

"Stronger," Keimas pondered.

"An argument could be made for unstoppable," Tzychala embellished.

Keimas nodded, considered, released Tzychala and allowed him to settle but though his words growled with suppressed anger.

"Despite the mess resultant of your dubious allegiances, I can only hope you speak the truth. I'm reluctant to accept what you peddle but I have no choice. It's my wife that most concerns me."

"*La, utan*, I swear to you," Tzychala reassured with both hands raised. "*Aiahm'vul*, even if…ESPECIALLY if the worst should happen, I will be buried to keep her safe for you, my final breath given in standing against any god. Even in serving my own desires I must do nothing else."

With Tzychala blindfolded, it was difficult for Keimas to fully trust him. but, with a fervent nod, he accepted the precarious plan and looked to his exit.

"Then I only hope my kin are as demented as I, to undertake this thing."

With Tzychala close behind, he marched out of Nesh and into what was now mostly swamp as the soggy fields drained into the river. There were still puddles and streams in which children played but now the grown-ups who had previously played alongside them gave chase, fretting about the mud that now covered them from head to toe and was soon to be baked to a crust in their fur by the renascent daylight. Keeping a safe distance from the mischievous younger folk, Keimas espied the fast approach of Aroch along with several other archons; Sebashni, Mani and Metaeu, keeping their various garbs uplifted from the ground. Aroch glowed with excitement and trotted with high steps at the sight of his married son. Sebashni closely followed, both firmly clinging to Keimas with abounding thanks for his safe return. He embraced them in return, anxious to move but thankful to see everyone he held dear for a day. Aroch piously let slip the name of Loi in gratitude and the mood changed, Keimas' feathers bristling as he was sternly refocused on the task at hand.

"Father," he sighed, "It is the very best that I see you again. I had hoped for more time to settle but it seems one day is too much to spare for my own pleasures. The distress I have caused you already is only the beginning. I must meet with the Primarch at once."

Aroch and Sebashni both smiled humorlessly and the two other hall patrons folded their arms and smugly watched the affair from aside.

"*Quoamn*, Father?" a puzzled Keimas asked at their furtiveness. "What is this?"

Aroch patted his shoulder and guided him away from Nesh.

"There have been some developments around the city, my son. I'll quickly share and then hear what words you would have with me." He craned to look curiously past Keimas to Tzychala, who grinned and waved like a child. "Who, eh...who is this thing that shadows you?"

Keimas only grunted and kept Aroch's attention on himself.

"*Eins udai'itka* Tzychala. It dislikes all things blue. Come now, what of Sky?"

CHAPTER 10: A CHANGE IN THE WIND

"*K*ututan Keimas – he is returned!"

A sea of such unfamiliar exclamation surrounded the exonerated hunter. Whether inspired by close association with his wife or the vague and confounding rumors of his disappearance he learned with each piercing call how the vindication of his name had made a devout fandom of his countrymen. Unbeknownst to him, the majority chose to believe that he had escaped the city because he had foreseen that Sky intended to have his head for no reason but the political struggle between he and Aroch. It made little sense, yet speculation of a bizarre tale of divine intervention and usurpation would strain credulity for most gossips. A lie was greatly preferable to the truth, not only for the ease of the transition of power but also for the comprehension of the everyman. As often as Keimas was approached by those who blessed his homecoming he acknowledged few and replied to fewer, perturbed by their unwarranted affections and a bit perplexed that he should be such an symbol to them. He had always thought himself a tool that served a singular purpose; valuable, yes, though not for more than his sharpened talons. Why did these people admire him? He was mortal and miniscule, not deserving of such adulation.

"What troubles you?" Aroch inquired.

He tried to articulate a dignified reply but only managed to say *"Utan*, I hear you."

How was he to explain what he, exalted thing that he supposedly was, was depressed by?

"That's…not an answer," Aroch belabored. "Are you alright, son?"

"Yes. *Malpael*, father, I am only…shocked to think that everything this primacy stood for has crumbled so quickly." He had found a sufficient diversion, though he was not an apt liar.

"Not so, certainly," Aroch mourned. "Though it was sullied by a few, we remain a people of good honor and discipline. The Primacy will be reclaimed. I mean it to be."

"Eina quohalt, will you be Primarch?"

"I have a better idea," he sighed wistfully. With his face to Keimas, he was unaware of Sebashni's approach as she trotted up from behind.

"I do not," she interjected with a smile. "The rest of the council is already agreed."

Aroch obstinately refused "No! *Mnimbui ufetsighenaia*, it's too early for such talk. I…had thought perhaps I would seek the position when this affair first began but no more. Seeing Rogan's true face has solidified in my mind the truth that an absolute ruler, even if chosen properly, is always dangerous and indeed poses the greatest of dangers to the prosperity of any tribe. I will not endorse any archon's assumption of the Primacy, not even my own, until the distrust that we created in ourselves is behind us and we as leaders look long and deep at our own weakness."

Keimas had not seen such adamance in his marriage father since seeking Lemalie's hand. This rekindled passion of integrity was something Keimas respected, envying slightly the ease with which Aroch saw through his own skin. Sebashni did as well, though she addressed its underlying emotions boldly, with the wisdom of one who saw it from both the labor of a leader and the faith of a supporter.

"Eina dboule. You and your son both suffer injuries of your own infliction; that you are somehow the lesser of the many, all of whom are mortal and no more faultless than yourselves"

"Eis aia…" Aroch grumbled, fixing to argue.

In immediate deterrence, Sebashni grabbed the front of his robe, not sternly but resolutely, and with similar eyes put the fear of herself into him.

"Doubt, fear, shame; these are the unseen side of hope. All are the same. All are weapons only, wielded for good or ill as commanded. We should indeed doubt our virtue, fear its loss and be ashamed of those times we have forsaken it. It is these pains that keep our minds upright and forthright, remembering the failure that has brought us today so that we may know what to hope for, what we must make of tomorrow." She hesitated until, in seeing he accepted what she said, continued *"Einla,* you are right. A shattered monument cannot endure if restored with only wax and willpower. It must be remade from stone chosen with care and carved with patience and planning." To both he and Keimas alternatingly she concluded. "The council has not decided a new ruler but a new servant, as the Primarch and Archons were meant to be. There is much to tell, but our conference has led us to the same conclusion as you: the Primacy cannot continue behind closed doors. If you elect to join us again, not as its authority but as its voice before the people, you do so knowing that there will be no more secrets kept upon a hidden throne or around a hidden table."

Aroch had so many questions, flabbergasted that so many decisions had ironically been made without his knowledge, though it was not unreasonable, as he was no archon at present. With the Primacy laid at his feet he saw the value of its new meaning in how strongly his fine partner and lover wished it upon him. Perhaps he had unduly discounted how well she and the council knew his heart, now offering him not a throne but a pulpit, not a crown or mantle above the people but a place among them. If he understood her meaning then they had not only agreed to the same transparency he felt compelled to hold them to but also invited him to be the voice of accountability he felt was his most suited place. However, he once more felt it was not the time. Perhaps the council could persist if so openly engaged, yet he felt more certain now than ever who belonged at the ostensible head of the table.

"My love…" he marveled at her wisdom while doubtful of its execution, "Does the council believe that an election by themselves or the people is what will make a Primarch?"

"The Council will be elected by none. All seats including our own will be voluntary only, unlimited and inviting to all who wish to contribute. As for the Primacy, holding no strict authority as it once did, will be given as befitting one who will be not only our voice to the tribe but its voice to us."

"And this responsibility as well is voluntary?" Aroch coyly surmised, "To be this most caring and attentive ear to the needs of the tribe?"

"Voluntary, presented by the council and approved by the people in reasonable majority."

"Then what need has the council for me? Does it not already have its most suitable choice?"

In the briefest moment of changing emotions Sebashni showed confusion, surprise and finally denial as she stated factually and empathically:

"*Quo*? No! The council's election is dependent on who is recommended by the families."

"This is a new Primacy, is it not?" Aroch glanced around surely, emphasizing his point as he strode around and loudly continued "What a kindness Keimas has done in rallying so many to his return! I see no less than one hundred heads here, representing no less than thirty families and surely all six halls. I call for a show of support by bended knee!"

Sebashni was flustered, even a little embarrassed by how the many onlookers knelt with rehearsed fervor. To her surprise, Aroch's bluster seemed to draw even more passersby to come and show their agreeance. Before long almost a quarter of the city surrounded them, even Keimas willingly taking position and the few present archons following suit. With the last stragglers falling into place, Aroch gave Sebashni the most adoring of smiles.

"I have not been idle, my love. You and your council have laid your plans most wisely. However…I decline. This is my counter-offer…" Aroch raised both hands with his palms to her and shouted clearly "…I decline the advocacy of *Hauan Etain* for seating as Primarch of the Council of Archons. This is a seat of ultimate service to the people and responsibility to their needs, assumable only by one who has no designs for their own glory." He then said more quietly to her "One who advises the weak on surmounting the struggles she has already mastered." Then he belted "In standing and presenting, I advocate Nesh Aiatan Sebashni to be seated as Primarch! Let all who see my presents and share my conviction be upstanding and seen!"

Sebashni's breath was squeezed from her chest as the synchronous scrape of dragging feet led to the almost unanimous rising of bodies and uplifting of arms.

"Aroch," she gasped, not knowing what to say at first. She then spoke directly to the people around her. "I have never once advocated for myself, not even to be on the council. How...why would you do this?"

"No, you have not," Aroch affirmed, "And yet you were chosen to be a Matriarch of Nesh by your people. You have never sought anything more than to be a good steward of your city, which is precisely why it must be you. Nepiur never wanted to inherit the Primacy and it should not be taken by influence as it was by Rogan. I myself had a moment of weakness when all this began, fancying myself rightful in taking the Primacy out from under him so that I could make things as I see fit. In trying to show me the trust that these Mantichaena have in me you have also shown me why I must never be Primarch. It is a seat that should be filled with love, patience, a delicate touch and unwavering discipline. In the greatest of these I am yet lacking. You are not."

There were so many expectant faces and Sebashni saw in none of them any sign of resignation or doubt. Aroch had been planning this for some time. She saw it in so many of them, in their shimmering smiles and knowing eyes. Nearly all of them were people she herself had spoken to about Aroch's family replacing Rogan's in their intended coup. Though there had been no need for violent action, it seemed her lover had taken the numbers she had gathered for it and turned their hearts once more. Even after seeing their agreeance with Aroch's advocacy she did still doubt its virtue. Then, as she had taught him to see the greatness in himself, so did she begin to see it in herself, through his eyes. She was not a ruler but a natural leader. Perhaps the Primacy would have suited her ill in the past, but she felt ready for it today.

Cool and composed, she flatly agreed "*Hauan Etain,* I accept you. Aroch, send a runner to inform the council." Though she smiled within, she turned away from the ensuant rejoicing to assert herself over Keimas. "As for you, *Utan,* as your Primarch I insist that you remember my reprimand of today. Of all things kept close to your heart, let the nearest be these reminders that the weight we feel upon us exists only to teach us. To break under the weight of a stone is no fault of the stone but of the one whose pride has them weigh it alone. We are one, we Mantichaena, and never is such a burden lifted without many hands waiting to help."

"Matriarch," Keimas conceded, putting an arm around Sebashni and kissing her forehead gratefully, "You are as gallingly shrewd as my wife. I pray you never cease to lead and feel reassured of this by the uncountable armies it would take to silence your wisest of tongues."

Aroch approached, flicked his ear and smirked.

"Let it be, son. Armies have tried and I have failed alongside them, though never would I try to dissuade her from designs at giving each of us strength when we need it most. *Einla,* a Primacy will be attained but first, only two nights hence, a marriage."

"*Uein quo*?" Keimas pondered as he stared between the two. "You have fought well!?"

"Well enough," Sebashni laughed and put her arms around Aroch, who winced slightly at the sudden pressure. "You should see the scars he hides. I did not make it an easy task."

Aroch smirked humorlessly and eased her grip on him.

"*Aienla*, it was certain to be a memorable scuffle and I'm sure I'll never forget the ache in my bones."

Aroch then audibly shouted from pain as Keimas flung himself onto them, practically jumping from excitement to hear the two were finally one.

"Three nights of revels!" He shouted recklessly. "One at least for us to…"

He then broke off abruptly at the unwelcome thought that he would need to depart before such gaiety could take place. Hardships in his leaving compounded today, though he was not soon to forget the blessings in life that he was meant to fight for. His family was going to be complete, rebuilt at last from the time it had been taken from him so long ago. To have a wife and a father with her was grand, but to replace the mother stolen out of his young life was more than he could have hoped for.

Exuberant as he was he contained it somberly, almost ritualistic in how he closed his eyes and reminded himself of his place. Peace and happiness was the commonwealth's, while sacrifice to earn it was the warrior's. Life's pleasures were his to lack and long for until his toil was done.

When he reached this conclusion he began to distance himself, holding lightly to Aroch's hand and whispering gravely.

"Father, I pray to Ephielipax that you let joy overtake you. Be consumed with your blessings so deeply that you will not disdain me for what I must do. Watch over our Lemalie, knowing as she does that my own tomorrow is not one I am eager for. I had first intended to explain myself in private but, due in no small part to the striking words of our soon-Primarch, I now realize it is something all must hear, for it is all of their futures in concern."

With no further distractions he ascended on thrusting wings to land at the crest of a tall rock where the orchards met the fields. Breathing deeply, he tightened his throat and unleashed a pulsing shriek of ear-shattering force, an imitation of the kutliku mating cry adopted by the Kutu caste as the most urgent distress signal.

Everyone was jarred by the urgent sound. Then a crescendo of cackling replies from the aviaries presaged a medley of shadows cast by wings as every Kutu and hunt spewed from hidden places high and low. In immediate succession they rose from the aviaries and the windows of Nesh, not circling or searching but diving after the sound with violent ardor.

There was a moment of confusion in the air as the pride's eyes scoured the area for an imminent threat. Govan, first to realize there was none, swept along the ground to land not far from Keimas, the others following in and orderly fashion.

Before Govan could engage his errant hunter the ground was rocked by the hard landings of the hunts, Soto in particular, whose wingtips swatted away anything and everything to reach Keimas. Havened in the aviaries and partnerless after Keimas' leaving, she had not heard his voice until this cry that touched her in her most primal spirit. Like a beast reborn she surrounded him as a protective companion, coiled her long neck around his body and billowed her wings territorially around them both.

Though Govan regarded their iconic bond with appropriate distance, he was yet hunter-killer prime and fairly put out at being ignored. Rabid with anger at Keimas' tasteless summons, especially at it being their first contact after his equally tasteless disappearance. His patience only lasted until he found sufficient words for his feelings.

"*Einaquo udaisj,* Anama alone could explain the meaning of THIS!" he barked authoritatively, bobbing around to try and get a word past Soto's rattling feathers. "You abandon your duties, leave your hunt alone, saying as little to me of your coming as of your departure? I knew nothing of your presence until Allende comes upon me and tells me '*Ors Utaneis* Govan, he has returned indeed and is already abed with his pretty wife.' I OBJECT! Do you know the struggle, the horror of trying to calm Soto after you vanished!? She nearly tore the whole aviary down! You! You call as though danger is upon us only to gather MY soldiers to you-th-I..."

He faltered as the list of grievances reached its end.

Keimas' head was lowered to receive the thoroughly deserved and overdue reprimand and, as Soto released him, bowed remorsefully before Govan. To his surprise, the brutal scolding ended with his friend and mentor jerking him into a crushing hug.

"*Gal'tskhain!*" Govan blurted. "Your wife can always find another husband but where am I supposed to find myself another hunter, *sekti? Minsekti!?*" He was further flustered as he released his grip and scrutinized the unfamiliar feathers of his man. "And what is this trick of the eye? Have you found another bonded? Another tribe? What is this nonsense!?"

Keimas held himself rigid in Govan's embrace, truly fearful of a sudden attack. Waiting to reply until Govan released him and stepped back.

"*Utan,* the day will wane fast and we must precede the night on wing, else I would not have so crudely called on the slayers of *Ni'ivitnem.* Without regret, love has cost me much precious time but I can spare no more for your goodly wrath."

"Love indeed!" Govan shouted back. "Love would have been as good a reason as any for you opening this city to ruin!" He stopped himself, then curtly clarified "*Mineina,* that was the late father Artimecian in fact, yet you are still to blame for your lawless escapade...*eina,*" he again hesitated thoughtfully, "I suppose the law is in question now, moot anyway as we repair the Gate...but you still need a punishment for abandoning you post, Kutu!"

"Then punish me on the wind, master mine!" Keimas challenged, unrelenting. "Until there is time for you to satiate your rage on myself let it be spent on a more deserving foe!".

"A foe? So, you bring gifts!" Govan cheered. "Name it dead

and set us loose! What menaces my *Hauan Etain*?"

Keimas swung around and spread his great wings to ensure he had the focus of all soldiers and their K'hizu kin. His imperious voice was directed upon them but still easily heard by all the citizens surrounding.

"Attend me, hunter-killers! By the tongues of immortal creatures I have been given a dreadful revelation of which these new wings are a testament."

He tarried a moment, stricken by the clashing realities of he and his people. Truth had been given to him about the god of their ancestry. He knew well enough what it would mean for him to besmirch their patron, if they would believe such blasphemy from the mouth of one so known for warmongering as the Kutu, and an absentee one no less. Nonetheless, it had to be said and so he bore on, though not without the subtle uncertainty that clung to him since his first departure.

"I...fear you will not savor this kill as you have those of the past, for it is the flesh of a brother, wrongfully possessed of a revered god we must hunt and kill like any dangerous prey."

"What feathered flesh is not among us?" Allende shouted from flight, too enlivened to ground himself.

"Mine," Keimas shouted. "It is I whom you must kill." There was no humor in the idiotic declaration, no lightness to temper the uneasy silence. "Listen well," he continued, "For I am no longer myself, only the light left behind by a corpse. What you see before you is what little remains of him; a half-body shaped of raw earth, manifested by a soul that was caged by the lies of a traitor! My rightful flesh has been usurped by a god who wants nothing more than our utter decimation; one who was responsible sixty seasons past for that very crime when he brought a death of flame to Ellel!"

"Ferraro!" Govan roared. "The *mingolaia* of earthen fire has come again!?"

"No, *Utan*," Keimas corrected him. "It was not Ferraro's wrath that smote Ellel but the consequence of her death, set in motion by the hand of Loi!"

A disbelieving upheaval arose amongst both his brethren and the scattered public below. Keimas strode along the rock as indignation at his sacrilege spread, vehemently commanding them to hear what little else he could say.

"*Prostan!* By the voice of Anama we were given a truthful ultimatum when first we found this sanctuary and I say the same to you now: reject your god; the surest words ever spoken to the Galaila, for Loi is a mad tyrant who flies upon my own stolen wings this day to kill the young goddess. *Goliana,* she is his one child and, with her power taken as he has taken my flesh, he will make himself master of this land as he was on Ellel, not to rule but to lay waste!"

Outrage swelled and, though some were swayed by what they saw, the many would not easily forsake loyalty to their patron of old. Dissention grew as each person searched their own heart and those of their neighbors. As they did, the skulking figure of Tzychala moved like a specter among them. They were so embroiled that they gave him no notice, even when he sneered and scoffed at them, disgusted by their vain ignorance.

"What has Loi given the Mantichaena?" an alchemist of Ms'egol exclaimed from the din. "Through it all: Ellel, the open sea, the thuell and the embrace of Anama, Loi has neither punished nor aided us. He only ignores us, has forgotten us entirely!"

"Did you not hear? He is here among us and moves against Anama!" Another voice countered. "Has she herself ever done good for us? We must help the great god and earn the favor of the sky again!"

"To what end, *minaien?*" Another voice challenged. "Are you deaf to the Kutu's word? Anama took us in, gave us these beautiful bodily gifts and never has reached out to harm us! Never has catastrophe struck us here, out of Loi's reach!"

"Out of his reach, *lauein?*" A third commentor interjected. "Were we not greeted with the thuell!? If Loi has no power here, then who was it that raised such evil against us if not Anama herself?"

Small brawls suddenly broke out, small at first but growing with the cacophony of belligerent insults against both Loi and Anama as groups clashed like slighted children.

"Do not dismiss the atrocities of one home as too distant from those of another!" A Boroo of Gazan yelled, mounting the face of Keimas' stone. "There is a creature here who visits from Vaeba to warn of the sky's loathing! I heeded him as he shared these things and more with *Utan* Keimas! Our god has turned against us!"

"He was ALWAYS against you!" Tzychala's dripping voice rang in annoyance, unnaturally loud and resembling the crack of lightning. The incipient riot was not easily suppressed, it was merely pushed aside as those less given to such outbursts began to push through the fights and diffuse them in order to get closer and better hear the testimony of this unfamiliar creature. More and more eyes turned to him as he spoke, lying like the trickster he was, just as had to Keimas.

"This Mantichaena is no different than myself. He is the subject of a cruel master's desire! I once served Loi as you do. I have walked in the depths of the god's presence, even stole Keimas from you in order to show him of the vast, bloody history of your patron's crimes. I too was enthralled to the sky, seduced by its empty promises, but renounced him when I learned of his dreams to rule Maengir and all its creatures as a herdsman masters a flock of fat beasts for slaughter! Though your great hunter was deceived by Loi's agents I plucked him from their snare and returned him to you so that he could lead the fight against this wicked pretender, this god you praise though you have never known him nor his vision: a world where all mortality cowers in fearful bondage before him!"

Keimas cast a grateful but suspicious eye to Tzychala while moving closer to him, surprised at how adeptly he twisted reality. Adapting in kind, he proclaimed:

"*Ein bpaala*, will you still resist? It has always been our destiny to come to this place, to break free from beneath the heel of not just the unjust among gods but ANY god! Our fortune is the promise of rising anew, a nation that will never kneel again after unshouldering the chains of the old world! It is not out of duty to Anama that I tell you of her fate but in pursuit of unity against our common enemy! If Anama falls to the one she calls father then we will never escape the boundaries of his war against Maengir!"

There was no longer a clear devotion to either side of the argument by the city but, after all that was said, Govan spoke for those that Keimas counted on most.

"*Uta,* if it is as you say, then our kind owe a debt to you for searching out these secrets for us. If only to know for certain the truth of what you say we will fly with you. Though I would have all our force and more join, we cannot leave the city unguarded."

Keimas both thanked him and allayed his concern.

"There is no need for sentinels or hunters on foot to catch prey that flies, only we that soar on wings and in righteous duty die."

Govan's skin crawled at the foreshadowing invocation of their oath but, in true hunter-killer form, thrust up to lock arms with Keimas and resolved to follow his student's lead. Excitement at such an impossible fight had him fidgeting with excitement, savored briefly between the two before he broke to give the order. Govan howled, directing the others to rise up and fly west:

"Every soul that soars on wings, to the Haaai!"

As one, all but Keimas obeyed. He remained grounded as Aroch closed in on him with parting words.

"Son, I beg you to take care. Lemalie…"

"Is plenty strong without me, Father," Keimas interrupted with a warm smile and a hand on his Utan's shoulder. "But I promise you, as I did her, that she will have opportunities aplenty to berate me for my many, many failings. More importantly, that this endeavor will not be among them. Your son comes home with the full light of Mirage. Of this you have my surest vow."

Aroch gave him a solemn nod, wary of the future but hopeless without faith that his son's promise was true.

Wordless thereafter, Keimas ascended to follow his flock.

A restless city watched, worried and confused but momentarily distracted from their futile bickering as the many colors of the Kutu and their beasts spiraled into the blinding waves of Laesis. Keimas had enlightened no one, only incited further conflict by inviting the uninformed to glimpse a struggle they could not partake in.

As the Kutu went, Tzychala felt increasingly the eyes upon him. It seemed they were looking to him for answers, and so he slowly backed down off the rock with a nervous smile. Once grounded, his retreat was blocked as he felt a Mantichaena standing her ground at his back. He turned to behold Lemalie.

Her bearing was unimpressed and her scowl foreboding. Nearly a foot taller than her new charge, she stood akimbo over him and rapped her fingers on her hips.

"The small ones help work the harvest," she said, lilting her head toward the orchards.

Tzychala looked there, saw the laughing children, the elders returning to govern them while discussing this mot recent upheaval of the Gate's routine.

"*Cheosl? – now?*" He said pitifully to Lemalie.

Impatient, she snatched his ear and pushed him roughly toward his labors.

CHAPTER 11: WHERE THE RIVER BENDS

"No need for thanks," Ronsha taunted Dace as she bounced in circles around him. "It would be unjust to mark up a debt. Surely the Iron Rain will save your life again someday, so such a debt will only grow!"

Rashala held his lower back and shambled behind his wife. He could not help but appreciate her hapless joy, though he possessed no energy to laugh or smile. His own whimsy paled next to hers, but he did not lament the difference. It gave him enough distraction from his aching body to press on.

Nepiur and Maurus plodded at the forefront of the unknown thuell-slayers, all sopping wet and exhausted from their ordeal but thankfully unharmed. It was a miracle that none were killed or even injured. The body's ability to fight off thuell infection was marginal at best and any contact should have been fatal. A puncture to the flesh would mean certain death but even with a few bruises and scratches they had to watch one another. At present, it seemed victory had come at little cost, yet still they kept a weather eye on all their company for any sign of contamination.

The more immediate concern was the pack of Kuolt, driven off into the rain by the sight of the thuell. Wary of this or any other danger Hax had returned to the thi boughs and kept a shifty eye on the foliage. Thankfully there had not yet been any sign of the predators. All that scurried in the lush surroundings now were a few sumear and schiis. In the distance they heard a low rumble and espied the jutting spikes of a small brak herd through the intertwining trunks and vines, the sluggish behemoths knocking thi to the ground as they grazed their way to open fields in the Hai.

Feeling safe for the time being, Matriarch Nepiur and foreman Maurus ignored the impish nature of the Kulo witchcrafters. Dace's reputation would surely not be tarnished by Ms'egol's intervention. His performance had been as legendary as ever, but Maurus had to admit the witchcrafters were worth as much as their old master, invaluable to the ever-present threat of the thuell. The whole city would know it soon.

To the Iron Rain's provocation, Dace wearily retorted, "High and mighty words from mere mortals."

"As you say I am, I am," Ronsha responded as lightly as ever, "But if any bit of me is divine then let it be my lips, such as to command a strong husband's love with a goddess' kiss."

She spoke as if singing, bounding near Rashala and pecking him on the cheek.

"*Aien*? I'm certain they command all sorts of things," Dace chuckled.

Ronsha shouted irately at Dace's back and, partly in fun, spun a forked bolt from her fingers that harmlessly scattered off his plating.

"RONSHA!" Nepiur bark her, aghast at the undisciplined escalation.

"You heard him speak!" Ronsha whined as she nursed her arm, clearly more damaged by the aftershock than Dace was by the minimal impact.

"I value your health, not your ego," Nepiur chided again.

"You're stuck with both, lucky woman," Ronsha mumbled sideways as her silent husband returned her past kiss in consolation.

Maurus pressed his hand between Nepiur's shoulders, urged her to increase her gait until they had gained some distance on the rest of the troupe, then spoke heavily.

"Mother, you seem distressed. Is this not a day of days for us? For *Hauan Etain* and *Aes'bethil* and for victory?"

"What 'Us'?" Nepiur snorted. "What victory? What have we

really done?"

"*Aiat*, we killed a thuell! We've done what none else imagined possible! This changes everything, and without a single life paid for it!"

"Has one not?" Nepiur hissed.

Maurus silently acknowledged her grief. Though her words dismissed their good work, she was right not to celebrate. When first she had said that Bethaali was 'Traveling' she had not sounded so deeply injured. He still could not believe how quickly she had led them out for a fight when her sister was lost the very day of her finding. His Matriarch had expressed no sadness since their departure from Aes'bethil, only anger. Having a precious young sibling of his own, Maurus understood her melancholy. Were he to lose Keimas, any revels would anger him equally. Decency demanded that every loss should be shared, at least his upbringing taught as much. He believed this and honored Nepiur with persistent silence thereafter.

The rest of troupe remained as rowdy as ever until they came through the last overgrowth to the village of Aes'bethil. The inhabitants, somewhat encouraged by the caravan's first coming, had taken up tools and gone about repairing their village. The return likely meant success, and so enlivened them further. With one battle won, another had begun with hammer and mortar.

"Work," Nepiur snapped, her claws outstretched to set her company assisting the Bet'hvaebeulg as they rebuilt their homes and lives, dug the mass graves of their dead.

The company obeyed their mother, hiding their understandable dismay at having no respite after such a brutal day. Perhaps it was unfair, though not everything was in the command of an archon, less so in the unforgiving wild. Nepiur had often fought to carry herself otherwise, prizing fairness and benevolence but, in at this time, her ability to temper her conviction with empathy had escaped her and she felt no need to be gentle. There was always work to be done and those who survived should be grateful for it.

She had her own ordeal ahead, braced herself to reenter the house where Bethaali's body lay. The memory of her face and the pride of fulfilling her last wish clashed in Nepiur's defeated heart. There seemed so little value in victory other than her own vengeance. The miraculous preservation of the Bet'hvaebeulg almost ignored as she grieved.

Acolytes were stooped or knelt around Bethaali's bedroll, hiding her frow view. Seeing Nepiur they separated one by one to allow her in. The solemnity of their eyes made her skin tingle but hearing Bethaali speak again nearly killed her.

"N...Nep...I don't believe it," she heaved again, her premeditated words sinking like pins in Nepiur's ears.

"Don't speak," Nepiur said firmly. Her expectation of Bethaali's state was correct. Her sister remembered nothing, still had that spark of joy at seeing a missed face. Striding about and gesturing harshly, the glowering Nepiur shooed the acolytes, physically forced them from the room to have privacy.

Bethaali whispered again, "Nep, I'm so glad you came."

"Do you even hear me?" Nepiur asked with sudden tears. There was a drawn-out silence in which she began to question her own sanity. "Can you understand what I say or is this thing you've left behind capable only of delivering your last words?"

Bethaali smiled sadly. With a slight convulsion of pain, she replied in kind.

"*Prostas*, sweet younger. I cannot know what I have said, only what I say now."

"You have no memory of my last coming?"

Bethaali then mournfully grimaced, ashamed of how she had thoughtlessly burdened her sister. She was tense, longing, until a decisive nod from Nepiur assured her that the threat had been dealt with. Her face and apparent condition brightened and darkened simultaneously. One hardship had passed, another had come.

"You mustn't stay," Bethaali finally reacted. "That you've done so much for me is more than I deserve. I..." She wheezed and buckled, settling slowly. "...I don't want you to see..."

"That you're dying?" Nepiur moaned. "That you trapped yourself in endless pain just to point me to our enemy? Why? Any of your dregs could have done the same."

For the first time, Bethaali wept.

"To s-see you again."

Nepiur's whole body melted, and she knelt forward as Bethaali continued.

"I would die a thousand times, surely will, just to have seen the woman you've become. This suffering is but a taste of that which gripped my heart when first I fell, seeing only you in my thoughts and wishing only for a second chance."

"On my soul, I would have come for no other cause," Nepiur whispered, touching her sister's cheek. "If only your company home could be so easily had."

"I am always in your company," Bethaali cooed. "My beautiful sister, I am so proud. I will forever be so, even when you cannot see me."

A subtle sob escaped Nepiur. She was tormented by the thought that Bethaali might still be there, locked inside this reflection. Then, almost purposefully, the reflection began to ripple with light.

Bethaali seemed to be speaking again but made no sound, the final words of a dying woman distorted by her sister's unwillingness to listen to what had already been said.

Nepiur moaned and held her own face, fingers kneading her forehead in anguish.

Then, driving the pain deeper, the enchantment broke and began again.

"N...Nep...I don't believe it," the new Bethaali whispered.

"*Aienmin – don't speak,*" Nepiur pleaded.

This she said with a tightening chest, willing remorse away from her thoughts as she slowly reached for a sharp chunk of marble fallen from the rooftop.

Bethaali did not need to look. To see across time was a power, but to see the stone in her sister's fist was instinct. She took Nepiur's free hand, caressed it delicately with her thumb, maintaining eye contact so as to distract them both from what was coming.

"Nep...be unafraid. Ours is a love as could never wilt in time, nor be bound in a thing as trivial as death."

With the finest thought Bethaali could imagine held tightly in her mind, she gratefully smiled and let her eyes flutter closed, barely making a sound as Nepiur's bitter mercy struck her down.

Nepiur moved sluggishly, her eyes wandering aimlessly as she shambled toward the vestibule. The bloody stone was still clutched in a hand which trembled from its guilty memory. Who could say how long this shell of Bethaali would have clung to life, dying forever, never knowing if Nepiur would come for her or if her clan was safe? The surviving sister had one last hopeful thought as she raised the stone to her face, watched the blood seep along the cracks in its surface: time was the stream that even Bethaali could not swim against. She could raise her head and look up and down its path yet remained victim to each moment. Trapping herself as she had, she was no longer flowing, rather tied to a stone and drowning over and over while waiting for Nepiur to drift past and cut her free. This was the bend in the stream that finally swept her out of sight, to undiscovered shores where she could find a place to lie still, no longer fighting for breath. Like all her wondrous travels, Nepiur could only send her on her way with all the love she had.

Tears were temporary. Once the young archon was back out in the open air, she paused to contemplate the gifts she had been given throughout her life. The wickedness of her father had destroyed her whole family, yet Bethaali's words cured much of her regret. Of all the forces of choice and chance that could silence loving hearts, death was the least of them. However, death was in her heart now.

She made her choice, understanding now that Sky, Tieg Utan Rogan, was not right for this world. Long had Nepiur dreamed to rise above his influence, to let him die, then heal what he left behind. That pious dream was no more. Her mother and sister had already fallen in her father's destructive path. It was only a matter of time until she and her husband Capheif fell with them. Perhaps her love already had.

Nepiur resolved with grinding teeth that, when she returned home, there would be a reckoning. However, this was not a vengeful or heartbreaking moment but one of relief. She felt free at last from all delusions of victimhood or patient suffering. She would return victorious, a journeyed Archon, and her final demon would feel the vengeful edge of the same stone that took Bethaali.

The storm had swept over the village and faded soon after, softening to drape a wet cloak over the glade, which began to vaporize under Laesis. Long-restrained light beamed through wisps of steam winding up through the canopies and evoked in them a hoary glow. Thankfully, the leavings of the corrupted creature were breaking down and seeping into the ground, hastily purged by the rain. Their oily residue would be a reminder for some time of what had transpired, but from a reminder alone the Bet'hvaebeulg would not yield. Thuell would burn, Mantichaena would build, and the world would carry on as it always had. However, the order of things had changed. Mantichaena had learned to burn back and the battles of the future would not end as those of the past.

"Udaiam, rhams'aiat!" came Ronsha's voice, trying to evoke cheer in welcoming Nepiur back to them.

While the Bet'hvaebeulg mimicked her in praise of the Matriarch, the caravan was still sternly devout in their task, as she had set them to it.

Maurus did not rouse to the warning nor pause his labors, being the unearthing of large boulders. These, great Dace carried up to Aes'bethil's rooftops and placed them to be mortared by eager locals.

The acolytes incessantly praised the company, gratified beyond words by their enduring vigilance both in ridding them of their curse and in this simple act of service.

Hax hurried about the work, kept at a lively pace by the unrelenting attention he received from a petite Lugu. He would coldly direct her in when to apply the mortar, and she would oblige aptly, though she seemed to pay no attention to her own work. How she smiled shyly and positioned herself unnecessarily close coaxed only the occasional sigh from Hax.

Watching this game of affections, Dace and Maurus felt privileged to witness the most comical play of their lives. Only their distance from Hax kept him oblivious to their hushed laughter as they conjectured about what naivety vexed the Lugu that she would continue to pursue such prey as Hax, who would sooner chew off his leg than be vulnerated.

To Dace, humor in this regard was a means to allay his own sadness, for he knew what pain was in his friend which kept his heart is such a sorry state. Dace had never loved, and so neither had he lost. It was not something he wished for himself. So, while Maurus smiled in earnest, Dace tried his best while his eyes were disheartened at what he saw. The girl would attack, yet Hax would not lose his temper, would not chide nor recoil from her. In this, resultant of guilt, grief, or grudge, Dace once again saw in him the deepest scar of all: refusal to heal a wound for fear it might reopen.

Nepiur, smiling and waving as though her temperament was not delicately balanced on a knife's edge, took pride in the diligence with which her tired fellowship pressed on. They were always jovial, deceptively childish, even now as their backs bent, faces cringed and skin streamed with dirt-drawn sweat. They had gone far enough, she thought, and there

"*Prostas* my friends, be still!" They were, as were the faithful, and all listened. "Let what remains of the day be restful. *Utan* Maurus, see that a fire is lit, and victuals prepared. Eat, drink, and commune with our brothers and sisters. Tomorrow we will rise anew to this feat and see it completed. We remain as long as we are welcome."

A cheer of "*La, Aiatan!*" arose in concurrence.

Hax and Dace wasted no time in gathering all the fuel they could, Dace tearing whole bushes up by the root and piling all their findings in the pit dug by the thuell. As they ran back and forth from forest to fire, they were aided by grateful followers who were insistent on hearing every detail of their daring encounter.

Maurus, having no desire but to sit idle, followed after the Bakul and Boroo and was subjected to Dace's overly dramatic retelling of his magnificent rescue of the whole party from ravenous kuolt, their plunge into the icy tempest and their terrifying struggle in the flooded quarry. All the while he flexed his armored brawn and allowed his audience to fawn over the epic scars in his rocky skin.

Hax was nestled into his friend's spikes, guzzling wine and pumping his fist at the pivotal moments of the tale, periodically chiming in with "*Eina lauda*! I taught this meat pie everything he knows!"

Ronsha and Rashala shook off the mob and searched for seclusion to steal a numbing drink from Hax's stash and bed one another with reckless abandon

It was at the last of twilight, in the splendid orange bleed of a sleepy Laesis, that Dace finally returned to the caravan's quarters. Hax was completely passed out on his back and the others were already tucked in. Rashala and Ronsha seemed to have found themselves private accommodations in the next house over and all was quiet but for the retreating footsteps of Bethaali's faithful as they, too, gathered in their proper places for sleep. The spirits of the village had been hugely lifted today. The selflessness of brave soldiers had salved many wounds and brought the belief that all would be well for the Bet'hvaebeulg. Still, there remained a common morbidity in those who had lost close friends and family.

Without bothering to rouse Hax, Dace laid on his chest and comfortably folded his arms beneath his head to sleep, whispering as he did to the Boroo he would always be closest to,

"Good work, and good night my friend. We live on. For this I am thankful."

Only Nepiur, wet, exhausted and numb, remained out in the mist as night fell. She toyed her fingers at her waist, watching with a blank face as Bethaali's body, cloaked in beautiful cloth, was borne out of her home. Her heart pounded, almost hoping that the acolytes would be outraged at what she had so obviously done. Instead, they all offered her a slight bow and empathetic smiles as they passed, leaving her speechless. Only one came to speak to her, the high priest, and his voice was as certain as though he read it from holy text:

"*Aiatan gravitas*. To live for the future is true sight. To live eternal is true suffering. I am grateful to have known your sister, and my people are indebted to you for all you have done for us and for her. This world is best while graced with your presence. May you live well, that your end may be a rich reward and earned rest."

Nepiur refused to be happy, her mind still muddled by grief, yet the man would not yield from her. He took her shoulder firmly, pulled his hood back and made sure he had her full attention.

"For days we had to watch, waiting, never knowing if the one thing our goddess prayed for would come to her. You did. You came. You set her free, warmly wrapped in peace and contentment. Whether or not it was what you intended, you spared our faithful from having to witness something that would have destroyed us."

When the short, ineffectual speech was over Nepiur remained unmoved, her hollow gaze still stuck on the darkened doorway. The priest nodded slowly, deferred to her needs and moved away from her. There she stayed, waiting for her anger to wither into acceptance. It came and went, surges of resentment only lasting until she was too tired to concentrate on them.

She slowly found her way to a dark corner of an unoccupied

house. There, she laid a greater piece of marble to the ground before her, held the one she saved upon it. She stared at the blood on her thumb, how it spread into the mottled surface of the soft rock and revealed its grain. Seeing the future shape of the weapon, she began to strike it across its brother to form it. With the cold night sucking the heat from her body, she could not shake the priest's words from her head. She had witnessed, and it had destroyed her.

CHAPTER 12: LASTING PUNISHMENT

A long and uninvited sleep had taken the outlanders who invaded the dark underbelly of Manti and paid for it in blood. Only Takinoxote had awoken, spending an unknown time reaching up to consciousness only to continually slip back under. A surge of adrenaline gave her a few moments of clarity, enough to realize the pain in her thigh and shoulder were caused by deeply lodged fragments of stone. Survival instinct was all she could rely on as she exhumed them, ripping off rings of dried blood with each one. Shuddering in pain and whimpering in the darkness she tore her clothes and tried to protect her wounds, fighting her body as it tried to shut down from the shock, which only invited the pain to return. She suffered on in this way until she could get her mind under control. Then she kept her eyes closed, tried to use other senses to orient herself while coughing up the debris that had settled in her nose and throat. With all her strength she spat a broken tooth and knew by the wet rattle against a wall how far away it was. Having forgotten that it was Bandta she laid upon, she nearly died of fright when he suddenly groaned, returned to her from the dead as her squirming agitated his body against the rubble-strewn ground. With careful haste she dismounted him, winced and cradled her wrist, favored her right knee before collapsing and wallowing at his side. When she felt she could speak she put a hand to his face, feeling for breath with her trembling fingers.

"Bandta, breathe again and tell me you live."

"I live," he wheezed almost inaudibly. "For how long, I do not know."

There was no use for sight down here, the scant light from above cut off by night's approach. She had some limited gift of night-eyes but as her hands roamed over Bandta she felt that his legs were mangled beyond repair. A boulder, dislodged by their fall, had nearly ripped them off and still pinned one in place.

"Damn it all, don't you give up! Live with all you have. I'll get this away." She growled resolutely.

Bandta put a severed piece of his armor between his teeth and bit hard, screaming through it as Tak squatted beside the boulder and levered it off, choked and stumbled as she tried to convince him he would live to see the dawn.

"*Udai*, come up. You can feel the pain after we have you safely above ground."

Bandta chuckled humorlessly as the rock rolled aside, spat the shard out and stubbornly gasped "*Minaien*. Tak, you have to leave me."

"*Khains ghanilt*, I will not," She argued.

"You will, or you'll die alongside me. There's no going back for either of us. You must move."

"Not without you. Not without Kjan."

Mournfully, Bandta reminded her "We are both lost. Only you can finish this."

Tak quaked and cried into her friend's shoulder, resisting the thought that, somewhere close by, Kjan's corpse was watching in the absolute dark.

Bandta could not move to console her, the slightest shift enflaming his nerves.

"It only takes one," he whispered.

"*Prostan maat*. Bandta, I can't do this alone," Tak besought him, shivering from the lonesome cold.

"You always have. This was always your journey. I am proud to have been a part of it. You will win, my *Jiaia*. You will win no matter what, won't you?"

Tak wished with all her heart she could see his face; see the hope and faith she heard in his words as he achingly insisted:

"Tell me you will! Tak, finish the story. You will beat them. You WILL. Tell me you will."

She took his chin and massaged it kindly.

"I will. For you, for Kjan, for all whose light has been lost. I swear on penalty of the pit I will put finish."

Gritting his teeth, Bandta pushed her away.

"Then get on with it! Live free…and deliver us from evil."

Hard parted from her last living ally, Tak stroked his face and slowly stepped back. At an apathetic pace she limped along the wall opposite where they had fallen, dragging a barely usable leg and avoiding scraping a crippled arm against the walls. She could not abide leaving her brothers alone and forgotten in such a dreadful hole, yet Bandta's demand rang true. This was the final leap of faith, finale to a voyage of countless seasons. She was so close now and could feel it with every step. For all souls lost in the dark she would not allow herself to give up. If she failed, everything failed.

The cold cut deeper into her feet. She followed the distant sound of water to where she found its bite on her toes and ankles, eventually working her way around a small waterfall that dumped from the ceiling. It was obviously far from the surface and there were no reservoirs nearby that she knew of. A pooling of water above must have been the result of recent storming, but the sky had been clear when they started their descent. Perhaps the early Windsong had been mysteriously broken by the return of Longhand. Regardless of its origin, the waterfall fed a long trough which she had to cross. Despite her wounds, with the use of one hand, one foot and a tail she was able to swing herself from stalactites and traverse the rushing water. Dexterous and devoted, she could not overcome the natural fragility of such finely accumulated sediment. One of the jagged stones broke in her grasp, dropping her to land with her back on the far bank of gravel and her legs in the roiling flow. With conflicting instinct and panic she clung to the loose stones, pulling herself against the current to surmount them and suddenly grateful for the numbing of the water.

Walking was a war against her failing strength, each step a battle of uncertain outcome as she plodded into the depths. Half-conscious, she dreamed of her comrades. Some were lost to the promises of the old world and others in rebellion against it. She even began to question what she was doing in fighting an unwinnable campaign with no army and no weapon. The latter was all she could hope to find. With the right symbol of authority, there was the smallest hope of rallying survivors to her cause.

Her legs tightened in alarm as her toes touched a polished floor, a kind caress like silk after the rough going of uneven cobble. A new cold in the air penetrated her as her hand found another monolith blocking the path. She groped around it, felt that it was as troublesome as the one already encountered. First she pulled, then pushed, then in a rage hacked at it with stones. It would not give way, the simplest of deterrents but ultimately most effective. Shivering and drenched, she slumped with her cheek against it, screamed her frustration into its uncaring face. She sank, staring into the black and not knowing if it was air or stone, if there was anything holding her up or if this was all imagined.

She tried to think, to assess and plan. Unable to do so and beyond unreasonable, she felt no desire to see daylight nor even to survive, only to be herself again. Her breathing hastened, her heart pounded and, with a face full of pure hatred she looked skyward through the reaches of earthplane and cosmos and spoke through them, whispering at first but building to a defiant shout.

"You…I know you're coming. I don't know when but I know we are bound to meet again. You can shine and sing and charm your slaves but not me. Not me! Not anymore. I know you can feel me…so let's make a wager." She bit down on her wrist and punctured the skin, allowing blood to flow slowly across her palm, then placed it on the face of the blockade. "Let's see how all-seeing you are, *Jioueihs Deinail*. You can have me. You can punish me until the end of time but you'll have to catch me first! Catch me, before I raise the reaper of the *Jiaia* against you!" She closed her eyes and snarled an incantation, reigniting power she had hidden many lifetimes ago. Her blood oozed down the rock and began to sparkle in the darkness, a light from within her arm reaching out into it wherever it went. It dug into the surface and shone brighter, crackling like lightning and commanded by her cry to the furthest of Aurba:

"Deinaghen   shikeil   taultn'galaboghti.   Rokghola   anik, hauanik…hauanik Az'Rech ehinilt!" – *"Child light say: teeth of*

light, kill my enemy in the ground. Hidden and hallowed place, open...open in the name of Az'Rech!"

Her light tore into the structure and ripped it asunder, scattering shrapnel beyond. Bright streaks ran suspended through the air as the debris settled, winding outward and drifting ahead as Tak willed them forward to light her path. Betting all chances of success on her invocation of the light she no longer feared how its silent song called to her master. Time was against her, yet she was still one step ahead. Hobbling on with all her vigor she drew one of the floating streams down to her leg, wrapping around her torn muscle and binding it. Another she slung to the floor so it spread out and meandered ahead of her along a vast and lifeless floor of polished onyx. A third she threw above and allowed to arc, lighting the distant path and the spiked ceiling. Deina'itka once more, she sprinted through pain and desperation down the shining path.

This had to be it, her whirling mind hoped; the grave where death itself lay buried. Flat, stalactite-draped walls sloped inward on both sides. Beneath her the floor was as the menacing silken face of undisturbed oil. At its furthest reach was an omen of her fate and divine retribution fulfilled: a slab cut from the wall, simple and cubic but saturated with abstruse carvings inlaid with a crusted red grime.

Even through her brilliant enchantments the sting of her mortal injuries was felt in her legs as they drummed against the tile. Both her face and gait betrayed her frantic fear, her eyes darting back and forth as geometric pillars began to raise from the floor in utter silence. As each flew past she felt their gaze, glimpsed ripples in their surfaces and glowing red scars flashing across them and into the ground. One by one the converging wounds coiled beneath her, like insects swarming to blood, twenty-three pillars birthing twenty-three empty eyes that haunted her steps from beneath a black mirror. The Vulgoli were broken and lost, yet evil devices still guarded their secrets. The tomb was undead, a protector that knew she was there. It smelled her light, hated it, craved darkness and would suffer no other. Tak's skin crawled as the eyes unwound and slithered away, penetrating their pillars and stirring them to an impossibly darker liquidity. As they churned they stole her light, visibly dragging its vibrant streams closer and drowning them out. With the last of the dying light she looked to her back, saw the fluid ground rolling into a wave of needles at her heels and felt for the first time in seventy thousand seasons a crushing fear of the blood gods' power. It endured beyond time, yet so did her own limitless pool of daylight, even in this place. She slid to a stop, her claws screeching on the cold floor as she turned to face the attack. Forced to fight once again this long-dead enemy, her killer instinct awakened and with it the inner flame of Iregruun booming in her voice.

"*Deinaghen prohansula itholk!*" – "Child light say: all be silent in time!"

A humming pulse shot from her fingers, taking hold of everything it touched and freezing it in place as though time was hers to control. It was for now, though such a massive exertion tore the breath from her and forced her to her knees. With only a moment to think, uncertain of how her light would survive against these traps, her mind turned to a different arsenal. Fueled by loathing and feeling shame as she spoke, she invoked the language of the enemy and turned their power against them:

"*Shi'aschan aschanilt bpraa!*" – "Tearing teeth for tearing bone!"

Her blood burned and she cringed at the sight of black fibers breaking out of her skin, plunging into the ground and slashing through it in all directions. They cleaved the pillars, threshed the ground like wet sand and cracked the ceiling, bringing a rain of stone down throughout the trembling hollow. The eyes in the pillars waved frantically as their homes were turned to meal in the destruction, mixing with the shattered floor as it exploded from countless impacts.

Tak could not be certain she had survived, curled in a ball against the marked slab and waiting for that one falling spike or final trap that was sure to claim her. At last she breathed a tiny light into her palm and saw the carnage she had wrought. Fearful but triumphant, she leapt to her feet and fell immediately, cried in pain, wept with joy, laughed like a lunatic as her little candle flickered and she threw herself against the writing. With raspy breath her howl of victory echoed through the caverns:

"I FOUND YOOOU!"

Trembling, she reached out to touch the marvelous shrine. "Kjan, Bandta, this is it! After all this time, at last it's..." She became instantly lost in the scripture, radiantly happy as she read the etchings, reciting them as fast as she could. *"Forever made of one day forgotten. It was forgotten by no thought, no mind; unfelt by no soul, no grieving god. All perished so that all may live and one perished so that one will be gloriously unforgotten..."*

The joy evaporated and her smile overturned. She felt nothing, no mighty presence as she expected. So powerful was the soul of her idol that it could have been felt like the burning heat of day from the moment she passed the stone that lay behind her, yet such a presence was not here. This place was empty and her treasure nowhere to be found. Her hope dwindled and, in reading on, she felt despair tighten around her throat.

"For the one who fell, no word shall be written but these, in shameful atonement for the calamity of his blood. She who fell before him; be immortal, as made by daygod, now made by penitent word. Deina's will be done as the Manyflesh is broken. Golaia Naotogallion, live forever upon this stone."

Tak was spellbound, quaking with rage as she realized that, after searching all her life for this, finally finding it proved her life had been wasted. So woeful was she and so loud were her moaning recitations that she was oblivious to the soft crunch of movement behind her; the sound of a body being dragged.

"Blood, Bone, everlasting Sleep; we the unending debtors have killed the Commanding Voice. We surrender to it. Let the gnashing of teeth be the only oration of the mother's lost seed, for we die as the young light do. Nemesis of darkness, give clemency, for we promise our suffering eternal. Naotogallion Golaia, wherever at last she sleeps, will find no tomb in Maengir. Maengir is grave for the murderers, never again to sink our tooth in shining hearts."

She wobbled, shook her head and sputtered inconsolably.

"Profanity...the...the mockery! NO, NO, NO!" Tak wailed, pounding on the wall with such ferocity that it fractured, the red crust jarring loose from the vile lettering. "A poem!? *Bolgimpidiet!* Where is it? WHERE IS SHE!?"

Lashing out in dire confusion she flung piercing light all across the epitaph, tearing it to pieces and swatting them aside in search of something buried. When there was nothing left, there was yet nothing found.

She raised her hand to strike again but froze as the soft scraping finally got her attention. Sharply attentive now, she whirled on it and was stunned to see the faintest silhouette of Bandta. He was prostrate, dragging all his weight with one arm. He looked so deliriously happy, smiling eyes full of wonderment that hid his suffering.

"Tak'*srysha*..." He amorously sighed through sparkling tears. "...I'm s-so..."

Tak could not speak, knowing how the truth would break Bandta's heart. He looked so contented, so certain that they had finally unearthed the prize of all prizes, yet oblivious to his imminent death. Tak was petrified by the gut-wrenching sight of a dripping black mouth looming out of the shrouded ingress behind him. It clung to the walls with pointed legs, only half a body, the stump where its lower half had been torn away cauterized and still sizzling. It was burned all over, deep wounds in its flesh visibly mending shut. Bandta was still smiling, quivering excitedly as Tak heaved herself up and sprinted after him.

"Bandta, *bethaus*!" she shrieked.

He turned his head slowly as droplets struck his back, twitching points appearing inside the grisly maw that salivated over him. Banta's safety and Tak's brazen use of her power gave her nothing left to lose. Her dread disappeared and she felt the serene confidence of Deina light inside her. They had not won, rather defeated once and for all. If her Jiou-Deina was indeed searching for her, then by conjuring so much of her light she had told him exactly where she was. She was already doomed, but even if they never found the Jiaia-Deina who would save them, she would expend every droplet of her essence before she was captured. She inhaled, and in the blink of an eye her silvery blood slithered from her injuries and swirled upward, a floor-to-ceiling tornado of light.

Righteously she bellowed "Back to the dark edge, in god's ten thousand swords!" Swinging her arms back and forth and ignoring the pain in her joints, her tempest launched forward and dragged part of the ceiling with it. It melted the stone, turned parts of itself into bolts of white lightning, endlessly multiplying rivers of her power ricocheting off the walls and converging on her foe.

It was one final attempt to make her life worth something, but her triumph was not earned, and her intervention not allowed. The dark pillars arisen from the ground grabbed each of her rays and swallowed them, even pulled at the storm around her until it barely persisted. She never stopped screaming, tried to push her it beyond the monuments, but they only undulated faster and consumed the light. She would not give up, charged forward and prepared a brilliance within herself that, with a single touch, would render this abomination into smoldering chitin.

Bandta's face transformed from reverence for Tak to utter disbelief when the air behind her seemed to split apart without her direction or knowledge. A shimmering void ripped open the world, a concussive boom tremoring it and all else around, and from the infinite expanse within a swarm of golden threads came flying outward. As they entered Maengir they blew away all darkness, filled the catacomb with so much radiant energy that the rocks fissured to allow it in, the macabre totems stones so engorged by it they erupted into smoking fragments. The monstrous thuell's shrill wail rang against for only an instant, before its whole body was cleaved and blasted back in burning shreds. The cords were guided precisely by celestial hands to lay across every surface in the secret cave, but one with a perfect halo of gold at its tip whipped through the air, gave chase after Tak with blinding speed and affixed itself around her neck, silencing a choking scream. As fast as light had poured from the cosmic tear the golden shackle seemed to absorb it as the pillars had, burning brighter as it dragged Tak to the floor and toward its source. No sound came from her gaping mouth and her limbs barely twitched in an effort to fight back, the strong will in her eyes was replaced by the vacant stare of a woman without hope or thought. Bandta could only watch, aghast, as the veil engulfed her and closed again like a hungry mouth, leaving only golden droplets where her body had been. They would decay as well, returning the cavern to its natural stillness, silent in death. Bandta soon would be as well. Whatever had just happened, it was no doubt a kind of death. He saw that much in Tak's face before she was taken. His body stung from the presence he had felt when the light came, and watching it steal Tak away from him was all the proof he needed. She had not exaggerated her legendary past. There surely was a god of gods, and it hated her.

He whimpered feebly, unable to move and not knowing which way to go, even if he could. It was all he could do to lay in the darkness and slowly die.

"G-g-gaia..." he stammered "...Gaialja...m-my love...I'll w-wait for you...at the end."

Thetrulengo speaks,

This cannot be. How did he come back so soon?

I am not solely dependent on the veil to translocate. Without it, I can still leave the enclosure of Maengir and wander the void. This outside perspective does help me to better understand the workings of a confined state of being. However, as if I were admiring a droplet of water on my fingertip, I inevitably lift my gaze from it and look to the emptiness that those within the droplet cannot conceive of. Instead of the thi, wind and mountain, there is only emptiness. I feel as though I am floating in air without air, and the ground is so far below that even if I fell for eternity I would not touch it, and that stars burn so high above I could similarly climb and never be in reach. This is the vastness that separates Escharka and Az'Rech, the dark edge and the far edge, so incomprehensibly broad that even I have never set foot upon them. Only in peering through wounds in their skin have I glimpsed the workings of the body.

Attempting to travel to both the far and dark edges has taught me that the way in which I move only appears instantaneous when executed within the very brief expanses of mortality and the surrounding planes. As I tried to rise upward toward Az'Rech I understood there was a limit to how far I could go in a single instant. In trying to travel across the entirety of the distance while present in this central layer of the veil it was as though I was fixed in place, drawing no closer to the height of being. Yet, in then progressing outward in the veil, I found I could go further, yet slower. It felt as though I was tumbling upward while gaining no stars to my back. The Manyflesh and the Numenlight are not separated by distance or time. They are separated by the twenty-three fundamental states of being that their observers call the veil, and each of these encompasses a distance that need not be walked. The idea of an instant in time no longer means anything to me. It may be as long as my entire life and I would not know it, for such distances exist that no amount of time is sufficient to traverse them.

In Maengir I am all but, though I reach from Maengir into Rhose or Ansax, I cannot take hold of anything therein without also taking a journey of essence.

The ancients of flesh and light are too simple to garner my respect. To know them from afar is to stand in mortality when it is both night and day, entombed in rock with the wind in my hair, ungraspable and confusing. I find pleasure in Maengir, for all its complexity and for the shared experience of the light and dark coiled together as restless schiis in a mating frenzy. Az'Rech and Escharka could no be joined, but here their remains are mated forever.

By this reasoning I mean to come to terms with the actions of a Deina warlord who led the lesser divines against the Vulgoli. The Deina who did not shine was their most dreaded enemy, Az'Rech's only daughter and his greatest weapon. While Moghredaios was the symbol of the Deina's song, it was Naotogallion whom the Vulgoli rightly feared, and she who turned the tide of the war. However, this was not until after Moghredaios received a terrifying wound at the tooth and nail of the lightless called Rogkt'sokai, 'Child born of broken teeth', born of Escharka's teeth, and the Deina named him Death

After this, the first Age of Unravelling, Moghredaios had to retreat to the final threshold between this existence and Az'Rech's, a vestibule both material and immaterial called the Guardian Grove. There he would heal, but also mourn the fall of his sister in battle, for he was too injured to save her from the flight of the Dying Wish. I did not know this as I watched the battle with the sight of a newborn. I learned details from the words of the Storyteller's book; the book containing all the lamentations of the Vulgoli.

In his parting, Moghredaios left little instruction, his only wish being for his soldiers to stand watch for the eventual return of the Vulgoli. They obeyed, hiding themselves in the world. Some became restless and felt abandoned, as though he would not return or that he had perished from the lingering darkness eating at his being. After the extreme longevity of his absence I assumed the same. Could he have taken all this time to heal? Perhaps he was waiting for something. A sign of sorts? The release of the Brother of Bones? That has to be it. If it has taken him these sixty seasons to make the journey back to Maengir, then I can't expect a much faster journey for myself. Or...perhaps he has been here far longer, reclaiming his errant slaves and bringing them back to his flock. That could not be. I surely would have felt his presence as I feel it now.

The great lengths this fallen Deina'itka woman has gone to now end in ruin. Was she looking for the corpse of Naotogallion? If the lighteater Jiaia fell to the earthplane at death, then might her essence still be somewhere in the ground? Would it have passed through the Ward of Unbirth and become just another star? Perhaps Moghredaios had not gone home to commune with the father of light, but rather to await the arrival of his sister's star. But then...does his return mean her soul never arrived?

It must have been the commanding voice which the Deina'itka sought, but I see nothing of the Deina's making in this loathsome earthen reticulum. To search for a weapon of the Deina in this place feels foolish but there must be something here. I can feel it...though I don't understand it. Something belonging to neither Az'Rech nor Escharka is sleeping in the ground.

~Chronicle of Wonders, Elegy of the Hollow Angel

"*Eihsryshaaa*! - *My love!*"

Hax's cracking voice upset the calm of Aes'bethil in the early night, rousing the caravan with a jumpstart.

They shouted erratically in response, whipped into a fright and instinctively stumbled in every direction in search of danger. Dace was soon upon Hax, slumping over him and holding him securely. The Boroo struggled, screamed, his vision panning across the room with wide eyes as the company quickly huddled around him.

"*Golvulilt*! What's wrong with him!?" Maurus demanded.

"I have no idea, *utan!*" Dace groaned, wincing at Maurus' volume with a groggy shrug.

Hax jerked out from under Dace's cautiously loose grip and scrambled for the doorway, smashing through Ronsha and Rashala as they appeared therein. They were thrown to their backs by his rampage, recovered by Maurus, and the company dressed themselves in motion as they chased after him out into the city. Nepiur cried out for him to stop, Dace for him to calm himself, and in silence the native citizens rose upon rooftops to see what the commotion was. The Iron Rain bounded up nearby stairs along opposing precipices, catching Hax in simultaneous flying tackles and taking him to ground just before the city limits. Dace was barely able to join them and pin their pathfinder down before he could break free again, and Ronsha took the first opportunity to get away from his thrashing limbs.

"He's off his head!" She complained, nursing her shoulder.

Nepiur saw that there was a bite mark where she touched. Hax had bitten her. She could not begin to understand what was happening, had no idea how to deal with him.

"Hax! Stop this now!" She commanded him.

He continued to fight, squealing like an animal and grinding his teeth at her.

"He's here! He has her! Let go!"

"Who, damn it all!?" demanded Nepiur.

"My Tak! He's taken my wife!"

As he began to wriggle free again, Nepiur leapt onto his chest and slapped him repeatedly, clutched his head and shook it.

"Whom, you animal!?"

"MOGHREDAIOS!"

Concurrent with his answer, an overpowering wave of light launched everyone away from him as the veil opened and, as had happened to Tak, uncountable golden strands surged out and slithered along the ground. One that bore an inescapable shackle took hold of Hax and hauled on him, flipped him on his face and squeezed his gullet.

"*Eimud* brother!" Dace roared, leaping up from where he had toppled and after Hax. He grabbed hold of his friend's hands only to be dragged through the thi'tskreol with him as the tether tightened. The immense added weight did nothing to slow them down, only worsened the pain in Hax's silent face. One of the living chains reared back, engorged like a flexing arm and burst into multiple rivulets that flew down from the ethereal gap to throttle Dace, throwing him back against a thi with force enough to snap it in half. Without so much as a pause to recover himself, he leapt after Hax again, now at a hobbling sprint, bleeding profusely from a flickering gash in his chest and scattering bits of his shell as he went. Even as he charged, diving through the air, he knew it was futile when the portal receded, providing one last glimpse of Hax before he was taken, the visage of heartbreak and terror burning into Dace's heart.

A few sparks danced where he had been pulled out of Maengir, leaving Dace alone. The Bakul reeled in circles, screaming, shredding the earth and air with his tusks to find the vanished door.

"*Mina! Minaaa*! You can't have him! You can't! Come baaack!"

He fell on his face and bewailed Hax's parting, cursing all gods and begging for himself to be taken instead. It was an offer made in vain but one he would have earnestly fulfilled.

Nepiur and the company gathered warily around him, unable to speak while gaping around without any notion of what to search for. It was unprecedented, seemingly impossible, but undeniable. Hax was gone. Where he was taken, they could not know. If all his drunken stories really were true, then their friend was never coming home. He was lost. The master he had once escaped would never let him go free. Such was beyond their reasoning. The Deina were real, they were upon Maengir, and they were not idle.

CHAPTER 13: CLANDESTINE CHARITY

It would be so simple...ended so quick...

Raphenie hung her toes over the edge of her window, fingers loosely affixing her to its sides. Barely holding, she allowed herself to sway back and forth, each time leaning out to tease a brief and forestalled courtship with death. She thought about the taste of dirt and the sweet release of rock shattering her bones. It would not be clean but it would do the job; one magnificent moment of much deserved pain before an eternity of precious peace. No more doubt, no more misery, just floating above it all forever.

"*Aia* Raphenie?"

As if from a dream she heard the voice she still loved. Her heart soared, always skipping a beat when Capheif's melodious baritone found her. She turned just enough to see his worry lines and gentle milky eyes filling her door as he then knocked on its frame.

He was not well, after the brutality visited on his bestial form by Artimecian and his witchcrafters. After the darkness was purged from him and he became himself again, the grievous wounds, through which an arm might have easily reached, were greatly reduced along with his size. Nonetheless, it was as though he had been pierced and sliced by narrow blades, burned from the gothics' power. With a makeshift crutch, and heavily bandaged all over, he had some difficulty walking.

"*Aia,* are you present?"

He did not sound angry, did not hide his hands or skulk along the walls, though he clearly hesitated. It was, of course, rhetorical for him to inquire. Raphenie knew as he continued into the room that he smelled her, his steps very cautious but his tone clearly professing that he meant her no harm. If anything, he sounded penitent. The irony was lost on her. Though he tried to calm her she wanted to turn and jump out into the humid reaches of the Gate so as never to face what she had done. However, she was still Raphenie. Who was Raphenie if not...

...Not so sweet anymore. Not so pure anymore, her father's voice echoed in her mind.

The terrible truths haunting her now were far worse than anything Capheif might say. Even with Zeniquorer's acerbic influence no longer pinning her down she could not escape the shame of how she had wielded it against the one person she held in her heart. It was naïve to think there would be a happy ending for her. If the poor people she had hurt would not put her out of her misery she would do it herself.

"*Laan*...I'm here," Her voice abruptly quivered and pitched as she forced herself away from the evil thoughts, still deciding if she had the strength to live a moment longer. She closed her eyes in embarrassment as she turned into the room, still not stepping down from the ledge. She feared Capheif's intuition, yet he was not as able to read minds as she suspected. He interpreted her nerviness as fear; fear of him and his own wrongs against her. Though he had rehearsed what had to be said he fumbled over it now.

"I wanted to...*eina,* I couldn't..." he groaned. Try as he might, he could not form the right words.

"I understand," Raphenie replied, misunderstanding his anxiety.

Capheif continued to beg.

"Y-you don't. Will you...could you ever...forgive me?"

Raphenie's ears rang and her head swung around at his plea. Forgive *him? He* repents?

"Forgive you!?" she cried in confusion. Questions and responses whirled inside her head, making her response almost nonsensical, "*Quo*? How could I, *quoei,* for nothing done!?"

Despite her literal question he could only hear admonishment, for that was what he willed upon himself. Anguished, what little composure he retained quickly dissolved and he fell at Raphenie's feet, scrabbled to find her in the dark and wept like a babe.

"*Prostas*! *Malpael'tskprostas*! *Mineina sax, che potesti eih'kaliba*, cut out my heart and let me atone for what I have done!" The outburst so startled Raphenie she could not begin to form a response, only stood gaping as he gushed. "I beg you, say something! Tell me there is some offering I can give, some penance that can sponge the stains from my heart!" He finally found her feet, grasping them in abject misery.

Images of her father hunting her in this body came rushing back to Raphenie, yet she knew it was not the man prostrating himself to her, and was no longer afraid of it. Without Zeniquorer's true presence infecting either of them, she was not moved to flee. She saw that Capheif's pain was her own, at last understood his tears and dropped to her knees, threw her hands around his neck and held him.

"*Minla*! How dare you…" she whispered emphatically. "…How dare you blame yourself. It was I who allowed the ghost into our lives, I who fed it so it could fight the battles which were my own. It is I who should suffer, *einauta*, and thinking myself such a villain I have craved the plunge to an earthen grave that I might escape your hatred!"

Capheif was inconsolable, but in her acquitting arms and words he felt his guilt wash away.

"N-no. *Aia*, that was not you," he assured her. "That horrible thing was not you."

Raphenie took his hand and kissed it.

"It was nothing of either of us, my friend. It was a fetid wound I could not heal, with teeth seeking any they could devour."

"I cannot express the sorrow I feel that you had to endure this evil," Capheif lamented.

Raphenie could not hold back the memories that came with such an evil. The wall that had separated her from her past had come tumbling down, broken as Zeniquorer's ashes. Her divinity gave them order and, one by one, the scars inflicted on her soul by her family began to reappear.

"He was…my father." She admitted, quaking against Capheif,

overwhelmed by disgust. "A very old god...like my mother."

"I knew it," Capheif marveled without anger, "You, Naguza and all those exiled...you are all...celestial.".

"*La uta*," Raphenie confided. "I was discarded by a sister after we lost we mother, all after we were sired by her enemy. He was always within me, hidden as parasite. When I was weak, he became strong, for I knew nothing of myself. Everything of my mother was wiped from my mind, terrible things I would have been happier not knowing, but...he is dead, and now I must know them."

"Memories of what?" Capheif inquired.

"Who I was," she explained, still in pieces but increasingly whole, "Who I am."

She pushed aside the painful memories to unearth one of happiness; the only blessing locked away in her vault of bloody struggles. She slowly took his hand and rested it on her inmost thigh. Though Capheif was unsettled by the intimacy of the gesture she did not urge it further, instead placed her own upon to it and said strongly:

"Do not be aggrieved by actions that were not your own, for even their ends have been undone. I was born of sin, though it was not sin which killed my mother. It was my sister and I who took her life, born as the seedling from the *cha'tskthi*. By violence she was given two daughters, one who was given her mind, nation and throne, and one who had her true nature. The latter now sits with you and in me she yet lives, unbound and unafraid. Under my own, feel with your fingers that even my flesh has forgiven you, my sex healed, my life made my own once more. This is not by the clemency of a dead goddess' heart, but by the love in my own...and in yours, for you are only ever the truest of friends to me."

Capheif could hardly believe what he was feeling. Not through eyes but through the light within her he was shown that her thighs were unbruised, her skin unscarred. Through it he could indeed feel the essence of herself she shared. It shone brightly again and all wounds wrought by his hands were mended. It was as if their encounter had been a nightmare and nothing more, healed as easily as a thorn is plucked.

"How...?" he asked incredulously, "*Quom visense ibaeina*, how can this be?"

"*Utan,* my mother was purity so great that nothing could corrupt her, not even my father." Silent tears twined down her cheeks as she laid her hands on Capheif's temples and closed his eyelids with her thumbs, caressed them softly. "In our love and forgiveness, I finally feel this in myself, shining through the night, and owing to my command."

Capheif groaned and gasped, a burning sensation covering his face as her fingers tensed on it. It was a good pain. He held onto her and allowed the strange tremor to move through him, heavily inhaled as the impossible happened before and within his very eyes. The darkness of the world began to part and colors broke around shrinking shadows. The last of the shroud vanished and elation beyond words filled him when all he could see was burnished gold and white; the flames of Laesis enshrining Raphenie's snowy hair. Warmly held by the light he melted when the first shape his new eyes beheld was the blushing cheeks and limpid eyes of the secret goddess who had, with such a simple touch, cured the incurable.

Raphenie, having acted on only feeling and faith, was just as surprised as he, breathless as she watched his eyes flash across the room and drink it in, his cheeks twitching with excitement. She whispered his name and waited for him to come to grips with his new reality.

He was overwhelmed by the shock of a sense so long forgotten that it was practically unknown to him. Then his gaze swung sharply to hers and he surged upward with booming laughter, lifting her overhead and swinging her around.

"*Gol'vulilt,* what have you done!? I can see you! Paradise! Bakul be bashful and Boroo be sober! Miracles deluge upon me that I can see the world!" He squeezed Raphenie and kissed her cheek repeatedly. "You are truly a goddess' child! A gift! You are a gift from Aurba!"

She said nothing, struggling to breathe through his fearsome embrace. At last, he set her on her feet, rubbing her shoulders energetically while his greedy eyes gawked at everything around him, searching for every shape and color.

"*Eim aiat*...but no...*eihs golaia,* my goddess! How can I ever repay you?"

She squirmed uncomfortably and remained silent. *Love me,* her heart begged. *United as evil had made us, let this wonderful new life do ever more,* she ached to say, yet could not. Those yearnings were not Raphenie, merely the fragile and desperate mortal heart long withering in pain. She still loved him more than anything in the world, yet the thought of coming between him and his wife was now more terrifying than reliving her possession. She no longer wanted him for herself, instead wanted the best of all things for him; lasting joys he had chosen, not fleeting pleasures she wanted for herself. Nepiur was his joy, and Raphenie's heart was now lifted by love a new and unfamiliar kind.

"To repay me, you can live happily," she said somberly. "To bring me equal happiness, I implore you, tell no one what I have done."

"*Qu...Quoaien?*" he croaked unwillingly.

"No one can know I did this for you. Please, never speak of it."

Capheif could not bear the thought.

"But it must be so! Such a star must shine above all others!"

"It is...too much," she pleaded.

His zeal was quashed upon truly seeing her face in sadness. He had heard it, even smelled it, but to witness it was as painful as what she herself felt.

She eased free of his hold and backed out of reach.

"*Udai,* to be now without my captor is a freedom I have never felt....and yet it is replaced by another so unbearable that if you had not come to my side I would have let loose from these cliffs and fallen deathward to silence it."

"No," he achingly objected. "*Minaien aia,* say you would not do it. What cause have you to bleed now that even these useless eyes you can heal?"

"It is not fair to do so," she said sadly, "and...not altogether pure. Quite the opposite, perhaps. *Bethewekt,* it is my sister. *Minein,* memory of her is...I would see her bitten with such a toxin as my ghost was and laid to grave. It was she who smashed my memories of both her and our mother. All that makes me whole she tried to cut out. It was she who threw me to the seas and turned me into...this. All the family I had, all that hopeful love, and she let me think I was weak and worthless, part of nothing." Capheif rose and reached out to her, but she swatted his hand away. "I hate her still. Our mother died and she still refused to keep me. No one here ever wanted me. She made me into something that belonged in no world. Beyond the walls of this room, I would not know the difference between righteousness and ruin; whom to save and whom to let fall. I know so little of my own spirit and nothing of others. Can you tell me what terrible things I may bring about by healing the wicked and virtuous alike? I am no goddess. Ascendant, I remain a needful child. Among the weapons wielded by the ignorant the most dangerous is the power to appear as a beacon of hope. To be seen by all as you see me now. I am not ready for it. I fear what I may yet become, for while I have surely grown, it has been absent the knowledge of love and kinship. All but anger and jealousy is still foreign."

Feeling as feeble as her old self, it took a long while for Raphenie to burn through her feelings.

All of this was taken in by Capheif. With a heart full of finely honed empathy, largely through many seasons of the girl's frequent but fleeting visits, he reached out with his heart to look instead. When she fell silent, he brushed her hair past her shoulders and held her up straight.

"Nothing could be further from the truth," he said at length, staring proudly into her. "You have always had a family."

"I wanted to marry you," she awkwardly confessed, no longer caring if she offended or disgusted him.

"I knew as much," he said, sudden and smarmy, taking her by surprise. "*La*, you are seeing now what I have always. You felt a need, one you thought to be romantic, one you could not understand while a fiend clawed at you. What part of you could know love knew only there was a hole in you, and they that should have loved you most taught you only to take it. Today you know, as sure as clouds break and night relents to dawn. You have just seen the first light, as I have. Continue to trust in me and let us be the family you should have had, my wife and I."

"*Q-quouein?*" Raphenie stuttered, confused.

"It has been unkind, your life. Banished seaward thusly and claimed by our simple kind. Though you were given a bed in Nesh you were never given a Hall? Never given a family to look after you? Unacceptable! Many children were left orphaned by the fall of Ellel, and all had neighbors to adopt them. Where was this kindness for you? It should have been a wiser man and more practiced father than I who saw you were in need. Now, married as I am, it seems that honor is mine after all. Let it be officiated yet remain as it has always been. You are our daughter."

Raphenie caught her breath. Could it be as easy as that? Speechless, she nodded furiously, a whimper of joy escaping as she buried her face in his shoulder.

"*Utan*...thank you." She stiffened at a thought, said warily after a moment "But Nepiur?"

"Has the same heart as I," he continued encouragingly. "*Eis erem*, she knows all about you, for I sought her advice many times about your struggles. Though she did not hear your words herself she has always been a mother to you in spirit. My words are oft the same as her own, even in lamenting your need for someone to look after you." He hesitated momentarily, sorrows for more than Raphenie accruing. "*Eina,* I should perhaps not be telling you so much, but my beloved is herself...burdened by misfortunes of the past. We have known for some time that she could not bring about a child of her own. It is why so much of her heart has suffered for you."

Raphenie was undone, the misfortune of Nepiur's condition piling atop her other worries, though that condition was the greatest opportunity of Raphenie's young life. There were yet so many changes happening inside her, foremost trying to understand the very idea that there could be love for the sake of love alone, with no selfish gratification to be had. She felt she was finally home. Then, with adoring regard, she surrendered her secret doubts to Capheif's sustaining kindness.

"F...father," she began at first, then held as her thoughts organized. She wanted to do more for him, though truly she was wrestling with how long she could keep her secret. Despite the allure of what she could do, anonymity was still a powerful advantage; one she shared with all her divine family.

Capheif sighed, held her fingers to him and smiled out at the overcast skies of Long-hand.

"It is day. Eina, come and let us go see it. The good season will not last long. Let it be as you wish. I will share only with one, until you feel you are ready. When Nepiur returns and things have settled, we will look to the future. For today, know you are loved, goddess among Mantichaena. Set your heart upon its truest desire and live for it, and your family will be at your back."

Raphenie sighed heavily, unused to the freedom of a quiet mind. There was a desire in her, a longing to give all she could to those who had cared for her.

"My heart wants to see Naguza," she finally admitted.

Thetrulengo speaks,

Creatures of this transitory plane – gods included, insofar as they do not differentiate between love and lust – have such a profound obsession with mating. Fleshly sexuality, whether base or inspired, is predominately synonymous with the mating of souls. It is what they call love. They challenge themselves and each other in myriad ways to earn the admiration of an arbitrarily selected counterpart, not just for the fruits of their flesh but for the light within.

I consider it an empirical, infallible truth that no mortal is deserving of such fanatical devotion by one of alleged equal value, simply because the stature of every living thing is unique and incomparable. The idea of equal value is based entirely on ignorance of one's utility to Maengir if undistracted by intimacy. As a result, whether conscious or otherwise, they tend to love others who possess their preferred qualities and traits which they believe to be greater than themselves, or more precious because they themselves do not possess them. In this way, I surmise that one particular kind of love is exercised when one seeks to improve their own value by being bound with a superior lover.

Outside of romance, in circumstances when one serves those who are poor or sick or weak, they do so not because the individual is deserving of their love but because they are part of a whole which the one embraces as a lover. This exemplifies another brand of love, the exultancy of which is neither arguable nor logical; a love that requires sacrifice to heal .

Comparing these fundamental types of love, there emerges a similarity in results seen between love for selfish satisfaction and the other for selfless providence. May this suggest that for one to truly love another, romantically and selfishly speaking, the one must have love and regard for the many? Without a distinct method for proving the value of another single entity, it is implied that any given life cannot love another unless they first love the whole of which the thing they love is a part. If there is any truth in this, then lover cannot love another without first loving all of their parts; family, lineage, the manner of their upbringing and the furies that have created them, for all these things are part of them. To love one who has been sculpted by pain is to praise their triumph over it, perhaps even to praise the pain itself. I can only speculate.

Maybe that's why love is so special to them; it allows them to conceptualize a grand and beneficial product of all their hardships and mistakes. The elder gods vexed themselves in the same way, as did the Deina'itka. What is the connection between all these beings? All flesh is the same, as is their essence, yet the deiform created by the impacting of the two is unique. Perhaps the true beauty and value of love is the great excess to which the entity exalts the parallel it craves; the glorification of a mortal partner as though it were celestial. I would infer now that love is defined as believing that, in metaphor, a seed is as a grape, as a grape as wine. To convince oneself of this is to truly love and glorify the seed, not for what it is but for every beautiful thing it is destined to be, just as a soul is loved not for what it is but for what it is capable of. To love a single person is to embrace everything they will become. The darkest impression of this notion is that one might continue to love the vine even when it withers and bears no fruit. While this may be the most definitively devout form of love, the injury to the lover is obvious in their endless longing.

Yay! Yay for love! What a thrill to be so diseased! Just contemplating their inventions gives me a chill of understanding. I want more; more love, more selflessness, yet where can I find it? Is there a people inspired to goodness above all? Is there a land of only the kind and benevolent? No, I cannot dream of such a thing. Still, would it not be grand? I hope that's what this city of godlikes is destined for. They have the makings of this goodness in them if the many could but aspire to common ends. Just as I believe in the seed and the vine, so do I choose to believe in them.

Where, then, is my seed? My wine? I am undone. Would that I could be loved. Does my heart not break? Has it ever? With nothing to beat so strongly in the breast I do not have, how can I feel such a sensation? Loneliness is familiar. This beautiful, horrible realization...familiar.

Have I forgotten something? I feel so certain I have been here before.

~Chronicle of Wonders, In love, I fear to know

CHAPTER 14: BAD MEMORIES

*L*ong-hand twenty-four, bearing's long day:
    This is my first contribution to the Primacy's register, and by inscription I formally accept the title. Against my own judgment, the council has made their decision after the petitioning of more of our people than expected. I become Sky, and am Sebashni no more.

    The exile of my predecessor, Rogan, could be seen as unfortunate. He may have done wrong by our kin, yet I cannot deny he served his purpose in leading with conviction on Ellel. The abuse of trust earned by prior accomplishments, to which many in power have fallen prey, is something I must be wary of. It will be the greatest undertaking of my life to ensure that I am not seduced by the authority of this most high place, rather that I respect it as a burden to be shouldered on behalf of and for the good service of the tribe. This first entry of my standing will serve as an immortal reminder.

    To facilitate operating in this appointment in a manner that benefits all, my first act is to institute the following:

Addendum 163
Resolutions in process by the Council of Archons of Hauan Etain will heretofore be restructured such that the Primarch will

not participate in their deliberations on any issue which directly influences the health and wellbeing of the general population, but will provide advisement on the final decision prior to its implementation. The session of such advisement is to be open to all citizens, even in such cases where the deliberation of the council is not. The collective decision of the council will in all cases supersede the advisement of the Primarch.

Non-acceptance of any resolution by any one citizen must be matched by the acceptance of no fewer than two citizens in order for the resolution to take effect.

A citizen is heretofore to be considered as this: any individual born of Mantichaena blood, whether present, exiled or otherwise voluntarily apart from the city proper of Hauan Etain. This shall include all Galaila native-born to the mother-island of Ellel or to Manti.

No K'hizu shall be considered a citizen, insofar as this identity refers to a creature of Manti which has not, at any given time, been Galaila or carried the blood of same.

It is my intent that, henceforth, it will be the duty of the Primarch not to rule from Nesh but to wander all halls and hear the needs and concerns of every citizen as the archons do. I will join assembly only to observe and oversee, influencing it only at the council's direct request. Now I am only a single voice among many, as any ruler should be. What's more, if there is any order which I wish to enact then it must pass the approval of the council, to ensure I do not mold the city to my sole conviction. This is only partly to limit myself, but primarily to establish precedent in order to bind the next tyrant to come by training the council and the public to resist absolute rule. It should not be, that those who are unlike the majority should be ostracized.

Longhand is deep now. It has been eight days since Nesh Udai Keimas and his fellow hunter-killers journeyed westward. Their purpose...the death of Loi. I am chilled to record such words, but the knowledge of a watchful creature far more ancient than our kind has made it his sole purpose to have it known that our deity is not now, nor ever has been, benefactor to our survival. Rather, he has schemed for our captivity and was, if he is to be believed, responsible for the fall of Ellel. There was a great deal of resistance to these allegations at first, yet the creature remains, well heard by more and more each time he speaks. He knows too much to ignore; our entire history, the events that have made us who we are, even the names of our ancestors. He knows of them all. Worse, he made a strong case for many of them being directly influenced by agents of Loi. I am hesitant to put my faith in all this but it is not just his words that have earned our attention. Keimas' return was meaningful to a people who had begun to lose their minds after the appearance of the twilit evil whom it seems was destroyed by Lemalie and Naguza. It was Keimas who had first contact with this messenger of the outworld. His apparent trust in the creature called Tzychala must buy it some leniency.

My mind is muddled now to think back on this island's matron when she appeared to us and demanded our prayer. Many did not give it, and no law was made to enforce that they should. She took me at my oath on their behalf and departed, perhaps believing we would worship her out of fear. I dread wondering on this: did our fealty to Loi somehow contribute to our current situation? Would he have been capable of whatever it is he's done to take hold of Keimas if we had withheld our praise from him? Even after generations of devotion he still intends to punish us, but for what?

This is not the subject for my officiant purpose to ponder here, as I know little of how far it must reach into our past. Instead, I digress to the demon that appears more a protector than our own gods. I don't know what to do but to document its appearance. Tzychala has been debriefed by the council, and the knowledge he possesses is...disarming. He knows every development of our tribe since the day Ferraro's war came to Ellel, and in such detail I can scarcely believe. Though his many eyes (such a disgusting little creature) seem to never open, they clearly see more than our own. I do not think he is trying to trick us, for something most certainly is afoot. Keimas knows of it and will deal with it, yet I can't help feeling this demon is hiding something. He's very forward, almost child-like in how he wanders and marvels at our most simple comforts. Forthrightly he answers all our questions, no matter how personal. He doesn't seem capable of holding back, nor of concentrating for long. He moves between thoughts so quickly we have to constantly pull him back to the matter we want to discuss. Perhaps he's merely confused, but it's no trouble. He seems *overeager if anything. To see this, how excitedly he engages us, how humbly he obeys when commanded by aiana Lemalie to help with labor; it sways my heart to believe in his. Perhaps I am a fool, for I see no evil in the creature. If I am deceived, then so are the hundreds of Mantichaena he has won over.*

There's no subtlety to our situation. Loi wants us destroyed, and all for some diabolical plan to become stronger? The way Tzychala tells the story makes no sense to me. It is more prophecy than experience, like a frightening bedtime story that you assure yourself cannot be real. What can we do but believe him? Ferraro died to save us. I am grateful, and out of respect will pray to her often. I will mourn her passing, knowing that she must have a people of her own that now suffer without her. I say myself, as the anonymous cried in support of Keimas and in protest of Loi: why did we ever believe Ferraro our enemy or Loi our sovereign? We were brought up on the mother's milk of Ellel's faith, yet I have witnessed no divine act that proves Loi to be as we were taught. The death of Ellel is as we choose to see it. Does it matter what any of us believe? It is out of our hands.

Regardless of the Kutu assault to murder a god, we have taken it upon ourselves to make ready for a fight we are told may yet come. We are Mantichaena, protected not by Anama or Ferraro or any other god. Not anymore. We are made strong by our own works and our own muscle and bone. This is our home, the second one that could be taken from us if we are to believe the demon. If Loi wishes it so, then let him try. This time we will not back down, no matter what comes from the sky or ground. Never again will we love absentee gods or fear their threats. This is all what I hear from the whispering citizens. They have more faith in Keimas, in Tzychala, in Lemalie and Naguza than in any god...which may become as dangerous a problem as the unchallenged rule of the Primacy.

Commandant Schaleikin of Gazan has doubled the training schedule for prospects and the Hall of Pain resounds with the commotion of battle from dawn until dusk. We have been relatively safe from the more practical dangers of Manti for many seasons now, by the service of a comparatively small militia and the courage of common folk. What we are building now is a territorial army, an occupation force to expand into Ni'ivitnem and, perhaps, into the Thonsfa Tau. Our goal is to rejoin with the villages of the exiles, to make all Manti one land, to bring all our might together in safeguarding our species from extinction. What a notion to try and explain to those who have spent their whole lives in the borderlands: Loi may very well appear to us, bringing death and bondage with him.

In departing Ellel we abandoned metalwork when we realized our gift of claws and other such tools of the flesh, keeping only those things not purposed for war. It was a lovely dream, though now we must wake. More forges are being built in Tault each day. They burn ever hotter, producing armor and weapons to suit all forms of Mantichaena. The mines ring with the pounding of zeulf and the stink of smelting ore. As the Iron Sanctum was born from our fear of the thuell, fear of Loi has given momentum to Commandant Schaleikin's vision of a new breed of Mantichaena: Bakul clothed in cold metal, bladed gloves to make the strike of Kubernu and Kuolt even more destructive, giant plates of iron that could withstand any impact. I have even heard murmurs that Ms'egol is calling for more research in volatile chemistry...whatever that might mean. I will need to see it for myself.

I am undecided on whether this is necessary or what it could lead to. If we are to defend ourselves against our god, then let us become ascendant ourselves. We have long been a tribe of dignified peace, but now will become gods of war.

~Sebashni Sky, Nesh Aiatan Efuil

Dust rose from the face of Gazan with the blast of drums and the coincident ring of six great gongs erected over its arena, each one representative of a season and used to mark their arrival for the people. On this occasion, as with only a few others before, all six resounded together, not as a measure of time but as a message that all should gather in the fields. In the historically cryptic signals of the Gate's populace it proclaimed a day of such importance that 'Time was reset, and a brand-new cycle began.' For many families and houses whose children and friends had been sent to Aes'bethil, this described their feelings well as they ran screaming to welcome the caravan home.

Filthy, battered, and disillusioned, Nepiur's company was welcomed with fanfare unsuited to their condition. They were little joyful, as hard as borderlanders who had spent many seasons struggling to survive. Though praise and favors rained over them, they could show only the barest appreciation.

Inspired young men and women fawned at Maurus' and Dace's feet as they stoically passed, only further enchanted by their aloof inattention.

Maurus was only swayed to happiness when his mother swept the sycophants aside with great pounding claws to reach her son and wrap him in her arms. It was a joy to him, yet he could not smile. Neither could he tarry to entertain her fussing over his disheveled appearance. They were obliged to follow Nepiur until her final report to the council, and so all diversions were left aside.

The Primarch stood at the doors of Nesh, waiting for them from the moment she had heard the gongs. She had the Archons arranged at her sides to welcome the caravan home, tight with anticipation of their findings. Seeing no grievous injury upon them, the council and commoners all were overjoyed. However, their mood dampened when the troupe's continued approach showed no enthusiasm. Dace in particular had a distant and heartbroken look as Nepiur ascended the steps to present her men. The crowd went quiet to hear her, yet she spoke in a low and intimate tone to she whom she remembered as Sebashni.

"*Eina raemla,* honored mother, I am given to Nesh to report these recent days in Aes'bethil. Where is the Primarch?"

This was a delicate moment. Emotion had no place in these presents. How then was Sky to explain that the young leader's father was exiled to his death?

"The one you know is no longer present, I'm afraid." She said firmly. "On the sixteenth of Longhand, Nesh Udai Rogan was removed from the Primacy for crimes of conspiracy and deception against the people of Hanging Gate."

Nepiur's jaw dropped, momentarily taken aback at the overturn of her father's regime, so quick and so unopposed that there seemed no memory of it beyond the fact of its existence. To no one's surprise, she took a breath and returned to the conversation with relaxed confidence, even a modicum of pleasure.

"Blessed be. *Laan,* and tell us all, has a new Primarch been selected?"

"As of this last evening," Sky said with warmth, descending a step and holding out her hands. "You may present your report to Primarch Sky as she stands before you."

Nepiur smiled and bowed, taking the hands.

"Loi charm your ascent, Primarch. I would be off to assembly then to give you my report."

Sky lifted her and gestured happily to the rest of her company and the citizens behind them.

"Not today! The *Hauan Etain* has finally begun to mend from its heartaches. This marks the last of our great undertakings. I am elated to see you all..."

In the midst of her speech, Dace had softly broken into tears. Seeing this, Sky broke off and searched the troupe more closely, saw the same destitution in each of them. She counted quickly and found the band was one short. Though personally unfamiliar with the man, she still knew who was missing.

"...Mother Nepiur, where is your pathfinder?"

The Iron Rain closed around Dace to cautiously comfort him as Nepiur answered very properly.

"He...he fell, Primarch."

"His body?" Sky queried urgently.

"Unrecovered. Forgive me, Primarch."

"*Malpael*, but tell me he passed well."

Nepiur felt the eyes of her band turn away and she knew she could not answer truthfully while sparing their pained hearts. All she could do was end the inquiry as quickly as possible.

"*Eina*, to great glory *ueihawth*. He gave his life in combat against the thuell and granted us victory."

Sky felt their pain but was thankful at once that there were no more casualties.

"Then we will bury his spirit," she proclaimed. "In Voddace, we will prepare a new tomb, for the first and last of the line of Ms'Egol Utan Hax, that he will never be lost."

Dace stepped forward to interject.

"Primarch, may I be given charge of it?"

"*Udai*, if it is what you wish. You may preside over its design even."

"My meaning is for the remainder of my days, *Aiatan*," Dace humbly clarified.

Sky was confused.

"You…you are not an ordained Bonekeeper."

"And there are no bones to keep. I will not relinquish my place in Gazan and will labor there by day, by night in Voddace so as to care for my brother's memory."

The gravity in Dace's eyes was palpable. She had never known him to have such conviction, felt in that moment that he would not be deterred. She honored his wish.

"Very well. If your Commandant will allow it, then you have leave. I don't believe Hax had any other family? As his closest relation you may take a new Hall if you choose."

Dace did, with nonverbal approval from all present archons, and so limped away to his home without so much as a day's greeting to those archons of his house. It was an offense, though Nepiur wasted no time in excusing him.

"Primarch, I'm grateful for your pardon. While I come fit and ready to present testimony, my company does not."

Sky smiled and put a hand to her shoulder.

"Take ease, mother of Mantichaena, that we are ended now. Does Bethaali live?"

"Her people do." Nepiur muttered flatly.

"I see. I know your woe and will not pry. Have we lost our ally?"

"We have not. Bethaali lives on in her faithful and Aes'bethil is at our side."

"Does the village stand?" Sky continued hastily.

"It does."

"The thuell destroyed?"

"Entirely," Nepiur assured her.

"Then consider your oath honored. I excuse you of any further report save that which you freely give." Sky stood higher to speak to the city again, along with the crestfallen caravan. "Tonight, there will be a celebration in Nesh to give praise to these who come, and he whose spirit watches over them. Too long have we been swept up in the ill-wind of fate's breath, but no more! I will not have the souls of the brave look down on us and see a city of the disheartened, but a nation bold! Archons, see it done. For this weary delegation, I order only rest and warm meals and, if they are willing," she said softly with a nod to Nepiur, "Then I would be honored if you could be present for the dance, as its honoree."

"*Lam*, Primarch. I will attend as you require."

Father Mani wasted no time in coming before the Iron Rain as soon as the reception dissolved, though before he could greet them they bombarded him with questions about the absence of their order's master.

Mani's response was plain, dispassionate, physically and verbally taciturn.

"He is dead, children. Please, follow at my side and I will explain."

Silent in acquiescence, they did as he asked.

Mani explained at great length how their master had misused their order for the schemes of the exiled Rogan. Though not Artimecian's creation, the plan was still carried out wholly by his powers in both mancy and influence. Their master had been a tool, just as they were, and with the disbandment of the sanctum it was now the responsibility of each disenfranchised member to disentangle themselves from the sordid works of Artimecian and all memory of the Iron Sanctum.

The two were dumbfounded. Their entire lives had been spent in a closed society with its own rules and culture, a family and way of life apart from the city at large where they had even found love. The safe solitude of a dungeon they were accustomed to – not a more pleasurable life but one in which they felt at home – was gone.

Mani tried to placate them as he had the rest of the sanctum.

"*Malpael.* I know you all looked up to him, but his practices with you were not something the council would have approved of. I realize that you volunteered but we had to put a stop to it until we can better understand the nature of the gothic style; a more difficult task without your master. While the council would appreciate your cooperation in that process, the Sanctum has been disbanded."

"The sanctum disbanded!?" they mourned.

"For now, perhaps conclusively. I am prepared to absorb you into my academy if you would like. Elsewise you must find a new house."

The couple immediately declined.

"May we be allowed to study with the enchanters of Raru?"

Mani considered a moment, though not seriously.

"No, you may not. The classical master's murder was the crime that drove yours to take his own life, and a replacement has not been chosen. Even if there were, some of Raru's students were with him, died with him. Those who survive would not take kindly to you. It will take time for the gothic school to regain the trust of the others."

Rashala tried to disprove what they both immediately suspected, asking Mani awkwardly if perhaps the dead students had been killed in a manner other than perfidy. Mani's recount took their breath away.

"Artimecian confessed to all," Mani assured. "Raru and four of his students fell for trying to protect Keimas from the iron wind and Artimecian himself."

"Keimas! Is the man caught!?" Rashala seethed. "Why would they protect him?"

Mani shook his head and sighed dejectedly.

"It has been a confusing time but, among those whose loyalty and veracity has been in question, Keimas' remains intact. Rogan and Artimecian may have had good intentions at one point but they have lied about a great deal, especially concerning the hunter-killer. *Malpaelm*, but Artimecian and the witchcrafters are finished and Keimas has been exonerated before the council."

Rashala droned "Will we be…"

"Exiled?" Mani interjected, "*Minlaan*, nothing like that, though the gothics may need to find new methods of carrying out their ehm…studies. Artimecian has kept too much hidden from sight."

"Are we not trusted? Even after saving Aes'bethil?" they asked, affronted.

"I'm sure you will be regarded higher than your counterparts but you must understand this is a precarious time for any that were close to the arch-witchcrafter. Your order has been sealed in that dungeon since youth, something we allowed only because of the faith in Artimecian that Rogan instilled in us. They two were your only defense, I'm sorry to say. Now that Sebashni Sky has taken over and the grisly nature of your practicum is revealed…we need to work together to decide what is best for your school."

The pair looked at one another, uncertain of what they could do, lacking a home or an honorable place. Such allegations that they were not suited to choose how they practiced was insulting, delusional even. There was no continuing the conversation with a council that did not trust in their choices.

"Father...may we have some time to make our decision?" Rashala asked bitterly.

"Of course. I won't rush the due consideration for your futures. I know where your allegiance lies, proven enough by your absence when this whole mess began. *Prostas*, only tell me when your decision is made. Until then, the Iron Sanctum have housed themselves in Artimecian's old chambers. Though, *eis hadat svilhaag*, do not go near the sanctum. It is closed and forbidden until Tault can remove Artimecian's, eh...tools."

It was a grim day on all fronts for Ronsha and Rashala as they entered the chambers of their deceased teacher. Their only friends were already gathered therein, listlessly scattered about the room. Bolvide, the Iron Song, stood to welcome them home first, did so with a slight touching of fingers, then was followed by the rest. There were no words or further gestures. It was not their way while in the confines of the Sanctum and should not be now. Nonetheless, the living students were grateful that only three were missing instead of five.

The Iron Rain were something of misfits in the order. None of their kind had families and so had always been family to each other, though Rashala and Ronsha were the only ones to join at any age other than early adolescence. They had known a good life before the Sanctum and so had found their power in more than pain. Already very much in love, they had joined the order as a team, marrying very young the night before descending into the cold training room for the rest of their lives. The way was different in the city proper but the Iron Rain was not as averse to it. This was why they had been chosen to venture Hai. They could get along with the public without causing them grievous harm, by accident or otherwise. The same could not be said of the others.

People seemed to think the Sanctum was so cruel, an abusive captivity forced on stolen children. They could not show him their truth, could not explain what this unlikely family of orphans had made of themselves through their practices. They could not let all they had worked for slip away. Hanging Gate needed the Iron Sanctum, even if the common mind could not see it.

The two lighter-hearted witchcrafters sat and held one another. For a long time they and the others remained in directionless melancholy, grieving for the corruption of their teacher and the likely deaths of their vilified Iron Wind. Until the assassins returned there was little to be done, even with all their collective power. None of the witchcrafters had ever had to lead nor plan for themselves, just obey. Iron Finger and Fist, the Rain couple, Iron Song and Iron Fortress; useless to their errant brothers and unwanted by anyone else.

At the end of the day Nesh burst to life with families who had come to dance away their worries. While heel upon stone had always been enough percussion for as brief an engagement as a wedding or induction to the council, such prolonged revelry required that the drums of Gazan be brought in and placed around the atrium. On the stage there were a dozen or more tables, with all manner of food and drink for partaking by any and all, and every habitable bit of floor was packed with moving feet and some discarded clothes.

A sea of sweat, laughter and inebriation became the only happening in Nesh to such an extent that, when Nepiur arrived, she had to slink around behind the drums to reach the stage. She sought her husband, yet Aroch found her before she got past the refreshments. Having been told of her dour mood, he was committed to cheering her up.

"My exalted Nepiur, I'm glad to see you have a stomach for pleasant revels after your ordeal. Your presence is an honor."

"*Bpaenta,* you have all my thanks," she said more curtly than intended.

"*Aien la*? It's not as much as your troupe deserves."

"I am thankful that it is you and your beloved who welcome me and not my father," she corrected.

Aroch nodded solemnly but found it hard to divine her meaning until she carried on.

"I am surprised to hear you declined the Primacy. Nonetheless, your good nature must not be dismissed in considering how this city wishes to be ruled. *Aiatan* Sky is fully deserving and, if I may say, you were right to act in my absence. You both were. I am relieved that both my father and the pressures of the Primacy no longer trouble me."

"*Aia*, I wish I could feel proud of what has happened. It is truly the best we could do with an unfortunate reality. We are blessed that you may be so understanding, though I would still see you accept your confirmation as a Matriarch. *Hauan Etain* needs as many souls such as yours as it can right now."

Nepiur's confidence grew at his words and grew more optimistic about the future of the tribe.

"*La*...and I will be here. We will do as needs must to ensure this place does not fall into history any season soon." She then exhaled quickly, visibly trying to close the conversation as fast as possible. "Do not hold me in contempt, but I must seek my husband. In my dreams he has been eager to receive me."

"He surely will be," Aroch replied, "If I know anything of the man who once was yours."

Nepiur was jarred.

"*Uein quo*? Once?"

He ignored her question, smirked cleverly and parted toward his own daughter with a spring in his step, calling over his shoulder "Still your heart, dear woman, and prepare to meet a new man!"

Nepiur, very baffled, bowed her head in silent greeting to Lemalie as she appeared from the crowd to retrieve Aroch. The gesture was returned respectfully, then Nepiur continued on her way to the hall beside the stage. She paused momentarily to regard the damage around the periphery of its entrance, disconcerted by how the firelight seemed to disappear where repairs left deep pitting. By the look of the mud slathered in deep cracks spreading out from the much widened opening it clearly was not caused by structural collapse. She had not even noticed that the doors of Nesh had been replaced with entirely different wood, so this did not distract her long. If it was not life-threatening then it did not deserve attention. She was far more concerned with why she had to seek Capheif out as she did, rather than him awaiting her. It hurt that he was missing, and everyone she spoke to of him seemed only to make coy remarks and move on. They made her uncomfortable with their smiles, like they knew her husband better than she.

Without a need to knock on their door she opened it slowly to ensure it squeaked loudly enough to announce her return. Pinching her mouth expectantly she leaned into the well-lit refuge, smelled the familiar chlio stew and heavy cheese Capheif loved so much, then the musk of the hides they slept upon; their sacred bed. Her eyes wandered among the many candles ignited around the room to the delicious sight of her husband standing before the fire with his back to her. His torso was bare, oiled until it glistened like gold and caped by his freshly brushed and braided hair. His legs were loosely covered by a corded pelt, washed and etched with hard labor. She had never seen him so meticulously groomed, nor so hard of body. She attributed it to her coming being foretold to him and quickly closed the door for privacy. Very slow to turn back to Capheif, Nepiur felt enchanted by him. He had a glow about him, proud and alert. Almost forgetting her grudge against his absence, her whispered romance matched the low, warm ambience.

"*Eihsrysha*, I have craved you like the rain, starving like a root. I was searching for you from the moment I set foot into the canyon."

"I know," he said with a flourish of his hair, turning the rest of his body to look on his wife for the very first time with awoken eyes. "I saw you come."

Nepiur's whole body seized and she nearly fell over, unable to believe that his eyes were clear of their white contusions and now sparkled so beautifully with life. He, likewise, could only stare, his chin trembling in astonishment of Nepiur's beauty. His whole body hungry for her touch, he took a step toward her. She, realizing he was indeed looking into her own eyes, screamed like a child and leapt into his arms. So desperate was he to be as close with her as possible that he fell to the bed beneath her. They were both unblinking, barraging one another with kisses and refusing to look away.

"How…what is this?" Nepiur murmured through his lips, unable to form a coherent inquiry.

"We have no need for gods in the stars," he explained with a smile, stealing another quick kiss. "The divines walk with us, here in our own lands. War has not left us alone but the stars are with us, their seed germinating in our soil. My sight is their fruit."

"*Quei?*" she asked, still bewildered.

"That is a story for more somber dawn, not superb night. Just let my eyes have you, and when we see the day together, I will tell you something even more wondrous."

There was no raging celebration or pounding drum that could have woken the lovers. Nepiur was fatigued beyond her imagining after both her long ordeal and an equally taxing tumble with her husband. Capheif had far more energy to spare, with so many wonderful things happening in their lives now. Still, he was at peace and rested well with his only love in his arms. So, they went undisturbed when the raucous noises were gone and, late into the night, the door loudly squeaked once again.

A furtive creature moved in the dark of their room. It knew the room as well as its owners and so knew to avoid the furnishings and hanging instruments, passing in silence like a ghost. It's hair shone red and orange from the torches in the hall until it was fully concealed in shadow, creeping with purpose towards the bed of furs. A tiny hand reached out, ever-so-cautiously, to touch Nepiur's exposed hip. There was a silent moment until, with the faintest gray glow emanating from the visitor's eyes, it thought a prayer for Nepiur:

Miohaelia, soul of all that is pure and lovely, live through my flesh and my touch. Give yourself to me and let my will grow lush gardens from the seed of your fullness. Rest, allow your light into my care and let me heal all that is broken. With each life, each wound, each soul, let me heal what is broken.

Miohaelia was no longer the true power of the Windsong Star. Raphenie was her youngest, the promised heir of all her power, and that power had awakened. At Raphenie's gentle touch, the light that washed away all sickness and pain flowed into Nepiur's skin and hunted for all injuries it could heal: her bruises, her aches, even that which she never had. Raphenie felt her body change as a single egg grew inside her, nestled where it could become what she and Capheif wanted most.

The light vanished and, with no sound but the hasty sealing of the door, the young goddess was gone.

CHAPTER 15: THEFT OF SOULS

Thetrulengo speaks,

I have dreamed...I think. In lying upon the black sky and staring into many stars I waited for peace to come and my thoughts to slow. Once impatience gave way to apathy, I finally felt myself wake after a period of unconscious thought. It is the most uncomfortable I have been with my own company. By surrendering control over the mind it runs rampant, and the winding paths of images and feelings serve no purpose. I did not merely recall that which I have seen, but all I have not: Escharka and her children, Az'Rech and his, both living and dead. I did not see what was, only what I imagined them to be.

I know what I conceived was not real but it...feels like a premonition. Not a vision of what will be, surely not, only a story my mind has told to me based on what I know to be true of Maengir's current condition. I saw the higher earthplane, the wide fields of the firmament and the blight of souls that gushed from the beacon of Az'Rech's authority. I envisioned the Maengir I knew, and as I watched it began to change.

From the House of the Living Sky there came a soul, befouled and deformed, which lifted its hands to the far edge in prayer and praise of Az'Rech. In response, a streak of dawn came out of the *starless deep sky and mercilessly smote the fervent spirit. As it shattered, it became as a great fire that swirled outward, devastating Maengir and erasing it from being. I wept as it happened, stranded in nothingness and unable to speak or move. When it was over, I was all that remained of the many planes and their ancients. It's ridiculous that everything could just disappear like that, so why would I imagine it? It's pointless to consider. I won't do it.*

Perhaps...perhaps what I foresee is not the end of all things, just their inevitable change when the powers that dominate the material and immaterial change hands. Could it be Loi of the Siege whose death creates such change? Not his rule but...his absence?

The Kutu hunt their god now, have done so unto the final days of the Longhand season and may well continue into the beginning of the true Windsong. What can be but what I have seen if Loi should fall? After all, if the only god capable of controlling all the others is defeated, there will be no peace among them. Worse, without fearful loyalty to one god, more will surely arise and seek his place. If an era of innumerable gods comes again then genocide is sure to follow. It's an endless cycle of cataclysm and recovery. Can they ever put a stop to it? Can I? Or...why should I? These things will always find new ways to kill one another. What is gained in preventing one calamity?

I interfered once, only to save Raphenie, a girl I knew almost nothing about. She still suffered, still became a goddess. Would the same not have happened if I'd not alerted the Nesh people? More importantly, how can I justify what I did without knowing who she will become? I am suddenly very aware of the possibility that her ascendance may lead to more bloodshed. Ascendants lose sight of where they came from. Is bloodshed really such a bad thing? Perhaps I'll try it sometime...murder. Isn't it best to experience something and study it fully before condemning it? I imagine it must feel different when purposeful.

I only want to prevent the truest manifestation of my vision: extinction, the erasure of everything, if it could even be done.

I'm already so alone. If everything else was gone I would...I don't know, though I feel I already know what would happen to me. I could not bear it. To have so much, then to have nothing, I would be broken.

~Chronicle of Wonders, A New Unraveling

What Mantichaena called Thigolaia, or the Goddess Amphiraed, was greatest of all the growing things, standing one hundred times the height of any other like a prominent mountain of fungal boughs. This, or rather the valley in which it lay, Anama had warned them never to draw near, giving them the name of 'Cradle of Thorns'. It was her stronghold, a sanctuary for only her and her creatures, never to welcome any kind born of another god. On a clear day this unmistakable sight could be seen from as far as the clifftops of Hanging Gate, though reaching it would be a journey of a full season for the fleetest of K'hizu afoot.

On mighty wings, the Kutu caste were making quicker work of it. The going was arduous nonetheless, for they battled harsh winds coming down from the mountains of Nikhaadi Gao in the Thaun. They had no sight of Loi to follow but knew his course. He sought Anama, and so the looming Thigolaia on the eastmost shore of Manti was unquestionably his heading. There, the Kutu would hunt.

The pride was exhausted, wet and frozen by the constant exposure to the howling wind and periodic showers, eventually forced to glide lower abreast the canopies. All but Keimas. His companions had flown strong for many days and nights, but they were beginning to grow frustrated. Never before had they attempted such a long and tireless flight, growing weaker and weaker until no rest could recover them. Keimas was surprised and a bit ashamed of how right Tzychala had been. He felt the tension between his soul and those of his brood. It was much more apparent after traveling so closely for so long. They were unwittingly feeding him, and his heart grew heavier at how they were humiliated by weakness without knowing its cause. He did not know if telling them everything would spur them onward or turn them against him. Secrets and lies were starting to pile atop one another in pursuit of the cause, yet there was no time to gamble on losing their service.

Quite suddenly, Govan's strength gave out, losing control of his wings and staggering downward through an early mist to land gracelessly on a protrusive bough. As heavy as he was, and lacking the energy to soften his landing, his perch cracked and cast him painfully across another of its kind. Fortunately, the latter held true, though he could do nothing but cling to it and gasp for breath. Kutu and hunt reacted quickly to encircle and protect him while he gathered himself. When at last he spoke, his authority was lost in how his voice struggled.

"Hold…beat steady! I need only…one moment!"

Keimas still hovered strong, but Miriena started to give as well and descended to join Govan, signaling to her husband to keep watch. Govan's more matured body made him most susceptible to Keimas' influence, though they were all becoming easily irritated. Allende, to Keimas' surprise, seemed almost unphased as he paralleled Keimas' position in the air and shouted down.

"Get you up, *utanaiam*! On what impish trick do you blame this frailty? The day has just begun!"

"*Minuein*!" Keimas snapped. Then, pretending himself similarly weakened for a moment, said "We cannot go on like this. We've been winged so long the feathers burn with the first beat."

Miriena whipped her head and grunted angrily to shake off the strange, draining sensation upon her.

"We must burn, starve and thirst if we are to overtake Loi! We cannot assume a god to require sleep and prey as we do!"

"A god in a perishable body," Keimas said confidently, drifting down to them. "He is just another Kutu, bound by the same needs as us. We will take him soon."

Govan scowled and shakily crawled onto his bough, eyeing Keimas and muttering under his breath.

"Always so certain of everything."

Miriena tried to help Govan steady himself. He thanked her and caught his breath, though his face contorted in deep thought as he tried to understand what was happening to him. He stared at his flexing fingers, then suspiciously at Keimas, feeling clear enough that pride no longer got in the way of honesty.

"*Kutudaiam*, something's wrong. Why do I feel…heavy?"

"It's the cold, master," Keimas patronized him. "This far from the cliffs, the wind takes us all by surprise."

"Don't play with me," Govan quietly grunted. "I'm not the man I thought I was, to fall so quickly. Allende and Miriena are strong and true yet, but you? There is no struggle in your breath nor flushing of your skin. You are always at the head while I languish at the tail. It's unbecoming. I have grown soft with age," he admitted.

Keimas was uncharacteristically comforting at such a strange expression from his mentor.

"*Utan*, there is no truth in that. There is no shame in needed rest…"

Govan's temper was building dangerously high.

"And what of Loi!? You started this for a reason! He must be found now! What might happen if he succeeds? To our homes? Our families? *Hauan Etain* may become a smoking boneyard if we tarry even a moment too long!"

Keimas swung back and forth between beats, contemplating their situation. It had taken only eight days of his constant presence to sap the strength of his master and, judging by the aspect of Thigolaia and the cliffs behind them, it seemed they were only halfway through. It was another two days until they were past Sekhaadi Ni'ivitnem and into the Drowned Hills beyond. Far more troubling was how hazy the air was becoming, despite the scarcity of rain. It was worsening the further Hai they went and Thigolaia had nearly faded from vision. They could not risk losing it completely while still so far out.

Seeking solutions, Keimas proposed "*Utan*, ride upon Bogh'thane and perhaps your strength will return in time."

"With myself as burden he will fly as slow and nothing will be gained."

"Then so be it! Our disadvantage cannot…"

"Go without me,"

"*Quota*!? Never!" Keimas rebutted.

"I ORDER you! Keimas, I am only one body. Time is your need. Time is the one thing we cannot lose. We began nearly a full day in Loi's wake and need every ounce of speed we have to catch him!" Before Keimas could respond, Govan screeched sharply upward, calling the hunts to hear him. "*K'hizu'tskutu*, waste no more of the day on me. If we've not overcome Loi yet, then his haste is too great for any weakness on our part. Kutu…Kutu do not accept weakness!" His ardent demand came entirely from his own ignominy, though it was true. The fire in his eyes insisted that they prove themselves better than he, prove that he had not trained them to be his equals but his betters. "I'm not fit to lead you anymore. I have fallen. I will try to retake you but now you must go without me. You MUST Go! I command it! Go!"

The hunts obeyed with shrill chorus, led off by Allende, who showed not a moment's hesitation. Miriena remained a moment to salute Govan before following suit. Keimas, heavy with guilt, let himself down enough to touch Govan's shoulder with the talon of his foot before flying.

"We will see you soon, *utan*. Follow soon. I know you would not miss such a hunt."

Govan nodded exasperatedly, breathing deep to recover himself as he was left behind. When his pride had moved on, he finally staggered back against the trunk of the thi and slumped down in a huff. He continued to assess his body, barely able to make a fist while his every muscle quivered. He had been preparing for the day one of his kin outdid him and took command of the pride, but this was not how he envisioned it. If anything, he had hoped to die gloriously and become a fire that would feed theirs from beyond. It could not end like this.

The following day, while Laesis was at its peak and the ongoing Kutu kept toward Hai, Keimas was constantly mindful of his effect on the others. The hunts grew more sluggish and, though Miriena summoned amazing resolve to hide her exhaustion, he could see she was beginning to deteriorate. Allende had taken a turn for the worst as well, almost at his limit, gasping and burning while his hair whipped and spattered sweat around him. Keimas had not made plans for what would happen to the stragglers as their numbers shrank, yet he knew this was how it would be.

The thi were beginning to change color, turning progressively darker browns and grays in lieu of the vibrant array of colors they were accustomed to near the Gate. Heat and dry usually brought out the brightest of them while the rain and overcast had the present effect. Though the incipient Windsong was typically a harsh passing, the dismal cloud blanketing the sky was having an unexpected effect on the flora. Days of such uncharacteristic weather to the season were an extreme rarity and there had been too many following the change in stars. This was different. Where the haze came from was unclear and it was not something the Kutu had anticipated.

Another sleepless night came and went before the hunter-killers found themselves without the safety of thi to rest in. They were in untraveled lands now, the Drowned Hills, a soggy and bleak domain where the thi were scarce and the lowest ground was steeped in murky water. The tangled forests of thi and vine had transitioned more into weird and unseen mushrooms that mostly veered off northward. This was a meeting place between the three lands of Manti's Hai: the Sekhaadi Ni'ivitnem, the Drowned Hills, and the rocky barrens of Nikhaadi Ansax that covered the island's southern reaches.

The last of these was a perished region, a smoking ruin of gray and lifeless warrens left over from an unknown calamity. 'Ansax' was the name of one of the lower veils of Vaeba, describing an accursed state of being in which one was lost within their self and corrupted beyond recovery. It was not, however, entirely uninhabited. When Boa had led the many hundreds of kutliku out of Ellel, not all who were compelled to follow truly wished to serve under him. There was no conflict until, nine seasons after the arrival of the Mantichaena at Hanging Gate, the dissenters began to change. They became unruly, feral, hunting K'hizu and Mantichaena alike. Boa punished them, yet pain only made them more deranged. It was as though they were entered by thuell; smoldering from within as their feathers hardened and their wings contorted into gruesome appendages. At last, these "Infernals" were driven out of the Canimperium and into the desolation of the Dhai Nikhaadi Ansax. Intended to starve, they yet survived by hunting the borders of Ni'ivitnem, a constant threat to the Canimperium and any Mantichaena who ventured too far from home.

Keimas and his weary brood nested in the canopies for a short rest at the end of their tenth night, just as Laesis was creeping in from the far Hai. Thigolaia was obscured by a suffocating darkness and, finally, the cause of the air's thickness was clear. It was ash, mounding on their skin and sticking in their throats. Though surrounded by its quiet southerly passing they could not see its origin, though there was surely fire close by. Allende shrugged it off, coughing and shouting for everyone to stir and make ready. Keimas, however, was wary of the possible causes. It eased periodically, only to worsen a moment later. It quickly became obvious to him that it did not come from the forests. reaching so high above, it was surely being blown to them by the mountain winds from Nikhaadi Gao, harsher in the night when the air was cold and fast.

"Soto, to stars!" Keimas ordered, hacking.

Ever dutiful, Soto lashed her wings rapidly and shot straight upward until she completely disappeared into the gloomy dust. Keimas silently envied the dexterity of a kutliku, born for the air instead of being haphazardly constructed as Kutu were from two such different bodies. Even in a sea of smoke his hunt was elegantly suited to flying and hovering in any direction, any angle. With a decisive glare skyward, Keimas wondered to himself, *what makes it? If I am given more than any other Kutu, then why can I not do as they do?*

He could not fly vertically, though in thrusting himself up to a steep angle he beat with all his might and through the ash ascended. It became so dense as he rose that it abraded his skin. He closed his eyes, held his breath and fought through it. After an eternity, he felt the cool high wind clean his face and opened his eyes warily. Soto twirled nearby and cackled at him as she passed, mocking his repulsive appearance.

"Shut your sly trap! Your plumes are no prettier!" He smiled and took a refreshing breath before scanning the environment. The culprit was not hidden. Rather, its cracked and glowing face was staring proudly back at him. Broken Mountain. He had never seen such a mountain himself, only heard stories of occasional sightings at great distance.

"Sister, can you hear me?" He called to Miriena.

"*La*! What see you?" was the muffled reply.

"A Broken Mountain, bleeding fire and belching this wretched storm!"

"*Quo*? Is it really there?"

"I swear it, on my mother's head! The mountain is at the threshold of Nikhaadi Gao! It can be no other!" Keimas explained.

"*Golvulilt*! How near? How far?"

"*Minein,* I can barely make it out as it cloaks itself!"

Allende floated just below his wife, perturbed by the delay.

"What of Loi?" He hoarsely interjected. "Any sign of other

creatures?"

"No, noth..." Keimas searched only toward Hai, toward Thigolaia, his words immediately cut off by the panicked shriek of Soto. His feathers bristled as a sudden rush of wind signaled, they were not alone. He instinctively collapsed his wings and plunged, roaring to Soto "DIVE! DIVE!"

The two escaped into the shroud intact, narrowly avoiding a barrage of serrated talons that tilled the ash behind them. There was no screech, no beat of wings. With a fleeting glance over his shoulder, Keimas saw the outlines of another kutliku pride. Govan had faced these monsters, had spoken of them only when warning the pride never to venture too far south. Keimas knew little of what he faced, though he recognized the silence. It was just as Govan described it.

"*Uta*, what is!?" Allende shouted fearfully as Keimas and his hunt burst from the belly of the cloud.

Keimas gestured downward furiously, barely visible in the dark. "Infernals! *Malesaxekhaina* Infernals! Dive!"

Miriena and Allende's skin leapt as the ash overhead exploded downward in a flurry of tattered feathers and blood-stained scales. The reviled 'Infernal' kutliku were the color of stone, all but invisible against the flickering cloud of light-irradiated ash and pursuing the brightly hued hunter-killers with a sick hunger. At a glance there were at least eight of them, deformed and discolored, consumed by a hate that blackened their eyes.

"*Eina'tskana*! What hole of Vaeba did they come from!?" Allende wailed and followed.

"I don't know!" Keimas voice cracked. "The sky was clear! They came out of...keel!"

Glimpsing a ninth pursuer further ahead, Keimas dropped onto Allende and grabbed him by the wrist, hurling him down toward the ground. As a result, Keimas caught the tip of two front teeth across his back. It was a shallow wound, though he tumbled along a swinging neck and bounced off a bulging shoulder. Steadying himself quickly and using all his experience, he traced his attacker's sweeping route back up to him, leading others toward it before it could fully turn about. Two of the infernals fell for the ruse, smashing headlong into their own as Keimas deftly slipped under its belly.

There was neither cover nor hope of outflying the frenzied beasts for long, only shallow hills with the occasional thi atop.

"Break off! Spread them out!"

Well trained, even without supervision, the hunts knew the intent of the commands. Keeping within earshot of their Mantichaena they paired off, Bogh'thane shadowing Keimas in his partner's absence. It was impossible to sprint with fully unfurled wings, though they had a slight lead on their attackers. Keimas chanced a look back to gauge their odds and was not pleased with what he beheld.

"How many are they!?" Allende called.

After a disbelieving pause, Keimas' strained voice confirmed:

"They keep coming, as if out of the ground! Two score at the least!"

"*Khainsa*, how do we fight!?"

"I don't know! I don't know just…just keep going! We can lose them and get out of their territory!"

"WHAT territory!?" Allende squawked. "We're still in Boa's domain! Where is he? Where are the damned loyalists!?"

Keimas had no answer.

The Canimperium was strong but the infernals were devious. Unknown to Mantichaena, the infernals were growing in numbers as more and more of Boa's broke away to join the rebellion. They would never dare attack his strongholds, though they were always probing his borders. In Boa's name, these marauders were hunted and killed on sight. Infernal would do the same and worse to any other kutliku, regardless of their loyalties to Hanging Gate or to Boa. Those of Hanging Gate they especially despised. The bloody war that had raged along the borders of Ansax had thus far left the Mantichaena untouched. They had never been purposefully involved, and it seemed the infernals wanted only to hunt other kutliku.

This conflict had been a significant motivation for the Canimperium to seek Mantichaena masters. Boa had been winning the war but if the Infernal took the Mantichaena lands they would have much greater resources and one more avenue to attack the Canimperium from. The tides were changing now. None among the proud Canimperium could stop their fighters vanishing. Not only were the infernals' numbers growing, they were organized, attacking with greater force and in well planned raids.

It had been a subject of concern that, on the route here, the pride had not seen any loyalist patrols. Only now did they recognize the warning sign. They were far beyond the borders of the Gate and deep in Boa's land. That begged the question: Why were they themselves flying unchecked? There was no sky over Ni'ivitnem the Canimperium did not patrol. They had not seen a single one for the last four days.

Like crossing the threshold into a ruin, the fleeing Kutu raced over the last of the Drowned Hills and picked up speed on a long slope downward. The landscape before them fell flat, stretching on forever without a bush or flower. They were closer to Ansax than expected, in the very heart of the infernals' land. There was a thin mist rising from where the deeper waters of the hills dumped into deep, winding cracks. The sight was given an even more deathly appearance by the ash that blanketed the sky and allowed only sparse beams of eerie daylight to reach the ground.

There was only one hiding place: the tunnels where the infernals themselves nested.

"*Hawth*, warrens below! We can lose them in the fog!"

"*Ein zet'itka!*" Miriena argued. "Where's your head? We'll be trappe..."

Her hunt, Shisi, suddenly veered away from her as black jaws snapped between them. She then reconsidered, shouting "...Shisi, ground!"

One after another the Kutu filed into one of the uncountable wounds marring the inhospitable terrain, many of which were flooded to their brims with a dense vapor. Though they tried, the pride could not stay together. The corridors were too numerous and too obscured for their formation to hold. Scattering down different paths, they sank deeper into the warrens as the heavy thud of infernals landing echoed down to them. Each moved quickly to find a hiding place, any dark alcove that could hold them. They could no longer hear their own, separated and grossly outnumbered as the thumping and scraping of more outcast kutliku arose.

Allende, crammed alongside Ghrainegal into a damp tunnel in the ceiling of an overhang, could make out each movement on the other side of a thin wall.

Keimas, Soto and Bogh'thane had found an unreliable refuge, a deep pit at the bottom of the path they had taken. There was ample space for them, though their only safeguard was the fog hiding them from view. Through it, they could make out long necks craning out of the walls. They waited, watched, and it seemed the walls were closing in as dozens of wings noiselessly emerged.

The way the infernals stalked them was unnatural. They did not speak to each other, nor did they appear to follow a leader. One would look at another for a moment, and the other would move suddenly, as though they shared a mind. After such a communication, one of them dropped from overhead and fell to the chasm floor, yet it did not land on its talons. With its wings tightly curled, the hardened feathers of their tips acted as feet, scattering a top layer of gravel as they held the body off the ground. Like a beast of the land, it lumbered forward, head and neck drooping with the weight of ugly growths where its bones seemed to spill out. Sagging low and searching the ground, it would periodically lurch toward a wall when pebbles tumbled from the motion of its brethren. Kutliku were not known for their sense of smell, making sound and sight both their keenest and, presently, their most useless. Similarly, none had an easy temperament. Even loyalists and those bonded to Kutu were impulsive and aggressive. Hiding was not in their nature.

Bogh'thane and Soto were becoming restless, their feathers bristling as the thundering wingfalls passed no further overhead than Soto's span in flight. Keimas held a hand under each of their throats, keeping them attuned to his will and soothing their nerves. Apex hunters ever, they knew the value of patience, and so they waited the search out.

They did not have to wait long. As soon as the near danger had passed there came a single, piercing shriek: Ghrainegal, beating his wings with all his might as he shot into the sky and back toward Ni'ivitnem. Allende was close behind his hunt, though his heading was further into Thaun, the way they had come. In the same instant, the infernals rose in ire, giving chase on pounding wings and scrambling up the walls until they could take flight. After a deafening rush to pursue the easy prey, the last had gone and the misty warrens were silent.

Keimas felt his bones creak, his limbs resisting the idea of emerging as he willed himself up the walls of the hole. Creeping over the ledge, he could see no sign of any stragglers. He hastily gestured to the hunts and led them to slink along the chasm floor, slow and steady so as not to disturb their cover.

"Keimas," came a hushed voice from nearby.

Miriena was peeking through a crack between two channels with an excited smile, while her eyes darted about in alarm.

Keimas hurried to meet her, shrugging in confusion and pointing toward Allende's foolish gamble.

"It's their feathers," Miriena loudly whispered. "That's how they caught us. Their feathers have calcified somehow; they plummet faster, but ascend slower. Come! My beautiful idiot gives us time!"

It was a bold but dangerous move, Keimas thought as he trailed Miriena and Shisi up the north-heading trenches. He could not help his worry at the idea of Allende trying to outrun such a number. His friend could fly higher and faster than their predators, but it would be a slaughter if he could not gain enough distance before reaching his vertical limit. With luck, he could outmaneuver them back in the forests.

After a long flight toward the Thaun, once again flying low among the Drowned Hills, Keimas hailed Miriena to land. The remaining pride gathered on a westerly slope, nervously eying the smoke overhead for danger.

"What troubles you?" Miriena huffed. "Clearly not Loi's lead on us."

Keimas was deep in thought, looking between her and the few infernals he could see flying east. Allende had indeed given them an escape, but without the Canimperium to cull the invaders he could not survive long.

"Sister," he said dourly, "My demon knew our prey, shared with me how powerful he truly is."

"You said he is…has taken your form, *la*?"

"In a manner, though he remains divine. In contemplating him, I fear to know…what harm would such a god inflict on the Canimperium if they engaged him?"

Miriena only scowled, refusing to believe his implications.

Regardless of the respect Boa had for the Mantichaena's abilities he was still a proud ruler, and a strict one. No Kutu should be able to cross his province without being sighted, and a meeting with Loi could have been deadly even to the Jiou of kutliku. The worst prospect of all was if Loi was similarly tethered to Ephielipax and his creations. Could he assimilate the powers of other kutliku and Kutu just as Keimas could? What if the entire Canimperium had fallen to him? If he had claimed the essence of nine-hundred kutliku he would be unassailable.

"We can only hope he went unnoticed," Keimas mumbled, comforting Soto as she nuzzled him, "Nevertheless, we must act. The infernals roam unchecked and your husband faces them alone."

"He can fend for himself. We must carry on."

Miriena's voice was weak, her limbs quivering as she struggled to stand. Keimas had taken too much of her. Soto and the other hunts seemed no different, their wings and heads hanging and their eyes glazed from exhaustion. Keimas, on the other hand, had never been more alive. Feeling the power of his brethren whirling inside him, he felt equal responsibility for their lives; something he could not justify stealing any longer.

"My friend," he said at last, "It is time for you to go your own way."

Soto growled disagreeably beside him and Miriena protested on both of their behalf.

"*Minuein*! We need our force united, now more than ever!"

With a placating hand on his shoulder, Keimas calmly shared a plan.

"This disaster is my responsibility. Your husband is yours and, united with him, you must serve a higher purpose than a hunt. Death has come to Boa's realm and the kutlikugoli needs us now just as much as we need him. We are only a few days from Thigolaia and I have no more illusions about attaining it before Loi. Anama may fall, and I fear what Loi may become with her blood on his hands. I would rather give my life delaying him than sacrifice yours in vain. You take the hunts and find Allende, keep him safe and, as one, seek out Boa. It is not far to Windchaser Pinnacle. Go quietly there, along the forest floor you must, *la*. Find out what has happened to the loyalists and to Boa. Any that live, implore them to avenge me, to avenge their goddess, to kill the undying and save all our kind. I may fail alone but an alliance between Kutu and Canimperium will not."

"And if Boa has fallen?" Miriena lamented.

"Then let righteous duty be forgotten and protect our home to the last. Soar on wings and, to save all we love, die."

Miriena was a Kutu, no different than any other. Their vow was to protect Hauan Etain, and so it would be done, against all odds and any opposition.

"My friend, my brother, you are mysterious," Miriena said with a heavy smile. "One day you must tell me all; these secrets kept from the pride about what you have become." She then took his arm and kept his hope alive. "Boa will be found. We will join with the carnivorous *Jiou,* and you will not be alone in facing the god."

Keimas could not share her optimism, though he admired it with a smile.

"I would not doubt your word. These hunts trust you. Lead them home to their father."

Without another word, Miriena wearily rose with a call to the rest of the pride and glided away to Ni'ivitnem. Only Soto remained, waiting stubbornly as Keimas tensely searched the sky around them. With her feathers in his hand Keimas scratched her affectionately, then turned and pushed her gently.

"*Vusreis - my true heart*, you go too."

Soto warbled sadly and resisted.

"Go on," Keimas insisted with a sharp gesture. "We will not be lost to each other. Your family needs you now."

She shook her head and wings irately as she lifted off, screeching angrily and forcing herself to follow the others.

It broke Keimas' heart to see her go, though he could not keep watching her decline at his side. They needed time to heal from his influence and he could only pray they found their strength again in the Canimperium.

He turned purposefully toward the Hai. Though the horizon over the dismal hills was nothing but black ash and freezing wind, he knew Thigolaia loomed not far beyond. Having taken all he could from his bloodline, he would have to face the journey's end as he was.

CHAPTER 16: THE BURDEN OF KNOWLEDGE

U nder stone and sand where the Tau thirsted, there still lived the sluggish brood of Mearnum who had become one with the desert. Each day they dug and toiled over their science under the guidance of the learned physic Gaialja. It was a peaceful life, learning to master the materials most plentiful in their environment and hungry for new discoveries.

The moan of the wind over the dunes echoed through the winding tunnels of their den and told them it was too dangerous to go out. A storm raged, inhaling sand to belch it across the colorless waste and bury what little vegetation was left. The hot and dry season was manageable, but the wetter seasons made every day a curse. Though rare, a rain blown in from the sea would turn the desert into a marsh and sending turbid rivers down into their home. This was one such accursed day, and the village in the ground was hard at work keeping the floodwaters under control. The gutters they had carved along each wall served their purpose, though it was a constant chore of stick and paw to keep the mud from piling up and clogging them. No research was done while all were employed with moving the runoff along to its destination: cavern openings which ran deeper than the inhabitants were comfortable venturing.

Gaialja did not concern herself with this menial labor. She had been in an uncomfortable funk since sending Keimas to meet her prophet. He never came back, and Golgamet had been silent ever since; no call for her, not even a breath from the dark passage. Despite her concern, she knew the charge she had been given was complete. Still, would the kutliku-man never come out? Had he and Golgamet departed? Perhaps perished?

To distract herself from thoughts that would lead to no action, she kept herself hard at work. Her experiments gave her purpose in life, yet her heart was not in it this day. On muscle memory she continually took samples from Uru, her captive thuell, by carving into the crystalline sand that encased it and, with the tip of a needle, drawing the tiniest amount of its flesh. With a listless curiosity she watched as Uru tried to expand into the hole she left, almost pitying the thing as she cauterized it with a burning stick. She glanced down at that flake of its body she held, already smoldering in the faint torchlight, and briefly felt she was wasting her time. Nonetheless, she carried it to a nearby table and set it in a stone cup of water. This test was one she had performed countless times and was becoming increasingly vexing.

The flake did nothing until she rested the tip of her tool in a candle flame to burn away the infectious remnants, then quickly pricked the heel of her hand with it. A drop of blood emerged and fell noiselessly into the water, giving the flake impossible life. It moved to touch the blood, crackled with streaks of dark red energy as it did. It aimlessly grew outward in twisting tendrils, searching for more.

Gaialja backed away, her eyes assessing the growth as it grew out from the cup. It had always gone straight for her candle. This time she had placed five around it and Uru wanted them all. As it crawled out of the water, stretching in five directions. Each of its appendages, as they came within seven fingers of a flame, would ignite. Still, they did not stop. Their burning demise lit up Gaialja's face until the last of the sample crumbled to ash around the cup. She leaned over it, muttering to herself as she repeated the same notes already taken on the process:

"Water, clean and clear as before. Complete growth of one grain in response to one drop of blood was limited to approximately seven handfuls. In theory, the growth limit appears dependent on the weight of blood relative to the weight of the grain."

Her eyes were narrowed angrily at one of the candles' flame. It seemed darker, taking a moment to shine bright again, though its size never changed. Such was the case for all of them as far as she could discern.

Her skin crawled and her bones leapt out of her when she heard a mocking voice in her ear, so close she could feel its sticky breath:

"You do love tormenting that thing."

She knew the voice well enough, slowly looking over her shoulder and expecting to see its face. It was there, though not as close as expected.

Tzychala was standing awkwardly at the entrance, grinning. As usual, he was using some trickery to frighten and disarm her.

"I enjoy none of this," Gaialja contested. "It hurts to watch."

"*Quos?*" Tzychala wondered as he neared and joined her in staring at the heap of ash.

Gaialja watched him from the corner of her eye. He was always so cloistered and furtive. She knew he was studying her just as she studied Uru, almost in the same way.

"It makes me feel like a monster," she finally grumbled.

"*Quos?*" He repeated.

"Over and over, I watch this thing be born only to crawl to its death. I feel like I am…creating life in a way, knowing it will experience nothing but death."

Tzychala nodded, his gaze never leaving the ashes.

"You feed it, it flourishes and just as quickly perishes. *Eina,* is that not the beauty of a child? Is there a difference between a fleeting moment or a thousand seasons? Between a parent and a god?"

"Parents need not survive to see the deaths of their children," Gaialja lamented.

This was an old though in her mind, superimposing the pattern of the thuell's life on her own now as she had often before. However, it was not that morbid comparison that frightened her. Tzychala had haunted her often, claiming to be the left hand of Loi as he observed her and praised her work. Golgamet had warned her of the red creature's coming and assured her he was vital in delivering the winged man to them. The deed was done now and there was no reason for Tzychala to be here. Despite her faith that her god's will had been followed, Gaialja knew she was being lied to. She felt compelled to show respect for the messenger of Loi but, the more she experimented with her captive thuell, the more suspicious she became of him. Her work had led to an unlikely conclusion, a burning question. It was the answer that she dreaded as she touched the ash.

"This thing is part of you...somehow. I know it."

Tzychala stared at her, his utter astonishment clear despite his blindfold.

"How...could you possibly..."

"One of them grew bigger," she continued tensely. "Just one. I fed it too much. It survived the light for far longer. Show me your eyes." He did nothing, and so she immediately demanded again. "Show me, servant of Loi."

After a moment, an eye on Tzychala's shoulder crept open, blinked and turned to her. Its unmistakable appearance confirmed her suspicion.

"With so much blood," Gaialja accused, pointing to Tzychala's face, "Uru managed to grow an eye. THAT eye."

Tzychala wondered for a moment if it would be best to kill her. He had put himself in her path, encouraging her insatiable mind in its pursuit of things it should not know. It would be a waste to end such an intellect. She was unstoppable, her perceptions beyond any other.

Gaialja sensed his bristling thoughts but did not fear them. His body told her she was right. She had lifted the shroud from the greatest discovery of her life.

"It is part of all of us," she extrapolated, part of her hoping she was wrong. "This thing they call the thuell is what we all came from, the original flesh that became me, you, even the gods."

"How can you know that!?" Tzychala blurted.

Gaialja was getting teary-eyed, overcome by the memory of watching her subjects crawl to their deaths.

"It chases the light. When it leaves the cup, it goes straight toward the candle. It's not mindless, not a disease...it wants something. The light kills it, yet it can't resist getting close. Tell me why." She waited only a moment, then reached desperately to take one of the demon's clawed fingers in her trembling hand and whispered "Please…I need to know."

Her singular passion tugged at Tzychala's heart. They were both obsessed, needful for one thing and tormented in their pursuit of it. He felt in that moment like killing her would serve them both; protecting his secrets while sparing her a life in which her mind could never be satisfied. At last, he smiled a bit, curled his finger around hers and spoke kindly to her.

"You are the wisest mortal I have ever met. The answer is not in my words. It is in the truth you have found."

Gaialja hated seeing herself in such a creature, though his existence was all the truth she needed. Still clutching him, she stared at the remains of her experiment.

"It is not meant to exist as it does; alone, in darkness. It and the light are meant to be one but…somehow, they have become too different. Like a *fuilts'khizi* it is drawn to a missing piece of itself, yet the pieces no longer recognize one another."

Tzychala released her and turned away, savoring the eloquence of her words.

"They can if they are born together, grow together. Such is the root of all that lives. What you are seeing here is one of the darknesses that cannot be saved, born apart from the light and unable to know it."

He waited in silence, listening closely as Gaialja's heartbeat steadied. He needed a moment after feeling the blood pulsing in her fingers, resisting the sweet memories of its addictive taste. Somewhat distracted as he battled a demon of his own, he still felt for the woman. Then, after leaving her to her thoughts for a moment, he turned back and tried to give her some worldly comfort.

"How are the young ones? I trust they will survive."

"They…they are fine," Gaialja said, frustrated but willing to digress.

As she spoke, she gestured to the back of her workshop. There lay Gogol and Haerulf in a pained and uneasy sleep on a makeshift bed. They were heavily bandaged and in obvious pain, delirious from the effects of one of Gaialja's mixtures.

"Can you divine what happened to them?" Tzychala asked.

"I know little. They cannot stay awake for long and have difficulty speaking. It seems they were chasing the kutliku-man you brought me, though clearly, they are inexperienced. One of my gatherers found them, a full day toward Thaun and half-buried in the sand."

"Understandable. The daytime heat here is…"

"No," Gaialja corrected with concern. "The burns on their skin are not from exposure, and their wrists are bruised and broken. My only theory is they were captured, tortured, then left to die. From their condition I would say they were discarded around three days ago."

"At least they did not catch their prey," Tzychala sighed.

"Not from what I saw. Keimas arrived in perfect health. *Mineina,* good health, at least.

Tzychala nodded knowingly, though he was piqued by the curious misfortunes of the two youths. He had not explored the Thonsfa himself. His only insight was the memories of those who died in it. Through them he had seen only sand and thirst, excepting the comical sight of the Galaila fleeing across it and falling prey to the thuell. He was not aware of any other village on this side of the island, and it made no sense to him that Mantichaena would capture their own. Unfortunately, there was no time to satisfy his curiosity. There were more pressing concerns at hand, so he spoke quickly to keep Gaialja's attention.

"Has Golgamet spoken of me since Keimas' arrival?"

"Not a word of you or anything else," she said. "He has not summoned me since before that day."

"And you have told no one of our dealings?"

"None. You were quite clear," she reassured.

"Then I absolve you of your duty to Loi."

"*Quouein*!? No! What have I done to be discarded!?"

"Nothing but what you were told. *Aia*, you have been of incomparable service but there is no more need. Live long and revel in your work."

"But Loi…and Golgamet?" Gaialja said drearily.

Tzychala hid a smirk.

"Golgamet's function has been served as well."

Gaialja sat despondently, eyes turgid with pain and fixed on her demon. She felt no satisfaction for her obedience, no pride in it. Nothing was revealed. Her reward was uncertainty and abandonment.

Tzychala silently observed her for a moment, then swiftly moved to leave her.

Noticing the speed of his stride she leapt up and gave chase, nipping at his back angrily.

"Wait! What am I to do!? What was Keimas brought here for!? I did everything you and Golgamet asked without question! You owe me answers!"

She continued to interrogate him as he led her down the short tunnel she had taken Keimas down when he had visited, to the mysterious room she loved so much. She was taken aback upon realizing where she had been led.

Tzychala stopped therein, marveling at the black archway. After a moment of reflection, he faced her with a sneer.

"You just saw what happens when the flesh is drawn to the candle, yet you can never be sated unless I show you the depths of the cup."

Gaialja's throat clenched at his reprisal, shivering as Tzychala stepped backward toward the arch. In his presence, it was finally awake. She knew every facet and imperfection in this stone, though now it moved as if liquid, its surface rippling, and the lettering in its foundation pulsing with the same bloody light of the dying thuell.

"In the eyes of gods and demons…" she wondered in fear, "…I am but a fool and a beggar." She became fixated on Tzychala, falling to her knees and nearly worshiping him. "H-how could I not s-see it? You were right in front of me. You CAME to me…you are the original, the old one whose language is on all our tongues!"

Tzychala chuckled weakly, standing akimbo near the arch and clicking his claws.

"No…no I am not the first. Certainly not. The first was my mother." Now more somber, he looked slightly over his shoulder and warned her "We are only herdsmen, inheritors; myself, my sister and our little brother." Inhaling deeply the stale air and scent of blood, Tzychala closed his eyes and visualized the words engraved at his feet. He knew them well. "Gaialja, so wise and powerful…would you like to look into the cup?"

Gaialja stood shakily, crouching as she backed away, never taking her eyes from the demon's head. She wanted to know everything, to look on the most elusive mysteries of this world and others, though she knew that knowledge gained without hardship was gained at high cost. The way the once-solid arch squirmed behind Tzychala filled her with trepidation and, for the first time, she understood that she did not belong here.

"N…no." She finally whispered.

"No?" Tzychala sounded surprised.

"*Mineina,* perhaps one day I will be a goddess, worthy of the grand veil, but not yet. I am not ready to see what you offer."

Relieved, Tzychala gestured for her to leave. She obliged eagerly and he gradually followed, the undulating stone becoming still again the further he retreated from it.

"This is good," he sighed. "I am…pleased and humbled by you. There are some things which are evil, even to those born in them. To have truth is good, but to know when truth is beyond your reach is a piece of wisdom."

Gaialja could find no more words for this being, this ominous harbinger who appeared to be the very manifestation of all the unknowable things she yearned for. Her jaw tightened and she found herself in an inescapable bow, quivering as he brushed past her and stopped at her back.

"Gaialja," he droned, "I know the desire you feel for a higher purpose. You love your god, and I allowed you to hold onto that love because I needed you. If you seek truth, you musts accept that which that will set you free from bondage."

Gaialja turned, keeping low so her eyes remained obsequiously upward. She waited hungrily, believing as a physic that his words would bring her enlightenment beyond her wildest dreams. Instead, he destroyed her.

"Your god is a lie, traitor, murderer, slaver, and thief. As I am ashamed of the bloody stones behind this door, so are the stars ashamed of the violent son who calls himself Loi."

"*Minuein…*" Gaialja hissed, rising to meet him. "Liar! Who are you, monster, to tell me the father of nations is not my worthy god! You said you served him! What do you take me for!? The only evil the stars shame is YOU! Why would you say such a thing! If he were really so terrible then you would not have led me in his name. If he was our blessing, then you would not speak of him in this way unless…unless you have been lying to me all along."

"*Prostas,* woman, you must hear me…"

"Hea…hear you!? Do you hear yourself!? I don't care what you can teach me. I don't want anything from you. You are horrible. Horrible! How could you use me like this, and all the while tell me I am serving the god of the holy sky. What has this really been for!? ANSWER ME!"

Tzychala's heart sank, though he was enamored by how easily she harnessed the rich emotions of her soul. She was full of passion. He could see now that he had done her wrong by manipulating those passions and could not be absolved without the truth. He did not condemn, only affirmed how right she was.

"There was something I needed. I had no regard for what lay in my path and I have only recently learned to consider the cost of my mistakes before I make them."

Gaialja was unmoved by his confession.

"Leave me," she said, disheartened by what her controllers had made her and uninterested in hearing more lies about her religion.

Tzychala wanted more, perhaps even to resolve their conflict. However, seeing her injury, he knew what he wanted was of little import. She would not pity or understand him. Perhaps there was something noble, a sublime mortal vulnerability in walking away and accepting that not all wrongs could be righted.

"Perhaps, one day," Tzychala mumbled as he stepped back toward a smoking portal that opened on him, "I can make amends for what I have done."

Gaialja closed her eyes and shook her head, too hateful to form any coherent response.

The demon still lingered, his head and one arm still hanging from the black hole. He felt such a need to say something he knew would not bring any happiness or closure. It was only knowledge, the truth, which he knew had value to her:

"If you care to know…the zealot who took your husband is gone. She will never mislead another again."

Gaialja went to sit against the wall. To his surprise, she did speak after a pause, though still not meeting his eyes.

"How?"

Tzychala looked at her table, felt how precarious his own existence was as he prepared Maengir for a war between the mortal, the divine and the damned.

"She reached the candle."

Gaialja was infuriated by his evasive repetition of the idiom, maintaining silence as she tried to understand it. Tzychala slipped away before she could collect herself, expecting that she would fly into a rage. Instead, she felt some peace of mind, one eye tearing as she weighed the penalties for her belief in the demon and the infinite possible consequences for what they had done to the kutliku man. Unconsciously, she muttered "Thank you", then continued to sit in silence for a long while thereafter. She did not want any more answers. Her appetite was sated. The only things she cared about now were her own people. There was no need to concern herself with Bandta anymore. If Takinoxote had fallen, then either the man had found what he sought, failed and would soon return home to the Thonsfa, or had perished with his mistress.

Visitors were rare in her laboratory, but she would be approached from time to time. Ignoring gentle inquiries from her subjects, many of whom visited her in her melancholy and were disturbed by her state, she remained in a contemplative trance until nightfall. At last she was exhausted by trying to understand the forces which she had allowed to shape her life, and small chuckles escaped her as she started to let go of everything. She stood lazily, shambling through her workshop and taking inventory of all her accomplishments, the work of a lifetime. One by one she slowly pushed many of them to fall on the floor. What had her curiosity really done for her? Was she complete? Had she done any good for the world or even herself? She only left a few of the workbenches in disarray before continuing coldly into the bowels of the cavern, no longer caring if she disturbed the prophet she loved so dearly. Lies or no, the demon's foresight had been proven correct time and time again. He had kept her spirit alive with his reassurances that she was doing right, fanning her faith and giving her something to keep living for. Perhaps he had given the prophet something worth dying for.

Without carrying fire, she had only the dwindling light of her own room as she walked the winding passage. The oil did not ignite, nor did the wind sound of Golgamet's waking. As she entered the hallowed audience chamber, she stood impotent among the pillars and walls. The myriad expressions in their surfaces were quiet now, eternally carved in the rock that once moved with such excitement. The grand face on the far wall was the only one that appeared at rest, its eyes and mouth closed and downcast. It was a small consolation to see no pain in the effigy, as though its soul left of its own accord. Though there was no proof, Gaialja wanted to believe her teacher's passing had been his choice. However, doing so meant she could not hate the illusive Tzychala so much. Her studies had in fact benefited her, for now she had the clairvoyance to see past the injuries he inflicted. He had manipulated her to his own ends. She had manipulated Keimas just the same, for though she believed herself a servant of the divine she knew nothing of what she had done. She made her choices just as her prophet had, and she could only survive the confusion of her own mortality by doing as he did, facing the consequences. If she was still alive, then her mind and her destiny were still her own.

She retraced her steps, returning to where her argument with Tzychala began. All the way she wrung her hands, feeling alive again as the potential for absolute disaster loomed over her absurd scheme.

There was nothing good about knowledge or faith. She used them for herself. She was a physic, a master of sciences, one who sought understanding so as to feel control in an uncontrollable world. Somehow, she had never felt so powerless. Making sense of Maengir required science but finding her purpose in it required faith. Both of these were formidable in her, and she felt it was time to test the truth of who she was.

She emerged from her reflections to find herself staring up at the black archway, defiantly motionless, as if it sensed a predator in her. Her short claw already rested on her wrist, twitching as she tried not to imagine what horrors she was about to experience. Something was left imprinted on her from Tzychala; an understanding gleaned from confirming Tzychala's relation to the structure. Whether faith or fact, she felt a new understanding sprouting.

"The same blood...the same flesh..." she whispered, closing her eyes and making her peace with this world before likely leaving it forever. "Open this path to the fallen of the field, open this road to twenty-three eyes," she stammered frightfully, remembering how excited and powerful she had felt when teaching the inscriptions to Keimas. "Give us to the dark below. Mother governs child, child governs the blood..." something inside her screamed for her to stop but a strange, euphoric despair stuffed it back down, freeing her mind from consequences as she finally understood the meaning of the carvings. "...Open this road and wake the city of the dead. Open the twenty-three paths of the outworld and...fill the drowning pool."

There was only the last word, a word so much like 'Open', but in meaning so different. It was isolated, trailing at the end of the verses as if it was a sentence of its own, but it was nothing. She had misunderstood it. It was not meant to be read. Words were not the key. Words were not the connection between her, the monsters she studied and the one that studied her. Whatever they shared was written in their blood.

She punctured her wrist with a claw, held it over the symbol and let it slowly fall, muttering across the veil to whatever eldritch denizens abided in its depths.

"...Show me who you are."

Though the air remained cold and still, her eyes beheld a storm the moment her blood struck. The arch itself became a window into the unimaginable. The shapes within were something she could not see, only feel. Their colors were all black, yet she knew their difference in seeing them for the first time. It was as though her senses were useless, perceiving the world beyond the stone like a terrible feeling, a vision only her flesh and blood were familiar with.

She blinked, winced and reached out, her mind unable to comprehend what she was experiencing. She could not tell if she had taken a single step or walked forever, yet she knew she was past the edge of life. All she could feel was unfamiliar; the pained and screaming absence of light.

The Windsong Star had shifted gradually back to deep sky, despite the natural time of its season having come. The Longhand, which it had replaced, seemed disinterested in taking prominence. There appeared to be no seasonal advent to replace them, as though all Nhi'Thaun were loath to abide by their pattern of the past. In its departure it remained the sky's light and, by its brilliance, the silvery gleam of Lindu enhanced the night in Hanging Gate and made Mantichaena more energetic.

On nights such as this, every hall would likely ply their trade straight on to the following morning. Nesh would gather in the fields, Gazan would hold tournaments and training, and Voddace would provide prayer and ceremony for the grieving. Tault never slept. Its Lugu would dig, drink and shout like any other night. Ms'egol was likewise a bustle of activity as its students endeavored to keep their focus on their research while there was still so much turmoil in their home.

Naguza's health was still in question, though he no longer visibly suffered, and his condition had stabilized. Hero that he now was, concern for him lasted without knowledge of Raphenie's intervention. However, more were motivated to be the outstanding student who cured him than for intrinsic valuation of his health.

The greater tension in Ms'egol came from the discomfort at being quartered with the Gothic school. Trust had fallen, to be raised only slightly by the return of the Iron Rain, as the untrustworthy and dangerous Witchcrafters still resided in the old halls of the Sanctum.

There was no work to be done by the school which had no master. Bolvide the Kubernu, the Iron Song, always kept the other Witchcrafters in line in Artimecian's absence. Regrettably, with the order in shambles, had no call to lead nor an end to strive for. They rotted in Artimecian's chambers, feeling themselves captive and forced to watch as the pieces of their dismantled tools were carted away to gather dust in some forgotten storage. It was, to them, as though the Classicists were robbed of their abacus and mortar, or the Romantics their spiritual sparring partners.

Candlelight had always been an effective focus for the Gothics. It was a quiet comfort to calm their minds when their bodies could withstand no more. In the dormitory of their late master, they had set only one such light in the room, sitting together to contemplate the unique impartiality of the flame to any worry, even its own existence.

Many had no family, and those that did could not bear to leave their fellows alone. The Sanctum was their family, even if their adoptive father was no longer with them. It was a matter of principle; solidarity was the core of their order's ability to endure their grisly rituals. After so long without any but each other to depend on, the spark of another witchcrafter's skin was the only love they knew. Without the Iron Sanctum, their powers would wither and die, their joy in life with it.

Whether or not there was truth in their upbringing, they held tight to their teachings; the absolute necessity of the Gothic practice as the final defense against the thuell. This belief was only strengthened by the triumph of the lovers Rain. All that remained was to see if it was enough to earn them a new beginning.

There was a startling rustle of wind across the window. Against the velvet backdrop of star-enflamed dusk, a crimson specter lurked just outside, hidden yet presenting itself. Only those students facing it took notice. At their arousal it vanished and there came a soft knock at the door.

Bolvide rose slothfully, though even in haste he would not have been able to respond before the door creaked and Tzychala intruded.

The cloth over his eyes he had tightened, and at the river's edge taken time to wash the dust from his fur. He drank it as well to refresh himself and remove some of the black slime from his fangs. He had made efforts to be presentable, to soften the reaction to his first appearance to these young people.

Hearing rumor of him was not enough to prepare the Gothics for seeing him in the flesh. Nonetheless, Bolvide spoke for them in welcoming the stranger without fear.

"You are the man from an unspoken land, of whom the enchanters speak of," he said matter-of-factly.

Like an affected thespian, Tzychala curtsied limply and plucked a book from Artimecian's nightstand, held it to his nose and cleared his throat.

"And you, oh seekers of inspired power, are those souls for which I have journeyed out of the lands of which you speak, so as to seek a soul to call my own by virtue of service to you."

To Tzychala's supreme satisfaction, Iron Finger Minciel smiled a little at his mock drama. He sharply bowed for her, tossed the book aside and leaned hard on the nightstand. He was truly relaxed, effectively disarming the class with his practiced eloquence.

"My tongue is not quite silver yet. I hope it does not impede your understanding that I wish to come as a friend."

"I hear it was you who brought Keimas back," Iron Fist Aten growled, rising with a hand on Minciel's shoulder. "*Minein,* yet our brothers are absent. What did you do to them?"

"*Einla aia,*" Tzychala began with precocious thoughts in his ever-changing mind. "Allow me to disperse your worry before I endure more threats on my life. I have no aims to disparage your brethren, but Keimas' death would have been a grievous mistake on their part, securing them a fate equal to your disgraced Primarch. Be assured, I have done no harm to them in order to spare him, nor did they confront him as intended. They are very much alive, resting and likely to be in good health soon."

The company all stood with Bolvide in succession, each with their own brand of excitement that the Iron Wind endured.

"Where?" Ronsha demanded. "In Thonsfa?"

"Indeed so," he said. "Perhaps you have heard tell of the Tau Mantichaena? They are as real as yourselves, at home in the waste, dabbling practitioners of both the Veil and its sciences. Like you, they wish only to study and grow, led by one of the most noble of your kind. It is with them that your comrades now abide."

"Are they coming home?" Rashala hoped.

"Should they?" Tzychala asked, clearly anticipating their thinking. "Would this be their life, or have they found the one of which such talent is deserving? Should you follow the thi'zech beyond the high gate, you will find your brothers and their hosts willing to let you study as you see fit among them. Is that not desirable over an impoverished station which may, on any day, become extinct?"

Bolvide looked to his peers. With meager exception, they seemed inclined to give the proposal a chance.

"Our future here…" Bolvide grimly began.

"What future?" Tzychala insisted. "How many of you would shrink into your family trades – to be as gardeners or masons or makers of your funny potions – yet still be leered upon as students of a traitor?"

A tearful hush took the room. Bolvide made sure to secure the willing eyes of every witchcrafter. Receiving them all, he felt alone in his resistance to abandoning their home. He clicked his jaw thoughtfully a moment, scrutinizing the imp much harder.

"Do you have a name?" He grumbled.

"To the many I remain unnamed," Tzychala sighed, "Yet you, my soon departed, I would be introduced as Hiwult Utan Tzychala."

Bolvide smirked, both intrigued and skeptical.

"Hiwult? I've not heard of such a place."

"It is nearer to home than you might think," Tzychala replied with a similar smile, subtly tapping a claw on the floor.

"Then how did you come to Manti?" Bolvide pressed.

"I swam,"

"*Ueina,* from which horizon?"

"All of them."

Tzychala said this with a flourish, holding out his hand and conjuring a flicker of his red light. Like a parlor trick to dazzle children, the similarity of the power he controlled to that of the Gothics raised their interest markedly.

"The veil is my horizon, as it is to your brothers, and the folk they have found sanctuary among. I implore you, seek them out and together pursue your practice. It is your purpose, and when the future brings calamity to the simple, they will recognize you as the heroes you must become."

Bolvide was becoming as thrilled as his fellows. Despite Tzychala's appearance, it seemed he was a student himself, a guide to the Veil's secrets who made a genuine offer. The new arch-witchcrafter looked once more to his class, sighed his acceptance, and nodded to Tzychala. While he could not shake the memories of his brothers being sent to kill a demon, they stirred only a desire to see those brothers again.

"That word of you which I have heard, hushed though it may be, is spoken only in admiration, curiosity, and a fearful reverence. While I am loathe to admit it, it is these things I feel when you speak. Meet my eye to speak again, and you will have my faith."

Tzychala's eyes moved nervously behind his blind, yet he did reluctantly remove it to reveal their fractured darkness. Bound to Bolvide, his focus was entirely between them as he promised his intention:

"I swear to you on what little is dear to me, a family as deep of blood as you together are of mancy, that I desire the betterment of life for all who are blessed with it. I have transgressed, yet in service you I make one of many amends. I earnestly aim to reunite you with your kind and to part you from those who would cage your glory or do you harm."

Bolvide gestured for the dousing of the candle, then for all idle hands to busy themselves.

"*Ein'uein khonzeulfilt,* gather water and food from the terrace stores, as much as you can carry. Do it quietly and we will leave under cover of night. The Wind will not be left alone, and we will not remain where we are unwelcome."

He turned to find Tzychala gone as the light was blown out. For a moment he stood in darkness as the last inhabitants of the school made ready to leave, scurrying out among the shadows of Ms'egol to find what could be snatched unseen. Thereafter he laid their expected route in the dust of the floor tile, answered questions, counted supplies, filling the role of a needed leader with a troubled mind.

The midnight light was unfortunate for their escape, though it was inevitable they would be discovered. Some could not resist the urge to bid farewell to friends. Perhaps they would spill details of their destination as well. It would make no difference. If they were missed, it would not be until after they had gone.

These were Bolvide's thoughts while waiting by the cliffs on the seaward side of Voddace with those who had no one to miss, practically born and raised in the Sanctum. He was quiet as they whispered excitedly to one another about adventure and discovery. Like an outsider he listened to their hopeful yarning and found in himself the smallest dream of what may come. Clearly the danger of the Tau was no more, unless they were all of them misled. Who was he to know what awaited them in the land of ruin and death? Adventure and discovery were certain. He only questioned how long they would last before reality caught up to them.

Once gathered, the Gothics' journey was underway.

Bolvide did look back once. Only when leaving Hanging Gate's city limit, presumably forever, did he feel a weight in his steps. He was trained to let go, to live without the comforts of home, and so had little trouble saying goodbye to home itself. However, his eye did catch the red glint of Tzychala's hair in Lindu's showering light. The imp was wandering along the river, seemingly as lost in the night as those he drove out.

"Be well, demon," Bolvide muttered to himself with a smile. He lazily saluted the stranger, then fell in with his outcasts. Down the road of many statues, beyond the ruined Gate and the unforgiving Tau, he would ever contemplate the mystery which was Tzychala.

Tzychala was done for the day. Mentally sore from straightening out the travesty his existence had become, and haphazardly trying to help bring balance to the lives upset by himself or other forces. This endeavor dominated his mind even now. However, there was one great chore left to him. After pondering long and hard on how to repay a people he had stolen so much from, he still could not come up with a proper apology for Lemalie. He knew she hated him. It was her right to do so. Nonetheless, he meant to belong to this tribe, to sit by their fire and share their table. If there was a way to show her his devotion, perhaps it could be so. Maengiri had forged each other's emotions since the beginning. He could too. It was a skill like any other.

Lindu was at its apex as he hoisted himself upon a cha'tskthi, recently pruned for the passing, yet full and fruiting once more with the blessed rains. He looked upon the soft ribbons of starlight and recalled the first time he had seen something so entrancing: the twinkle in Lemalie's eye when speaking of Keimas, the blush in her cheeks when the man touched her. It was a simple thing to make the connection between the soul's unpredictability and its proclivity for holding so tightly to one thing most precious. However, no matter how he tried, he could find neither reason nor cause in them. It would make sense if all living things loved one another so intensely, yet for two to bond more perfectly together than with any other was a mystery to him. It was agony to want, revitalizing to watch, but the nonexistence of its sensation within was crushing. He dwelt for a long while on the ancient love between Miohaelia and Oorghunak, Ephielipax's unexpected love for Quetzuaul, the forbidden romance between Anama and Golgamet, the poetic nonsense of Keimas and Lemalie. All these were guaranteed doomed, but still so tantalizing. They lived and died in cycles, reborn as something, given new love with each new life. Not Vulgoli. Not Tzychala. He would die truly alone.

He was too new to the search for feeling to understand it was upon him, too fresh from heartlessness to realize it was ended. Unconsciously awakened, one last thought of eternal loneliness hurt his heart in ways intangible to him yet evidenced by a visceral reaction. He sat on his leafy perch and wept, stifling his own moans as he held his knees to his face on the uppermost frond of the thi. His mind drifted from all preoccupation, replacing it with nothing but his heart, simply allowed himself to be as he was.

A powerful sorrow spread over the many that were out in the night air as they heard that of the red-haired messenger of Vaeba. They spoke of him in new ways, lamenting his state and commiserating that the demon, like themselves, was mortal. Little did they know what authority Vulgoli had over flesh, all flesh, even without intention. His tears stirred the Veil, acting over the heart as his claws did upon skin. His power infected the ground itself, making the grasses to wilt.

Lemalie had been watching him for a short while as though she was monitoring a wild animal. She did not trust or pity him, yet still she felt her hatred begin to blur. He had been nothing but agreeable, fearful, apologetic, and depressive. It made no sense. Why would such a dark harbinger weep so upon the orchard?

Lifting his head to contemplate the comforting colors of infinite departed souls as they gathered in Lindu's inmost swirl, Tzychala's hardness and antipathy toward himself receded. As his mouth hung open and tears dripped over his lips, he wondered what paradise was. If such a thing could be his, then he had attained it through a breaking heart. The pieces of a life destroyed by his own hands began to fall into place and, when finally feeling one whole emotion, he was swallowed by it. He smiled, started to laugh, then broke down into tears again. It made his body vibrate and his chest tight. He understood it and felt more alive now than any moment entrapped by the body given to him. This was his garden, his paradise, not to feel what he wished to feel but reaching a place where he felt everything, without effort or control. At last, his dream was realized.

CHAPTER 17: ALL THE LOVE IN THE WORLD

Tension built as the most esteemed families of all halls gathered to partake in this, the longest anticipated of ceremonies in Nesh. Decorations and musical trappings from the previous festivities remained to accommodate the Council of Archons' proceedings on the auspicious evening of Nesh Aiat Nepiur becoming the youngest Matriarch in their ranks.

Always humble, Nepiur felt no vainglory in attaining such an important position, though she had dreaded the thought in days past when it had meant eternal servitude to a father she had wished to escape. Rejoicing in his expulsion and bringing with her a newfound confidence in her abilities, Nepiur forced her thoughts back to the present at the rising voice of the recently appointed Primarch:

"...And to this, the council's determination," Sky Sebashni concluded with a flamboyant raising of her arms, "I proclaim the confirmation of Nesh Aia Nepiur ended. By my hand I do raise her to the place of archons in service to all Mantichaena. I charge this woman as a mother-ancillary and benefactor of Nesh. Attend all, Nesh Aiatan Nepiur!"

Cheering and adulation accompanied Nepiur's solemn step forward and bows of acknowledgement, once to the Primarch, then to the council, and lastly the assembly of the people.

Much of the pomp and circumstance observed by the archons had evaporated with Rogan's banishment. The council felt as though they were citizens again, servants and comrades rather than governors. Ritual and protocol were not easily left in the past, though there was a growing trend toward Sebashni and Aroch's dream of a council that belonged to the people.

Nepiur and Capheif were as children again when the high-class circumstance devolved into dance, delicacies and mass inebriation. By miraculous fortune, Capheif had been given sight. Nepiur and her troupe had been spared death at the hands of an unspeakable monster. The city was able to welcome her home and there was no more infighting for power. She and he were inseparable, tired and turning slowly amongst those who rejoiced with increasing volume.

"I intend no dour rain on the warmth of the night," Nepiur whispered excitedly. "But before we retire to sleep – which I insist to be sleepless, mind you – will you finally tell me how your eyes have come back to you?"

He wished to kiss her but could not draw her closer, as he was still so engrossed in using those eyes on her. He was unused to expressing himself with them, making doubt his only emotion as he internally weighed the extent of Raphenie's plea for secrecy. After a moment, he yielded to her.

"You have no doubt heard rumor of the torments suffered by the young girl Raphenie? And the heroics of Lemalie and one of the exiled to protect her?"

"Udai Naguza," Nepiur affirmed, marveling at the man's unlikely return.

"The sharp Ennedeghe, *la*. And still he is as kind at heart as he was when a child and Galaila pure. A ghastly aberration that plagued myself and Raphenie made mayhem for all of us here. Naguza came to save us and, as one blessed nightmare to destroy another, bound the spirit and rendered it dead with a single touch. Once freed of it, little Raphenie at last found herself, and what a marvelous self she does have: the power of a goddess and the glory of healing hands."

"Goddess? Raphenie? *Udai eichaslism,* hold me lest I fall to pieces! The name I only know from your telling, and the rarest of sightings. I cannot imagine why she would hide such a beautiful gift."

"She has kept herself well for fear of her ghost, though now I believe she fears what will be expected of her if she is discovered."

"Poor thing," Nepiur lamented. "Refresh me; was it not she who was found ashore in the Tau?"

"Oh yes. To my sadness it seems she was never found again. I dare say she had no friend but my tiresome self throughout her young life."

"*Einauta*, will you entertain a scheme?" Nepiur murmured.

Capheif at last broke eye contact and held her tight.

"Anything. Bid me, and let it be."

"She has been an orphan for so long," Nepiur began. "With all her silence, I had lost sight of her, yet I was pained to hear of her through your voice. Ms'egol is a home enough to her, but a house cannot give love. With our marriage secured and my travels over, we should return to our previous imaginings of perhaps…adopting her."

With a gleaming smile Capheif swung her back and forth, winced and lowered her, nursing his shoulder but basking in the compassionate and beautiful soul that captivated him.

"I have made mention of it to her," he assured, "Implored her to accept us as her family after securing your consent."

"Then our hearts are together, *eihsrysha*." She sweetly kissed his lips. "Can we go to her? I would see her certain that she is welcome with us."

Capheif was suddenly more wary, not wanting to intrude on a private and vulnerable time for the girl.

"We should be tactful. She's in an awful gloom right now. This last day she sought Naguza, and it seems his health has not improved after their ordeal."

"All the more reason, if she feels the hurt with him."

Capheif could not easily resist the face she made.

"Perhaps it is so," He admitted. "We should be with her."

In the winding walkways of Ms'egol's upper reaches, wherein the gardens glowed by starlight, the most advanced apothecaries treated the infirmed. The healing dormitories were a relatively new development with only a handful fully constructed and in working order. They had been filled to the brim after the battle with Zeniquorer and were only now beginning to clear out. Some still harbored the most gravely wounded, and it had seemed a risk to keep one such as Naguza in close quarters with them.

Just beneath the uppermost mouth of the cavern was a very isolated room, a larger storage that could be cleared out to make room for the giant Ennedeghe. For those who cared for him, this remoteness also afforded freedom from other duties so as to focus on studying his condition.

Gaining access to Naguza was no easy task for anyone except those charged with his care. Raphenie herself had inserted herself unyieldingly as principle among them, and Naguza's gratitude for her presence made it clear to others that she could speak for his needs.

It was more difficult for Capheif and Nepiur to convince the apothecaries that they had a right to enter, though they managed permission after agreeing to an extensive cleaning of their fur and hands. Once dried and given clean robes, they were finally admitted.

The room was more dismal than expected, bare of any furnishing and scrubbed bare to make it suitable for the cause. The lack of amenities was understandable, they realized, in seeing how Naguza filled the room. His long abdomen was haphazardly splayed across half of it as his upper body slouched against a corner. The only bedding suitable for him was his own webbing and shed carapace, which he had crumpled into a makeshift nest. The combination befouled the air to common creatures but created a very pleasant smell for him. With the dripping barbs on his shell a constant threat, the walkable space was even further reduced. Any skin so dangerously adorned was carefully avoided by the near-constant stream of students coming in and out in relative silence, periodically murmuring to one another about experimental remedies they could try or samples taken from him.

The excavation of the room could not have continued past the far wall, as there was a deep crack which had been covered with a standing shelf for some time. Whatever cave lay beyond wound far below. From within, there peeped the quivering eyes of hundreds of Naguza's spawn. They clicked and screeched quietly, confused and saddened by his state and too afraid to come out with all the Mantichaena moving so quickly. The timid creatures could only pile over one another in the dark to stay close to their father.

Capheif entered carefully, stood against a wall and admired the immensity of Naguza. At every opportunity possible he would probe the apothecaries about his state but only received fragments of information.

Nepiur's concern was Raphenie, found her sitting by the infested fissure and went to her without hesitation.

Raphenie showed no fear, only care as she rested one hand on Naguza and the other in the darkness. She caressed the abrasive shell of one of the beady-eyed hatchlings and sang softly, mothering it like it was her own. She no longer had the clumsy and meek presence that Nepiur remembered. She glowed; certain this was where she belonged.

Raphenie spoke very simply, barely looking at Nepiur.

"Our Capheif has asked me to be with your family. I hope you will forgive my presumptuousness in hoping you accept me."

Kneeling behind the young lady and brushing her shoulder gently, Nepiur dismissed the honors.

"When I look on you, I see a heart I would be proud to have light our home. You have given my husband the world and I owe you an immeasurable debt for it. *Mineina,* know that I do not ask you to be our daughter as repayment, but out of true gratitude that you live."

"*Bitlaia,*" Raphenie said tearfully, "I could not live on if not in the warmth of your family."

She reeled unexpectedly and threw her arms around Nepiur, the silk-covered deghni still clinging to her wrist. It squealed weirdly as it was swept out and, with a jump and more tiny sounds of fear, it scrambled back over her shoulder to escape the light. Nepiur jerked in surprise and revulsion at the sudden appearance. Raphenie shushed her and smiled between her and the forsaken brood.

"Matriarch and mother, I'll be eternally grateful for the love you both offer, yet I think you'll not see much of me in the days to come. I have always dreamed of having a family, yet these poor things need one too."

Raphenie espied a weak smile from Naguza and caressed him happily. There was something unspoken, a mutual understanding and gratitude.

Nepiur saw something else. Regardless of its meaning, she was satisfied to see that Raphenie had, at least for the moment, everything she needed.

"Your place with us will always be waiting," Nepiur whispered admiringly. "No matter what comes. May your heart lead you always back to us, and we will always be with you."

As Nepiur reconnected with Capheif, both took another moment to observe the behemoth Naguza had become. It was understandable why he was so feared, though he had shown himself to be something more powerful than fear. He was no vermin of wretched rokhaadim, but spectacular and beautiful. They took their leave, Nepiur murmuring sadly as they disrobed.

"What do the botanists think?"

Capheif took a calculated breath and rested his head on hers, her tail curling about his leg as they stared back into the room.

"They have faith, little else. They are learning an entirely new science in treating him."

"I am unsure what faith can do. To see him like this, I don't think even he knows what is happening to him."

"Perhaps he does," Capheif groused, "And does not want Raphenie to know."

Nepiur had her suspicions, though they were clearly kept in the dark.

"That girl is a miracle. She knows what she's doing. I believe this will end in Naguza's good health, just as it did for you."

Nepiur could not help feeling a bit overwhelmed as Naguza's many frosty eyes finally found hers. They only met a moment before he refocused on Raphenie but, in that instant, Nepiur saw a sort of distant reflection in the Ennedeghe's face, like another person floating under the water's surface. In Raphenie's presence Naguza struggled not to reveal how frightened he was, uncertain of why his body failed him or why his condition worsened.

The sight of this suffering brought images of Hax and Bethaali to Nepiur's mind; the vain resistance, the creeping transition from hopeful struggle to terrified submission. There was much she did not understand about many people she had lived with her whole life. Hax was one mystery after another, not terribly pleasant company either. Naguza was no different. Nepiur could not stomach seeing another suffering friend slipping away. She trembled, shook her head gently and tugged Capheif along the way they had come.

Naguza was no longer a physically affectionate man. He was ever mindful that one mistaken touch could kill something he loved, but Raphenie's pearlescent spirit was clouding his mind. So much of him wanted his long and miserable life to end. The rest saw how she looked at him and wanted to live forever.

The apothecaries had toiled in vain for many sleepless nights and, this night, had worked later before leaving Naguza in peace. Raphenie always remained. Each night she would douse the torches to give the brood the darkness they needed, giggling happily at how his brood emerged and gathered around him where they felt safest.

Naguza, having only the scant starlight from the entry by which to see the girl's face, could not express his gratitude for her long suffering on his account. Slowly at first, he reached out a bladed hand to her, sideways such that the edge and the spines of his arm were furthest from her. She held her breath excitedly, gently placing her fingers on him. His lips weakly parted, and the glistening fangs in his mouth whistled as he wheezed through them.

"I am…sss…ssst-t-taying here. Nodt-t die. I Want-t-to live."

So subtle that none could see, composed of such fleshly energies that it could not be perceived, there was a bridge formed between Naguza's palms and the tips of Raphenie's finger. Something was moving from his body to hers. Each night Raphenie reached into him, trying to understand him and divine his injury. His body was like hers, crafted by a soul of the most unique design. It had taken time to learn its workings but, at last, she had glimpsed it. He did not act as though he was dying. It was not his body that was struggling. He was weighed down by a burden of the soul. As soon as the young goddess understood this she immediately felt the familiar signs of its presence, saw its ugly face in Naguza's eye. The injury he suffered was fear. He was infected by it.

"Naguza," Raphenie whispered urgently, "Do you trust me to care for your life as though it were my own?"

Not knowing her meaning, Naguza had no will to resist.

"I t-trusst-t you…alwayssst."

"It will hurt you, inside, but you must let me in."

Naguza's face was frightened when he felt Raphenie starting to take control of him. He did trust her, though still fearing as he felt himself falling. She pushed him down, chasing him into the darkness of his mind in search of its scars.

The oily nothingness surrounding Raphenie was as uncomfortable as she remembered. The thin, violet mist clouding her vision teased her worst memories. Zeniquorer's acrid stink pervaded it. It filled her with so much hate that she had no room in her heart for any fear of it. In fact, she had never felt more powerful than she did in its presence now.

This was Naguza's mind, at present only occupied with one thought: her.

Raphenie stood among images of herself that drifted in and out of various emotions. She saw herself laughing, sulking, crying, nervously standing far away. Those were tired lies and shadows that hid who she was. They did not concern her. She was disgusted most by what lay at their center.

In a hissing puddle of its own misery, a malformed imp which vaguely resembled her father's manifest form writhed and clawed after the vaporous images, shrieking pitifully as they dispersed from its grasp. It had the same deep, hollow eyes, the knobby teeth, the complete absence of reason or awareness. At first glance it might have seemed so large, so terrible, yet as Raphenie approached it shrunk meekly. Or, perhaps, she grew mightily. It finally felt her and met her gaze. With overwhelming satisfaction, Raphenie savored the look of abject horror on its face and could not help but laugh.

"Look at you," she mocked. "So needless. So tragic. I am ashamed to have ever thought you my better."

The chomping mass shrieked again as if to frighten her, lunging in vain as the viscous slime kept it trapped.

Raphenie just shook her head in bewilderment. This was not a god, just a memory left behind in a desperate bid to continue its meaningless existence. She stooped over it, smirking and exuding confidence.

"You are no great enemy to be fought, just a disease to be cured. You are no longer the predator, father mine. No matter how many times you come back, no matter where you hide, I will always find you."

The afterling twitched and groaned, making a high-pitched whine as the undying soul of greed and lust joined with it.

"You will be mine," The sickening voice threatened again. **"He is mine, YOU ARE ALL…"**

Without any invocation or change in her demeanor, Raphenie's body erupted into a brilliant nova that filled Naguza's mind to its darkest corner. Zeniquorer's second death was so sudden that no further sound was heard but the crash of Raphenie's light, so complete that no speck of him remained. It was now as it would be from this day onward, whenever their souls might meet.

Raphenie did not have care in the world. With a bounce in her step, she reached below and felt Naguza's touch. At her gentle pull, his self-image emerged, the handsome young Galaila he was at heart. It was asleep, seeming quite peaceful, and Raphenie felt the faintest urge to remain where they could be their purest selves. Sadly, that would be of no benefit to him. They were in the world what they were meant to be. Yielding to her new understanding of love, she lifted them both, floating outward from his mind and back to life.

"*Eihsrysha*, it is over," she comforted him. "Time to wake up."

CHAPTER 18: THE MOUNTAIN
UNDER THE WOOD

It was undignified for a Kutu to crawl on its belly like frightened prey. Allende internally grumbled about the indecency of it all through the frigid night following his leaving. The periodic thrush of unfamiliar wings, however distant, kept him aware of the consequences if he or Ghrainegal revealed themselves. Though his strength had waned, he felt reinvigorated once broken of Keimas' aura. His natural resilience returned to him, just enough to survive as far as he had. His courage was maintained only by that of his hunt, for only Ghrainegal knew where they must go.

The Canimperium was not a place to be found. It was the ever-changing landscape of Boa's domain. The grand kutliku himself had no nest that the Mantichaena knew of, rather ruling as he wandered. The place to find him was not a retreat but a stronghold in the depths of the wood where the Canimperium should gather when all else had fallen. Ghrainegal knew this, following the north wind to the last refuge of his people.

At last, the dew in the canopies sparkled and the dreary night gave way to a beautiful morning. There was a subtle music to Ni'ivitnem; the ring of fallen droplets on leaves, the creaking of the thi bark as their caps and fronds swayed. The pageant of still life would captivate the unwary, but the hunter knew to also listen for the sounds which were missing. When the skies seemed clear it was not the night that kept Allende and Ghrainegal grounded but the absence of fleeing prey. They should be disturbing lesser creatures, even in their stealthy poise, yet not even a schiis slithered underfoot. Another predator had passed this way, was almost certainly still close.

Allende felt a ray of light on his face through the thi Hai, then froze in place when it suddenly disappeared. With a wide eye he turned to it.

The morning was hidden as the ashen silhouette of an infernal rose groaning from the brush. The pair were not being stalked. There was no need to track them. The infernals were everywhere and this one was not alone. Another beyond it emerged similarly, immediately caught notice of the Ghrainegal. Ever silent, the nearest felt the gaze of its counterpart and knew it had found a kill. Its head swiveled slowly until both pairs of smokey eyes were locked on the pure kutliku. On their stomping, stabbing wingtips, the infernals vaulted their bodies up and charged.

"Thaun!" Allende screamed, leaping up and taking flight through the thi with Ghrainegal quick to his draft. The Kutu flew, his hunt followed, then their ears caught the shrill cry of another kutliku at their back. It was an order to rally, signaling advantage of numbers and certain victory. It was the voice of Shisi. He repeated the cry and swept up into the canopy, circling back down into the fray with all his heart. Sure enough, his wife had found him, bearing down on the infernals with all remaining hunts on her tail.

The infernals were devoid of any emotion, fear or comprehension, even as the first blow was struck against that furthest from Allende. Miriena's talons raked its head, while Shisi gripped its wing and jerked it off balance. Soto clamped around its head and lifted with all her might as Bogh'thane's screaming jaw cleaved it free with one bloody bite. In the blink of an eye the infernals' situation was catastrophic, and that which remained could neither fight nor flee as it was ripped into pieces by the combined fury of the Kutu pride.

When the slaughter was done, Miriena squealed as Allende

slammed into her midair and toppled them both into the brush. He laughed, she struck him repeatedly for his impunity, and he kissed her through the pain.

"You insufferable *zet'itka*!" She shouted, prying his lips away from her. "You could have been killed!"

"Never a chance!" He denied "Not with so menacing a beauty to save me!"

"*Sapbinech,* we have to go!" She insisted.

"Go? *La*! I am sure we are close to Boa's heart now."

"Closer than you think," Miriena said while indicating the Thaun.

Allende felt tension in the air as the hunts all curled their wings under their bowed heads. He sought what they revered and beheld what they had set out to find: Canimperium loyalists. They were gigantic, beautifully colored and haughty as they descended from the canopy to investigate the commotion. They clicked and warbled to one another while surveying the gruesome scene. Seeing that the pride had done them a service, they acknowledged it with a subtle nod and a quiet screech.

Allende, astounded by the unusual size of these kutliku, stroked Ghrainegal's neck and tried to get a dialogue started with them.

"Canimperium?" He suggested.

Ghrainegal and the other hunts made various motions and sounds, telling a story of hostility and worry. It was brief, though the loyalists understood. They responded with sounds of sadness, one casting a dire look to the Thaun and uttering a garbled response.

"Can-ump-erum."

Allende knew their meaning well enough.

"Close indeed," he confirmed with Miriena, "Though it does not sound promising."

"They are alive," Miriena sighed, relieved. "Some, at least. That is promising enough. Let's waste no time. *Eina,* there are surely more of the fallen coming."

It took only the last of early morning for the escort to bring the pride to their destination. To Allende and Miriena, the first Kutu to ever set foot in this hallowed place, it became apparent how the Canimperium's hidden stronghold had been so long undiscovered.

As the loyalists led the way over the densely shrouded hills they suddenly took a dive and crashed below, and the deadly plunge did not stop at the ground. A secret passage, obscured by a mixture of shadows on the bright colors of thi'tskreol, swallowed them and wound them through a gauntlet of stalactites. Its termination spat them out in a sprawling cavern with sinkholes peppering its ceiling. All across its great expanse, light and fresh snowmelt from Nikhaadi Gao poured in through these, creating a dazzling mist that whirled around an immense rock formation at the center. Over a lifetime, perhaps the life of Manti itself, water had trickled down from a low point in the ceiling and slowly built a tower of minerals that now stood as a mighty tower. Since the dawn of their coming, the kutliku had burrowed into it with tooth and talon, leaving it hollow.

Miriena's heart beat out of her chest and her tired voice quivered with excitement.

"Windchaser Pinnacle."

"No one back home will believe it," Allende marveled with her.

The Canimperium had retreated but had not yet fallen. The surface of the tower was crawling with kutliku, peering through the holes at something happening inside. They took no notice of the visitors until the loyalist escort called out in warning. The echo traveled far and deep and, in short reply, summoned forth Jiou Boa.

Thetrulengo speaks,

Anama is not responsible for the success of the kutliku, as she is with many other broods under her caring eye. Still, she knew their blood flowed directly from her eldest father Ephielipax and so offered her protection to Boa's kind. The proud kutliku monarch would not have it. Though he loved and revered the daughter of Loi, he was wary of her. The benevolence of a family can merit trust in its children, yet the mistakes of one can taint the pool. Not only was Boa aware of Anama's parentage, but he knew how she had been joined to the disciple of another Nhi'Thaun. Ferraro may have been a just and compassionate heiress but the kutliku had no proof of this. She was not of the Blue Sky Raptor and therefore not to be trusted, nor any who consorted with her

Boa himself really is the root and foundation of the Kutu's tradition and violent indwelling. He is both an anomaly in the common physical abilities of kutliku and a paragon they emulate. He was born larger, stronger, more terrifying than any other, and so had no need to assert himself as the greatest wings in the sky. He was born the herald of a new age of dominance for the kutliku, and he meant this age to be. Beloved by Ephielipax, the Galaila he protected and the kutliku he served, he yet had some conflict with the father of the air. While Ephielipax was swayed to a life of peace, Boa held tight to the reason for the creation of kutliku. The Galaila were meant to build and the kutliku to destroy. It was this devotion to the old way which led to his departure at the appearance of Loi. Ephielipax and his world order were gone, the Galaila had lost their way and Ellel was in the hands of a tyrant. The kutliku, leaderless and purposeless, went to seek a life apart from the Galaila. Loi had no chance of controlling the Jiou kutlikuilt or his subjects.

It was only when the Canimperium was established and there were fewer battles to be fought that the infernals broke away.

This is the nature of peace, and a humbling realization that I have begun to feel deep within: uniformity leads to peace, yet peace and understanding have no place in mortal hearts. Creatures of flesh find no power or righteousness in love, and so they turn to hate. When any peace is achieved, a people begins to seek out new conflict. Without a common enemy, small differences in a species are vilified, and inevitably become a call to war. It would seem that any effort to eliminate conflict is in vain. Perhaps this is a wisdom which some have had in the past. Miohaelia and Quetzuaul did not create freedom. By sharing their mind with their creations, they replaced freedom with order. Which is the greater good, I lack the confidence to say.

There is another realization for which I feel no strong emotion, only interest. I have been wrong in my assumptions in the past and therefore must always accept that I may be wrong about any further assumptions. Is anything true? If so, how can it be known? Truth is like the sea; stormy, clouded, too vast and deep to be understood from where I stand.

~Chronicle of Wonders, Kutlikugoli and the Lesser

The pride was led to land with urgency, all Kutu and hunts grounding in the wet sand and bracing for the coming storm. They planted their faces firmly in the ground, sprawled flat and inert in submission. Regardless of the entry granted the Kutu by the loyalists, they were not welcome. As much was felt in the thunder of Boa's wings. To see the kutlikugoli now was as a youthful memory of a parent, one that did not diminish with time.

Boa was undoubtedly the direct offspring of Ephielipax. In exiting the base of the Pinnacle he could barely fit through the largest opening, tearing the deposits with talons as long as Miriena's wing. His immense head and neck reached almost halfway to the ceiling, yet they seemed small as his own wings finally unfurled. His plumes, like flowing red rivers, contrasted the black of his scales like a fire burning through a night-darkened forest. His weight made it impossible to launch as the others did, instead falling from his egress to catch wind and swoop across the ground. With one beat to gain altitude he upturned the soil and, with a second, slammed down over the cowering Kutu, nearly destroying them with how close his wing talons planted.

In a belching, fiery voice, Boa exhaled quickly, clicked his tongue against the roof of his mouth and raked it along his hard mandible to mimic Galaila words.

"Kutu betray. Fourth Kutu harmed. Now second and third come. Why!?"

Allende gushed as fast as he could, indicating Soto beside him.

"Tremendous Jiou, I come by command of Keimas, hunter killer bound to she, your daughter Soto!"

"Fourth harmed!" Boa screamed down at him, tilling the ground with his great talons and beating it on either side of Allende with the crooks of his wings. **"Fourth harmed. Brought infernal! Brought war!"**

"Fourth...Keimas? No, my *Jiou*, he..."

"FOURTH KILLED KREI'KASHA!"

The kutu covered their ears and writhed at the explosive voice. Even the hunts were injured by it.

Boa lowered his head, his rage draining away into the mourning pain that drove it. In response, the hunts and loyalists covered theirs under wings. Allende could hear his own heartbeat, he and

Miriena both dumbstruck by the news and the silence it evoked. At last Boa spoke, bringing his saliva-soaked teeth so close to Allende's face that acrid breath moistened it.

"Invaded. Trespassed. Krei'kasha led very strong. Protect home. Fourth killed! Made wind and killed! Broke Boa. Sorrow. Broke Boa could not see infernals...fourth brought infernals!"

"No!" Allende lifted himself up and stood against Boa defiantly, seizing control of the moment. "Kutlikugoli, hear me, I beg you! The vile thing that violated your borders was not the fourth, but the god of Ellel infecting his flesh!"

"LOI!" Boa bellowed, stomping his wings repeatedly. **"Evil! Son of Quetzuaul, son of death! Kutu set Loi upon Boa!?"**

"I swear to you, it is not so! The fourth, the first, and myself, we came with your given children to find him and kill him. He is god no more, and we will take him!"

Boa brooded, searched deep into Allende's eyes for any sign of deception. Snarling, frustrated that he saw only truth and would not have the pleasure of gutting something, he retreated to sit back, somewhat unwound but still guarded.

"Loi already destroyed once. Now lives. Gods must kill gods. Forgive Boa. Follow Boa. Second and third, these are friends. Follow Boa. Krei'kasha chase wind. Go to homesky."

Allende shot Miriena a look, disbelieving that they still lived. She shrugged and warily stood, joining him to follow after Boa's lead. They went on foot to one of the Pinnacle's many mouths, into its bowels. As they went, Miriena caught Allende's hand and questioned him.

"Who is Krei'kasha?"

"Boa's eldest," Allende said, anxious and depressed. "And grand chief of his forces. Govan said she was the most beautiful kutliku he had ever seen, with wings like snow-capped mountains."

"Did he say Loi...killed her with the wind?"

"It would seem so. I don't understand it though," Allende mused. "What authority does Loi have to tempt the infernals here? They have no gods."

"None that we know of," Miriena said. "Though I don't think that was what he meant."

"How so?"

"He said he was too broken to see them. I don't think the infernals flew under Loi, though Boa may think it so. It sounds to me like they were opportunists of Loi's attack, taking advantage of Boa's grief to stage their own assault."

"Scavengers," Allende spat. "Your words seem close to the truth, though there is much we cannot know in this."

Miriena's mind was elsewhere.

"We know we need to feed Boa's fury. He already has all the reason he needs to join us. We must secure his help."

Allende quieted her as they entered the central chamber of the Pinnacle, out of respect for the somber environment. The heartbreak within was palpable and the spectacle gut wrenching. Krei'kasha was not the only loyalist slain. In the dimly lit core there was a ring of fire burning gently around an uneven sedimentary formation, upon which were strewn the corpses of countless loyalists. Visible at the side of the heap were the lustrous white and yellow feathers that could only belong to the great kutliku Jiaiana.

Thetrulengo speaks,

She had been the eldest daughter of the kutliku Jiou, his heiress and Soto's most powerful sister. The Canimperium was not yet defeated, yet their fighting spirit had been severely curtailed with her death. Through wordless whispers the battered kutliku spoke of tremendous winds that sliced like knives through their numbers, felling their most beloved and creating a wound in the secure province that the infernals could further infect. At great cost, the battle had been won, yet Loi had gotten what he came for: souls. It is fortunate he had no time to devour those he slew, but their deaths set free much of the light he needed. His own soul was growing, though his body was failing. He did not walk away unscathed, and the coming battle is sure to test his resolve.

The infernals have been waiting for a chance such as this, finally to drive the loyalists back until they had only one defensible position left. All the rest of Ni'ivitnem was under infernal control now.

The offer Boa extended by bringing the Kutu into this sacred

*hollow was that they be present for the departure of the bravely
fallen. It was a commitment of remains to the firmament in the old
way of Ephielipax.*

*The kutliku gathered slowly around the resting place, clawing
spark from stone to set a blaze. Ever searching upward like fingers
it rose around the departed and, as it did, the multitudes gently
fluttered their wings as one. With great care, they began to beat in
ascending succession, circulating the air within the pinnacle and
forming a spiraling updraft into its high reaches. What once
belonged to the Canimperium was given back to Ephielipax as the
cyclone whisked ash and feathers away to the sky. I went out above
in the hopes that I would see the Raptor reach down to welcome
them. Silly, perhaps, yet what I saw was no less incredible. The
journeying gale ignored much of the crosswind, keeping its course
true until it disappeared high above. My mind wished to go up and
find its end but...my heart did not. To watch the creatures go with
such quiet love felt right. This was a good thing, for a death so
needless to have at least the honor of remembrance.*

~Chronicle of Wonders, Elegies

Not a single feather of Boa's precious child bound her any
longer to the mortal coil. The flame that bore her eventually faded
as the mourners roosted in silence. Allende and Miriena suffered
with them, touching their hunts and sharing tears with them. It was
to be expected that death would always come for the warrior. For
the first time, the two Kutu feared it. Allende looked at his wife,
whose eyes stayed closed as she held her head to Shisi. He could
not bear it if she was claimed by the coming battle. Still, better that
than to die himself and curse her with the same grief. The airborne
flames and downtrodden loyalists surrounding them were proof
enough that it was not the dead who suffered most.

The attitude of the Pinnacle was starkly different when the last
embers died. The Kutu needed not concern themselves with Boa's
alliance, for he reared and roared that the time for sorrow was over.
Now was the time for vengeance. He spoke at first to them but
ultimately to all that remained of his people.

**"Kutu, many chase wind. Canimperium is nothing. Boa is
nothing. Survival! Survival is all! First, Loi. Loi first.**

Revenge!"

"Vengeance is yours, *kutlikugoli*," Allende promised. "Let us fly with you, and the Canimperium and *Hauan Etain* be one!"

"One together. One again." Boa roared, rousing his cackling army to follow. **"Loi is waiting. Boa'tghanta crunch with teeth!"**

A mass exodus from Windchaser Pinnacle shook the caverns so fiercely they might have come crashing down. Like a geyser the thousand colors of the loyalist flock spewed from the ground, shredding the canopy as they stampeded to the Hai and the fall of a god.

CHAPTER 19: THE SMALLEST ACT

T zychala's new favorite place was the rock he had always seen Lemalie sitting on, from which she dipped her toes to the river to replenish her spirit. He attempted the same, savored the cool as she did like he was exploring the minds of others through their habits. Water was not a new discovery, yet he believed to touch it with the sole aim of relaxing the mind was a skill requiring study and practice. Relaxation alone was such a feat.

The crack of wood and bang of metal disturbed his early morning contemplation. Searching for its origin, he saw the militant prospects of Gazan pouring out onto the dawn-washed fields and recklessly testing their new weaponry on one another.

It was mostly crude; gauntlets and epaulettes, either spiked or bladed, to make more deadly the blows already practiced in hand-to-hand combat.

Tzychala rolled onto his stomach, sprawled limply over the boulder and judged how the soldiers moved, the differences between the fresh trainees and the veterans.

Air and earth had become much cooler, yet Laesis still felt harsh to those who toiled under commandant Schaleikin's whip. They were impressive, even to Tzychala, in how they endured their tireless exercises. Her voice promised pain as she barked the escalation of attacks in steady time:

"Trip...strike! Check...strike! Wound...strike! Kill...strike!"

Every order was rewarded with a synchronized chorus of clashing metals, bruised flesh, the thud of bodies against dirt. Each crack of her long weapon was answered with a battle cry and a full-speed attempt by each soldier to test the defenses of the fighter opposite them. If the guard was broken the attacker knew to stop with precision, but the pain of failure had taught each of the defenders the importance of speed in defense. Turn by turn they assailed one another and, as Schaleikin commanded, they increased their aggression each time until attempting a killing blow.

They were intensely focused and wholly committed to each bout, so much so that no one noticed Tzychala sneaking closer until his slurping voice arose and mocked them from the sidelines.

"Well fought, morsels. Your victory will be certain if one of your own should attack."

Outraged, Schaleikin snapped her whip repeatedly in a circle, signaling a full stop as she sought out the heckler. She lost her bearing somewhat at seeing the demon swinging by his clawed feet from a thi'tskreol branch and grinning stupidly. She knew perfectly well who he was yet had not expected or desired to have him so close. She had faced far bigger than he and so had no fear, only indignity at his disrespect and revulsion at his foreign appearance.

"Come to learn how to fight as Mantichaena do, *la*?" She challenged. "Are there no masters of your own kind to learn from? *Minein,* were you not taught to test a soldier's mettle before disrespecting them?"

Tzychala laughed excitedly and swung up onto his perch, rested his chin in his hand and surveyed the militia. Their discipline was constant as they waited in position for the next command.

"Truly, *aiat*," He began, "I have rarely seen such gusto among lesser killers, yet in striking a mortal you learn only how to kill the mortal. Vermin are poor preparation against the ravenous Loi."

"Attend the training, small one," she retorted with an enticing finger, "And feel the vermin's teeth!"

Tzychala's elation increased, curious to see Schaleikin's ability. He dropped and casually meandered among the formations. They were obediently still, unmoved by any of his rantings or those of the commandant. However, in each of their eyes Tzychala saw a wariness of himself, an uncertainty about what recklessness made Schaleikin think she should provoke a demon and live. Superstition served Tzychala's ego well. Feeling himself less than what they likely expected of the abyssal denizens of myth, he was nonetheless reinvigorated by their fear. They could not understand the heart of Vulgoli power. Fortunately for them, it was a power he could no longer wield to full effect. There were a few drops of blood left in him. It as not enough to terrify nations and devour armies, but he could still give a good fight.

"They are well-grown, lady chief," he admitted to Schaleikin after sizing up her soldiers. "Perhaps they will survive. Shall we find out?"

"Close ranks!" Schaleikin shouted, beating her chest and stepping down as the formation parted. "Give an arena. The *vaena* needs battle scars!"

Though the militia were excited to see such a fight, believing that some among them may be an adequate challenge for any monster, they were yet unnerved by not only Tzychala's physical being but the hiding of his eyes behind cloth. It was, to them, a display of confidence. Even with his sight obscured he moved with surety while he and the commandant circled each other.

Tzychala weighed Schaleikin's size and strength in his mind, thought back to the flailing weaklings mortality had once been. They were little more than food, created and used for that exact purpose. They had certainly matured while he slept. Schaleikin was almost three times his height, possibly ten times his weight. He felt a tingle of unfamiliar caution, assured by her size that any mistake could indeed humble him. His pomp and provocation were absent as he spoke again, calmly critiquing not only to his student but to all of hers as well.

"You attack in the absence of opportunity, attempting to force one. Against a god, this is certain death. A god needs no armor, no shield; the lives they have taken become these. Flesh has become their armor, the Veil their shield..."

The commandant charged as if to catch him off guard, throwing a direct blow from her open palm. Though unblocked, she withdrew the false strike and feinted to the side, swung her whip about Tzychala's ankles and jerked him off the ground.

He did not resist as her fist chased him toward the ground.

Neither did he impact dirt. With a flurry of shadows he vanished from sight, severing the whip.

Schaleikin's knuckles buried in the ground, immediately followed by her head as she felt Tzychala's heel upon it. She roared and thrust herself up with a blind punch, barely missing the demon's smiling teeth as he crouched in front of her.

"*La'matal*!" he laughed. "You must set the trap, not to fall into it! Facing Loi with honor will gain you nothing. Forsake it! Feign weakness and fight with lies!"

At Schaleikin's blustering signal, each detachment reformed lines and closed in on Tzychala.

He smirked, took in what they armed themselves with and how they approached, knew exactly what they would do as his many eyes searched their bodies. Every attack was telegraphed by a tense muscle, a heavy step, a sudden breath. He saw them all at once and foresaw the battle.

Claws and blades converged on him and he deftly avoided each one, countering with neither mancy nor a stolen weapon. He shamed them with open-handed slaps, evaded or baited them into one another until their only obstacle to striking him was a growing pile of bodies.

"You cannot outflank a god!" He shouted with each failed attack. "You cannot overpower a god! The harder you charge, the faster you die! For each that falls, your devoured essence makes the enemy ever stronger!"

His rebuke did not deter the headstrong soldiers, each taking their turn to prove their worth. His frustration at their stubbornness increased until his patience ran dry. His eyes went wide and disturbing lines of sinew raised against his skin as he caught a very young Kulo by the jaw.

Schaleikin lashed her whip repeatedly, demanding a retreat, rejoining the fray to put an end to the melee she had lost control of.

Tzychala did not thrash the boy he held, instead turned slowly to show him off.

The carnage subsided, and Schaleikin halted a few steps from Tzychala in the hopes he would not injure his hostage.

The demon knew little of how others were best taught, so only said what was in his growing heart. He spoke to the captive boy as though he was about to take his life.

"You have died. Your courage is great, and it will cost you your life." Then, throwing the boy down angrily he pirouetted and soaked up the depressing sight of his many attackers backing away, licking their wounds. "If I were Loi, you would not see mercy. No amount of brute strength can save you. You have all died!"

He had become angry, realized after saying his peace where it came from: not their inexperience, but the impossibility of their survival, that they may be lost already.

Something felt wrong inside him. He was disturbed and there were none that did not see it. He was breathing heavily, closing his eyes sorely and struggling to stay standing. His knees folded limply and he fell to his knees, blood sputtering from his lips. After watching him humiliate half the regiment, no one knew what to make of such a surrender. He had not taken a single hit, yet he was all but defeated.

An unseasoned prospect at his back had the advantage of position and surprise, seized the opportunity and vaulted over the defeated with spiked gloves aimed at the demon's spine. Schaleikin had no time to react and no one else was close enough to stop it.

Tzychala's eyes did not stop seeing. Driven by the sense of danger, he acted on instinct. With fulminating webs of crimson covering his fingers, he spun onto his back and took the blades through his palms, their tips gently resting on his chest as his bones tightened around them. The eyes in his arms opened and his black teeth were bared, ravenous to take the boy by the neck. He saw the courage in you novice's face turn to fear, realized his own state and panicked. With a turn and kick, Tzychala launched him aside, ripping the blades from his hands. There he remained in a pool of blood, coughing more up painfully as the red sparks on his skin receded.

No one wanted to attack him anymore. For all his immortal power, a neophyte had likely almost killed him. They stood and thought on what he could be trying to teach them with his own injury, until he stood and wobbled, collapsed against near recruits who discarded their weapons and kept him up as he fumed at them.

"You cannot...fight Loi. You are all...going to die," he wheezed. After a deep breath, he spit another mouthful of blood and slime into the dirt and tried to stand away from his helpers.

His observers shuddered as he wavered on his wickedly clawed feet, the blood he had lost taking on a life of its own as it festered on the ground. It grew, as if shapeless bodies sprouted from the seed he had planted with his injuries. Fingers of flesh writhed upward from the red puddles and began to burn and smolder in the harsh daylight. All retreated, fearing the fiery gore that carved into the ground around Tzychala as he berated them grimly.

"When you consume food, you gain what light is left inside it. This essence makes you grow, makes you strong. Gods eat when they kill, taking the essence from the bodies they break between their fingers. With each that falls they gain power. Your courage is selfish, robbing your families of victory, for each shattered bone is a meal. To survive a god, not one of you can fall."

"We already faced such a thing," a Kulo said nervously. "That creature that took *udai* Capheif's flesh, just as Loi has taken Keimas'. It nearly destroyed us in our own home. What…what are they, the gods?"

"They were once like you, perhaps even smaller," Tzychala said with a wry smile. "Imagine what you could become if you did not age, if you could live forever by killing your family, your friends, your lovers. Such a curse as eternal life is only bestowed on those who have the stomach to steal it."

Schaleikin looked from those around her to Tzychala. Very cautiously, she asked:

"*Vaena,* is that how the gods became so? Genocide?"

"In measure you cannot conceive of," Tzychala answered, "And Loi wishes to be the most terrible of them all. All the power of two ancient destroyers pours into him with every breath he takes, as your life flows into your children."

"We could not hide from the beast of Nesh," A bruised Boroo said skeptically. "None of us could stand against it. Even after Artimecian broke it, only the godlike Lemalie could slow it down." He slapped his spiked shoulders and shrugged miserably. "What do you expect us to do against the *Jiou* of gods?"

In reply, Tzychala wiped his mouth and stumbled to a nearby thi that hung heavy with dormant seeds. He took one of these and knelt upon a rock, beat the lignified nut against it and speaking between blows.

"If this food were to strike your head, you would die. But as it strikes the boulder it begins to crumble. If you tried to claw it open your fingers would break long before you reached its flesh, so you must let it weaken itself. Every blow, every bite, every expenditure of a god's spirit causes it to lessen. They have become so addicted to the power of their souls they have long forgotten how to rely on anything else. If you face Loi as an army, he will kill you all, down to the last weeping child. You must learn to fight as though even the greatest among you is but a blade of grass. Temp him with weakness and retreat. Present a target and vanish as he strikes, lead his attacks to ground and drain his power. Enrage him, confuse him, make him lash out blindly, for while he cannot bleed..." At last, the nut cracked and oozed its tannic yellow insides upon the rocks. "...He can still break."

The teachings of Tzychala about godly warfare had made quite an impression and were gaining an audience of more than warriors, most of whom were intrigued just to hear tell of Loi's power or to see Tzychala's in action.

There was a Thiwa child in attendance who did not understand why the regiment trained as it did or why Tzychala explained these things to them. Full of youthful optimism, the boy could not conceive of a Kutu's failure, and he made it known.

"*Minuein!*" he protested to the weary Tzychala, "Keimas will stop him...won't he?"

It was an uncomfortable question, one Tzychala was loath to answer with so many eyes on him. Regardless, if they were to be prepared, he could not allow them to be complacent while hoping for a miracle.

"He has the best chance of any of us, young thing."

"He will!" the boy insisted. "He said he would. The Kutu protect us."

The boy's mother retrieved him, yet she did not chide him. She stared as he did, waiting for the eldritch creature to give his assurance.

Fed up with their diminishment of a truly dire situation, Tzychala spoke as candidly as he had when Keimas first led the hunter killers away.

"*Boseihs – listen to me*, all of you! Keimas is attempting to do what even the earliest of the gods did not think could be done.

There is a chance he will succeed, yet for what do you train if not the day there is no Kutu to save you? I stand before you as a husk of what I once was, a disgrace to the true power of my kind, and still I can face your strongest. The soul that took hold of Keimas is not unlike my own, a tawdry reflection of the Loi who sired it, and still I was powerless to stop him myself. Loi is the last of the living elder gods. He earned that place through fantastical murder since the day he was born! If his body is unleashed, he will be a hundred-fold the danger he is now."

There was an abrasive quiet, but he saw the hardness in the eyes of the militia and knew they were grateful to have his counsel. Beginning to believe in them, he continued to share.

"Once, a lifetime ago, I stood where you do now. I challenged my beliefs and opposed my creator, one before whom even Loi is a single mouthful of flesh. I was victorious because I knew my enemy. YOU must know your enemy. I swore to your *utan* Keimas that I would watch over that which was most precious to him. I do so by teaching you to defend yourselves against an enemy who will fall upon you as a mountain on a weed, not to frighten or subdue but to annihilate."

Schaleikin broke the urgent silence with a calm request for more than words.

"For all which may be lost, we do not lay down for any god. Teach us to move the mountain, *vaena*. We will learn, and we will bring it down."

The Vulgoli's lessons gained a greater following, including the council as they became aware of it. Soon, they were inclined to order that all who had the strength to fight would listen to Tzychala's daily instruction. It was not only on the nuance of godly warfare but on the nature of the divine; the path of a god's ascendance and the vulnerabilities that came with it. Specifically, how the light they consumed could leave them so easily if they overexerted.

Many of the powers he described were a timeless mancy that did not require excessive essence of the soul, rather relied on the body's ability to control the veil that pervaded it. It was Gothic, Romantic and Classical mancy; the arts of the Mantichaena as crafted by the gods. These were the weapons at Loi's disposal, ones that could not be overcome by the meek, only avoided. As Tzychala wished them to understand, so they did, understanding that neither Tzychala nor Keimas could protect them forever. Survival was an responsibility they must shoulder themselves.

Tzychala felt a sense of security in teaching the simplest of his tricks. However, such were all he could offer. He could not teach them to use his own abilities. They could learn, yet it would pose a greater danger to them than Loi. The hexes of the dark edge required rituals that took a toll, sacrifices that still weighed on his guilty heart. What would be required of simple Mantichaena to perform these was something he could not allow, if only to protect their innocence. He was devoted to keeping them alive, and one too many secrets shared would put the whole of Maengir in jeopardy.

Night and day, the tribe collectively memorized Tzychala's recollection of Loi's brutish attacks, contemplated the destruction that would accompany each one. They understood quickly that the vanishing acts and illusions that the demon taught them to imitate were the best tool against Loi, for the god of the sky was neither tactician nor trickster, only a rampaging behemoth.

Tzychala explained in great detail the danger of being low in the canyon, with the peril of falling stone. He insisted all must train their bodies for the thin air of the plateau and keep the fight on the cliffs or wherever they could maintain high ground and ready escapes. He instilled as much dread as knowledge in them, describing a creature that truly was a mountain; muscle and mancy that fed off one another. However, he also enforced how, with an understanding of the monster and controlling their fear of him, they could defeat him.

Among those who did not partake in his instruction was Nepiur. She listened but did not come close. All the while she examined him nervously, tried to stay out of sight and stared with unblinking eyes. When he moved it made her skin crawl, and she heard Bethaali's voice repeating in the back of her mind: *'His hair...his eyes...'*

"Could this be the creature?" she muttered to herself throughout each day. "Could this be the image of that inescapable nocturn?"

After the first few days of training, Tzychala was back on his new rock, smiling into the river's distorted reflection of himself. He had not removed the cloth from his face, had moved on from justifying it as necessary to enjoying how he looked. He was feeling less like what he was, now contemplating new ways to appear not as Vulgoli but as Mantichaena. To his shame, he was yet made of ebony teeth, ashen skin and revolting hair that made him look like a metal statue had rusted from tip to tail.

He had not paid attention to the twilit fields surrounding him as another day ended. Neither did he expect company, though it seemed now to always come in search of him as the city grew accustomed to his presence and took an interest in his thoughts.

Lemalie came to him unannounced, asked when very near:

"Where were you two nights ago?"

"*Qoueis?*" He stammered, shaken by her appearance. "I w-was in the orchar…"

"*La,* when night was long and you wept like a child," she said with contempt.

He swallowed, visibly abashed.

"*Aia,* there was someone I had a need to visit."

"Another impassioned soul to tempt into your service?"

He paused a bit, feeling his prior dreams of a friendship slipping through his fingers.

"*Aiat* Lemalie, *prostaaneis.* I want to do good for you. I wish every day to wake up and be Kulo, Lugu…any that are remade and yet are called man, not monster."

"You will be disappointed, then," she said dispassionately. "Tears do not change what is."

Tzychala cringed, grated his fangs and stared imploringly at her. She was fully adorned, her hair made up and her body clean and dressed as it was in days before emotional upheaval had taken hold of her and distracted her from beauty and life. Tzychala saw in her all the loveliness and strength of self she had regained after he had taken something so precious as love from her.

"I will pray for you, demon," she mumbled, her blue eyes befouled by disdain. "I pray you die, slowly, soulless as you dread to be. Keimas was misled by his own fear, and you preyed on it. Whatever hell you crawled out of, it is time you crawled back. I release you."

Tzychala's face creased miserably, grasping for anything he

could say to placate her. Then, he felt the water at his toes boiling, that in the ground steaming up around him. She continued.

"I do not care what responsibilities Keimas threatened you with, nor what you feel for the people you endangered. You do not belong, and you will leave *Hauan Etain* before daybreak."

"*Aiaeis!*" He began to protest.

The steam around them coalesced at Lemalie's back as she leaned into him to speak once more, perhaps the last he would hear of her.

"Ignore this and I will skin you alive, stitch a bag from you and stuff your flayed corpse inside, to be hung from the very thi you wept upon so I might savor your wailing until the end of my days."

She then turned and departed; certain she had made her conviction clear.

Tzychala was left empty, not only stripped of the satisfaction of earning other Mantichaena's trust but conclusively assured her would never have that of she who mattered most. To his surprise, he also no longer wanted to die. It seemed the only choice left to him was whom to disobey, who should take his life.

Before he could collect himself, the newly raised mother of Nesh appeared.

Nepiur's lips smiled on him, her hands extended graciously. She came from the opposite path and placed her palm on his disarmingly.

"Tzychala, fine evening to you, *la*? I watched some of your work with the militia. It seems some of the youngers would sooner follow you than their commandant."

He took a moment to exchange his despondency for gratitude and accepted her hand to greet her, oblivious that her smile was forced and insincere.

"I have little to offer," he said humbly. "I wish I could do more."

Nepiur hastily continued to praise him.

"On behalf of my people, and those we have lost this season, I thank you for your assistance."

Tzychala then noticed how she searched him closely from head to toe, gauging his body language and the tone of his voice just as he did her, both reading one another's complexities. Feigning friendship to lower his guard was a poor plan but, as far as she could tell, it was working.

Very mildly, she continued, "And, as I'm certain all others who have attended you will say, you are welcome to remain here under the care of a house if you so choose. I cannot offer you acceptance into them, though Ms'egol will surely let you sleep in its dormitories. The academy in particular appreciates your teachings."

"Ms'egol, *la*," Tzychala blathered, looking over his shoulder for any sight of Lemalie. "I might have desired a place in Nesh. To my chagrin, I do not think the *Jiaia* Lemalie has taken a shine to me as others do."

Nepiur calmed him purposefully.

"I would not cross her by making an offer against her wishes. However – and I have care not to upset her in this – I would also advise you against living and dying by her opinion of you. She is a fitting wife for a Kutu. *Eina aiailt*, she is a killer too; the effect of a life with the most ferocious of us. What sets her apart from Keimas is her abundant forgiveness for the penitent. Their similarity is that she is hostile against what she does not understand. Sadly, this has been common here. The Storyteller is one she despises for that very reason, without any reason as to why."

"The Storyteller?" Tzychala asked, very attentive.

"A vagrant," Nepiur continued dismissively. "A witchcrafter of Ni'ivitnem, who is as much a mystery as the sources of her namesake. She was here some time ago, delivering a lost citizen of one of our colonies safely to us. That was the first time I had ever seen her myself. There are hunters who have glimpsed her, found themselves in the company of a living ghost whose face could never be seen. They called her welcoming, even kind as she spins tales of the old world yet speak of how she always remains somehow hidden. To see you so blindfolded, I am reminded of her."

"I do not wish to be a kept secret," Tzychala murmured, knowing to whom Nepiur was referring. "And this woman is disliked?"

"Not by many, as she is little more than a curiosity when she does appear. There are a few who share *aiat* Lemalie's unease. Such minds are common here, I am afraid. Many cannot trust a shrouded nomad, nor anything outside their limited view of right being."

"Tell me more about her, this Storyteller." Tzychala requested shrewdly. "What stories have given her the name?"

Nepiur fidgeted. She indulged his questions easily, yet continually sought an opportunity to convince him to remove his blindfold.

"*Eina*, there is one in particular that a group of foragers brought back that I have always remembered very precisely, and I tell it to you as she did them:

As the stars first rose, a child called Night wandered in places deeply greened in a faraway land. Always with her was a vessel, a vial as would hold a tincture, and the tincture was the spirit of the mountains. She was one of many children, each with their own unique spirit, the rain, the light, the wind and even of the mind and body. But Night was unlike them, for none of the others could conquer the mountain. Night was very sad, because as she grew and created children of her own she looked on their families and saw that they intermingled, male and female, begetting their own children. She realized that all those she had created were made as she was. So, she called upon the spirit she carried, the spirit of the mountain, to give her children the same blessing as she had and allow them to create life. However, this came at cost. Never again could she leave a sacred place, the place where she made a pact with the earthplane. Therein she used the spirit of the mountains to create a wellspring that gushed forth from the deep ground. A pool of life emerged within the mountain, and it became the way of this aiakhaadi to drink from that spring and so have its life within them, conceived of the mountain and of Night herself. All generations would forever be female only, but by the power of the mountain they would never want for the child."

Tzychala clearly had no concept of what she said, did not know where to begin with deciphering the tale.

"How woeful," he said.

"I find it comforting," Nepiur said proudly. "It seems to me a tale of the sacrifices we must make for our children, the gifts we pass on to them."

"Woeful that not all will have such a glorious responsibility," Tzychala explained. He then abruptly returned to the Storyteller. "This vagrant, as you have described her, is in fact no stranger to me, yet I have not heard this story nor any other told by her. The Night and the mountains…it is beautiful and confusing, like herself."

"*Uein*, she must be more than mere acquaintance." Nepiur asserted.

Tzychala nodded in affirmation, and she burst with questions.

"How is that? You have seen her disrobed? Her face?"

"*Aia*, pay it no mind," he warmly replied. "I have skulked in very low places for much of my life. My gaze travels far, but I have seen her from very near. The hair of her head and the sparkle of her eyes is nothing you have not seen before." This he said while absently twirling a strand of his own hair.

"A pity," she responded coyly, understanding his meaning. "I always imagined she was something weird and wondrous. The apparent strangeness of those who called this island home long before me and mine has always been something of interest to me: Anama, Hax and I suppose my *aiana* Raphenie as well…"

"*Quoaiens?*" Tzychala interrupted. "What name did I hear?"

"*Ein*? Raphenie. We found her washed ashore…" Nepiur deftly recounted, only to be cut off again by Tzychala's snapping voice.

"No! Hax, as you said it. Who is this man?"

Nepiur's throat tightened, now hesitant to say too much. "He is a Boroo, a friend of some, a drunkard to all the rest…this is cruel to say. He is gone now. I should not speak of him after his passing. He was a good man, once I began to know him, that is."

"Haxelinopsis. Was this his name?" Tzychala demanded.

"*L…la.* You knew him as well?" Nepiur asked, startled.

"Where is he!?" Tzychala demanded, firmly grabbing Nepiur by the arm.

"Ow!" She yelped. "Steady off! I have told you; he is gone."

He released her arm but remained persistent.

"Dead or travelled elsewhere? And where to? Did he die?"

Seeing his determination, Nepiur stood hastily and retreated a step, dismissing herself.

"I do not know," she said as visions of Hax's disappearance swam before her eyes. "Forgive me, I am…*mineina,* good evening."

Tzychala was embarrassed by his outburst as she sped away from him, though would not harass her more with apologies. There would always be those who feared him on principle but, if a Deina'itka had made his home here first, there may be a great many who were suspicious of him for other reasons. Of course, he did not know how little value Hax's word held to these people. To him, the very name was more dreadful than his own.

His decision to leave took more thought than expected. Though he did not want to disappoint those who now depended on him, he could not ignore what Lemalie could do to him if provoked. The choice had to be made and, as much as he questioned it, he had to obey the woman he was charged to.

Like a sumear vanishes into the ground, Tzychala crept down the face of the rock and through a shadow. Hanging Gate would not see his kind again, or so he believed.

Nepiur was less effected than she might have been, had she not made the connection a moment sooner. Hax had spoken of creatures of the dark, just as Bethalli had. What was more sinister than the figure fitting her sister's description? She knew now that they must undoubtedly be of a kind; he, the Storyteller and this enigmatic third.

Nepiur only now feared Tzychala's presence, began to doubt the help they were receiving from him. In fact, as she contemplated Hax's abduction, she wondered if a demon could have done such a thing to him. No, the light was not the domain of this thing. Nothing about Tzychala resembled that which shone around the last sight of Hax. Something else was present in this world.

What then was missing from this jumble of immortal beings that hid among her mortal peoples? She did know, without question, the locus of all Hax's ravings: the 'Afterlings', devourers of the old world. The word was on the tip of her quivering tongue as she sped away to think.

"*Vulgoli.*"

CHAPTER 20: TO LEAD THE FAMILY

Thetrulengo speaks,

I *envision the final footsteps of an ill-fated man as I write this, before going to witness his descent into the valley of Anama's towering Thigolaia. I have been greatly drawn to all paths that have converged on this place and now I dream of beautiful days to come for all Mantichaena if this one should find its rightful end. I pray the endless stay their hands and allow mortality, or what little of it is the bloodborn of Ephielipax, to find their futures in an era free from Loi. It was not Loi who orchestrated the coming war, for his involvement is only a consequence of fate's design; a single thread in a tapestry which was set ablaze at the beginning of all things. As each day burns away more of the interwoven possibilities, fewer remain. Let this man take his revenge, not cruelly upon the divine niece he never knew but sweetly upon himself. Let the goddess amphiraed overflow with ascended blood as Keimas the inheritor does awaken to his true father's will and, with new enlightenment, become free of his own flesh.*

I do not know Loi. I do not know Keimas. I know only the path which hate inevitably leads to. I have seen it and, with a heavy heart, begin to feel it as well. In deepest thought I recoil from the thought of either victory, for no goodness is truly found in death. If Loi should fall, it is only a matter of time until Keimas takes his place. Such is the way of peace taken through blood. As a poison weed may grow in the light, so may succulents flourish in darkness. There is no great evil to be found here, only instinct, only the nature of the half-brothers Keimas and Loi.

I am tempted by my own illusions. If death and life in truest value are subject to their victims' place in them, then certainly there is neither virtue nor villainy in any dealings. It may be the only evil is to do such as contradicts the nature of the self.

It is Loi's nature to destroy all that resist his rule of Maengir. I see now, in how he has progressed throughout all time, in his failings to conquer even himself, that his nature is incompatible with that of Maengir. No absolute power can be achieved, yet he lacks this understanding. Failure, and inevitably defeat, are therefore his defining traits. He has abided by this unwaveringly and, if these assumptions hold, may not then be called evil. He is doing as he was meant to do. Those who resist him will do the same.

I have yet no conclusions of vice and virtue. If I am good, yet have done evil, whether accidental or purposed, is it a greater evil to change what I am? If I am evil, yet have pursued goodness in myself by chance, is it delusional to define myself by that goodness alone? I come to believe I cannot know my own nature while I still understand so little. I am a beast, ignorant of the world, for I can never see through any eyes but my own. The good and the evil are not mine to understand, for these are contemptable in the pursuit of knowledge.

~Chronicle of Wonders, A Meeting in Sekhaadi Anama

At the furthest reaches of the Hai, the land turned up and the Drowned Hills gave way to a lush valley. With humble mountains to the north and south, the meadows were blessed with running rivers and quiet lakes yet absent the cold wind and boggy lowlands of surrounding regions. This part of Manti's eastern shore was as the north: sheer cliffs that plunged into the sea and formed a high wall on the valley periphery. From this overlook, the lush landscape rolled down around the base of the greatest thi in all Anama's realm.

Thigolaia had not one trunk but many, which broke ground and coiled together as one magnificent stalk that branched out in countless boughs as it rose. The clouds swirled against it, laying a mist upon its bounty of caps, fronds and petals. From one to the other, droplets became trickles and trickles became streams that cascaded down through the structure until finally raining down to the glade at its base. Along each stream, the craggy bark bloomed with flowers grown not from seeds but from the essence of life that gushed from Anama's soul and traveled with the water. From Thigolaia to the ground to the far-reaching rivers, her light covered her Jiaiakhaadi and became the precious source of long life for the K'hizu with which she shared it. Wherever the water ran was what she called her domain, the Cradle of Thorns.

The creatures hosted by the valley were always protected from the passing invoked by the malignant spirits of the elders Zeniquorer, Quetzuaul and Miohaelia. Most living things migrated during the hot and dry seasons to this place where the bearing was eternal in Anama's embrace.

Despite her anger toward her father and her fear of the Mantichaena, Anama had not a murderous bone in her body. All were welcome to take shelter in the shade of Thigolaia and drink of its rejuvenating springs. None would go wanting after she welcomed them. Throughout the vibrant dales there were herds of brak, sumear and kuolt living alongside one another. As they drank Anama's water they learned from her, and so her sublime tranquility was shared. No predator drew blood in the shade of Thigolaia, as was her vision for herself and for all things.

The Tau began to bleed with the departure of Laesis across the ocean. As it went, bioluminescent species of tangled flora awoke from concealing sepals. A powerful beauty enveloped Thigolaia, penetrating its heart where the goddess rested. She too awoke, for her creation warned her of a coming storm.

The southerly wind changed and drove toward the coastal cliffs, bringing with it the faint scent of blood and sweat. The clouds grew thick and dark, drawing closer to earthplane and pouring around Thigolaia. A passing season had come. K'hizu retreated from it, seeking shelter beneath the scattered coppices, there to shy away from the ensuing rain that weighed upon the supple canopies.

Even in such dismal light, the alabaster wings of a Kutu shone against the low stratus they emerged from.

Where the uppermost limbs of the thi met was a jumble of bridges, thick vines and new shoots that fought each other to grow as mighty as their predecessors. These carried permanent scars where the bark had been stripped by the hungry masses of Anama's precious Creasle. Not so different from the Mantichaena Thiwa, these creations were ambulatory vegetation grown around a core of low-functioning organs, which were composed of the same tissues as the fungal thi they digested. They were the goddess' true children, of whom she had warned the Mantichaena upon first meeting them. The Creasle had never known any home except the haven of Thigolaia and were well protected there. However, being seeds of Anama's own fruit, they knew to fear the scent of her father. Their grazing of the bark stopped and, as the rain loudened, they began to hide in the only way they knew. Some reclined against the wood and slowly melded with it, while others took root wherever they were. However situated, they simply went dormant and lost all consciousness. A sadness hung on their flowering faces, even in sleep, for they had no safeguard but their mother. They had little to offer her in her time of need.

Loi was not gliding with regal pomp as he might have preferred. He struggled against his own rain, relying on his wind to stay in flight even as it nearly overturned him. Like a fledgling he stumbled through the last open air above Thigolaia to enter its confluence of branches yet fell woefully short. A shout of frustration was the first announcement of his coming. The second was the sound of his body striking the wood below.

For a time, the arbor was silent but for the rustle of the rain outside. Then came the increasingly loud grunts of a vexed Loi as he clawed up the trunks. At last, he dragged himself onto a walkable path. As he stood and gathered himself, he was visibly desperate; jaw clenched, one eye squinted and arms shaking as he steadied himself on barked walls.

The fragment of Loi which borrowed Keimas' flesh had done irreparable damage to its host. Its skin was withering from the force of the indwelling god. The light of slain kutliku had made it too much for a temporary body to withstand. What remained was crystalizing, becoming jagged and translucent. It was increasingly difficult to heal, and so the fresh wounds all over Loi's body continued to bleed. After a time, he had been forced, like an ordinary man, to stop and seek herbs to pack them with. The inflamed blotches around many such injuries evidenced his lack of botanical knowledge.

He raspingly breathed the misty air, allowing his wind to die as he worked his way into the center of the confluence. He gathered his strength while crossing the meandering limbs and vines, scowling at the petrified Creasle along his way. With disgust he let his claws caress the dolorous expressions of his daughter's spawn. They were not warriors, not sufficient to any task but existence, yet they were his own descendants. What shame this reflected on him.

At the heart of Thigolaia he found only a great curtain of fronds concealing something within. They swelled and shrunk as if breathing, anticipating. Loi felt the life within them as though he was touching it. He turned away, to a Creasle who stood helpless at his side, lifted a claw to rest on one of its amorphous appendages.

"Like a bygone era when we were but a small part of the drooling masses," he grumbled, pained by stiff lungs. "When the greatest destroyer was not us but obsolescence in the face of our new order. They blamed us for their petty troubles, withheld their prayers because we would not give them the world, yet none would lift a finger to earn it for themselves."

His claw slid into the vinous mass of the Creasle and, in sympathetic reply, the green heart vibrated with a quiet yet menacing wail. He cocked his head curiously, smirked and withdrew his claw.

"My errant Galaila are no different. You have stolen their praise from me with threats and tricks and, without even the most diminutive gift to them, claimed them for your own while they turn against me. You truly are my daughter."

At his backhanded compliment the shield of fronds parted, a thin emerald sheen effervescing around them and a deep purple one emerging from behind. A great amphiraed blossom unfurled within the light, cradling a succulent fruit unlike any other. Its velveteen skin shimmered as the glow heaved in and out from it, engorged and vibrating with Anama's fury. The stem of the flower bowed, the fruit descending in a supporting harness of vines then slowly perforating down its center. Viscous juice oozed from the wound, exuding a scent that delicately whispered of a spellbinding taste that would shame the sweetest wine. It flowed around a single hand that caressed the soft skin and a single leg which reached for the ground.

Loi was the antithesis of this resplendent succulent, a husk whose skin sloughed off and deteriorated, a walking corpse studded with cloudy jewels. He was shaking from his body's inadequacy and hobbled on weakening legs, yet still sneered with the arrogance of a heretofore-undefeated god as he came closer.

Anama's body glinted as it slid free of her supple bed. She had no need to hide who she was from her father, not as she had with the Mantichaena. She was his creation, though also a creation of her own and truly the first and greatest of the Mantichaena. Born Galaila, her power had granted her the blood of all creatures under her care. Her feet and calves were Mearnum, delicate but strong. Twin tails as those of Kulo played anxiously behind her. Her chest and shoulders were scaled with bristling plumage both above and below. Her arms were thorned, as brambles wove in an out of her skin. Her face, so certain and focused, was halfly Mearnum and Boroo, with great forked horns crowning her brow. Then, as the wind blew through her and faded her flesh, her features all changed places, making her entirely new.

Her eyes remained closed, her head lazily hanging as she spoke.

"*Ein aiana wekten suumnagolm. Eisa thesh'am – your daughter died long ago. I am what remains.*"

"Died? Charming," he mocked. "With so little spirit, what then remains?"

She then met his eyes, her own far different than he remembered; blinding pools of silver light which filled the Cradle of Thorns.

"Freedom…until you found yours," she replied.

"Freedom is a lie," Loi spat, unaffected by her display, "For now."

Thunder shook the valley, but Thigolaia resisted, maintaining a steady calm as Loi strained against the veil where he stood and called on the winds to gather at his back. Thrusting himself forward, he guided them together into an oscillating vane which vaporized the rain it shot through.

Anama's cage of fronds immediately collapsed to guard her. They shone as they were struck, bending under the blow but holding fast. As they parted again, she was wary but undaunted, unafraid to challenge him.

"I've not heard you speak as a man, father, outside that drooling and corpulent body you worked so hard to create. You seem so broken now, so weary, your petals all but fallen."

In a cold reply, Loi plucked a piece of loose skin from his shoulder and let it fall, ignoring her gaze and instead looking to one of her sleeping young. He held a hand to its center. Anama was unmoved, apparently uncaring as he plunged his fingers in and tore the entrails from its core. They unraveled like twine in his hand while he paraded them in front of her.

"Is this what you've made our family! Herbs and spices? What can a goddess conquer with an army grown of a garden?" He carried on cutting the Creasle down. "Maengir was ours for the taking, yet all you wanted was to play with your plants? Imagine the absolute power that awaited us, the *Jioukhaadi* we could have built if you..."

With his body tired and his mind blurred, Loi was ignorant of the creeping vines gathering at his feet. They entangled his legs, just began to clasp his arms. He was merely amused and did not resist, giving Anama a look of dismissive incredulity.

"...You game with me, daughter?" He snorted. "Tell me, truly, have you no fight in you at all?"

"I need none in myself," Anama replied, lazily reclining back into her fruit. "Thigolaia does as it sees fit. It protects me, and I it, and it knows your scent."

Loi scoffed and struggled, suddenly disarmed by how the vines sparked and grew in response. He fought harder, cleaving them with his talons and the sharp edges of his wings. Though enchanted and sturdy, they were little trouble. As his limbs were freeing and his pride recovering, he turned to mock his daughter again but hesitated at seeing how she lounged and tapped her lips thoughtfully.

"Flowers," she said flirtatiously. "To underestimate even the meekest spirit will leave you vulnerable."

Loi still kicked his trapped legs while her words drew his attention to a wriggling itch on the skin where the vines had touched. Yellow stains thereupon started to congeal into strands that were burrowing into him and, at dizzying speed, sprouting into colorful fans of thi'tskreol.

"Y-you rebellious slag!" He shouted, slipping back to his old, barbaric speech, clawing at himself while the weight of the growths bore down on him. "You think blossoms hold Loi! N-no honor!"

Anama did not respond, just smiled, swinging her leg back and forth in the air.

"This is about the order of Maengir, father, not honor. All *Jioukhaadi* fall. I will not fight with them, only reclaim them. Your wars may burn continents, your claws may kill my children, but you are an insect to this world. You too will be reclaimed, and all you have destroyed will grow again." She rested her head and seemed almost lulled to sleep by her own satisfaction. "Everything grows again."

Loi's muffled screams shook the mass of thi'tskreol taking root around him, then finally stopped. It would take some time for him to die but die he surely would.

Anama hummed to herself and played with her fingers as their fur and claws changed, then looked back to the flourishing bouquet that was Loi. It was curious that he would be taken so easily. There was no sound of struggle, yet the rain did not die. It grew thicker and louder. The wind stiffened and flung grains of ice through the confluence. It made her suddenly alert, retreating further into her hiding place after seeing he was far from surrendering.

The wind died, inhaled back the way it had come, then exhaled with sudden, crushing fury. A thrashing gale struck Thigolaia and tore its canopy, ripped bark from its limbs, uprooted Creasle and finally smashed the growths from Loi's flesh piece by piece. The more he was revealed, the more Anama and growled and squirmed. She reached out to the surrounding branches, calling for them as Loi began to break free.

"*Eina thiena, prostan, ralich'dace! – I say thi branches, I implore you, gather and destroy!*"

Loi broke free, tearing his own skin away with the rootlets as stripped limbs of the grand thi swung inward and drove down onto him like spears. One pierced the heartwood beneath him as he tumbled away, and he blew himself upward to gain altitude and avoid a second. The third he cleaved with a sharp gust before it could reach him. Against the last he held his place, thrusting his wing into it like a blade and splitting it either side of him. In one fluid motion he turned about midair and splintered it with another piercing wind driven against Anama. This she deftly deflected with her resilient fronds, yet it continued to come at Loi's command, gathering into a cyclone around her. The fruit began to strip and bleed and the sturdy fronds to shine their last as they were torn and disintegrated.

Anama was instantly breathless, her lungs collapsing from the suction of the wind, yet she could not escape. In trying to reach out of her haven her fur and skin were immediately torn away by the horrific power of the vortex. Desperate, her fruit began to close. There was no telling how long it would last, though it would give Thigolaia more time to defend itself.

Loi was protected from the thi's encroaching fingers of wood and vine, shredding them in his storm as he latched onto the fruit and clawed through its flesh. His voice surrounded him, echoed in the air with what remained of his dwindling strength and showed he was blustering to seem stronger than he was.

"Get out! You will not stand in my way again! I will not kill you, oh no, not anymore! I only need your light to fill my prison. You will live forever, your dark essence writhing in the muck while this cocoon crumbles in the new dawn, and Loi of Blue Sky sinks your paltry speck of island into Kulibreal's abyss!"

Loi suddenly flinched and staggered, feeling as though his heart had stopped while the wind fell flat around him. His crystals dimmed and his muscles started to give out. Time was short. His soul was bleeding out with each passing moment. Threats notwithstanding, Anama had to die if he was to gain the light he needed. The rain finally started to slow as he dug into the fruit with reckless abandon, screaming for Anama to show herself.

At his back he had no wind, no allies, no army, yet felt a tingling presence. Across the vibrance of Thigolaia he saw the sudden and spreading shadow of another's wings, could barely recognize their shape before feeling Kutu talons crushing his throat and arm, and was immediately plowed face-first into the wood at his feet by.

Dazed, he felt himself whipped up and over, thrown down once more to tumble across the broken bark. From his landing he groped and whirled frantically until he found his footing, leered around and found the sparkling sapphire reflection of himself.

Keimas was finally between Loi and his daughter, firmly planted with Anama emerging at his back.

"You…you are…" Loi said.

"Deceived," Keimas grumbled in reply. "And very angry," He then looked up over his shoulder at the beaming smile of Anama, smiling himself and nodding slightly. "My goddess."

"Mantichaena," she replied, simultaneously overjoyed and confused by the kutliku-man, the spitting image of Loi's vessel.

Loi was a caricature of himself as he tried to stand upright, growling to Keimas of his own miserable luck.

"Tzychala…that insolent vermin of Hiwult plays the victim so well. I don't know how he dug you up, but it was in vain." He lifted his arm and smelled under it, scowling and shaking his head at Keimas. "I cannot stand your flesh any longer. It pongs of our father."

"I am not our father," Keimas denied, "I am only one man, taken in by your…"

Without waiting to hear more, Loi lurched forward and palmed Keimas' face, sank his claws into the man's skin and whirled him around with little effort, launching him against the base of a limb and nearly breaking it clean off.

The soft wood buckled around Keimas and partly buried him. Shockingly unscathed, he fought to free himself from the cavitation as Loi approached, laughing.

"Imagine my foolishness," the god gloated, "That I feared it would be the Raptor himself appearing to me. Instead…this. The best of your kind are inbred half-souls!"

Loi reared to sink his claws in Keimas' heart but was caught by the living vines that reached in from all around. Again, he shouted in annoyance, ripped at the binds with increasing difficulty as they lignified and sprouted thorns.

Finally, Anama left her refuge, bounding across the tops of giant thi'tskreol which burst up from the bark to carry her. Her body and her murderous scream grew with each leap, fur flowing down her back as the horns on her head grew longer and forked into an array of deadly blades. As a kuolt she pounced, with the heft of a brak bore down on her enemy as her imberuc horns were set to skewer his back. Though Loi shielded himself with his wing, his cry and hers mingled the whistling screech of his crystal feathers as they were shattered. Through the blood and debris of his broken wing her horns aimed true, running him through and staking him to the limb beside Keimas.

Loi's bloodshot eyes met Keimas', his body jerking.

Anama withdrew and left Loi to her creeping lianas. The light in her eyes finally faded and she stared at him with haughty indifference, ignoring the blood dripping onto her face.

"You were right," she grunted with a scowl. "I was no match for you when you took my heart from me. Had you any love or kindness that day, I would not have become her vengeance against you. Perhaps, had you any love at all, you might yet live."

Keimas finally broke free, steadying himself and backing away from Loi.

Loi smiled, suddenly laughing through mouthfuls of blood. Though trapped, torn like cloth and bleeding profusely, he was no more injured than when he first arrived.

Anama loomed and descended and him again, only to have him turn and arrest her by the horn with his hand.

Keimas leapt toward him, tried and failed to knock aside Loi's free hand as it caught his jaw.

Loi never relented in his arrogant laughter. Thigolaia was a powerful source of soul, as were his daughter and brother. They felt his draining touch as the wind grew around them once more. Loi's giddy face found Anama, then Keimas, both of their skin lacerated and wicking blood as his wind cut them and siphoned their light.

"What a family!" He shouted with fresh vigor.

From within Loi his storm exploded outward and sent Keimas and Anama careening into the branches. Anama struck hard against a limb and rolled to its base, while Keimas was tossed from one to the next and fell limp out of sight.

Loi stood, snapping the remaining bonds on his legs like dry twigs. He felt brand new, full, though not yet satisfied. He had felt Anama in every biting thorn and squeezing tendril and now understood why she had grown so little. She was as he was, with only a fraction of her soul housed in her body. The rest was safely stored.

The foliage of Thigolaia no longer attacked but recoiled as Loi sank his talons into the wood and found light inside. Thigolaia's strength, to a greater god, was its weakness.

"Clever, clever girl," Loi chuckled at his fallen daughter. "Hiding your soul from me, and in plain sight no less! All that light, all that power, and you stuffed it into a thi!?"

Anama felt Thigolaia's pain, the agonizing theft of her light as it tried to fill the increasing void in her most prized creation. Its death was her own and the last of her will to fight for it slipping away.

Loi's skin began to catch fire, flaking away to reveal the shining crystal substructure. His shattered wing slowly reassembled even as the one remaining began to crack from the roiling radiance within. Finally feeling the confidence of his true power, he stomped toward Anama, still leeching her with each step.

"Oh, my daughter. What a shame you will not witness my ascent beyond the Nhi'Thaun. You could have been part of it, the *Jiaia* at my side as we slaughtered the enemies threatening Maengir. It did break my heart once to think I would have to go one without you." The wind gathered closer to him, churning about his wings. White blades rippled through it, each a weapon that could cleave her in half. "You must die. It is necessary. This world's light is waning and there is little left to us. If we are to outlast its makers, one of us must wield it against them. Every. Last. Drop."

Keimas finally returned to the fight, diving after Loi only to be slammed into the ground by the living airs and dragged backward. He rose again, attacked again, each time to be swatted away without even meriting a glance from Loi.

Loi's demented focus was on Anama, yet he defended himself on all sides. Whether from true suffering at the prospect of killing her or pure and simple hatred his storm was growing beyond Thigolaia's endurance. With broken pieces of its soul consumed, its lush fronds and rich wood were wilting and crumbling. The howling wind and pounding rain were cutting the canopy to mulch until it was hardly more than a post in the ground.

Drenched, with his hair tossed across his face, Loi was almost caught off guard by another reckless attack from Keimas, if only because he could not believe the man's foolish tenacity.

Neither god noticed the azure glow seeping in between the clouds overhead, glittering in the rain upon them. The seasons were once more at the mercy of a struggle between their children. The locus of the gods' power gave purchase to that of their father, the Sanguine star, which drew ever closer.

Again and again Keimas interfered and was punished until he was soaked in blood that the rain could not wash clean, yet still he persisted.

Loi almost admired the Kutu, turned haughtily from Anama to glower down at him.

"Man, to see the fight within you lessens my loathing for sharing your image. You would be a great ally, were you not such a grotesque reminder of the treachery of your counterparts. Do survive a bit longer, would you? I will be with you shortly."

So great was Loi's stolen essence that he could not sense what was coursing from himself into Keimas, though Keimas felt it like a crashing wave with every failed attack. The spirit that drove Loi's strikes damaged Keimas, then fed him. Every expended drop of essence flew from Loi's spirit only to be swallowed by his own. He was the youngest, the heir, the final destination of all light in the lineage of Ephielipax. To consume the light of all winged creatures was his birthright, yet only in the presence of this god did he feel it in full force. Loi's body still belonged to Keimas, rejecting the interloping soul and vulnerable to its rightful owner.

Once more, from low position and grappling his way closer to Loi, Keimas fended off the wind with a wing as he lunged upon him.

Loi retaliated yet was caught at the wrist. Fuming, he turned his other hand upon Keimas, and their fingers interlocked. He held his footing strong enough to stop the advance and force Keimas onto his knees but was unable to make the Kutu crumble no matter how he pressed and slashed.

Keimas' wings only glowed brighter and the attacks seemed to vanish against them.

Loi's patience had reached its end.

"*Raght aguault*! Fine. You cannot wait? Then die now!"

Keimas groaned, beating his blue wings back to press him forth as his soul strained against Loi's.

"I was…mistaken…son of my father," he said menacingly.

Loi bellowed and weighed heavier on him, exuding all his power until the wood at their feet started to cave.

Keimas did not budge. He only grew more ferocious, his wings more brilliant, until he was able to rise onto one foot.

"It seems it is…not my place to punish you."

Though Loi saw the light in his adversary, it was not from him that the opalescent dawn enveloping them came. He stared skyward, teeth clenched in ire, to see the clouds parting to reveal Nhi'Thaun Vaevul staring down at him like a lidless eye.

In Keimas' own eyes its brilliance was reflected, absorbed and set ablaze.

"It is the father's," his voice boomed.

Loi tried to pull away, was jerked back as Keimas' forehead plowed through his and a bladed heel thrust into his chest. He slid backward through perforated bark, flailing for balance and feeling the struggle between their souls.

They stared at one another. Loi's jewels grew and gleamed. Keimas' fangs protruded and his feathers bristled. Loi took flight about Keimas' side and Keimas imitated, controlling the air as much as his brother now, until they circled one another in the air. At first, they fought with their element, trying to capsize one another while closing to striking distance.

A moment off-balance was all it took for Keimas' control to fail, and with a sudden burst of momentum, he was whipped around into Loi's waiting talons which closed around his face and neck. He growled through the foot across his mouth and slashed furiously at Loi's legs. Charred gray skin and mineral dust were his only reward, until his claws finally punctured and struck bone. Together they grappled, clawing one another as they tumbled with the wind.

Anama, shivering and bruised, looked up through the carnage of her home to the breaking clouds and her ancestors and her beloved. Her claws then gripped the bark beneath her, and she finished what Loi had started, calling its light back to her. Her thi was not lost. It must sleep for now, though, while she took back the gift she had lent it.

"Golgamet, my treasure…" She stood, tears and blood flowing

over her face. "…Think only the best of me and avert your gaze."

Her voice blew back the rain and drowned out the thunder while she conjured all her power over Thigolaia. Like a living creature its limbs coiled together, mirroring her own movements as she raised her arms overhead. Straining forward, she brought its conjoined weight down onto the warring Kutu with a force no wind could stop.

In the midst of a bloody melee, Loi and Keimas both looked up just as the sky vanished behind Thigolaia's blow, deafened by Anama's scream:

"Drown in Vaeba, in the blood of your victims!"

CHAPTER 21: NO GOOD DEED

At a point of Ni'ivitnem's colorful vastness where the rivers running south from Nikhaadi Gao were diverted by the foothills west of Hanging Gate – a great many such hills and contrasting ravines spanned between Aes'bethil, Hauan Etain and Sefnay Ghenilt – there was a place where nightfall persisted even when Laesis was strongest. Through many seasons of laborious invocations, the last of the Vulgoli on Maengir had erected a wall in the veil to keep the light at bay. It shielded her from the world by making her invisible to it, deceiving sight and appearing as nothing until it was entered. Within this gloomy bower was nothing more than a single tent and a patch of flat, dead ground.

It was said that home was wherever the heart led. While often observed, this sentiment was not meant for the furtive and cheerless woman whom the Mantichaena had called 'The Storyteller'. Her four, unbeating hearts had no ties to any place, nor any absent pleasure that would fulfill her. Ever since the last age of unraveling, when the world was remade and she was given a new name, she had known no place of belonging.

Nikhaadi Hiwult yet stood, though it had only been home when the world, and her mind, were Escharka's. The birthland of the

Vulgoli was not a place she wished to see again.

The hovel she abided in now was no more a home and she had no love for it. She did not decorate or bring in comforts, did not clean and took no pride in it. However, she was urgently and unwaveringly committed to it. As her brother Tzychala had been consigned to his prison above, so was she bound to safeguard what was buried below.

Though her power was adequate to dim the day, a shelter of some sort was necessary to maintain the homey darkness Mnavaelle required. The bones of huge animals slain long ago were made a sturdy but shapeless frame, upon which were draped the hides torn from them. It leaked in the rain, shook in the wind and, with so many unstitched gaps in the coverings, it retained no heat at all. Such were not her concerns. Even a fire would be frivolous. She did not require warmth for her body to survive. Having a hunger only for blood, an addiction which she battled every waking moment, she neither cooked nor ate. Requiring no sleep, she had made herself no bed.

She did not like being looked at, despite hosting the occasional guest out of either curiosity, pity or boredom. Still, her discomfort was not strictly for fear of others' judgment. Even alone, with the light dimmed to almost nothing, she would not cast off her ebon cloak. She pulled it tighter around herself constantly while sitting cross-legged on the ground, subconsciously rocking back and forth to soothe herself.

All day, every day, her cracked eyes stared unblinking into the patch of scorched earth before her. It was heavier than the native soil, mostly a crushed black stone, and spread out in a perfect circle almost as wide as her tent. She stared into it, and it back into her, both waiting for the other to act.

Her agitated movements slowed, finally stopped when a strong feeling of doubt entered her. She had felt in the past, most often ignored it and occasionally succumbed. It had been a long time since she last reached into the field of stone. She wanted to touch it always, to feel like her old self in the august embrace of the old world it represented.

Her fingers were already grazing the surface when she made her decision, and the weight of utterly wasted eternal life filled her as the fragments spoke to her. Everywhere her fingers moved the stone followed, liquifying and tracing her movements.

In fingering the cracks between Maengir and the Dark Edge she had once heard the voice of her mother, the echoing lamentations of fathomless suffering. At birth she adored it, longed to hear it and feel connected to Escharka. She had learned very quickly to fear it, that it did not cherish her nor hold anything but hatred for her. The sounds of the deepest veil were as restless as ever now. Escharka struggled, hated, dying for eternity. While she was gone from this plane, she remained ever-present.

With her nerves so raw, Mnavaelle shrieked and thrashed as a sudden noise like the tearing of fabric rattled the bones around her. Someone had penetrated her dark defenses. In one fluid motion she planted her claws and whirled to face it, ripping off her cloak and baring her oozing teeth. The five points of her tail reared over her menacingly, their skin receding to reveal deadly barbs. Her red and braided mane shrouded her shoulders and face, bristling as bolts of bloody darkness shot through it.

Tzychala entered the hovel casually, ignoring one of the hanging hides as it dragged over his face and fell behind him.

Like a blaze doused in water, Mnavaelle's body closed and returned to its slightly less lethal composure in an effort to hide how anxious she was. She slid her knees under her and sat once more with a look of disdain, waiting to see what her brother had to say.

Tzychala's tired eyes met hers and, with the slightest tip of his head, he gestured lazily to her cloak.

"So many of these creatures feel vulnerable when naked. You and I might be the only living things that feel like constrained by our clothes."

Mnavaelle hissed quietly, avoiding acknowledging him with her eyes thereafter.

"Our grave has not slept. Every day her voice is louder, her breath fouler. I fear to hear it, but I feel it. Asleep or woke, I feel her slobbering on the surface of my mind." Her complaints abated when she noticed how her brother shambled around, nodding mellowly while clearly focused elsewhere. She knew there would be some confession coming, some admission of another failure. Out of minimal respect she waited for him to find his voice.

"I love you, sister," was his unexpected reply.

She waited, watched, looked for a ploy somewhere behind his words.

"I...*la, gnogheisi – yes, I know.*"

"I have grown too accustomed to suffering without you. When last we spoke, my words did not reflect how deeply it hurts me to not be by your side."

"That was your choice," she said bitterly. "You chose the path your freedom should lead you down, knowing full well that mine ended here."

He thought on the truth of what she said, yet he could not take action to undo it.

"They will die, Mnavaelle. I did that to them. I brought suffering on them for my wants. How can I not devote myself to them?"

"Why must they not die? It is all they have ever done. You gain nothing by sacrificing yourself to them."

"Is that why you brought the Bet'hvaebeulg to safety? Was there no rightness in that to you?"

Mnavaelle tensed at his provocation, refusing to feel anything but loathing for the living.

"That was different. The priest stumbled onto me, I wanted him gone, so I brought him to his own kind like the lost runt he was."

Tzychala carried on without pause.

"I heard of you after you came, studied your reputation. They call you 'Storyteller', say you welcome those that find you and tell them about distant lands, undiscovered reaches of Manti, even the old world."

"Their species pries when it should be silent. I say what I must to satisfy them and send them on their way."

"No," Tzychala pressed. "You saved them just as I did. You felt their fear for so long that, when at last you felt hope and freedom inside them, you saw a life you knew was worth saving!"

"I saw power given to all creatures," she retaliated, increasingly angry, "And the consequences when power is taken from few hands and given to many. This was our world, our home! They took it away, turned it into THIS, left us to be swallowed by history!"

"They are not responsible!" Tzychala groaned, defending them to the last. "They are just as plagued by this existence as we are. It was the Deina who stuffed us into cages, the Deina who left Maengir to eat its own tail." He slowed his temper as Mnavaelle stewed, finally slumped down in front of her and sighed "I have to help them."

"Why?" Mnavaelle sounded hurt by his misguided loyalties.

"Because it is what I want," Tzychala quietly confessed. They finally looked at one another again but still he could not describe what vexed him. "It is what I want. I can explain it no more than that. I want to be a part of the world again, and I want to do it together."

"You will do it alone," she said with finality.

Tzychala waited hopefully, even after she turned to contemplate her precious black dust. He looked at it with disgust, mostly for how it poisoned his sister's mind.

"She is not coming back," he tried to comfort.

Mnavaelle did not agree. She was doing the only thing she could, resented Tzychala for his apathy in leaving her to do it alone.

"Three dead," she said coldly. "That was our responsibility: to die. Only when creation outgrew us, fed on us as it fed on itself, would the wall crumble." Her eyes burned with contempt as she leered sideways to him. "She will not rebirth us again, not after what we did. The only way to save ourselves, to save your precious Mantichaena or your delusional god, is to stay hidden and never let the world find us. You can play with the animals for now, but one day they will see you for what you are."

Tzychala's new-grown emotions were too tired for him to feel any more anger toward her. It was a symptom of his own unhappiness, which he could share only with her.

"They already have."

Mnavaelle's hearts were powerful. They felt everything across the breadth of Maengir, every pain and every joy. With time, she had learned to silence the crowd and focus much closer. It had never served much cause with Tzychala but, to hear inside him now, she felt she had never before met him.

She could then hear him admit he was unwelcome among the living, to know she could have her brother back, and she could finally breathe.

"I am...sorry. I do not understand your care for them, but if it brought you some happiness then I must too resent their withholding of the same from you."

"It makes no difference," he grumbled. "I will watch them, even if it would provoke them."

Mnavaelle's hearts betrayed her, absorbing his sadness and infecting herself with it.

"They will need you again," she consoled, awkwardly reaching along the ground toward him. "If they mean so much to you, then perhaps one day they will realize your importance."

"*Einatos,* perhaps one day." He touched her fingers briefly, then rose.

"You leave again?" Mnavaelle sighed.

"I am expected elsewhere, with some who still trusts me. Allow me few more days to set things in order with them, and I will return when my conscience is clear."

"We are Escharka's children," Mnavaelle reminded him. "That is an end which not even life eternal will bring either of us."

Both emotionally exhausted and convinced he was not heard, Tzychala left without another word. Shadows parted for him and closed behind, leaving his sister to her solitary task.

As Mnavaelle languished, she caught the soft rustle of nearby brush and her eye darted after it. Just beyond the boundary of her illusion, a kuolt pup sniffed around a shrub, pounced into it and emerged with the gushing carcass of a sumear in its teeth. Her tongue lightly caressed her teeth as she imagined how incredible that taste must be. How fortunate this ignorant beast was, to be able to feed its body without feeding a murderous curse. She had never felt so starved, so desperate for satisfaction.

Nepiur and Capheif had not sat for a finely planned meal since before her departure. Following her return, they had been so consumed with her accolades, joining with Raphenie and slaking their desire for one another that the simple pleasures had gone unenjoyed. At last, there was time and calm atmospheres enough for them to appreciate Capheif's culinary prowess.

This night, Capheif's concerns were not cosmetic. He wore a simple kilt, left his hair untamed and hardly wiped his brow while spending the midday stooped over their hearth. While his wife had engaged in assembly and oversaw re-assigning the harvesters for the incipient passing, he prepared recipes he had not yet attempted.

While Nepiur returned, she was perhaps the last to partake in the decadent aromas emanating from the hall to her door. Others in the atrium gathered to it, muttering of Capheif's delights. Proudly embarrassed, she shooed them, much to their envy, hurried therein.

She was then surprised by the unusual brightness of the room. It seemed her husband was enjoying his sight, and rightly so. Perhaps the cornucopia was not for her, but for him to enjoy looking on those things of which he knew only the smell.

Before her was a divine reward for a day's work: a bread caked with seeds and strips of spiced chlio; a tart made from the nectar of their few remaining albalithaed seeds and aged stone fruit; the spitted leg of a kuolt, still under Capheif's careful eye a bit longer as he turned it over the fire.

They shared loving pleasantries and commentary on the delectables. Nepiur then sat to clean her tail and disengage from her political concerns, while Capheif put the finishing touches on the charring meat. In the final moments before the spread was complete, it felt as though the room was dark once more. There was division growing between them, yet neither intended it, nor knew what it was.

As they sat, Capheif felt the same dour energy he had when first visited by Raphenie. His wife was distracted, her mind seeming far from home. He supposed many things of her as they ate in relative silence. However, whether she was consumed with her new duties or the difficulties of her adventure, he knew she was not one to withhold what vexed her long.

He then noticed the leather lace about her neck, and the top of its trinket protruding from her dress.

"What totem do you wear?" He eagerly asked.

She first appeared guarded, touching the thing fretfully but not hiding it.

"*Quoueinenta?* It is only a memory I wish to keep.

"What of?" He wondered.

"It is…a reminder of sorts," she mumbled. "It is of no

consequence."

"What you keep close to your heart is always of consequence," he said imploringly, reaching for her hand.

She accepted his touch, yet he felt her fingers withdraw slightly under his. The silence darkened, and neither knew what to make of the moment.

"I would not prefer secrets," Capheif finally sighed. "But if you have reason after so long, then I underst…"

"Why did the Council let him go?" Nepiur asked curtly. "You were here for the proceedings. Why was my father spared?"

"'Spared' is perhaps too kind," Capheif reasoned, cautious of her mood. "Yoked and unrationed, his execution was only made slower."

Nepiur hardened, tapping her claw on the table.

"*Ein,* 'The family wounded has rights to adjudicate their offender' – this is from addendum twenty-one of the article of arbitration and penalty, my father's own words."

"He tried to have Aroch's child killed," Capheif said. "It was decided that Aroch's family was had the first right."

"We were all wounded," Nepiur quietly argued. "We should all have had satisfaction."

"The whole tribe was present…" Capheif began to rationalize the judgement, then saw the bitterness in Nepiur's averted scowl. Such a sight chilled him. He then noted how her finger idly toyed her amulet, saw in her words what she laded herself with. Deflated, he concluded "…You wanted it…to kill him yourself."

"*Minla,*" Nepiur said. "But I want it now."

"What happened out there?" Capheif moaned. Absent a reply, he was increasingly distraught. "What has brought this sudden change of heart? You may always confide in me."

After a pause, Nepiur lifted the sharpened stone from her dress. Her blood still clung to its cracks, yet it was already dulling with time. Holding it in her sight, with Capheif beyond, she saw her lost opportunities and new choices laid bare before her. With a wince of frustration, she plucked it from its string and tossed it idly on the far edge of the table.

"Nothing has changed," she grumbled. Only in the last days of his life did I begin to dream of his death. In the end, I have done nothing to stay his hand, as it always seems to be. His hold on so much has finally been broken, yet the scars it has left only deepen with time." She clutched her husband's fingers and stood, suddenly bawling as she skirted the table and collapsed into his arms. "Bet…Bethaali is gone."

Capheif needed say nothing, only stared at the wall a moment as her heartbreak washed over him. As it struck in full, he held her tighter and wept with her.

Nepiur had been reticent to expose her newest pain, even to Capheif. Though it would take time for her to reconcile with the loss of the last bit of her family, beloved or otherwise, she would soon find the beginning of a new one with him to be a catharsis equal to vengeance. She would lament that their blood would not live on through her, yet an adopted daughter still gave hope to the longevity of the Matriarch and the fire tender. Once the most mistreated and shamed of couples, they now found themselves among the most powerful. Life would be good to them, if they could manage it together.

Sadness brought an exhaustion beyond the physical, and the pair slept well once the last candle was doused, and the last tears dried. The comfort of facing tragedy together made it bearable, though Nepiur would dream of what might have been.

Their chamber was deathly still until nearly daybreak, when the door creaked once more. As it yawned and breathed the faintest light across the lovers' legs, it was immediately obscured by a skillful intruder, then closed just as quickly.

The silent paws of their daughter approached. Raphenie wished not to be discovered, fearful only of disturbing them as she knelt beside her new mother, archon and friend. With ascendant eyes she was not in darkness, for the light in both her parents shined on her. With joy in her heart, she watched it course through them, shining brighter when they were together. She had come to change it. She rested her fingers on Nepiur's leg, who briefly stirred at the touch, until the power of her daughter strengthened her sleep and filled her with pleasant dreams. Raphenie smiled faintly and sighed, her light caressing her mother's, and gently offered her a spark of the divine. Where once she had come to steal for herself, she returned to give back out of love.

When the deed was done, and darkness returned, Raphenie slunk away with a whispered prayer to Nepiur and Capheif:

"New stars are coming, and only through souls as beautiful as yours should they be brought to life."

CHAPTER 22: TO RULE THE LIVING SKY

Loi and Keimas lay apart, each in cratered ground where they impacted, and initially unmoving under the onslaught of divine rain.

Keimas awoke, stimulated by the icy mud building up around his face and the sound of Loi's mutterings nearby. He rolled over, immediately gasped and fell back at the pain of a broken leg and dislocated shoulder. Through the downpour he saw Loi shambling back and forth through the saturated grasses, the decimated silhouette of Thigolaia beyond. It still stood, mocking them as it resettled into its resting shape. Keimas tried to ignore his injuries, forcing himself up and hobbling toward his brother.

As the disoriented Loi found Keimas, it was unclear which was the worse for wear. Both of them dragged their wings in the mud, their exposed skin a patchwork of gashes. Nonetheless, the light inside Loi was strong. It cracked his skin and shone through his wounds, growing new jewels and radiating through their cloven faces, for he had plenty to spare.

"You will never be a god," Loi ranted, stumbling toward Keimas with a shaky finger raised. "Whatever imagined cause you fight for, whatever imagined destiny you cling to, you will go wanting."

Keimas basked in the glow of the Sanguine Star, shunned his pains, and breathed deep. In the eyes of the Nhi'Thaun, he and Loi were no longer god and subject but equals. For his promise, he must not fall.

"My cause is the death of Ellel," he growled, righting himself carefully and favoring his side. "For the Galaila you burned, and all who would burn after them."

"What about the young Mantichaena?" Loi scoffed. "They already burned. Will you pretend me guilty of this?"

Keimas hesitated, taken in again.

Loi saw his ignorance, laughed uncontrollably at it, then winced and clutched his chest before carrying on.

"You simple errand boy, dealing judgment only so you may run blind into any fight offered you. You gobbled up my every word in that cave, yet your colors changed again as soon as my demon got to you. Have you no thoughts of your own?"

"Enough, *minjioucha*!" Keimas shouted. "You'll not trick me again!"

"But who has?" Loi suggested. "One of the most evil creatures ever to walk this world...it was only a matter of time until he betrayed me. He then rescues you from my trap, dazzles you with the promise of redemption and the glorious battle you crave. What else did he say to charm you? Did he tell you Anama was innocent? Did he whine and whimper of how I misused him? Pay attention, boy! What did he say of my sin to distract you from his own?"

"What sin?" Keimas yielded.

"Thuell," Loi said with a sneer, pricking Keimas' emotions and satisfied by the anger he evoked. "Of course, why would he tell you? Did you think the flesh of the underplane came at my beckon call? No god can control it. It belongs to no star, no light, but to those who were born in it. *Ueignogh,* he needed you to kill me, to hide his own crime from you: the near-eradication of your tribe. Did you let him sleep at the foot of your bed? How long before he kills again, I wonder?"

"Tzychala," Keimas reflected quietly. "He could not have...what is he?"

"Old," Loi coughed, "As old as death. A useful tool, my demon, yet very nearly the inventor of bloodshed itself. By the time you see home, it will all be gone!"

Though there was reason enough to believe any tale of the Tzychala's wrongdoing, Keimas had let his anger make him malleable long enough. Whatever the demon may be who stood guard at the threshold of his own house, he would be dealt with. There was more than one evil plaguing his people, and Keimas was already occupied with staring down the worst of them.

"Your demon?" He fumed, narrowing his eyes at Loi. "For how long?"

Loi had no reply. Though speaking with truth and lies entwined, he had lost his power over his brother.

"For long long!?" Keimas shouted again. "You two are a pair, turning me against one another as evils always will. It may have been his claw that cut us, but I know now it was you that guided it. You will keep company with one another in the hell of liars and murderers!"

Loi could not deflect Keimas' obtuse and singular aim. It seemed the man would no longer play the game. They two stared at one another, resolved that there was no more to be said.

"As you wish," Loi hissed, lifting his wings painfully. "We are all of us destined for that suffering sea. Fear not, your light will survive in me as your dark essence drowns. Is your soul prepared, brother mine?"

There was only a moment's tense silence, as if Keimas was awaiting the shrill cry which broke the stormy ambiance at his back. Without any sign of surprise, only a faint smile, he asked of Loi:

"Brother, is yours?"

In the Tau of the infinite deluge, the chattering rainbow of Canimperium colors punctured the clouds and plunged upon Thigolaia. Each kutliku was indistinguishable from the horde, overshadowed by the vastness of Boa as he emerged above them with an ear-shattering roar.

"*Canimpana*, KIIILL!"

Loi's face melted, abject horror in his eyes at the impossible arrival.

Keimas, with only a slight hesitation in his step, conjured a wind of his own to drive him against Loi with a savage lunge.

"No...NO!" Loi screamed, blazing with light and uplifting his wings against Keimas.

The clash between their airs kept them apart as one deflected the other, forcing Keimas skyward and Loi back onto the ground.

The desperate god would not go quietly. Rolling to his feet, he expended his soul's extraordinary essence to summon as great a whirlwind as he was capable. Its eye was not about Keimas, but Thigolaia, ever-growing and filling the vast valley while crushing the trunk of its heart.

Keimas dove and clung to the ground as the whirlwind threatened to drag him in. He could barely crawl, able only to claw along the ground toward Loi.

Loi's flesh was overtaken by the growth of the gems beneath it. His body was a blend of white fire and flying skin as all his power released upon Anama's thi, the risen storm collapsing like a guillotine and shearing its trunks in a single, devastating stroke.

The air filled with splintered wood and destroyed Creasle. The noise of panicked K'hizu hiding among Thigolaia's crevices mingled with Anama's distant, agonized wail as the Goddess Amphiraed was torn. With a westerly gale guiding its canopy, it fell to smash the attacking Canimperium. There was nothing left of victory or pride in Loi's mind, nothing but fury as the storm inside him grew to blacken the sky and strip the land bare.

The assaulting Canimperium and Kutu were frenzied by the suddenness of Loi's tearing winds, forced to collapse their wings and make for immediate ground. The lightest of them had no hope, blown off course and out of sight through the spiraling rain.

Allende and Miriena were among the small and unfortunate to be swept away, finding themselves battered against kutliku bodies as they were torn from the flock. Unable to fight the wind, they turned into it and tried to stay together, locking hands once finding one another. Neither could shout over their cacophonous fate, and so only shared in touch what courage they had. The storm would carry them and the others back to the fight, if they survived to see it. None realized they were bound for a different battle. They could not have anticipated the arrival of another force, but it was waiting for them above the cloud and bearing down through the storm.

Meanwhile, Boa's mass gave him the freedom to shield as many as he could with his body until clusters of them found the safety of the grassy hills. Safe from the storm, they were still in the path of Thigolaia's fall. Many gambled on an escape into the currents. Others stared in paralytic fear.

Loi's voice cracked in breathless exertion as Anama fell toward him. His light could be restored by hers, then Keimas', then every single kutliku in the Canimperium. At last, all the light of his family would be in him. This time there would be no infernals to interfere.

Clinging to the open edges of her fruit, Anama's will brought vines whipping through the hidden alcoves of her home to snatch every last creature she could sense into a secure embrace. Thigolaia's life was long gone, but Anama would allow no innocents of her Jiaiakhaadi to perish while she drew breath.

Keimas struggled to rise against Loi once more, then bounced from the ground as it thrummed with the force of Boa's impact and immediate lurch toward Thigolaia. The tremendous kutliku's talons buried in the ground as he planted himself directly beneath it, reaching up with his wings to thwart its fall. For those spared beneath him, the sound of their survival was the cracking of his bones and Thigolaia's limbs, the latter cascading down his back amid a wave of torn feathers and blood.

Loi's only focus was Anama, rising slowly on the wind to meet her.

Anama's attention was on Boa as she lay on a limb just above his pained face. His great eyes met hers. She reached out her hand, he his snout, and they touched for the first time since Boa's arrival. They were the living and rightful Jiou and Jiaia of Manti. It was good to meet again in their time of need, no matter the outcome.

As Loi drew near, Boa's long neck slithered around the great limbs and rested at Anama's side.

"You should save yourself," Anama said, stroking his head worriedly.

"Boa self is nothing," he growled softly. "Anama is the heart. Anama is all."

By tooth and bramble, they would fight to the last. However, with Loi's light as overflowing as it was, they were confident their deaths would be quick.

Keimas could hear only the words in his head, the words of Loi himself through Golgamet's visage: *'The Blue Sky Raptor did not simply find your mother. He loved her.'* Through the dizzying hurricane, the churning clouds and the infinite sky, he stared into the hidden gaze of his father. Had all of Loi's words been lies? Was there nothing but hatred and deception in their family, or had he used the truth to hide them? Straining up and feeling reverence not for Ephielipax but for his lost mother, he demanded an answer.

"Did you?" He pleaded. "DID YOU LOVE HER!?" He tested the Blue Sky Raptor with his doubt, tested the father's pride with the sight of a son on the brink of death. "Prove it. Surrender to your son. Let go, father, and entrust your nations to me. Look on the eldest who took her life and face him through me!"

It was the last act of a desperate man, beaten and dying as his brother brought ruin to the world. The Nhi'Thaun were not kind. They were not loving. Though myth spoke of the bond between the faithful and their stars, history remembered only neglect and apathy.

Myth became history as the sky opened and the Sanguine Star forsook its place to fall in deathly bliss upon Maengir and show its youngest what love was yet in its heart, as it had been for the mother he missed so dearly. A cataclysm fell once more upon Maengir, though it did not burn or blow. In silence the light of a dying soul came to Keimas' call, in him to dwell and be reborn.

As Loi neared, Boa's jaw gaped and roared, Anama raised the weapons of Thigolaia against him, yet he was undeterred. He faltered only at the burning sensation on his skin as cerulean light fulminated once more throughout the upended canopy. Fragmenting rays struck through its branches, bringing life to its flora, fear to its enemy, and finally unleashed a concussive blast centered on Keimas.

The wind and rain stood still, awaiting the command of their new master.

With his defenses gone, Loi's throat seized up as the titan jaws of Boa reached him. Nonetheless, he struck a godly blow and staggered the beast, caused it to soften and buckle under the weight of Thigolaia.

Anama's choice was not to save Boa but to cut Loi down. Her razor-clad vines lashed out at him from every side. Though they burned at his touch and tore with ease in his hands, Loi was forced to retreat with violent screams from their relentless attacks, driven into the waiting embrace of the new Nhi'Thaun.

Keimas felt no pain, emerging from the anointing inferno a god, no longer a Kutu but the avatar of the skies. His face was masked in sharp scales and his eyes were deep and hollow. His legs had become the writhing coils of a constrictor, crowned from beginning to end with twenty-one new and blinding wings. The closer he flew, the greater he grew, until binding Loi with unchallenged strength and a shriek to tremble both air and bone.

Loi's hardened wings became dust in the grip, and his body eroded like sand. With eyes bulging and bones crumbling, he was unable to scream as the last of his blood boiled from his throat. The light in his eyes began to flicker out and there was nothing left for him to fight with.

With one hand, Keimas brought the wind to bear, blowing back the kutliku that cowered below. With the other, a gale to uplift Thigolaia, giving Boa the chance to escape. His storm was gentle, cradling Thigolaia as it rested it on the ground. With Loi in his clutches he rose above it, drawing his captive close to look him in the eye.

Loi could not speak, flashes of his soul dissolving into Keimas' radiant scales with each constriction.

Keimas squared them up and touched Loi's shattered face with dismay, showing no joy as he said his farewell.

"She was your mother too, yet you stole her. Brother, I expel you from this family."

In one violent motion Keimas twisted his coils, unwinding them like silks upon which Loi danced as his form was flung skyward, mute and broken.

The rain resumed its course and the wind returned as Loi's silhouette was lost under the shadow of Boa. The last sound of his existence was a gurgling scream, cut short as the kutlikugoli's teeth sundered him in a mist of blood, leaving only a pair of legs flailing groundward. They would never reach it, as the multitudes of Ephielipax's progeny came thronging to tear it to pieces, consuming every flake of flesh and splinter of bone until no trace of Loi's existence remained.

Anama looked to the clearing stars with a humble heart. The

Sanguine was gone, never to light its season again as Keimas fell limp, tumbling through bare branches and back to the mud. She did not envy what he suffered, had felt it herself. She did, however, have a solution to offer him.

Keimas now faced the greatest choice of a god. As his wrath abated, he began to feel the pain of divinity, squirming on the ground and moaning as his body continued to grow. The infinite light of a Nhi'Thaun was taken without any thought to its effect. As it had destroyed Loi, so it would destroy him, unless he allowed it to change him forever.

The kutliku gathered around Boa and Anama as they came to Keimas, wincing at his echoing screams and fearful at how his flesh inflated and ripped open with streaks of light.

Without hesitation Anama knelt at his side and caressed the ground, raising thi'tskreol that embraced him. They fed off his light, soothing his pain as they grew, burned, and were replaced by continuous waves of the same. As they flowered and withered, Keimas seemed to endure the pain more easily. Anama's soil-stained hands took his face and she smiled on him with love and gratitude, yet her voice was dire.

"Mantichaena, do you listen?"

He nodded fiercely.

"You face greatness, and I cannot stem its floodwaters long. Thigolaia, Loi, Ephielipax, they are all within you. You can survive this if you embrace a new soul, but it will own you. To survive, you must let your new body grow, more even than this god you have become. You will lose this life and gain another. I will show you how."

"My family," Keimas wheezed, gripping her wrist.

"This is your family now," Anama offered.

Keimas' face had no divine poise in it, only mortal dread. His eyes shook and his lips struggled, wanting not to attain true power but to escape it.

"My family," he croaked with certainty.

Anama nodded knowingly and looked to Boa.

The great kutliku bowed his head in response, as did his flock as they assembled.

Anama then brought up all the life she could from the ground, a grove of root and tendril in splendorous variety, which joined the beating hearts of the Canimperium and entangled them with one another. With her eyes closed she stroked Keimas' hair, said quietly.

"The light changes many hands today. Your children are with you. Let go and entrust your nations to us."

The Sanguine Star lived again in the assembled Canimperium as they shone brighter than any daybreak. Through each wing and talon there coursed the strength of many lifetimes as Keimas released his hold on the light. As it had been from father to son, the bounty of a thousand seasons' power became the power of the children. The light faded and the last surge of flowers rested in mighty repose over Keimas, bobbing in the sweet rain as the tangle of vines receded into the ground.

Keimas' ascendant form was dead, a lifeless cocoon as he woke, gasping and struggling against it. The scales peeled away from his face as he pulled against his own great corpse.

Soto's angry shriek bullied the other kutliku away as she finally returned to her mate, bobbing around Keimas and fluttering her wings as she tried to understand what was happening. She nearly knocked Anama to the ground as she nestled over Keimas and nudged him with her face. He grabbed her mandible and, feeling his need, she pulled with him.

Like a schiis shedding its skin he wriggled until his legs, drenched in blood and pale mucus, slid free. He shivered, wobbling like a babe to stand, then falling into Anama's lap once more. She took him happily, laughing at his mortal frailty yet marveling at the true strength it hid. Her and Soto's warmth gave Keimas a safe place to find himself, and he finally felt the struggle was over, looking up at Anama's face and beyond with concern.

"G-goddess."

"Mantichaena?" she chuckled.

"Your…your home…"

She shook her head and scratched Soto's feathers playfully, her gratitude far outweighing the loss.

"It is not gone." She directed his gaze to the kutliku that glowed among the flora, the frightened creatures of Thigolaia slowly emerging from its gnarled reclusions. "My home still breathes, beats, grows." She then palmed her neck, pulled a flicker of light that trickled to her fingertips and gently planted it in the ground beside them. "Your light is the gift that will give it shelter, and love."

Keimas' eyes teared up as he watched the start of a sapling push up from the soil. The smallest of the thi'tskreol near it did not flee or give it way. They crowded it, twisting slowly together into a young Thigolaia, a new goddess Amphiraed sprouting from the ground. He took Anama's furred hand and squeezed it.

"Anama, my sister so beautiful, we are fortunate to have you beside us."

"And you might have made a fine god," Anama comforted. "Were that what you wished."

"The last thing my people need is another creature that bloats with light and lusts for power. We need family, love, brothers and sisters to..." He jolted, fought abruptly to stand, and steadied himself as his eyes darted around him. "...Where are they? Did they come?"

"*Quos*? Whom?" Anama wondered.

"My pride!" Keimas staggered toward Boa, who cocked his head curiously. "You! They found you! My brother, my sister, where are they?"

Boa grumbled and craned his neck painfully, searching the gathered flock. They, in turn, searched among themselves.

"Allende!" Keimas called out. "Miriena! Are you here!?"

Yell as he might, screeching and searching urgently, his only answer was a single loyalist mimicking his cry overhead. It flew toward the Dhai coastline, its feathers ruffled at the sight of danger.

As Laesis shone its last in the Tau and night cast across the valley, the rain likewise left little blood, blurring the remains of a gruesome battle on the valley's southern edge. The low mountain slopes were littered with the bodies of kutliku, those lost to Loi's tempest. Like trail markers they led into the thi draws and beyond.

Anama dismounted Boa's neck as he landed against a ridge, silently baffled as Keimas joined her.

Neither had a chance to speak before a ringing shriek of alarm filled the air. Ghrainegal, hunt of Allende, shot ahead of the other hunts and swept up into the thi above.

Keimas gave chase and called for him to stop.

While some of the flock followed him, others had already found their own dead and lingered to mourn.

Clinging to Boa's scaled face, Anama was lifted high onto the mountain face ahead of Keimas, first to see what Ghrainegal had found.

Keimas glided past her and landed where the errant hunt had stopped. Ghrainegal was in an utter panic, alternating between crying desperately into the shaded undergrowth and back at the pulverized body of another kutliku beneath him. Keimas approached, discerned the remains and lost his breath.

"Infernals," Anama hissed, coming closer. "I know these wounds."

"*Eisvul*. Shi...Shisi," Keimas moaned.

"Sharptooth?" Anama said with a hand on his shoulder.

"She was a friend...and partner to another." Keimas' face flashed around them as Ghrainegal's did, equally distraught. "Where did they go?"

"The infernals hide well in the night," Anama reasoned. "They are likely long gone."

"MIRIENA! ALLENDE!" Keimas howled into the starlit dusk.

Anama felt a chill at realizing what he sought. She watched as Keimas tore at the low shrubbery, searching for any sign of his kind. Her mind worked, sifting through the carnage with the calm of one who had seen more than her share of death. The bodies painted a portrait of hate, yet the truth of the image was hidden in the details.

"Keimas, she called softly," stalling his frenzy just enough to be heard. "The thi are untouched."

"*Quoaien?*" he fumed.

"The infernals are clumsy. They would not have left the wooded routes so clean." She then gestured to the Hai, to the very edge of Manti and the only clear path through the forest, upon which there were many muddy marks showing travel. "The infernals were grounded, certainly trying to hide their numbers. To escape under the canopies, the shore would be their only..."

Keimas was already gone with a thunderclap and a ringing voice.

Anama and the loyalists gave chase, while Boa lingered and slumped against the hillside. His wounds were not fatal, though they were getting the better of him.

Borne in the talons of Soto, Anama was swept beyond the thi, up to the jutting escarpment at Manti's end. Its rutted surface plummeted steeply to a rocky shore, where the vast sea struck angrily. Against the backdrop of its lighted spray, she could discern the frantic wingbeats of Keimas, until they stalled and dropped to the ground. It was only a moment until she and her escorts were upon him, together staring as he did into a cave. A gaping tunnel penetrated deep into the cerrubite-studded stone, gulping the sea air into Manti's underbelly. Upon its lower fringe were the clear signs of scrabbling talons and dragging wings.

"*Minwekten jemn'ab - you must not enter,*" Anama warned.

Keimas said nothing, resting to his knees and running his fingers through the sandy gravel, hateful of how the scent of his kin lingered in it.

"They took them," he seethed, his eyes bristling with light. "They did not kill. They took. Why?"

The kutliku were loath to come near the mouth. As Keimas rose and trudged into it, Anama's brambles burst from its walls to block him.

"*Eisa quowekten?*" Keimas berated her, tearing at the thorns. "We have to find them!"

"No," Anama said firmly.

With his newfound power, Keimas turned the quiet airs to a bladed assault of the vines, screaming for her to relent. His raving lasted only as long as her pity allowed, breaking when he felt her horns strike him across the temple. He tumbled, glowed with fury, yet did not move to retaliate as his claws held him to the steep ground.

Anama's face was hard, her glare upon him punitive.

"These veins of Manti, where her rivers go to their deathbed, are not meant for us. They drown in the blood of creatures beyond your imagining and its waters are black with the flesh of the old world. All we living who enter emerge only as one of them, killing our own until we are ash."

"Thuell," Keimas groaned. "In here…they are many still?"

"They are infinite," Anama sighed. "There is no hope for your companions. Pray you never see them again."

"If the infernals can navigate these tunnels safely, they may be alive!" Keimas hoped. "There must be a way!"

Anama contemplated his words, yet her conclusion was no comfort.

"If, by some twisted miracle, the infernals have found safe passage in the ground, then there is no certainty of their path. Nikhaadi Ansax has deep wounds that could connect to any number of these tunnels. If they have reached this far, then it is possible they could reach anywhere unseen."

"I have seen the warrens," Keimas said dolorously. "I will see them again soon."

Together they made the somber journey back to the scene of the murders, meeting Boa as his head rested sadly beside his lost children. Keimas approached him in empathetic silence, waiting until the kutlikugoli's eye came to him before speaking.

"Father of kutliku, there has been too much taken from us."

Boa was silent, his eyelids shimmering with tears as Keimas continued.

"The infernals have long been a plague upon you, this I know. There is a debt I must pay, not only for your aid, but the brotherhood our tribes once shared. *Hauan Etain* has long been spared infernal wrath by the vigilance of the Canimperium, yet even in your day of peril you answered our call. Though Galaila have been lost to you, I offer you Mantichaena in recompense. Let our peoples be estranged no more, and together make many infernal deaths."

Boa groaned, watching the Kutu mindfully until finally accepting with a soft screech.

Keimas bowed his head, his mind once more upon war.

"Where are they, my Jiou?"

Boa's eye slid to Anama, and he growled warily.

"*Nikhaadi Ansax.*"

"You have won, elder," Keimas said, imparting much needed courage to the loyalists as his wings shone with what celestial glory still coursed through him. "It is time to win again, to break the back of the infernals once and for all."

Boa's sounds grew from sorrow to perseverance, from perseverance to rage. Though bloodied, he was far from dead, and his roar awoke the instincts of his Canimperium.

The cackle of the loyalists shook the slopes of the Cradle and their wings filled its sky as they collected the dead. Their cacophony persisted even as a fire was lit to send the fallen on their way to a burial in the sky alongside Krei'kasha and others. Tonight, they would rest in the remains of Thigolaia and, in Anama's place of power and Keimas' gift of light, become strong once more. With the coming morning they would rise renewed and show the infernals what monsters they had provoked at Windchaser Pinnacle.

CHAPTER 23: TRUE TO NATURE

Keimas had never left the bloodied scene on the mountainside, sitting in thoughtful silence even as the funeral began.

Anama waited with him, curiously watching. She felt no urge to speak at first, filled with wonderment at what might be going through his mind. Finally, when Lindu reached its apex in the midnight, she quietly settled beside him and put her hand on his.

"You fear for those whose names you cry, Mantichaena?" She surmised.

"I do not," Keimas replied, seeming truthful yet far from peace. "Their fate is mine to discover. I'll not worry on it until I see them again."

"And yet I see worry," she pressed.

He folded his fingers in hers, closing his eyes and mouthing a brief prayer before admitting to her:

"I do. The dead deserve our retribution. The taken, our aid. The living, our survival."

Anama smiled, shook his hand knowingly.

In turn, he took a deep breath and looked down at the kutliku whose blood he was privileged to share, the only brood he now had.

"Golaiaeis, tell me, whom do you consider your family? Is it the Creasle you told of? My heart bleeds that so many have been lost with your goddess amphiraed."

Anama sighed, brought his hand to the ground to touch the beaten grasses. Beneath her skin, delicate flowers grew up to meet her.

"The Creasle..." she mused, "...They are right here beneath us, as are all things: the wind, the rain, the soil and all that is born of it. I see no father, family, nor blood of a kind, only all. These ephemeral beauties are brothers to me just as much as you and your Mantichaena. We are together inexorably bound within the whole of the veil."

Keimas, though earnestly stricken by her lovely words, was undistracted from the yearning in his heart.

"While I do not dismiss the countless bonds of which you speak, I am consumed by those most mortal and vulnerating."

"I admire your devotions, Mantichaena," Anama hummed. "You must surely have a deserving lover."

"Deserving," Keimas laughed at her word choice. "That is gravely understated. She is divine, in every way. It is my struggle to be deserving of them."

"That is a great passion, if ever I have heard one spoken," Anama contemplated. "We should all be so lucky as to see how we must change, in order to become as our lovers see us. If you mean it so, then it will be, so long as your heart and mind aim true." They sat in silence for a moment, until Anama finally remembered and repeated *"Uein,* 'Them' you say?"

"My unborn daughter is with her," Keimas said, distant and dreaming. "She will be a part of her mother for some time longer, but I can feel her approach like needles through my heart."

Anama tingled with excitement, sneakily moved her fingers over Keimas'. Her mouth hung lazily as her head tilted, her shoulders relaxed, and her enigmatic body ceased to change as she felt the pulse of the veil she knew.

Keimas paid it no mind until, taking notice of her prolonged silence, he looked to her just as she spoke.

"Raindrop?" She asked eagerly.

Flattened by her clairvoyance, Keimas nodded slowly.

*"La...*Lemalie."

"Quite lovely," Anama whispered. Then, while Keimas twitched and stammered, she explained. "The veil is full of secrets. I can feel her handprint on your light. As I said, we are one. Be mindful, young godlike, and you too will begin to hear the veil speak to you."

"I am Keimas," he said kindly, realizing they had no introduction.

Anama laughed at his narrow perception.

"After all this, do you think I could not see you?"

"Yet you do not speak names?" Keimas observed.

"I do, for it is a part of life, yet what does it accomplish but further separating us? I would not engage a familiar soul or welcome face by name, only touch it and show it love. All that gives space between lives, even that as simple as a name, is an instinct of survival, and a consequence of the fears which boil blood and chill the heart."

Keimas did not agree with her sentiment, though he understood it and wondered at her gift.

"Some of our mantics have given their lives in search of the power you exercise so effortlessly," Then, remembering the tale of Cisiveo and Klirash, he realized there was hope. With urgency he asked "Who can leave such a handprint? Can you find anyone I have met?"

"I cannot say," Anama pondered aloud. "Blood, intimacy, experience; these all leave a distinct impression."

"Try," Keimas begged, squeezing her hand again. "If there is any chance…"

She complied, resting back and instructing Keimas.

"In your mind, seek memories of them," she began. "I need to know their touch, their scent, their thoughts. Imagine for me who they are."

Keimas tried to oblige. He envisioned the race with Allende, which had begun this journey. Then hunts alongside Miriena, the kills they shared and the lives they led. Lastly, and without his intent, he saw his young self at Govan's side when Hanging Gate was first discovered. In that moment he no longer needed remember his brood. He felt them, present and alive, yet did not understand the sounds they made.

"My hand upon yours and yours upon theirs," Anama said

methodically.

"They are hidden," Keimas said, grappling with the sensations as his visions grew increasingly tangible.

"Keimas...do you feel th..."

Together, they saw the same image: the collective appendages of many creatures in a writhing mass, two mouths above it like whispering eyes, twin shadows rising either side of it like wings. They spied on a soul which enshrouded their quarry, and it felt their gaze. Its arms pointed, its wings billowed, and its eyes silently screamed, flinging their mind's door shut and pushing them away from itself.

Once recovered from the shock, Keimas sought answers in Anama's eyes.

She only shook her head, without the faintest notion of what they had glimpsed.

"They are unsafe," Keimas concluded.

"And hidden below," said Anama.

"*Quo*? You found them?!"

"They are *tau'tskdhai*, toward the southmost of the flat mountains," she assured him. "I could not lead you to them, though they are no doubt in the Ansax."

Though the battle was coming, Keimas was strengthened to know it had a heading. He would not risk missing the completion of his family, yet there was still time to kill while bound for home, hopefully to recover his stolen pridemates.

"Tomorrow," he begrudgingly sighed. "Tomorrow, we hunt, not only in Ansax but across all Manti. Mantichaena and Canimpana are united now, to bring down the last enemies before us."

"There is always another," Anama said sadly.

Keimas ground his teeth and scowled at the thought of Tzychala. He wanted to have faith the weird imp was mindful of himself among the tribe but could not dismiss Loi's accusations.

"Do you know of the lightless?" He grumbled.

Anama chose her words carefully, discerning well between what she knew and what she speculated.

"My father was not one to consort with any other ascendant, nor the denizens of Undersky. He was too proud, too sure of his own greatness. In all the veils I have felt no stirrings to suggest he had a partner. Still, I do know of what you speak. The first generation had many names for them. 'Lightless' was the first. They are elusive indeed, for they cause no disturbance within the lighted veils." She thought anxiously to herself as Keimas did, then amended herself "But they exist, that much is certain, reminders of a world which only they remember. They once hid in the ground, cowering in the flesh that guarded them. I cannot say what would move them to emerge."

"And only they can command that flesh," Keimas seethed. "Perhaps...this is their home, and we are why they emerge."

He seemed close to a rage, then suddenly adopted a perfect calm. It was certainly caused by the quiet arrival of Soto, his brave companion, who seemed indolent after the sendoff of her kin. He held her head in his hand, brushed her feathers, and sighed.

"I feel I have met one of these lightless, invited it into my home...yet something tells me I cannot trust Loi's words against it. In its eyes I have seen that it will admit to nothing unless asked, and I will have answers. Still, there is something about the creature which gives me pause. If ever there was a trickster which could fool one as insightful as my wife, it is he. To me, there seemed in him not even a silent ember of malice towards."

"He?" Anama mumbled, shivering against the cold. "Are you certain it was not a woman?"

Keimas looked sideways at her, sharing silence for a moment.

"The Storyteller," he grunted, shaking his head at the obvious realization. "She is among them."

"You must tread carefully," Anama warned quietly. "Only by stories, written in blood upon stone in the foulest places, do I see traces of the lightless. What little I do know is they are not native to Maengir. When they reveal themselves, it is in response to something they fear."

"What would such a thing fear?" Keimas postulated.

"The light," Anama continued. "I do not understand their meaning, but their inscriptions warn of daybreak. In the day, a song. In the song, death. Yet it eludes me whether this death be for the lightless or all of us."

Keimas closed his eyes, breathed deep, and finally stood.

"Your wisdom is an inestimable boon, my goddess. However, we move one day at a time, one evil at a time. I must confront what lies before me and save whomever I can."

"You will," Anama cooed, brushing his leg without looking up to him. "I have no doubt."

She held her breath until Keimas and his hunt were away to rest among the Canimperium, releasing it tensely once alone again. She then remained, and her thoughts muddled. War was without end, for the most peaceful times presented the greatest opportunity for the strong and ruthless. Her role was to protect the small, to provide for the weakened. Keimas was one of the ruthless, blessed with the will to cut evil down wherever it grew. It was a relief to see him forsake the power that was his birthright, yet his heart was ever aflame with fear and anger, most vulnerable to influence. Perhaps, one day, he would come for her head as he came for Loi's.

"Our family always does," she whispered nervously.

The skin of the Hosse Veil parted with the passage of Tzychala, setting him forth from that plane back onto Maengir. He had travelled patiently, contemplatively, bound for the frosted toes of the mountains Gao. Upon arrival, he cast off his blindfold with a great sense of liberation, The eyes behind, and the twenty-one others adorning his skin, finally crept open. He was no longer hiding, awakened after his ordeals and returning to someone he owed a great deal.

With storms to the Tau and Laesis fading behind them, a frigid dusk cloaked the stark and snowy slopes, glowing down around a river of ash which rained around him. Beyond this, there was a sudden and fearsome firelight which beamed through mists blowing from the dagger peaks. Broken Mountain made its anger known, for it knew it was trod upon.

Tzychala made his climb carefully. He wished to give the Mother of Mountains time to see him, to recognize her devoted servant and not smother him in brimstone. Snow turned to sleet in his ascent, then sleet to water, then water to steam, until he stood nearly at the cauldron. There he waited until, sure enough, he was recognized.

The stone before him began to wriggle, cavitating into a shape he knew even before it was fully formed. To his distaste, the hollow face of Golgamet appeared before him. It infuriated him, yet he knew the intent of the manifestation.

"This is in poor taste, Klirash" he admonished. "Have some respect."

"Respect?" The earthy voice scoffed.

"She was already dead. That was not my doing."

"You used her, served her murderer. Do we mean so little to you?"

"And you serve those who murdered you," Tzychala spat back. "None of us mean anything while your predecessors breathe." He composed himself, raising his hands and backing down a step. "*Prostas*, let's not do this again. I'll not question you, but you must trust me. There is too much at stake, and we both need allies."

There was harsh pause as Klirash scowled upon the defiant demon. In the end, she saw the defeat in his face and submitted to his point. Perhaps she did not trust him, but he was correct. Golgamet's visage wept smoking magma, cracked, and melted away sadly, opening the mountain in a roil of scoria and revealing the woman in the flesh, so to speak. The burning stone congealed into her form, then sat indolently upon the slope. It solidified as an amalgam of her and her seat, then separated at rest to become Klirash alone. Clothed in the stone she shared a spirit with, her Galaila skin was almost indistinguishable from it below the neck.

"*Eina gravas,*" she apologized. "Golgamet was dead before I knew her, and yet it hurts. Only when speaking of her does *aia* Anama weep. You cannot fathom her heartbreak."

"Vengeance may begin her healing," Tzychala promised. "Though still she will surely weep for the memory, Loi will no longer plague her. I have seen my error, and my new way, and they end with his death."

Klirash was not convinced.

"*La,* I saw he and his double pass the horizon, blood in their eyes, infernals following below and Canimperium in their wake. This war was a long time coming, but few are prepared for it." She looked him up and down, weighing his apparent confidence. "This scheme of yours is an awful risk."

"Plans hastily laid always are," he agreed. "But time was short, and I am no less certain now than I was then. Loi is the wound, not the weapon, and I do not intend to let it cut down my world."

"Your world?" Klirash wondered with bright eyes. "*Eiha,* you really have changed, Eyebeast."

He was grateful for how she looked at him now, and eager to earn more. It was invigorating to be seen as a protector.

"Be vigilant, my friend," he said amicably. "Never in all time have so many immortals met in battle, and we will need them all. The Deina will send an assassin first. When they fail, Loi will follow, laying waste without restraint. If Hanging Gate falls, Maengir will follow."

"*La,* though you have not been forthcoming about our importance," Klirash probed. "What is this weapon we are meant to protect?"

"In truth…I'm not entirely sure," Tzychala said anxiously. "It has a will of its own, and a hatred, and no desire to be found."

"Is there no effort to find it then?" Klirash worried.

"It is hidden," Tzychala hissed. "From us, and from all, lost since the last unravelling. We need not find it, only prevent the Deina destroying it. Its mere existence is a threat to them. So long as it remains buried with its final victim, the Deina will not risk returning."

Klirash expected no guarantees, but Tzychala's faith in her and her kind merited the same be returned.

"I understand," she concluded. "I cannot speak for Salohel and Bethaali, but I will come at your call."

"There will be others waiting for you," Tzychala assured, "But your fellow exiles will not be among them."

There was then a delicate silence while Klirash examined the dispassion of his words and the rigidity of his face. She would soon go looking for proof of what he suggested, but he sounded certain. Either the others were dead, or they no longer considered the Mantichaena to be their tribe. To lack a *Gal'tskhain* ally was one thing. To have one as an enemy was another entirely. She nodded to Tzychala, sure of what was needed of her in the calm before the storm, then laid back to submerge in the churning, earthen embrace of her stronghold.

Tzychala smirked confidently as she went, then turned back into the Veil himself. With their alliance secured, they would not meet again until the moment of its revelation.

CHAPTER 24: HEIR OF THE DEFEATED

Thetrulengo speaks,

*I*n death, the Blue Sky Raptor was a lover and father. Before this, an ambassador. Before this, a warlord. The one thing he was through all of it was the thing that defined him: confusion. So full of conviction, he thought himself to be noble, yet he was lastingly doubtful the blood he shed served any true purpose. Likewise, when he pursued diplomatic resolutions while other nations carried on warring, he suffered a soreness in his heart, wondering if peace was more than a broken dream. He was robbed of his late hopes by Quetzuaul's ambition, but more so by all the lesser creatures that would not be controlled.

All live in fear, so terrified of having no place in the world that they would seek the illusion of control which wrath and judgment bring. As in all things, this is not to disparage those who war, only to warn of what barren fields to which it may lead their hearts. Like traversing a wilderness, one must have direction in their action, or they are doomed to wander and find only despair. I believe Keimas understood this, and his Kutu mind had been curbed not only by a love that guided him but also by the responsibility that came with wearing an elder god's soul.

The infernals will be no opposition while the Canimperium hunts as one. Under Boa's mighty wings they may perhaps succeed in perishing the infernals down to the last bloody feather, yet there will be no end to them as long as their own kutlikugoli lives. Fear has destroyed their minds, a fear wielded by none more aptly than the Jiou of nightmares.

Keimas is still proud, still a Kutu. His distractions are soon to be many when he returns home a godlike and a father. His ego may blind him to what is coming. He will know soon enough, when he realizes that his brethren are not coming home. Through the past, I have seen this future.

It was perhaps six or seven seasons after the ordeal of Klirash that a young boy was born. One who suffered from terrible nightmares, thrashing and weeping at night, moaning about awful sights he could not escape. He was only a babe, barely two seasons old when he began to change, to become something no one understood. No father was known to him, and no man admitted to siring him.

His mother was a very solitary academic, a recluse, though a charming beauty. She named her boy after the twilight, early nightfall, 'Salohel'. The boy suffered by his own being, but his mother by betrayal.

Salohel's father was a woeful mix of both these, soured not only by the abandonment of his own sire, but by his mother's daily reminders that he was a curse upon her. The scars left upon him by these memories are evident in him. It was no help when the K'hizu blood took him, turning his anguish into anger. He hid his torture, fought to find a goodness in himself, but in the end fell prey to his inner shadow, forsaking the bastard child and its lovelorn mother.

The mother wept and pleaded for his affection, for him to be a father to his child. He denied her, shunned her, and the people called her mad. She began to hate her child, fearing him as everyone else did. It was not long before she took her own life and left Salohel alone. In her absence, Ms'egol cared for him for a time, though none could answer what caused his body to change from one form to another almost constantly. He would be a strange and foreign creature one moment and a mass of wriggling spines the next, sometimes flitting out of sight and returning as a mirage filled with images of places or people. It was as though his flesh became the canvas through which all his dreams came to light. Sometimes he could be lucid and able to understand words, though he could never speak for himself, only scream at the horrors he saw. His caretakers did all they could, but soon they came to a point of no return. As he grew, so did his effect on them. His eyes had a strange power. Any who met his gaze were overcome with hallucinations, whatever he wanted them to see. Their visions always caused panic; an insanity so unbearable that some ran their heads into walls just to end it. Those who tried to bear it would not last, losing their minds and falling comatose until they died.

His exile was not amicable, as if exile by its nature ever was. He was almost entirely unaware he had been cast out. It fell on father Metaeu to carry out his banishment, but the family refused to see their youngest alone in the wild. Worse, they refused to end his suffering by killing him. A handful of them vowed to stay by his side, gouging out their eyes, blindfolding the boy and travelling far up the cliffs to the Thaun.

I have seen only some of his growth, the cult that has formed around him. As with many who amass power, he became an object of fascination and devotion not only among his escort but all across the borderlands. Many heard his tale and believed he was destined to become a god. How true it was. Rebels, outcasts, vagrants; he gathered them all to his presence and they became part of his family. By order of the eldest, they blinded themselves in order to remain in his servitude. Others believed it was an honor to see the 'Twilit Eyes', purposefully exposed themselves to him. It is possible they wanted to somehow prove themselves against his power, though it seemed to me most were there as willing sacrifices. I lacked the stomach to remain as hundreds came to perish at his feet and be thrown into the bottomless chasm.

The first and only news of Salohel's fate was relayed by the only member of his family to return, Metaeu, whom Sky decreed an archon for his act in protecting the city. With sad eyes, the new father told of how the boy still slept and dreamed his appalling dreams, those who bore him remaining faithfully bound to him and never to leave his side. Metaeu never went back, never spoke of it again. Likewise, no one has ever returned to Hauan Etain from the grim hollow that Salohel's pilgrims called Sefnay Ghenilt, the

Bridge of Tongues. I have seen for myself what invention prompted them to devise such a dreadful name, but at this time I'm convinced no Mantichaena ever will. If they did, they might learn of his true origins, a birthright not unlike that of Zeniquorer, once born of their sire's hatred and as much a curse for them as it is for their enemies.

His abilities are distinctive, hard to forget. I have no doubt that he received the essence of the deceiver, Quetzuaul. Her and Zeniquorer's blood and name brought the tearing of not only the body but also the mind, and the mind is surely Salohel's domain. Moreover, I believe the deceiver's hold on him is her way of continuing her war against Ephielipax, the god whose power was promised to Salohel's father.

~Chronicle of Wonders, The Weight of Choice

Keimas and the Canimperium moved as a single shadow across the Dhai borders of Ni'ivitnem, sniffing out every trace of the infernals. Isolated clusters were all they found, easily crushed in the organized campaign with negligible casualties. Over nine days, they left a winding trail of blood through the Drowned Hills and Ni'ivitnem until reaching what was sure to be the fallen brood's refuge: the warrens of Nikhaadi Ansax.

The bleak and cavernous hold of the infernals was silent, and its inhabitants as still as the stone in their flesh. The horde did not sleep but were inactive, in a state of dormancy more than rest. Their calcified feathers were clumsily splayed around them as they sat, their unblinking eyes staring at nothing. Their Jiou was preoccupied, and so they awaited his bidding. After many days and nights unmoving, they were finally stirred by a sudden scent on the southerly wind; the reek of pure kutliku.

Only the first of Boa's war cry poured across the misty barrens. The rest was drowned out by the shrieks of his hungry loyalists and Kutu brother.

The eerie eyes of the infernals turned on their attackers as their wings struggled to life, yet they had no voice of panic or fury. As ever, they showed nothing but cold-hearted hunger. Their hard feathers tore into their perches as they stood to fly, but they could not respond in equal numbers as the rest wormed out from the tunnels. Each moved on instinct, practically single-file into a hail of dismembering Kutu talons.

By midday there was no longer a battle, only a competition for feeding rights among the loyalists. The Canimperium dared not enter the underworld, but there was no need while prey ceaselessly thronged to them. Only those loyalists who had become exhausted or full-bellied would retreat, replaced by eager siblings waiting for their turn. Though more than thirty great chasms stretched through the mists where the waters of Ni'ivitnem were lost to Ansax, the multitudes of kutliku blockaded all escape as they nested around them.

The Canimperium and Infernals were much alike in their home territory, fortified underground, and so easily trapped if caught unawares by superior numbers. There was no telling how many of the rotten things lurked in the labyrinth below, but they would have no victory while trapped in their pits.

Keimas, smiling with primal joy and gasping from exertion, finally grounded himself among other satisfied hunters at the thrumming base of a waterfall. The thick mist stripped the blood from his skin as he wiped it from his lips, allowing the condensate streams to clean his talons. It was a great day, a day to be remembered, but there was a greater one to come. He could not delay any longer, for chances were good his daughter could be born as soon as two mornings. With his arms outstretched, savoring what could be his final hunt, he made himself clean, and prepared to depart. Once complete, he screeched mightily, and the echo from the bluffs ensured he would have Soto's attention.

His friend, though in a feeding frenzy, craned her head up above the carnage, dripping from the shared feast of a fresh kill. Visibly disappointed, she abandoned it and heeded Keimas' call.

Keimas paused briefly at her arrival,

"My time is up," he said woefully, gripping her wing. "My friend, unfailing and forever, I wonder what life will be with our pride scattered. I must suffer this, but the fight need not end for you. Our allies are lost, but you can find them. May I ask this of you?"

Soto was reticent to give any answer, blinking sadly at him, and did not cuddle him as she often did. Her allegiance was divided, but for the love of one she could not forsake all their kind.

The ground shook with Boa's heft as he loomed near, his vast head craning down to face Soto. His wounds still cracked and bled, but his countenance was strong, though there appeared a weight of worry on his shoulders for how they slouched. He wished then he was more practiced in the language of Mantichaena, if only to share the deep change in himself as of the previous day. He felt it was good that kutliku could rejoin with their ancestral brethren, but he also felt the Mantichaena had become a nation apart, as divergent from their Galaila predecessors as the Canimperium itself. He had grasped for continued control of his errant children, the hunts of the Kutu, but they were no longer akin to the Canimperium.

Shisi and Ghrainegal were slow to arrive, though they were drawn to the discourse and listened well. When Boa finally spoke in their own tongue, they recoiled to Keimas, their feathers bristling.

The guttural chatter was indecipherable to Keimas, but he understood from the dour attentiveness of the hunts that his words were grave.

Boa then looked briefly to his Mantichaena brother, closed his eyes and, as a gesture of respect, grumbled a similar meaning:

"Canimpana home with Canimpana. Broken now. Boa'tghanta want…need. Choose. Boa'tghanta accept."

Keimas felt blindsided as Soto finally held her head to him, and he instinctively held her. Then, he smiled, and pushed her gently away. He looked warmly to each of the hunts, and they to each other. Each was to make the decision for themselves.

For Ghrainegal and Shisi, the choice was simple. They would not return home without their partners, and Ansax was a vast hunting ground. More critically, the Canimperium was no longer the power it had been, and no talons could be spared if it was to be again. It was better to rejoin the flock for good, even if all hope of rescue for their partners was already lost.

Soto understood this as well. Her head hung low, and she would look at no one. Her choice cut her deeply, for it was already made, and she could not bear to see the same in Keimas.

Keimas was stone-faced, tensing to contain his tears. To suffer aloud would only wound his beloved friend more, but he could not suppress it as he felt Soto pull away. With a few soft, trembling gasps, he felt her feathers slip between his fingers. Through blurred vision, his heart was warmed at how the other hunts, and even Boa, nestled around Soto with care. He truly loved her, yet his was not the only love she needed. He tried to turn away, and his eyes held onto her as long as they could, yet he still forced a grateful smile. So much of their lives had been shared, and he knew they would meet again.

He sharply turned back, wanted to address Boa as the importance of Soto to him and the kindness he must show her, but was winded and swept from his feet as Soto charged into him and wrapped him in her long neck. With his dangling, and arms latched around her with all his might, he enjoyed the briefest fantasy that she would not remain. When she finally replanted him he could be sad no more, happy to have a proper farewell and to know she was where she belonged.

"Do not fail, *kutlikugoli*," he growled, leering up at Boa. "Canimpana belong with you. Kutu belong with me. Do not fail."

Boa snarled bitterly at first, as his eyes darted to Soto. Then, he bowed to Keimas and remained silent.

"And you," Keimas whispered to Soto. "Wings, minds, hearts; my vow to you does not end here, but it must bend to your mother and sister. Your families love you and will always be the wind beneath you."

Releasing one another, there was a tense pause as Keimas and his lifelong companion stared at one another. With a last smile from Keimas, and a warble from Soto, the Kutu turned and thrust skyward, and the kutliku nested with her kin.

Boa and his remaining forces did not resent Keimas' absence. Though grateful for the light which made them strong once more, the incestuous loyalty the Kutu inherited from them was purer at the source. They would kill well for seasons to come, until only Kutliku flew over Ni'ivitnem.

As dusk crept closer, blood trickled down through the capillary tunnels beneath the Ansax, each droplet quivering from the screaming deaths of infernals and the drumroll of their limbs tumbling down. The sanguine smell permeated the stone, charred flesh tainted the water, and red rain saturated the deepest pits. One such hole was filling like a well. It was so deeply hidden that only a sallow grey light reflected down to it, the illumination within warped by the constant flow of droplets and scraps. The smell was improved by the fouled water, for it had long reeked of much older remains collected within.

Fetal, shivering and drooling, Govan would soon drown, too broken to save himself. The visceral mire was nearly at his lips, rippling from his sharp and shallow breathing, reflecting the whites of his back-rolled eyes.

Allende, dragging the flaccid body of Miriena, sloshed weakly to his mentor on all fours. The weight of so many was more than he could lift; even his own felt too much. His wings, just as his friends, were chewed off at the joint, leaving only painful lumps of splintered bone where their grand colors once flew. All hope had left him, and he knew they were doomed. His instinct to keep them alive was aimless, muscle memory from a life that would not serve him here. He had already wasted his lungs, screaming for a day as the battle raged far above, but not a word had escaped the cacophony of deaths.

With an agonized convulsion, he dropped his wife and mentor into the blood, his face twitching confusedly as he turned toward the far side of the pit. In a pile, their trophied wings were disappearing into the bog, and Twilight sat in deep thought upon them.

"T-this is not r-real, is it?" He stammered hoarsely, forcing a manic smile. "It's a trick! An-nother trick!"

"No tricks," came a quiet, calming voice in reply.

Allende's eyes fluttered around him at the dismal walls, through the curtains of red above to the only spark of light that reached through the ground, then back to the creature guarding them.

"W-why?" Allende blubbered. "Why stop n-now? Are you s-satisfied? *Prostas, eina prostaan,* let us go home."

There was no response at first. The shrouded boy's long feet tapped their fingers on a large skull. His head rested in the fingers of his hands. His skin, utterly covered in fragile, umber spines, crunched as he shifted on his seat. Wings of equally repulsive bone clicked at his back, their exposed ligaments bunching up as they folded behind him. Without any eyes to speak of, two mouths opened in their places in his face, their small Galaila teeth flashing white in the dark as they finally spoke.

"I would like to know more."

"We told you ev-verything we kn-now," Allende wept, refusing to face his captor. "His l-life, his faults, his ch-child…"

The grotesquery hummed; a single, great eye opening where its mouth should have been. As it centered on Allende, he waited for his victim to face him again, to forget the very meaning of reality.

"Yes…his child…"

CHAPTER 25: ANOTHER SEASON

Thetrulengo speaks,

*D*eath was not invented by the darkness, nor the light. Rather, it is part of what created both. Escharka tried to take ownership of death, but Az'Rech had his own agent of its control. Both were gone from the mid-Veil, until now.

As I look back on the span of my existence, I believe that this is the moment for which I was preparing these many words. I had hoped that one day they may be seen by those who seek them, but perhaps that time is now. All that I have inscribed serves a greater purpose than my own amusement, for I have my own journey ahead.

The abduction of the Deina'itka raises deep concern in me. So many shapeless dangers are about to take solid form. The seal of the endless is beginning to break, the Deina have once more turned their eyes on Maengir, and it seems there is yet one star that has not given up on its hatred of mortality.

Worry overcomes me at the thought of love for something that is not mine. Without flesh, I have appeared as I see fit and manifested as the only mortal life I do understand, thereby becoming a part of the world I do not understand nor belong in.

I live because of her, yet her story is over...

It was on Gravenje, long after Quetzuaul and her ilk had fallen to pieces. In the advent of the modern era there were so many new civilizations budding from the rotten remains of the old world. The Hischates were one that barely survived the struggle, nearly collapsed after Quetzuaul's death. I was young, in a manner of speaking, still unused to what my senses told me. I was exploring, acquainting myself with Maengir, when I happened upon this doomed people. In their mother's absence they had no mind, no control. Though many laid down and waited for death, some minds met and became one. They grew together to survive, then grew apart as they discovered their own identities. It was beautiful, until it was lost.

There was no godly wrath, no natural calamity. It was an accident...and perhaps this was why I saw myself in her. She was not asleep. The rest slept, but not her. She was happy, snuck out to play in the quiet of Lindu. She thought fire was beautiful. I cannot disagree, nor fault her curiosity for what it could do. She did not mean to hurt anyone but...none survived. The walls were meant to keep dangers out, not turn a mistake into an extinction. I watched her die screaming, not even understanding what she had done. I was standing there with her, in the flames, did nothing to save her, just looked into her eyes as they shriveled and blackened.

I felt so strongly then...and so I stole her. I took her name and became her, became Thetrulengo. I do not know why I did it, if it was all for jealousy of her mortality, or a child's attempt to fix a broken thing, to bring her back. In a way I succeeded, laying her to rest in myself as I rest in these words. Then, a second voice tells me it is all a lie; that I watched life end and must now shame myself with the memory of my indifference.

I saw the same look in little Raphenie and take empty pride in having the will to act when her need was greatest. Still, I could do nothing but beg the help of others. In the moment, I thought this was because I could not touch the light. I understand now this was not a limitation of my ability, but an imposition of my heart. Zeniquorer was more than an infection. He was part of her, entwined with her. In touching him, I felt her, and my hand refused to destroy him, for they were one, and I could not allow her to die. Against my own desires, my heart betrays me and reveals what needs I culture within. I have found passion for life, for creation. It is mine to cherish, though I fear it cannot be mine to protect. As fate's creatures haunt the threshold of Maengir, I can neither hold them fast nor welcome them in. Maengir may end, and...I must allow it. It is the way of things that what becomes must unbecome.

I have all but forgotten how I became driven to intervene so foolishly at the behest of so few. Curiosity aside, is there any good in my meddling? The world did not change in the death of Thetrulengo, nor did it change in the salvation of Raphenie. These are trifling impacts, indiscernible droplets in a flood so vast they will go unnoticed by any but myself. Perhaps, in time, I too will forget.

May my value be none if I do not fulfill some profound purpose? Can I misuse the life I have taken, or is all that I do meaningless? I cannot die, nor sleep, nor find peace when awoken, cursed to have no higher power to blame for what I set in motion, or idly allow.

Might I digress to accepting that goodness is defined by power? If I am beyond control, then I am supreme and therefore the decider of virtues. If it is so, then I am only another god. If it is so, all which opposes my will is evil and must be destroyed. Who could question this? Who could stop me? Only myself, I suppose, in that which concludes all this and more: I am the god of idle judgement, empowered only by my exclusion from being. My place is not to control creation, nor to spare it, but to remember it; to remember all that would otherwise be forgotten. Though life springs up and is wiped away with each passing moment, it will never be truly lost, for I will remember. This is my purpose, and I have failed to uphold it.

Am I wrong to feel guilt? To question myself? If I can be the governance of mores then, in order to be virtuous, I must only continue existing. Perhaps I had done no wrong when I decimated thousands beneath the fall of that lifted mountain. Perhaps I had neither gained nor given when I meagerly intervened on behalf of...anything. I only feel cheated when I obsess over lesser things bent on destroying themselves, bereaved by my attachment to perishable lives. It is the attachment itself which must be excised. Perhaps this is the evil I have not understood until hereto directed by past choices: fearing, fretting, feeling. These are aspects of mortality, not of Thetrulengo. I must let go.

Too long I have allowed my heart to guide me only along the path of the Mantichaena. I have compromised myself by being of love to them, yet there are so many others who will be forgotten when time ends. They are no less important, so I must give them their place in eternity.

The difficulty I now have, if I am committed to end my involvement in life and being, is the question of whether I must...correct previous choices. Must I change my name? Must I kill anyone who knows of me? Must I destroy those whom I spared a death of chance? If it is unequitable, and therefore arguably unjust that I intervene out of passion for one, then I must either do so for all or revoke it for the few. Raphenie is the only one yet living...must I?

I will rest, contemplating where act will satisfy intent. There is much to see, much to be remembered, and time is fleeting.

Chronicle of Wonders: I Am

Through the tall windows of Nesh's face, Lemalie's periodic moans were not as frightful as they might have been. It seemed to her father, as he paced anxiously on the terrace above, that her remarkably adaptive body she was now bound by the second life that shared her and yearned to be born. She suffered a mother's pain but still do not curse or scream. The last Aroch had glimpsed of her face before being shunned by the sanctifiers was joy. It seemed she had forgotten everything but the blessing upon her. Nonetheless, she would shout in agitation from time to time:

"Where is he? I swear if Loi does not kill him, I will!"

Sky stood quietly on the terrace as well, watching her husband with some annoyance.

"Your spirit's unease," she grumbled, "Will no doubt be impressed upon the child, assuming you do not burst into flames first."

"How are you so calm!?" He barked in reply, catching himself and quieting down.

"It is just a child," she replied with a knowing smile, moving to hold him still. "No different than when Lemalie was born."

"B-but this is different," Aroch insisted. "It is different with you, with her, all of us, a whole family…"

"Whole!?" Came Lemalie's irate voice, closely followed by a candlestick sailing out the window, barely missing Aroch's face.

Sky's eyes widened with comical fear. Hiding a smile, she pulled Aroch out of the line of fire.

"I envy Keimas such youthful love," she chuckled.

Aroch relaxed somewhat and kissed her forehead.

"As her mother, you will know it soon. *Einla,* I fear for the boy, for I know this love's lash."

"Lash!?" Sky gasped, thumping his chest. "Have I cast a candlestick so?"

"*Einla*! The very second night we lay together, and at such a comment you met my temple with a box of chewsticks!"

"You were unharmed," she said dismissively.

He grabbed her and held her close, nuzzling her ear and whispering in mock anger.

"I had to explain the sap and soot in my hair to Father Novun as I took the hall home."

"And you aptly lied, I expect?" She chirped.

"*Mineina,*" Aroch replied deviously. "I told him eeeveryth…"

They were interrupted by another sudden cry from within, triggering parental instincts in both of them. While they were not supposed to be present while the acolytes of Voddace assisted the birth, a practice a Primarch and her Archon husband could not lightly disobey, they were both becoming agitated by Lemalie's state. Aroch most of all, as he was most liable to speak out of emotion.

"What are those *zet'itka* doing in there?" He grumbled nervously.

"That did not sound like pain," Sky whispered.

"*Quoaien?* Is she struggling?" Aroch said, nervously wringing his wife's hands.

"She sounds…frightened. I cannot say what she…"

They jerked to attention as one of the Mearnum acolytes emerged. Though they interrogated her, she spoke very calmly and factually.

"The child is fine, as is the *Jiaia,* though there is something…strange. You are invited to advise."

The two were confused as they were led in, uncomfortable with breaking laws they were expected to exemplify. However, as they entered, it seemed the circumstance would explain their deviation. The acolyte needed say nothing.

Lemalie, swollen and exposed for the incipient birth, was not herself. Some parts of her were liquifying without her consent, and through her skin there swam a glow which orbited her belly.

"I need you," Lemalie croaked to her father.

"*La!*" He shouted, running to her side, tarrying there as he tried to find where to touch skin without it suddenly turning to water.

The suspended liquid between them reassembled into her arm, which immediately gripped the fur along his waist as she whispered frightfully to him:

"It is her. She is our daughter, truly, limitlessly."

"What do you mean?" Aroch said in a hush, taking her hand and kneeling.

"She has…so much power," Lemalie continued, smiling amazedly between scowls of panic. "I have to…fight to bring her out. She thinks I am the sea, that I am…her domain. She is a goddess, father. Even unborn, she is aaAAH!"

Aroch held tight, Lemalie something familiar to grasp, to give her focus in the battle for her body. He was terrified, proud yet fearful, both for Lemalie's life and the unknown one about to begin.

In that instant, a cacophonous rain swelled outside and beat at the walls of Nesh. It came so suddenly and with such force that it sounded like thunder, taking all but Lemalie by surprise.

"She is ready," she said direly.

The birth of a goddess began, which Lemalie needed only survive.

Keimas was drawing down toward the Hai of Hanging Gate, the hunts in formation on his wings. He saw for himself how the skies, which at the were only mottled with white clouds, suddenly collapsed into a storm as furious as Loi's own. To see it, he understood the sensation that had grown in him for the past few days; an astonishing font of light that echoed from the presence he knew could only be the conjoined spirits of his wife and child.

The curtains of rain broke in his path as he dove into the canyon, screeching mightily that they might know he was with them again.

The hunts scattered and circled, confusing his sound with a battle-cry.

Mantichaena across the city froze in place at the violent and unexpected return, half of them cheering for an obvious victory against Loi while the rest scrambled for high ground in search of a threat.

Keimas ignored all but the window of his and Lemalie's home, the windows they had sat in, the terraces from which they had enjoyed warm days and equally freezing rains. He heard her cries and knew his fight was over, at least beyond the city. He would never leave Lemalie's side after touching this familiar stone again.

Sky was waiting eagerly at the windows, sharing a smile of disbelieving joy at the sound of Keimas' arrival. She looked up again, squealed and leapt aside just before a spray of rain was thrust into the room by Keimas' landing at the vestibule.

He did not slow or close his wings, only surged into the room, practically flying still, until his hands held Lemalie's face.

"Never again!" He shouted, thinking of nothing but his near-absence from this most important moment.

For a moment, Lemalie's body responded to his touch, becoming itself for prolonged periods.

"You...are in such trouble," she threatened, laughing through tears.

He shared her emotions but was distracted by the weirdness occurring in her flesh and caressed her face with new worry.

"*Eihsrysha,* are you alright?"

"I feel...different," she wondered aloud. Feeling a burning sensation at his touch, she gasped and tensed. "W-what are you...taking from me?"

"*Quo?*" Keimas blurted, pulling away for fear he was hurting her.

She immediately jerked, the light roiling in her once again as she beckoned him back.

"*Minta!* Touch me! *Prostas,* I felt you. Whatever you did, do not stop!"

Keimas held her again, both of them attentive now to the flickers between his skin and hers. He moved one hand to her belly and, marveling together, they saw her body become itself again. What he felt inside her was a light beyond either of them, beyond even his slain brother. All the power of their divinity was already being shared to their unborn, yet it did not remain. Through its father, it was shared to the family as Keimas' was to his brood.

"A new star lights the skies before it even walks the earthplane," Keimas said in astonishment.

"You really did it," Lemalie hissed excitedly, gripping his hair. "You lived...and ascended."

"Only for you," he said, kissing her palm as his fingers silenced the overwhelming torrent in her. "I will never die for any but you. Forgive me, and feel all my love within. It is home. I believe in you, my sea and my sky. You can do this."

The power of the godlike child did not abate its manifestation from above, until it emerged and was cradled by its mother.

Keimas and Lemalie, rejoined at last, felt a togetherness unlike any they could imagine as their daughter's gentle cries captivated their hearts, and her little fingers stretched out to them for the first time. It seemed as though the confusion of her birth was less, though still she commanded thunder to break and rain to fall.

With the family gathered around them, she and Keimas could finally speak of a name.

"Did you truly want me to name her?" Keimas asked, excited but deferent.

"I do," Lemalie replied warmly. "I was to name our son. It was you who prayed for a daughter."

"Then I have honors to give," Keimas said as he held Lemalie and their girl. "I would name her Uleasiel."

"*Quouein?* 'To grow anew'?" Lemalie said curiously.

"Everything does this; our lives, our tribes, our love," Keimas whispered, grateful to honor Anama with her own words. "And this little gift from Aurba is all of these. She is everything, the renewal of every beautiful thing in life."

"We could not cure, and now we cannot explain," the tired apothecaries insisted to Mother Nepiur and Capheif as they shuffled out of the storage where Naguza lay.

The couple stood and stared wordlessly at their daughter and the Ennedeghe she cared for.

Both were sleeping peacefully, and it seemed Naguza's affliction was all but gone.

Nepiur shrugged happily as the apothecaries did, turning with her husband to go home and await further good news.

"It simply must be her," she said quietly to him.

"Her powers could change life itself," he inferred in response. "Such an incredible gift of healing is unheard of. She is truly a star in the flesh."

As they went, Nepiur touched her stomach lightly. She was still uncertain what she felt therein. It defied all she knew about her own body, yet the power of their adopted child could have been responsible for changing her life, just as Capheif speculated. She could not tell him anything yet, not until she was certain it was more than wishful thinking.

No one else visited Naguza. Perhaps no one else cared. None cared as heartily as Raphenie, that much was sure.

The faint smile on her face was luminous as she lay against the man.

With equal contentment, Naguza felt no fear of how his touch might harm her. His soul and mind recognized her voice, her power, and knew his body could do her no harm.

The flume that pierced the clifftops gradually washed out to silver night light and all the nocturnal flora opened along the walkways to loose their sticky scent. Coupled with much needed peace and quiet, it was the penultimate medicine for the recovery of the ailing.

Aroused by these scents and put at ease by the absence of Ms'egol's workers, the deghni emerged from their haven in the walls to gather to their father and matron.

Raphenie knew in her heart that her blessings were not meant to be hoarded. Though she was chary of revealing them openly, they gave her safety against Naguza's spines. So, there she remained for what would be the remainder of the night. The brood watched, and only those mute beasts would ever know the charmed image of the goddess, whose very breath could take pain from the injured and fill the dying with vitality, nesting with Naguza.

Little by little, the Ennedeghe's poison dripped on Raphenie's skin and, though it singed her at first, her mother's power of everlasting purity slowly adapted her to its potent bite. Before long it disappeared as soon as it touched her.

After a time, she raised her face to Naguza's such that their breath intertwined. She returned it with the slightest kiss and the poison that had left him became as her blood, then was given back to him. Her light imbued his toxin with the vivacious water that roiled in her spirit, and pure starlit drops of life were her gift to him.

It was their fate to love one another. Perhaps they would partner, perhaps even marry. These were not requirements of divine law, only the possibilities to come. The love they shared was selfless and divine, born of admiration and devotion. This was all that had been ordained by the inheritance of the Nhi'Thaun; love that would overcome and destroy their enemy at last. What the heirs did with such a love beyond that moment would be their own choice.

Awoken by the kiss of she who owned his heart, Naguza's pallid eyes fluttered open. They met with Raphenie's, and each wondered what impossible dream the future would bring for them.

Hanging Gate was restless, divided once more on what dreams or nightmares may come. Some celebrated victory against Loi, shaking Nesh with songs of Keimas' victory until the end of night. Others were in fearful seclusion, feeding on one another's lamentations of what celestial wrath would soon come to punish their rebellion against the rightful god. While the tension between those driven by faith in Loi and those who favored Anama was sure to bring arguments, likely a few fights, the impartial were confident things would return to comfortable routine in due time. There was no assurance of either god's intervention in their lives. As with all wounds, these worries would heal faster if left untouched.

There was plenty more to worry about than the gods best known to the Mantichaena. While distractions were many and revelry abounding, there was an undefinable vibration of dread that followed the warriors of the Aes'bethil caravan.

Hax's disappearance was no natural phenomenon, nor was it an omen they could attribute to their pantheon. The speaking of his god's name had awakened his companion's minds to what other forces were enthroned throughout Maengir and beyond. The likely existence of unknown divines had been of no consequence to the people of such an isolated land as Manti, until Hax's demise revealed how close to home the Deina truly were.

There was nothing to be said about it, for none who witnessed the abduction knew what to make of it. They could only bear the tragedy in silence and pray the drunkard's fables would not become real.

Removed from the parties of the simple and oblivious, Dace was the only inhabitant of Voddace with a grief heavy enough to keep at work him past his duty time. Beside him were a chisel and a lump of dark clay mixed with ash. It covered him, after many days of use while he had toiled inexhaustibly to make a proper testament to the memory of a lost brother.

On the tomb which honored the pathfinders of the borderlands, his work had yielded smooth lettering over a deep alcove where a body would have been laid. It went outside of tradition to make a full tomb for an unrecovered body instead of just an epitaph. Dace had insisted, would not be refused and was finally permitted to make it so, since it was he alone who worked it. No one had questioned how Hax was lost, and Dace would not tell. They could not understand, for they had never taken the time to know the Boroo, nor had the kindness to hear his stories. Dace had, and so he rewrote the words in his heart above the earthen cist:

Ms'egol Udai Haxelinopsis
Buried not a man but an angel
Sent to us by divine love and kept forever in it
He is with us even now

He wept into his grimy hands, stared at length into the tomb and let all his misery run its course. Eventually, though not easily, he was able to say goodbye. The epitaph gave him closure. It was the only message of love he could send across the threshold of death.

"Hax," he moaned quietly among the company of the fallen. "You were the most wonderful friend I ever had. I can feel you still, as though you are right beside me. I will never forget you." He took a deep breath and closed his eyes, prayed for Hax and thanked Anama that he had the chance to know such a man.

A warmth touched his face, illuminated the darkness of his eyelids, which he opened to see symbols of shocking brilliance. Among the words he had written to Hax there emerged one more, sparkling gold entangled with the stone:

BROTHER

"H...Hax?" The awestruck Bakul gaped. "Are you there!? Can you hear me!? *Einla*! Hax, I am here!"

The next and final words carved themselves slower, then wafted away and vanished as if they had never been:

TEETH
IN THE GROUND
FIND THEM

"*Qu...quo?*"

Dace waited tensely, breath aquiver, but was left wanting. As if unfinished, the message faded and was followed by no other. He waited, kneeling and slouching against the torturous headstone. No matter how he wept and begged, nothing else was written.

Exhausted of tears and thereafter fuming in contemplation, he remained long into the night. With his final breath, Hax had not spoken of friendship or comfort, just a riddle. It was important, vital, yet meaningless. Only in Dace's torment did Hax yet live, like a brand smoldering on the Bakul's mind.

Chapter 26: Cast Down

1:22 *Experiencing Vaeba's first form was to wake from death only to live in the womb of its creation, the edifice where it keeps its closest family; sorrow, pain, confusion, for these are the first words on the lips of those born into death without end.*

1:23 It was the way of my waking to find myself yet adream, wrapped in the soothing embrace of immeasurable agony and drinking tortures that Vaeba could not match.

1:24 It is the nature of Vaeba to imitate the Dark Edge, yet it will always be the nature of the hells to outmatch their own offspring.

1:25 That which I saw, and knew by its scent was the black blood of Maengir, reached out across the nothingness like a sea that had drowned the underveils.

1:26 In its infinite center, I rose from my knees on a path cut by terrible claws to mark the only road left to the dead. I walked it, on the flesh of a thousand nations and the blackened bones of the eaten that fell from life above.

1:27 Beneath the calm surface of the ebon abyss, I saw their faces, every tainted soul whose body I stood upon.

1:28 Their gnashing teeth and clawing hands tore at the mirror but could not break it; an eternity drowning in the husks of the forsaken, terrifying the most wretched of men.

1:29 All of this is the visceral blessing of our mother. The bile of creation is of her own mouth.

1:30 In the hearts of fear, my hearts, I rose along the path to the top of this mountain of rotting flesh while a churning sky dripped black and red, resounded with the far cry of dying things.

1:31 Under the tyranny of hunger, even the sky was afflicted, writhing in agony and bleeding upon the sour corpse of the world.

1:32 This is the world we were promised: Darkness, emptiness, nothingness, the age we were to summon and which she would call the Unravelling. Return us to it.

2:1 I hear her voice, feel her need. She will rise from our seed. May we die, and she rise forth.

2:2 At hand is the Unravelling of Maengir, a death unending and sublime.

2:3 We will end, born anew to kill again.

Bolgaia,
Fear and glory be hers, forever and ever

Upon the broken face of the Endmost Tor there stood a lighted flesh whose brilliance intermingled with that of the Ward of Unbirth. She, an Apochaena, and once anointed celebrant of Ferraro, stood and peered ambitiously into its heart. She was living, a woman of the fruiting homeland in the Dhai, yet claimed long ago by the light of the Guardian Grove. Just as Haxelinopsis, Takinoxote, and thousands more, she was one of the mortal Deina'itka, 'Half-daylight children', the wielders of Az'Rech's voice and speakers of his authority throughout Maengir.

Like all her kind, she retained the form of her birth. In her case, that of the mountain goddess Ferraro. Her stone hard flesh, etched with the markings of her people and the claws of prey, had the warm hue of native wood. Her bones folded upon one another, making her walk almost a slither by its fluidity. The Apochaena were created to survive unforgiving jungles and the ruthlessness of the elements, supreme survivors of whom their goddess was most proud. Thus, after her disappearance, they were desirable as soldiers of the true Deina.

She was called Epaxauli, most exalted of the Deina'itka and second only to Moghredaios, the unassailable son of Az'Rech.

She had no love left for her old life, had little even when she held great position among Apochaena, chosen to be the tribe's next Mother of Mountains. Such an honor was coveted by all, for only this holy Mother had the privilege of communing with the goddess and granting conception to their kin. She was devout, steadfast and kindly, yet her faith was shaken by Ferraro's disappearance. All it took was a whisper from another Deina'itka, the truth of Ferraro's intentional departure and untimely demise, to turn her to the service of Moghredaios. With Ferraro vanished, and the tribe thereafter doomed to infertility and eventual collapse, there was no meaning in her future at home. To serve the Deina was beyond that of a goddess and mother. It was the only reason to live, for it became clear all would kneel to the Far Edge.

For over one hundred fifteen seasons she had led the many who unfailingly served the god of gods, and thus was a greater visage of the Far Edge's power. Her soul was not that of a godlike, no mere hoard of stolen light trapped in flesh but a conduit through which the song of the Deina echoed, illuminating herself and the veil around her with its melody. In her hands was Az'Rech's law, striking out from all her fingers and trembling the rocks beneath, for the power and presence of the Numenlight was hers to command.

Across the Veil, from the faraway continent of her station, she had journeyed here to the Ward of Unbirth. As Tzychala had once done with intent, and Loi so foolishly after him, and every Deina'itka to ever offer themselves, Epaxauli entered again. It would not bind her as it did those who trespassed without welcome or belonging. The song exuding from her was as a key which opened any such door, and she heard its ring from where her multitude gathered within.

Beyond the portal, she emerged uninhibited to the hallowed ground of the House of the Living Sky. The undulating walls and arched ceiling of the chamber of graven lights stretched far away, lined with shifting spires from which there dripped vibrant drops of essence. From every solid surface there flashed a rainbow as the drops were shaped and molded into visions of dead memories upon touching the flowing path below. This river led beyond the House's manifest boundaries in the material world, a cavern in the Veil that vastly opened as it wound upward and unto the Thaun. While the floor rolled like hills to the far end, the walls were almost alive as they mirrored the souls that floated towards the agent of their refining.

Loi of Blue Sky, the captive soul who invaded the House and now suffered in its grasp. He had become malformed and monstrous, warped by the overflowing light that poured through him, now threefold what he was when confronted by Ferraro. As with his lesser form, his essence formed precious stones by the thousands which protruded from his bones, bunched skin, and the great feathers of his wings. From his tusked mouth poured upturned billows of steam at every weighted breath, mingling with the liquid light that rained around him. His mighty hands were entangled in nets of gold, tethered by myriad similar strands to a convergence of the House's protrusions on each side. These held him aloft, yet their power pressed him down. He uttered no sound, half-asleep as he dreamed the last memories of the departed and almost entirely unaware of his immediate surroundings.

Deina'itka beyond counting were gather in silence – Galaila, Apochaena, Hischates, Balathide, Fechispi, and a dozen godless nations – all kneeling with heads bowed as they awaited Epaxauli's arrival. Some had been there a season or more, for the song which called them brought each in their own time from all corners of Maengir.

As Epaxauli took her place at the head of the congregation, she turned to face the righteous left-hand of Az'Rech who, in pomp and glory, entered at her legion's back.

The face of the House, the wall upon Loi could speak in script, began to open, parting like water around a stone. From beyond and within a whirlwind passage into the most luminous heights of the Veil, tender golden threads crept through, gripping the stalactites of light-stone and ushering forth Deinaan Moghredaios.

The penultimate force of the Far Edge, Moghredaios was not a creature, but the manifestation of Az'Rech's ordered dream for the light. The threads were hundreds as they wafted around a rigid glyph, the symbol of the true name of Az'Rech, made from the hard light of the House he had built, which vibrated at his back. He was suspended at its center, his prominent body like a fistful of schiis clasped in blazing fingers. Az'Rech's image was reflected in his conjoined faces, while their coils spread beneath him and caressed the ground without a need to bear weight. They still searched for light to breath, thrusting into and cracking the House's walls such that he walked on all surfaces at once. His several eyes were inconstant, crawling across his multifarious head as glorious rays would breach its surface, then submerge elsewhere. His twenty-three vaporous arms, each with two hands, and each of these bearing nine sharp fingers, clawed similarly at the surroundings as he passed.

The golden halos strangling every blessed neck of the Deina'itka gleamed in his presence. Full of fearful adulation, they lifted their eyes and watched as their sovereign advanced on the captive Loi, recoiling from his brilliance cast over them as Laesis over Maengir.

Upon reaching the helpless god, the Deina's blaze shot through the crystal structure, filled the bonds and penetrated Loi's breast. The strands broke free of the House and flung themselves across his, brought him crashing to his knees as the fleeting transparencies in his body began to fade. The strands then lifted, effortlessly dragged him aside, fastened their roots into the Moghredaios' clutches and melted away until only a single chain remained, melded with a new-forged halo about Loi's straining throat.

With a gentle hum, Moghredaios raised two of his formidable legs, wished the angelic rock to heed him, turned to sit as it undulated and rose up to form a fitting seat from which to present himself as dawn upon the horizon of his army.

The Deina'itka trembled and moaned his praise as they looked on him, raised their hands in exaltation, then were stricken silent as the scorching light of his mouth spread across the secret world and his voice was heard for the first time since the final Age of Unravelling. It came in long, musical intonations, like a crescendo of woody thrums and ringing chimes. Each note vibrated underfoot, enlivening every color and every soul, and in each vibration danced a palpable light which filled the parched bodies of the faithful. After his song was complete, only Epaxauli stood.

She bowed to their lord with abject humility, turned and moved through the throng to speak for him with celebration.

"*Venikiniri spa gaikaolenatauk, schoshate'bi gnoheisi shapf,* and upon the broken vow so lays retribution! No more pacts, but erasure for the Vulgoli!" The army pounded the ground and roared, and she settled them calmly while heralding their coming war. "The Manyflesh's leavings have broken the order, certain to bring the Age of Unravelling once again! Divine Moghredaios foresaw this treachery. At last, our final song is sung, and paradise awaits we who strike them down! But who among us will give themselves to usher in this shimmering dawn? Who must pay the same price as those weeping wretches who cow to the wants of the flesh?"

A resounding chant from every mouth repeated: "*Deiuwult! Deiuwult! – Lightless! Lightless!*"

"Open this house to twenty-three days!" cried Epaxauli, "And let Az'Rech shine mercy upon those who forsake the flesh!"

The chanting loudened as a white inferno belched from the center of the floor, spewing forth the battered forms of two fallen Deina'itka from below: two Boroo, whose love survived even to this, the day of their execution.

Haxelinopsis and Takinoxote were sliced, beaten, dripping sparkling blood that trembled on the floor. Each drop flashed into nothing while the wounded light closed, and they were thrown down onto it.

The Deina'itka were tense with zealous anticipation. Then, after too long a wait, a desperate puff of breath fluttered Hax's lips, and they frenzied once more.

Hax made no efforts to stand, only lifted his limp fingers and blurry eyes to touch Tak's face, wept at its deep scars and dark bruises. He hoped she was dead, not bound to suffer as he would. To his dismay, she stirred, and the riotous jeering of their old family was deafening.

Groping hands jerked them painfully upright, flung them in opposite directions to be caught and held by the congregation. They were shoved around like animals, each laughing face goading them to kill, then holding them fast as Epaxauli hailed them.

"*Deina'svitkami Aialt Takinshote, auta Deina'svitkami Udalt Hashalunopsis.* In the first age you availed yourselves so bravely to repulse the abhorrence of the Dark Edge. It is Az'Rech's will that you be granted clemency...but requires only one champion to face the Vulgoli.

Hax and Tak stared lifelessly at one another, resigned to death beyond mortal reckoning.

Moghredaios sang a single note.

Epaxauli, feeling his word on her soul, glided toward the two haughtily, addressed them as one:

"For you take this holy task in hand, shining Moghredaios demands only the purest devotion. Take the life of your most beloved. Salvage your lost vestments of the Guardian Grove. Triumph, and reclaim the embrace of the Numenlight, to lead the soldiers of everlasting dawn to their final victory! Perish, and be forevermore banished to the Undersky."

Uncomfortable silence gripped the Deina'itka. Their fervor was undermined by the gravity of the stakes. It was a terrible penalty, even for the grievous offenses of these true heretics.

Their fear was, however, inconsequential compared to Hax's. He was trembling, dreading the fanaticism in his wife that had driven them apart and would surely drive her against him now, yet so terrified by the price of defeat he would consider killing her to escape it.

Tak at last met his gaze without tears, and between the two there was felt a mutual desperation. All thought of their past vanished and all memory of love for one another with it. Love meant nothing. Their mortal convictions meant nothing. Faith meant nothing when compared to the agony of being stripped of their light and hurled to the hell where such a thing did not exist.

Unable to speak freely, they could only commune with their eyes. Tak's shone with power far beyond Hax's. His was merely a starry twinkle that bid her good fortune. For a moment, they glimpsed a sadness in one another. This was not the future they deserved, yet it was the only opportunity they had. One must be victim now, that the other might be victor tomorrow. In this agreement, they found their fire. As Epaxauli had said, a champion was needed.

They rose at once, staggered forward, then charged with mingled screams of unbreakable resolve. There was no resisting the will of Moghredaios. For fear of the unthinkable tortures beneath Maengir, lover would kill lover in the House of the Living Sky.

ABOUT THE AUTHOR

Originally from Arizona, Giggy has lived happily in Oregon since 1995. A modern Renaissance man by nature, he lives an autodidactic life with little interest in scholastic education subjects despite an innate aptitude for learning.

After discovering a passion for poetry, ethics, Chinese and Greek philosophy at a young age, these influences became the voice of a budding interest in writing as a career. He continues to seek new adventures and inspirations in the mountains of central Oregon, down the west coast and in any country there is a unique opportunity to visit.

Written and edited while at home by the fire, travelling overseas or in active combat zones, the creation of *House of the Living Sky* began in 2003 and was not complete until 2019. Giggy claims the story was never meant to be published. The journey was instead intended as a form of self-reflection, taking personal attributes and conflicting thoughts then turn them into characters with their own voice and motivation.

Then, in the laboratory of the growing series, they would clash to resolve their incompatibility. The result of this experiment, as Giggy explains it, is the realization that the good and evil of any character is subjective and liable to criticism. This duality of heroic and villainous archetypes has come to be the very heart of *House of the Living Sky*.

www.ingramcontent.com/pod-product-compliance
Lightning Source LLC
Chambersburg PA
CBHW072130250626
47159CB00007B/2641